D0985137

DEAR MONA

LETTERS FROM A CONSCIENTIOUS OBJECTOR

DEAR MONA

LETTERS FROM A CONSCIENTIOUS OBJECTOR

JONAH JONES

Edited by Peter Jones

Foreword by Wynn Wheldon

SEREN

Seren is the book imprint of
Poetry Wales Press Ltd,
57 Nolton Street, Bridgend, Wales, CF31 3AE

www.serenbooks.com
facebook.com/SerenBooks
Twitter: @SerenBooks

The illustration used in the cover design is the work of Jonah Jones and was
printed by the Canopy Press in the summer of 1945 on the front of its 'Record of
the Unit's Part in the War in Europe', detailing the activities of 224 Parachute
Field Ambulance.

ISBN: 978-1-78172-479-8

A CIP record for this title is available from the British Library.

The publisher acknowledges the financial assistance of the Welsh Books Council.

Printed by TJ International, Cornwall

Contents

List of Illustrations

Foreword

This book, among other things, is the story of a friendship, that of Jonah Jones and Mona Lovell. I have been invited to contribute this Foreword in consequence of two of Jonah's subsequent friendships, one with my father, the broadcaster Huw Wheldon (they had met first as educators at Mount Carmel in Palestine in 1946), with whom talk, and a kind of unspoken religio-chemical mutual understanding of the world was the bond, and the other with his wife, my mother, Jacqueline, like Jonah a novelist, with whom, as with Mona, he maintained a long correspondence.

During my childhood the Wheldon family spent every August at Criccieth. And every August would involve several trips to the Jonah Jones's (never 'the Jones's'), most memorably to Tyddyn Heulyn, the house Jonah built looking out over the Dwyryd estuary. Occasionally we would see Jonah in his workshop, first in the Market Hall at Tremadoc, later on the quay at Portmadoc. Jonah's son Peter, his father's splendid biographer and the editor of this work, was usually about, a soft, sable, intense presence, often amused.

To the young me Jonah was a compendium of the senses: the kindly hooded eyes, the grainy Cymro-Geordie accent, the welcoming whiff of his home-baked bread, his loving touch on slate, on dough, on his slate-thin whippet, Lowri.

I never saw him writing or inscribing, but of course I have seen his inscriptions in Westminster Abbey and Llanystumdwy, and I was lucky enough to have a short correspondence with him, as my mother had a long, so I own examples of his handwriting. My wife and I also own one of his scripted watercolours, a quotation from the Epic of Gilgamesh, which Jonah gave us as a wedding gift.

It is impossible to avoid the impression that Jonah, whether what he was writing told of bad news or good, enjoyed the physical process involved. He wrote in black ink, using what can only be described as his own font, a kind of straight italic, tremendously regular, the whole very white page filled, with no veering, the lines lusciously lateral, tremendously legible, and compellingly readable, determined to get life, as this splendid volume so well demonstrates. All that is missing here is that inimitable hand.

Friendships don't always last. That seems especially the case in those of high intensity. A tautness slackens, and connection fades. This book has a novelistic quality in that sense: it describes a relationship almost from start to finish. It is full of intellectual curiosity, candour, thoroughly engaged with life, even in those periods when Jonah is at odds with the world, depressed or sick at heart or in limb.

The correspondence proper runs from October 1940, when Jonah was 21 years old, and had been sent, as a Conscientious Objector, to fell trees on Exmoor, to December 1955, but the story of the friend-ship (perhaps 'relationship' is a better word) ends in August 1946, with a letter from Haifa announcing Jonah's intention to marry Judith Grossman (later known as the novelist Judith Maro). Mona's hopes were thereby finally dashed. Fifteen years his senior, her love for him had been constant, and at times burdensome. She was a mentor, 'the guiding light' of his young life, an ever-generous benefactor, and for the reader best of all, a mighty correspondent.

As was Jonah himself, who, despite denials, was a born writer, eager to understand the world around him, writing with the intensity of youth, first, while a forester, about ideas and his relationships with men and women, and his attempts at art, and then, having joined up as a non-combatant (in order to escape rocky relationships with Mona and with the poet James Kirkup, in which he felt himself to be the guilty party, hopelessly 'self-centred') about war, and then, at length, about Palestine.

At first ambivalent, confused (who has not been over the years?), aware of the wrongs done to the Arabs, and the difficulty of the British position, horrified by Irgun terrorism, he finally comes down on the Zionist side, embarrassed and ashamed at the British govern-ment (and its army's) treatment of the Jews in the aftermath of the war.

Jonah has something to say about all sorts of things, from Proust to the class system, male friendship to pacifism (about which he has complicated feelings), from sex to religion (and sometimes sex *and* religion). However, the remark that most caught my breath concerned producing a 'dressed piece of timber'. He writes from Jervaulx, in Yorkshire, in November 1941 – and this was long before he had any thoughts of being a sculptor – 'the skill of the hand is an amazing factor in happiness'. This seems to me to predict the man who so fascinated me, at his dough, at his slate, on his dog, running his big-bulbed fingers over Cambrian stone on the Roman Steps, under the Rhinogs, happily, I think. But 'the skill of the hand' also includes the act of writing, which is thought made concrete. This collection is important not just as a portrait of its creator, but because it gives us insights into the experience of the Conscientious Objector, the army medic (and parachutist), and, almost viscerally, into the experience of Palestine in the years immediately following the war and prior to Israeli independence. It is astonishingly both intimate and intellectual, private and public. I defy anyone not to be engrossed.

Wynn Wheldon
April 2018

Introduction

The conversation always reached the same point. Discussing this book, Mick Felton would start, "Len –", then hesitate before continuing: "I can't call him Len – Jonah!"

Mick had known my father Jonah Jones for over 30 years, and had published two of his books at Seren[1]. He could be forgiven for finding it difficult to accept that the man whose wartime letters we were discussing was effectively a different person from the cherished and respected figure we both knew. For that is what we have in these letters – the slow, often painful mutation of the young Leonard Jones, the librarian son of a County Durham coalminer, into the Welsh artist, writer and educator Jonah Jones.

I was completely unaware of the letters when I wrote my biography of Jonah some years ago[2]. Then, on a summer's day in 2013, I received an unexpected call from David Lovell, the nephew of the woman who had given Jonah – or rather Len – his first job as a librarian in 1935. While sorting out his deceased father's possessions, he had found a box full of letters written by Len to David's Aunt Mona through the 1940s. Would I be interested in seeing them? Trying not to bite his arm off too unceremoniously, I said yes and drove over with my wife Maggie to David's home in Wiltshire.

Waiting for us there was an old cardboard box tightly packed with bundles of mostly handwritten letters – 475 of them. Reading a sample it became clear that this was a treasure trove of vivid writing that filled many gaps in the narrative of Len/Jonah's early life. The letters transform our understanding of his early sense of identity, how he found his vocation for art and other questions. If this resource had been available during the writing of the biography, the first three chapters would have been substantially different. The letters also illuminate important matters like the experience of conscientious objectors during the Second World War and British conduct in the final phase of the Palestine Mandate. As such they make up a significant historical document.

My father was a great letter writer all his life, both in the sense of quantity and quality. The war years in particular were a time of huge social dislocation, with millions forced away from their homes and loved ones. Letters were effectively the only form of communication available, so were hugely important to those who wrote them and their recipients. The army recognized the role that regular mail played in keeping up morale among the troops, and the Army Postal Service provided a remarkably efficient flow of letters between the front and people back home. Letters written during the war provide a striking insight into life in those years which is of great interest now to readers and historical researchers alike. Our times, with their electronic communications, will not leave such an invaluable resource.

Who was this avid young letter-writer? Leonard Jones was born on 17 February 1919, the eldest child of Norman and Florence Jones (they went on to have two daughters, Betty and Gladys). The family had a background in coalmining. Originally from Somerset, Grandfather John worked for a time in South Wales as a young man, perhaps leading to the vague belief in the family that they were of Welsh origin. He worked his way up England as a mineshaft sinker until he settled down in County Durham. John was a considerable influence on young Len; he was a strict God-fearing patriarch, and the Joneses were devout Congregationalists. Len was thus predisposed to idealism and the search for moral living.

His father Norman was a coal hewer before the First World War, in which he saw service at Gallipoli and the Western Front until he was invalided out with battle wounds. He was left disillusioned by the war and by the hard times after. The family lived in some poverty for most of Len's childhood, affected as they were by the Great Strike of 1926 and the Depression. However, his early life was spent in what were then pit villages, surrounded by open country (yet close to the Tyneside conurbation), which left him with an instinctive love of rural living.

Len also got a good basic education, securing a scholarship to Jarrow County Secondary (later Grammar) School, where he did well. He was a bookish boy and also won an art prize. Then he won a scholarship to study at the King Edward School of Art in Newcastle, but family circumstances required that he get a job, so he attended evening classes at the art school instead. In November 1935, aged 16, he was fortunate enough to be appointed assistant at the recently opened public library in Felling, part of Gateshead near where he lived, working under the redoubtable librarian Mona Lovell. Now he had a salary (£1 a week) and "was plunged into the world of books", of which he took full advantage.

As a Quaker Mona believed strongly in the improving power of education and helping others as much as possible. She sought to maximize the potential of all her employees; to this end she drew up reading programmes based on her English degree course, which she encouraged the library assistants to follow. They were also urged to study for library qualifications with her help. Len proved receptive to all of this. She gave him what was probably his first experience of live classical music, ballet and theatre, and meeting her Quaker and other friends hugely broadened his social outlook.

And who was Mona Lovell? She was born on 15 April 1904 in St Mawes, Cornwall, the eldest child of a senior Customs and Excise officer. Her first years were spent in Cornwall, then the family moved to Bristol before finally settling in Bath. There seems to have been a liberal bent to the Lovells, and Mona was one of that generation of independent-minded women who were determined to make their own way in life and stand up for their principles. (Her younger sister Doris was clearly similar; she and her husband Alan Bradshaw moved to southern Africa, where they were among the very few white people who remained friends with the Englishwoman Ruth Williams after

Mona with her family in Bath

At the local Friends Meeting House. Mona is on the right

she married Seretse Khama, heir to the kingship of the Bangwato people in Bechuanaland.)[3]

Mona studied English at Bristol University, gained a diploma in librarianship from the University of London and in time became a Fellow of the Library Association. She had a keen interest in European culture, and made several extended visits to northern France and elsewhere in the late 1920s and early 1930s. She acquired penfriends with whom she corresponded for many years after (she was a great letter writer all her life). She also perfected her French, and probably learned at least some German and Italian during sojourns in Switzerland and Italy.

She began her career in librarianship in 1930 with a seven month stint at the Workers' Education Association library in Bath. The following year she did summer work at the Quo Vadis Library in Geneva, which specialized in Eastern faiths. Mona always had a deep fascination with religion and philosophy, and it appears around the early 1930s that she became a Quaker (her family were Methodists). Her conversion may have happened after November 1933, when she moved to the North East; she worked for three months at the Newcastle Society of Antiquaries in the historic Black Gate, and at the same time started a job as assistant to the Editor of the Northern Regional

Catalogue, a grouping of 33 libraries participating in the Regional Library system. The opening of a new public library in Felling on 1 July 1935 provided her first important post when she was appointed librarian, also taking charge of a branch in nearby Pelaw which opened four months later for two days a week.

I knew that my father had been close to Mona, who became a mentor to him and played a vital role in his development. Yet I soon discovered from the letters she was still more important than that to him. Mona was Len's soulmate, whose wide interests in the arts and similar outlook on life helped to anchor his sanity through the seven long years he served first as a conscientious objector working in forestry and then in the army. For so much of the time he was isolated in a world from which he felt disconnected; he could always turn to Mona, for she understood his interests and concerns. He called her "the guiding light in my life"; elsewhere he wrote "you have helped to mould my being these growing years".

Startlingly the letters reveal even more than this. For Mona was in love with Len – fifteen years her junior – and very briefly he thought he had the same feelings. When he realized his love was purely platonic, there followed years of unrequited passion on her part with all the emotional turmoil this brought. As if that was not enough, for a time Len was also pursued by his friend and fellow conscientious objector, the poet James Kirkup. So this is a love story full of drama and anguish.

Mona supported Len with unceasing generosity, not only with her

Mona, writing at her home

steady stream of letters but also with regular parcels of books lent from the library, newspapers, tobacco, food to supplement his diet and anything he might mention he needed. If he wrote about cold weather she would knit him socks or buy gloves. When he began doing water-colours she bought him David Cox paper and paints. Len knew that he could ask her to seek out things he wanted from the shops in Newcastle, like picture frames or art books. Sometimes he would pay her back for what she had bought him, or send her a picture, but over the course of the war Mona must have made substantial sacrifices to help Len. So many of his letters begin with the sentiment "Thank you for your parcel..."[4]

She was similarly generous towards many other people – Len chided her for "dashing here & dashing there" to look after people, neglecting her own peace. As the war went on, Mona tired herself out helping others. As a good Quaker she clearly felt that doing chari-table acts amounted to a vocation. There was too a streak of brisk practicality in her character. Sadly her letters to Len were lost long ago, but a small batch to her brother Tony (David Lovell's father) conforms to an observation made by him: "How I should know a letter from you if it were read among 100 others. You have the same style, or lack of it, & the same interest in mundanities. You are like Breughel for detail, especially in the sense that the details seem too characteristic to omit." (At the same time, of course, Mona's letters were often full of depth in both content and emotion.)

Evidently she was a remarkable and virtuous woman, but she was not a saint. It is obvious from Len's letters that she could be bitter and sarcastic, capable of remembering wrongs for years. He paraphrases her acerbic remark "you say you are a useful person to know perhaps, and that I need a friend, but anyone almost would do", to which she adds "I'm sorry I can't be a doormat" (Mona's own words). She was more than a little jealous, too, so that Len became wary of telling her about his meetings with other friends (especially female ones). Inevitably this had a wearing effect on their friendship.

The young Len who is revealed by the letters is a very complex character. His keen intelligence and depth of learning are striking (we have to remember his formal education ended at 16). He is essentially idealistic, but grows more worldly-wise, even a touch cynical, as time

Len, in 1944

passes. He describes personal integrity as a "holy grail" (a quality all who knew the older Jonah would recognize as one of his outstanding qualities), yet at one point he comes to the conclusion that he is "rotten inside". He struggles to do the right thing but can be surly, even cruel in Mona's presence, without fully understanding why. He is obviously a loner yet he suffers from loneliness, and exults (at first anyway) in the company of kindred spirits like James Kirkup, the Castle Bolton artists, his army comrade and fellow artist George Downs or the "inner circle" in 224 Parachute Field Ambulance.

In the early letters Len's youth is evident as he struggles with homesickness, bad food and miserable conditions on Exmoor. The vicissitudes of a hard job, but above all of complicated relationships, impose a steady maturing in his personality, yet he remains prone to spells of terrible uncertainty, even depression. His introversion becomes notably less marked once he joins the army – there is little time for it – but it is when he enters 224 PFA and finds a real purpose in his existence that he seems to reach a state approaching rounded manhood. Inevitably the experience of war changes him irrevocably. "Nobody can ever grasp what happens inside one on a day like 24 March [1945]," he writes three months after the crossing of the

Len, with a colleague

Rhine, in which so many of his comrades died. (Such is the effect so often of the horrors of battle, which drives an unbridgeable gap between those who have seen them and the civilians at home who cannot truly understand.) By the end of the correspondence, the tone of the letters is recognizably that of the older Jonah, as expressed in countless letters to family and friends.

In many ways, then, what these letters represent is an *Éducation sentimentale*, or a kind of *Bildungsroman*. Reading them one is frequently reminded of D.H. Lawrence's Paul Morel, the central protagonist in *Sons and Lovers*. Obviously both Len and Paul (like Lawrence himself) are the sons of miners who find fulfilment in the creative arts. Like Paul, Len's fascination with art helps him to enter a middle class circle; he becomes more sophisticated and learns new social habits. Both think deeply about religion, but in time move away from acceptance of any one set of Christian beliefs to "the bedrock of belief, that one should feel inside oneself for right and wrong, and should have the patience to gradually realize one's God", as Lawrence says of Morel.

Strikingly, Len's letters also recall Paul's complex relationship with women. Both have a charisma that exerts a powerful hold over those who love them, but both find more turbulence than fulfilment with the opposite sex; they come to feel a sense of failure and wonder if they are capable of loving another person. Yet both like and respect women, while having a sense of the centrality of male friendship.

Len is excellent at conveying the character of his closest friends; the self-consciously bohemian yet sensitive James Kirkup, the genial, apparently self-sufficient Yorkshire painter Fred Lawson, the grouchy George Jackson, George Downs (his first artist comrade in the army) and the members of the 'inner circle' in 224 PFA. He describes vividly the life of the forestry worker, both the hard physical conditions and the occasional moments of astonishing beauty in the woods. And he is very good on life in the army – the petty discipline, the boredom and frustration, but also the "wonderful brotherly feeling" among fellow soldiers. The letters provide an interesting insight into the psychology of wartime, with its spiritual fatigue, the endless impatient waiting for the end to come, the longing to resume private lives and careers.

While the tone of Len's writing is often gloomy or despairing, there is also joy and much of the impish, quirky humour which was so distinctive about the later Jonah. He describes a dream in which he has to "retire from public life" due to suffering from a disease called either Peebles or Dunstable, which he speculates must be connected in his subconscious to measles or constipation.

The letters provide fascinating illumination on Len/Jonah's evolution as an artist – and as a Welshman. Clearly he had an early interest in art, having attended evening classes in Newcastle. However he long expected to pursue a career in librarianship. The letters reveal that only gradually did his aspirations change; finding himself in Wensleydale with James Kirkup he began to explore outlets for his creativity, and having dabbled in writing he turned to watercolour painting, learning from Fred Lawson and the other members of the Castle Bolton group. A passion for art drew him to George Downs in the Non-Combatant Corps after he joined the army, and his conversations with friends in the 'inner circle', especially the printer and woodcut artist John Petts, clinched the transformation.

As for Len's sense of identity, what leaps out from the letters repeatedly is his deep love of England. Nowhere is this more powerful than in Wensleydale, for which he came to feel a deep attachment and regard as his home. Yet here and there are tangential reminders that the Jones family had a certain undefined sense of Welsh roots. When Petts gave him the opportunity in 1947 to work with him at the Caseg Press in Llanystumdwy, Len seized it eagerly and moved to North Wales. He never looked back.

As well as the personal aspect of the letters, they also contain a valuable element of historical record. We gain an insight into the experience of conscientious objectors during the Second World War. Len was treated as a pariah on Exmoor, exploited as defenceless by his farmer employer on Tyneside, but treated quite tolerantly in Wensleydale. He records the stark reality of fighting and conditions in Belgium and Germany late in the war, going on to document his reaction as a member of the armed forces in late Mandate Palestine, where he becomes bitterly critical of British Government policy.

This is one of the reasons why I felt these letters must be published. The truth is, I was faced with a dilemma as I read and transcribed them. To reveal them to the world is an intrusion into my father's (and Mona's) privacy. He wrote to her in early March 1945, shortly before a military operation which he knew he might not survive: "I feel letters are between friends only & I want the lovely personal sacredness of those letters to remain unspoiled by others' reading, even my parents." Reading those words, and then publishing them, feels rather like a betrayal. Yet the quality of the letters just seems too good, and their content too important, to leave them languishing in some archive. The story of Len and Mona should be read; let it be a tribute to two extraordinary people.

A few words about practical details. Most of the letters open with a simple "Dear Mona" and close with "Yours, Len", which I have omitted. Where the salutations vary, this has been indicated if it appears to have any significance. I have tried to supply a date for each letter where possible. After Len arrived in Wensleydale in mid-1941 he tended to write nothing more than the day of the week on his letter headings. In such cases I have attempted to work out the date from clues in the letters, and then work backwards or forwards. Where it has been impossible to pin down a reasonably definite date I have simply given a rough period such as "early-mid May". The problem diminishes considerably in the army letters, most of which remained

Mona in 1935

in the original envelopes in which they were sent; these are conveniently postmarked to give us a clear indication of the date.

I am indebted to David Lovell for allowing me to borrow the letters and a number of photographs, and for his help with additional material. It goes without saying that this book would not exist without his contribution. Both he and his wife Anne were most hospitable on the many visits I paid them to discuss the project. My thanks go to my siblings David Townsend Jones and Naomi Jones, without whose approval for the publication of the letters and my handling of them I could not have revealed their content. I am grateful to Mick Felton, Cary Archard and the staff of Seren for bringing their professional expertise to bear in the production of this book, for which Wynn Weldon kindly provided a generous Foreword. Finally I must thank my wife Maggie for supporting me patiently over the many months it took to transcribe and edit the letters. She typed out half the text, and offered a number of telling observations based on her historical knowledge and shrewd insight. With Mona Lovell she shares the instinct to go out of her way to help others.

Exmoor, Kirkcudbrightshire and Tynedale

Len's first letter in the correspondence is worth quoting merely for its tone, for it reminds how his relationship with Mona began – as a bright youth fresh out of school given his first job by an enlightened employer who wished to build on his potential. Written from the family home on Tyneside, the mood is light and cheery. There is no hint of the shadow of war, leading one to suspect that it was written before 1 September 1939, although it is impossible to date the letter.

Len's father Norman was for several years a first aid man at Follonsby pit, and the young man seems to have had an affinity for the medical vocation which would resurface some four or five years later. He signed this letter (as he did others occasionally) 'Hookie', a common nickname in the North East.

8 White Mere Gardens, Wardley
– Wednesday [impossible to date]

Thank you very much for the Bath buns. My share has already gone, so tomorrow I shall have to scrounge from one of the others.[1]

I didn't realize that your holidays started before mine finished, but I'm not too late to wish they're good. The weather seems to have changed for the better anyhow[…]

Mother thanks you very much for card & biscuits; she's very busy now jam-making still.

I had a strenuous holiday. I worked with Uncle Jack in the welfare, and even cut the full bowling green twice by myself[…] Oh! and I also massaged a man who has been in bed with a broken femur for 17 weeks and I actually had the honour of getting him out of bed onto crutches[…] I felt grand seeing him onto his crutches and hobbling about[…][2]

[Signed "Cheerio, Hookie".]

The next letter was probably written at least many months after the first, and the tone is completely different. Len had been sent to Exmoor to work as a forester. It was his first time living away from home, and the whole experience was a shock to him. A preoccupation with food, understandable in a young man doing hard physical labour, emerges as a recurrent theme.

Rockford Lodge Hostel, Rockford, Brendon, Devon
– Wednesday [probably 2 October 1940]

I'm writing this after my second day's work, and there are no traces of stiffness or anything. Thank you for your letter which I received just now after dinner 6.30.

I'm taking to the work OK but we are all agreed that there's something fishy going on. The Forestry Commission is trying to get a forest felled for nothing and as far as skill is concerned, we are most of us already quite adept at the art of tree-felling. All it needs is a little practice & if present progress is kept up we will all be quite proficient foresters after a fortnight.

My main impression so far is very bad organisation on the part of the M. of Labour & the Forestry Commission. We arrived for instance, at Minehead at 10 am Monday morning, were met by a M. of L. official who told us to mope around Minehead till 3 pm, when a bus would come & fetch us. At 3 we met, ready for bus, but we had to wait about, bored stiff & dog-tired, till 4.45 and had to go to Brendon by a roundabout way, arriving at the Hostel about 6.30. That meant 24 hours from Wardley to Rockford – not good enough. Next morning, our boss Mr Thorne met us at Hostel & told us to walk to the wood in the Doone Valley, & that it was 4 miles. However, it took us 1 hr & a half, and we reckoned it was over 6 miles. Then, once on the job, we were made into 6 groups of 3, and each left to itself to fell and trim its trees. We felled & trimmed 11 trees the first day. Today we felled the same number in the morning & then, after they had been marked out, we sawed them into logs. The first is about 8 feet by 8 inches diameter, the next 7 by 7 and so on. Then we stacked them into their respective piles.[3]

On our first day for our packed lunch we had cheese & ham roll sandwiches without butter or margarine in. After a complaint, we got marg. today, & the breakfast & dinner were much better. We actually had a sweet (rice pudding) today for dinner.

But pardon my many complaints. We are all very much on the *qui vive* for anything funny, & any victimisation will meet a strong united protest. We have a committee of 4 to look after such affairs.

By the way, we suffer many little discomforts and we are far far from civilisation, so I wonder if you know of any organisation parallel to the WVS[4] which looks after COs [conscientious objectors] in our position. We are really worse off than soldiers[…]

Rockford Lodge, Sunday 6 October 1940

I received your welcome parcel yesterday afternoon, Saturday, and as we now have a proper quiet reading room, the books will be invaluable. It must be awfully expensive for you, buying Thoreau (7d I notice) & then posting them on. It is just another thing for which I can never thank you enough[…]

Myself, I am fine by now, much less miserable and scrounging than my first letter must have implied. I am beginning to adjust myself to the work more, but still find it vastly different from librarianship. I am afraid exams[5] are out of the question, not so much because I can't study, but because this place is so difficult to get from. First a 5 miles heavy walk to Lynmouth. Then the 1 a day bus service to Minehead. From Minehead a single track line (most of the way) to Taunton, and from experience this is a bad service. From Taunton to Bristol is comparatively easy, but the total cost, including loss of 2 days' pay would be absolutely out of the question. It's a pity, but I must wait till the "end of the present emergency"[…]

I'm so happy to have friends like you – the other poor fellows seem to have no one except wives and sweethearts, which must be awfully conventional & boring[…]

Rockford Lodge, Tuesday 8 October 1940

[…]the hostel is not half so bad as it was at first. I think it must have been because some of our ration cards were not then handed in, but by now the food is really excellent for 25/- a week[...]

It was a joy to hear that people wished to know my address. As far as contact with friends [Quakers] is concerned, it is only possible in spirit and memory, as Minehead is nearly 20 miles, needing a special conveyance, and I'm afraid I could not manage 40 miles on a pony, not yet anyway, and it is rather expensive[…] I shall make an effort to get to Minehead as soon as I'm used to the ponies – it may cost only 5 or 6 shillings in winter for a morning but now the rate is 2 to 3/- an hour. No other transport is available.

Discomforts? Well, getting your knees wet and muddy as you kneel to saw. Jamming your fingers once every hour (not hard enough to resist yet). But the most important have partially disappeared – bad food altogether – and reading, last week impossible a little more possible though some of the chaps, a little thoughtless, disregard the request for silence. So you can cancel my complaint of discomforts. I was miserable last week. This week, I'm not a bit homesick but I'm feeling awfully job-sick. Trees, trees, trees, all the same, the same to be done to each – so dull compared with books.

However, I'm quite happy by now, and so will close with a wish [Signed "All the best, Len".]

Rockford Lodge, 13 October 1940

I was overjoyed to receive the parcel of dates, figs, books etc from you. What happiness it gives to find a parcel waiting for one when one comes back from work. The food is ever welcome here, as we seem to be always hungry, despite the fact that we have plenty of food from the hostel. It is probably because of the enormous amount of energy we must expend on this job, as logs, axes & whatnot are heavy things[...]

I find that the greatest pleasure here is being alone, and I shall endeavour to read in my bedroom if it is not too cold. This morning I went [for] a walk alone towards Simonsbath, left the road and crossed the moor back to Rockford. It is by far the best walk since I came here, and on the whole this weekend is the first time I have really appreciated the beauty of the district, excepting last Saturday's walk to Lynmouth[…]

I must thank you here also for the newspapers & writing-paper you sent me. The latter was most acceptable (this is it) and needless to say, the papers filled one of the many gaps in my life now, because intellectually this job & place is barren. It is work, eat, sleep and unlimited jawing most of the time. As the talk penetrates to the "reading" room, reading is as difficult as ever, especially as some seem to delight in breaking the rule of silence in this room even. My thoughts these days dwell mostly in the past & in the future when I shall be once more a librarian.

There is supposed to be a fellowship among COs but this is almost absent here. On Thursday, piece-work began enabling some, if not all, to make more money, particularly fellers, of which Myrddin[6] and I were one gang. But some of the cross-cutters, sawing the trees into logs, kicked up a stink because we two were single. The result was that we were taken off felling and a married pair took our place, despite the fact that they make a weak gang. One of them, the chief troublemaker, is an insurance agent in S Shields & has actually admitted that his wife is still earning £3 a week from his £12 book as he calls it. This same fellow, George Stephenson by name, a little shrimp with big specks [sic] on, grumbles constantly at the table, calling the tea varnish etc & thereby causing embarrassment.

Myrddin & I could do nothing but submit, though I am sure the feeling of the rest was with us. In any case, a rota scheme is in embryo, so we may manage to earn a little for Xmas. I don't like this piece-work anyway – there's too much competition. Sometimes I'm as sick of life as I've ever been in that forest, but once round a good dinner I improve 100%[…]

Our daily routine is rise at 6.15, wash (cold water in an outhouse affair) and breakfast (based on fried bread & fried potatoes with the addition of bacon or sausage when possible – no fancy post-toasties etc or porridge). Catch lorry at 7 – arrive Malmsmead about 7.20 – walk to forest & commence about 10 to 8. Break at 10 to 10.10 am, lunch at 12-12.30 – finish 4.30 – lorry 5.0 & so home, wash & dinner leaving 7 to 10 pm to be bored or to snatch a bit [of] reading if noise (or its absence rather) permits. We sleep in a linen sleeping bag covered by blankets & are usually too tired to notice any discomfort there. I suppose the whole business sounds awful to you, and it does to me sometimes. In fact, I quite often wonder if this is a bad dream. To make it worse, we are practically tied here, because we have been given to understand that had we refused, or if we try to leave, we are for the tribunal again. Some of us would like to risk it, but there are times when things are not so bad and I feel quite content.

There is one compensation – we hardly know there's a war on except when a Nazi plane (presumably) flies high over here at night in its way to Wales[…]

[This and the next letter signed "Yours, Hookie".]

Rockford Lodge, 16 October 1940

As I am well down in the dumps today (indeed most days now) you must not expect a very good letter.

First of all, there has just been a row in the camp. Darke & Lister finished felling today, and Wood & Harrison take their places for a week, & as there is good money in the piece-rate for felling it is essential that a good start be made. Wood & Harrison complained that D & L have chosen all the small trees & left the big ones for them to clear out, & mostly spruce at that (very difficult to clean). W & H even went on from calling it unbrotherly to un-Christlike & finished up by calling D & L (both Brethren) hypocrites which was all very nasty.

It was a horrible Christadelphian versus Brethren fight in a CO camp. Fortunately, I was out of it in the next room, & intend to keep out of all such silly rows[…]

This is becoming a concentration camp slowly, if various quiet hints are to be noticed. Someone, asking for his cards today, got chalked off. There's no escape, I'm beginning to think, and a kind of stagnation is getting hold of us. One never thinks anything out – no, you start at 7.50, hope for 10 then hope for 12, then a long hope for 4.30. And then the lorry driver usually contrives to have a load of horse manure on just before he comes for us & so we stink & go without a bath. Dirty, cut finger nails – hair matted with larch needles, mud up to our knees (it is now 6 in deep on account of much rain). My present job, cross-cutting the trees into logs, is the most monotonous job I've ever done in my life. My own mate, Myrddin, is down with the flu, and I am now coupled with the party's biggest bore[…]

Staple diet – potatoes, turnips & bread with variations on the same theme. Thank goodness you & my people are so good to me[…]

I have been simply aching to get all this, and more off my chest to somebody, but please don't let my people know, but honestly, I can't explain the sordidness of this existence. Too tired even to read, if that were possible.

To try & clear my mind a bit, I'm going to make a big effort to get to Minehead [Quaker] meeting one Sunday. I tried to get a pony last Sunday, but the farmer knew what I was & said he didn't "believe in they conshies" & refused me. You see how we are imprisoned. No wonder we have rows (I've not had any yet fortunately)[…]

[Note at top of letter apologises for being "much too self-centred. Must think of others in worse plights".]

Rockford Lodge, 17 October 1940

I write this in haste, so as to get on the heels of that awful last letter of last night, which was posted by mistake. I wrote it, sealed it, & thinking better of it, put it back in my writing-case. Myrddin, who is ill & therefore at the hostel all day, wishing to write something, used my stuff to save going upstairs for his own & found this letter. During the day, I felt I must burn the lot & came home intending to do so, only to be told by Myrddin that he had sent it to the post, thinking I had forgotten to do so.

So there's only one thing to do, & that's to apologise, & hope this gets to you first. I'm very sorry to palm all my troubles on you, but my only excuse is that most of it's true & that we all feel the same to a man. In fact there are worse cases than myself, and several married men are obviously pining. And the mud really is 6 ins thick[…]

I now have the attitude that I am being tested & that I must win through. That is the correct attitude, I feel, and I am now determined to stick anything, realizing that the filth, spotty skins etc are nothing to what the poor soldiers suffered in the last war in the trenches. But the first reaction (and it has not yet completely gone) is to fall back upon oneself & indulge in self-pity etc[…]

I beg of you to believe me when I say that I now cast aside the self-centredness & will stick it out. It's only the inevitable reaction to the ultra-comfortable life I have led. And I am not alone. As I have said, some seem on the point of breaking up. And one fellow (a bit cracked, I'll admit) has actually run away & been imprisoned as a suspicious character. We started 18 or 19 – now we are 13, with 1 down sick & another with a strained muscle.

We all pine to do the little normal things of our lives, which are impossible. How I long for instance to hear a little good music, have scrambled egg on toast at your home, talk about things I'm interested in with a friend, have a dainty meal, a hot bath and a thorough rest (already), and above [all] be an ordinary unprepossessing librarian[...]. All day, our contacts are cold, and even a brotherly affection, to be expected amongst such as us, is not what it should be for some unknown reason. The job is also crooked from start to finish – we simply are not getting a square deal & the whole thing is a great mystery to us[...]

I promise you I'll never write another wholly in that vein, although you must forgive occasional self-centred spells, as I have no 'real' friends down here.

Len wrote again on 21 October in a more cheerful vein, reporting that a knee injury was keeping him off work for a few days, which he was spending reading. He passed on thanks from Bill Hamilton to Mona for sending Hansard – Len's first mention of the future MP who would become a good friend. He wrote again on the 24th:

Rockford Lodge, 24 October 1940

As I was feeling awfully miserable again this morning, your letter (from home) was most welcome and encouraging. It was a relief to know you took that depressing letter in the right spirit, and your answer to it was not only encouraging but a real comfort[...]

I got back to work after my knee got better but am now off again for a week or so with rheumatics. I think the dampness and bad feeding must have caused it. Today, 2 more men are leaving for home, invalided out, one being my friend Myrddin, whose lungs are in a terrible state – he has never stopped coughing for days. He was 2 days at work after flu, but cracked up again, and the Dr says he mustn't do forestry again.

I hope I myself shall soon be alright again, because here the Forestry C does not pay you when you are off[…]

Rockford Lodge, Sunday 27 October 1940

This is my fourth day of rest almost over, and I feel so much better that I shall start work tomorrow, instead of having a whole week off. As I received your jar of malt on Friday morning, I attribute my return to health to that, and must thank you accordingly, since our present diet seems devoid of vitamins and composed mainly of starch in bulk. It was a sensible and most appropriate gift.

I think I should continue in better health from now, as 5 of us are moving on Saturday next from this damp and depressing place to a farm situated high up on the hillside, so high up in fact that Wales is visible on a clear day across the Bristol Channel. It may be a move from the frying-pan into the fire as far as food is concerned but for situation – oh! An excellent move. This river has got thoroughly on our nerves and you can imagine what such a move is like, from the bottom of a deep valley, canyon-like, to the hill-top. As for the food, the frying pan is slow death and the fire quick & therefore preferable, but really, I think we have been on rock bottom with this heavy diet. The milk, I am sure, is skimmed, a fault not present on a farm, and we may catch sight of an occasional egg, especially since there are only 5 of us, Bill [Hamilton], Bernard, Alec Parlane, Jim Minto and myself. Bill and I have already got our bedroom, which looks over the Bristol Channel.

When we informed our present landlady that we were moving she went mad and threatened to bring the police to turn us all out, as 4 others are moving into Brendon. She then informed us that she had been compelled to take us by the authorities who had instructed her to give us plain fare and not to fuss over us! Are we criminals or what? The village snobs certainly treat us as such, and come riding through the deer park where we work & look at us down their noses[…]

[Signed "Affectionately yours, Hookie".]

Rockford Lodge, 29 October 1940

The atmosphere is not too grand just now, as we have had the billeting officer (hitherto an unknown quantity) and he made things pretty hot for us because of our removal or our proposal to remove. We consented to stay if the food was improved and a fire every so often in our damp bedrooms. He then went to see the landlady who refused these requests so we won our point, fortunately, and although he had blustered in with tales of compulsion & soldiers under canvas etc, he meekly allowed us to remove[…]

Last night was hopeless for writing and consequently I am behind somewhat. And tonight I have rather a queer feeling, having witnessed "civilisation" at its worst today. A fox hunt neared its end where we were working, and we were overwhelmed by hounds sniffing all over the shop & yelping & then snobs on horses who curse when you won't tell them where the fox is. That part was all right but a little later we heard such a crescendo of yelping that we knew what was happening. Our reward came for hindering the darlings when we saw at the gate to our wood, as we were leaving, the poor fox's head, horribly mutilated and with eyes missing (dainties no doubt for some hound)[...] That's the second hunt I've seen & I've seen more meet. And once we were asked where the stag had gone. No wonder we can't answer the swine. A stag-hunt takes place next week some time, and I hope we miss it or if not, have the opportunity of misleading them […]

Poor Bill [Hamilton], next to me, is wrestling with shorthand as a pastime. He's a BA [&] a Durham lad, big and blond, & after leaving Sheffield Univ in June he's not worked till he got this job. BA a forester! Isn't it shameful – but perhaps I'm advocating an intellectual aristocracy. He's a Communist & his comments on fox-hunting are ripe[…]

Cranscombe Farm, Brendon, Lynton, N Devon,
3 November 1940

You are all very much perturbed seemingly by my slight lapse in health recently. As I don't seem to have assured you on the phone, I can only say now that I have recovered completely and am now feeling better than all the time since I came, and have actually been on 3 days felling now, surely a sign of fitness[…]

I now have no trouble whatever with knees or anything – in fact

I'm working really well these last few days and I know it, and have not felt any effects whatever, despite being soaked 3 days running.

But anyway, you were still sufficiently concerned to send me a huge sum of money, to use if I was in straitened circumstances. I don't know what to do with £5[…] You are a great friend to me, and I don't know how I should have managed the awful weeks that have passed without your help[…]

This is my second day in my new digs, and if only I had been here all the time, how much happier I should have been. How much lighter, more airy and open it is. We can see the sky by merely turning our heads, but at Rockford – oh, you could only see trees and rock on the valley side. There, it was artificial light all the time morning till night – here beautiful daylight. Then at Rockford the wood fires used to smoke terribly, making the atmosphere thick, but here, a sweet-smelling peat fire spells much better health. Of the food there is only one thing to say – that our new landlady knows how to cook and how to feed working men without throwing it at them. I am much happier already[…]

Len wrote again on 8 November, still content with life at the farm. The family there were "the only set of people round [here] to treat us as fellow human beings. The rest treat us as dirt, in the main, and we are branded." His next letter came four days later.

Cranscombe Farm, 12 November 1940

[…] I am by now thoroughly hardened to meet the little discomforts of which I have so often complained. It has now [rained] for a fortnight without any great breaks and even though I am wet through almost every day, it leaves me unscathed. I cannot say, of course, that I am content, but which person would making such a change in life. However, I am well over the worst and can analyse, a little at least, the reasons for my awful grumblings. First, of course, was the absence of home & its comforts. This not only meant difference of food & beds but more important still, it meant living with a crowd with which I had little in common. There was only one with any tastes in common with me, Myrddin. Another, Bill Hamilton, more political than myself was also a kindred spirit. Another, quieter, was Alec Parlane, who left us for Scotland the other day. With these three, I had to bear the crowd[…] [T]hose first weeks were hell. The second main reason for my misery was the food, which was a mushy hash as a rule, full of bulk and *sans* nutrition.

Then of course, the work would have been awful without the above discomforts. We were placed immediately on felling until a permanent foreman came and our utter lack of experience caused us to eat our hearts out. I have never felt so exhausted as on those first afternoons and looking back I really believe we all lived through our own little hell on earth.

Most of the discomforts in these three categories have now disappeared, fortunately, but another trouble has arisen, not so personal, however. There are 6 locals and 2 horsemen (local also) and 1 evacuated boy (15) on the job besides the dozen COs. The kid, working with us once, was rather cheeky about "conshies" and naturally we told him to shut up. The result – he got rattled – informed the locals of the general trend of our conversation, probably with a few lies and the next we knew was a row on the lorry and nearly blows. The locals, it seems to me, are waiting of [sic] the slightest excuse to beat us up, for we are hated in this valley, we know it only too well. However the foreman made the lad give a more correct version which proved that all we said was in fun or fully justified & the locals are as nice as anything again today[…]

The boys have sorted into their respective groups so that I am living with the ones I should choose, though two, Lister & Minto, left last night[…] leaving Bill, Bernard & myself. I sleep with Bill & genuine brotherly love has sprung up between us. We also work together & are happy together & each cannot stand any other company down here. I have no hesitation in saying that we are the best pair of pals on the job[…]

I must thank you for your repeated kindness – raisins are just as delicious as dates & I am really enjoying them[…] I bought some rubber overpants and have found a great help in them[…] Your kindness has left me suddenly rich![…]

[Signed "Affectionately, Len".]

Cranscombe Farm, 19 November 1940

[…] This Lyn valley is a pretty place but I shall always associate it with the unhappiest weeks of my life up till now. I may have had a comfortable existence hitherto of course, but still these weeks have been unhappy ones.

Even friendship I find is limited. Bill, to whom I have become attached more than any of the others has got on rather well with the pretty daughter of this farm, & Bernard and I have obliged by going to bed immediately after supper to allow the dears a few moments alone with each other. Last night, I wished to finish a letter home after supper & was determined not to neglect it, so that long faces ensued & I was finally asked if my letter was so important as all that. I finished it in bed, but when Bill finally came to bed I had to remind him that my affections for my family were not transient, & contrary to his supposition, were rather important to me[…]

Len got away from the area shortly after this, joining his Exmoor comrade Alec Parlane in south-west Scotland. First he had some time off at home – and clearly his visit to Mona did not go entirely smoothly. Reflecting on the reasons, he realised that his experience on Exmoor had changed him. His almost five months in Kirkcud-brightshire would be a rather happier time for him; he lived separate from the local community with five other pacifists, with whom he got on well, and when there was interaction with the locals they seemed less hostile than the Devon people. Ultimately, though, Len's Scottish experience ended in disillusionment.

Summerhill, Laurieston, Castle Douglas, Kirkcudbrightshire, 2 December 1940

I have just finished my first day's work after my holiday, and apart from my back, which is aching somewhat, I feel none the worse.

We are busy digging drains, making the land around here fit for planting young trees. It is hard work, particularly for the back, because one is bent down all day, and we are up to the eyes in mud. It is interesting work however, up till now, and since I am working in congenial company I am quite content. As you no doubt know, I am with 5 other COs, very good lads and much better than the Exmoor crowd. There are also 3 other locals & a boy, & they also compare very favourably with their Exmoor counterparts, for no foul language & mockery is

The forestry gang, Len is kneeling on the right

ever heard, in fact they work with us and we are all good pals. One of them is the ganger, a dour hard-working little Scot, who sets a hot pace which we try to keep. How much more willing we are here than on Exmoor, and if ever we feel downhearted, instead of wrangling among ourselves, we just commend it to a higher Power at night before we go to bed. You would be surprised to see how different the two camps are.

On Exmoor, every man for himself. At Summerhill, six lads living out Communism in its simplest & most wholesome form.

Besides all this, I like the country much better. It is rugged humped country with lochs in the hollows – there is one where we were working over a mile long. It was so sunny and still that the reflections were a lovely sight[…]

There is one thing on my mind just now, and I wonder if you would help me. What was the matter when I was home? Why were you so fed up with me the first few days. I wish you would tell me in a friendly way, so that it can be cleared up[…]

Summerhill, 7? December 1940

I received your "strong" letter this afternoon, and must thank you for being so frank with me. I can only say how sorry I am that such words are necessary from a friend who has played such an important part in my life. Nevertheless they were necessary.

Last Saturday I was quite pleased to be leaving home again, after longing for it for 2 months. I knew, at the end of that week at home, that I had definitely not fitted into my old niche in my circle of friends. I knew also, on that Saturday, that it was my fault entirely, and that it was better for me to be leaving home again & better for my friends also.

What was the matter? I'm not quite sure. "Every man for himself", as you say, seems to fit me, and it is a lame excuse, no doubt, to say that I was on Exmoor and was one [of] the men included in "every man". It seems very weak, that I should be so influenced by a circle of fellow workmen, but there's no denying I was a different person, a "stranger" from Exmoor, and I cannot blame you for not desiring any more to do with such a person. I need not say how sorry I should be if you really decided upon such a course, and must beg you not to judge upon one week, a week which passed with such a whirl that I had no time to reflect upon what I was doing or why.

Perhaps, after all, you have viewed me in too good a light all along, for I am only too conscious of faults in my character, which I have tried to conquer & which still crop up to my own discomfort. I am aware for instance, of a coarseness which seems to dog my path wherever I go, a coarseness due, I suppose, to the fact that I have had a colliery upbringing in my most impressionable years. Then there is the old self-centredness, which even now is showing through[…]

What I am trying to say is that when such things occur as they did last week, they seem utterly beyond my control; it is something innate & present all the time which erupts at its own pleasure[…]

Excuses, however, cannot mend what has been done, and it is up to me to redeem myself & conquer this outside spirit. I promise to try, and venture to say that in my new life it is already departing. The contrast I made of Exmoor & Laurieston still stands, and I hope, with corresponding results upon myself.

One thing is vastly different, namely, that here, on a windswept hillside, in a disused shepherd's "bothy", I have a home away from home, a home shared with 5 of the best fellows I could wish to meet. We are secretly proud of our little shack, for no outside person has anything to do with its running. We alone keep it clean and tidy, & cook & eat our food in it. We make our own beds and we sleep in them, and all that is implied in that word "we" makes us a happy crowd, considering various little difficulties & tiring work.

You ask about the cooking etc. Each day a cook is chosen, usually Monday – Jim, our leader, Tuesday John, & Robert, George, Alec and Len respectively on the remaining days. The cook gets up first with his orderly (who was the previous day's cook) and attends to the breakfast, but his main duty is to take our grocery order and the milk-can down to the box at the main road, ten minutes walk away. The breakfast is usually made by anybody who is up, however, & George & I take alternate mornings making the porridge. The menu for the dinner is usually decided by Jim, our leader & John our purser in conjunction the night before, with any suggestions from the rest of us, though the choice is simple – potatoes, a vegetable, soup, some form of meat, & some form of sweet if necessary. Quite simple fare, but plenty of it & quite well cooked[…]

After devouring this fare & criticising it in the time-honoured fashion of men, we all set to and wash-up & tidy generally & then settle down to read, write, sew or whatever. We have no supper or evening cocoa here, and after Bible-reading & Prayers at about 9 to 10 we retire, not before preparing the morrow's lunch[…]

We are felling an old birch wood & burning the trees so as to clear up for replanting with better trees, larch & spruce[…]

Mona's response to Len's apology "comforted" him, he wrote on 12 December. "It is you who seem repentant this time and why? I was wrong – I know it now, and it is I who should be repentant." He explained that his companions made all the difference compared with Exmoor: "I have no particular 'close' friend to the exclusion of the others – we are all good pals with no cliques and gossip or anything." Len described the men, who were mainly in their mid-twenties – Jim McCaw, "officially chosen as our leader", an assessor for Glasgow City Council; John Armstrong from Edinburgh, "the only non-Xtian pacifist among us (humanitarian

The young Len, with Mona

grounds)"; Robert Hewitt, a sub-editor on the Glasgow Citizen; George Gilchrist, another Glaswegian and a tomato-grower; and the 30-year-old Alec Parlane, "a fellow Tynesider & Exmoor victim", who was a window-cleaner and Sunday-school worker. Len had known him formerly at Byker Young Men's Institute. "And I am the baby of the house, but fortunately have already been able to reassume my ambulance duties by attending to cuts & squeezing Archie's [Alec's] boils, and massaging sore muscles etc. Otherwise a nuisance no doubt, because I am a big eater, but make up somewhat by 'sacrificing' the sugar in my tea". Len added: "I'm very fit now and swinging the axe, a 7 pounder better than ever[…] We cut and limbed three big spruce, the biggest I've seen, on the roadside[…] It is very interesting work".

Summerhill, Sunday 14 December 1940

[…] The boys are very busy planting still but Jim (the big local) & myself are still snedding[7] trees blown down in last week's gale. It is sometimes a disadvantage being big, for the boys say planting is quite light work, if tedious, and Jim & I are sick of snedding; the cross-cut saw is blunt as old harry[…]

Your news of the PPU[8] interests me, and I am strongly on the side of you & George [Carr?][9]. Mass movements confound me; I gain more comfort in knowing you, George, my six workmates & a few others are with me & I with them than in gloating over the 130,000 of the PPU. If it were more our concern to make boily[10] for John[11] than to make Germany friends with England, I think things would be considerably better all round. Unfortunately, the boily falls into the background when one begins considering a mass appeal against war or whatever. If only we could keep the boily to the fore, how much better[…]

Summerhill, Sunday 22 December 1940

[…] I am very happy this weekend, because by now our domestic machine is working so well & smoothly that we have far more leisure[…] I noticed the temperature was 38 degrees Fahrenheit. And also that I have put on nearly a stone since I came here, being 12 stone clothed (without overcoat)[…]

Is it correct that 4,000 are dead in Coventry or just a rumour. If it is true, I cannot understand how this bloody war goes on. We have a very keen sub-editor, and I am always slating him and his snappy headlines, knowing that such things are used to keep people going through fear of enemy brutality etc etc. "Beware of Quislings", "Report all rumours and defeatism" and so on[…] We get no daily newspaper, however, and even though Robert gets his weekly supplies & I my *Sunday Times,* we are spared the daily round of rubbish that makes up our press & wireless news & are consequently grateful[…]

Two themes emerge in Len's next letter that would resurface regularly over the following years. First is the longing for a return to normality of men torn by the war from their home lives and hopes of self-fulfilment. Secondly, he notes the banal effect that hard, monotonous physical labour can have on the mind.

Summerhill, 9 January 1941

[…] I am still finding it hard to resign myself to a long spell in exile here, and even find the thought frightful at times. I made one sweeping resignation by having all my hair cut off, thus not daring to come home. I now look like a well-fed Nazi[…]

You ask what I put in my journal. Not much I'm afraid – somehow my thoughts are an utter blank these days. It may be the heavy work with the axe that does this, and some "gentler" occupation with the spade will perhaps provoke more thought. I jot down anything interesting I see, like six bad-tempered swans trying to land on the frozen loch, and fluttering about with the queerest noises. Otherwise I think not at all and that is my biggest regret. Big muscles apparently mean little minds.

God knows when I'll see you all again. I hope this war ends quickly. In our most depressed moments, how we wish for that happy day when we can return to our homes and jobs. To see the months passing by in this job where none of us is in the least interested hurts sometimes, especially when we reflect that the longer we are in this job the further we are from real jobs. That's the main trouble here – our job isn't "real" to us[…]

Summerhill, 18 January 1941

I received a letter from you yesterday and a parcel and letter from you today and they were all grand. You certainly have the right idea of our needs and mine[…]

The jacket is now on me, and is warm, thank you. It has come at a good time, for like you, we are having a cold time[…]

We were discussing Joad[12] at dinner tonight, and Bertrand Russell, and then got round to free love, somehow. Sometimes our discussions are quite serious, other times silly, as on free love, though we took it all most seriously[…]

Your mention of "Everyman, I will go with thee, and be thy guide, In thy most need to go by thy side" is a wise quotation. Yes, my reading goes with me, sometimes giving me the greatest joy, and my friendship too. Many hours each day are spent with you and my home, "in the spirit", and you are always by my side in that sense. Solitude is becoming a need for me, and I often lunch alone now, usually reading the *TLS* or, at present, the *Biographical Dict of Eng Lit*[…] On the whole,

I'm quite happy in the thought that I'm free, and that I could find worse situations[…]

[Signed "Affectionately, Len".]

Summerhill, 20 January 1941

[…] I'm feeling in a bad temper, being bit rheumaticy again with this biting wind and having a bad cough which refuses to leave me[…]

I am afraid your pampering these last few years has made me a bit soft & I take it very badly when our boss here makes us work in a blizzard to keep his books right. The Forestry Commission looks after every little tree, as God with his sparrows, but with men – well, as I said I'm a bit soft.

I have finished *Madame Bovary* and am grateful to you for recommending it. It has left a lasting impression as a novel & as a work of art[…]

And on the same subject, your remarks on "free love" seemed fresh & good after our wordy discussion that I remember now again. Men such as us discuss in a rather stupid way, you know, though one must admit that we are handicapped by the total absence of our women folk, mothers, friends, relatives, sweethearts and so on from our lives. Women can be so sane in discussion[…

Because of the [sawing] horse being broken at the weekend, very little sawing was done, which meant doing it at nights during the week, so I've just done an hour. However the saw was giving a lot of trouble. We thought it was the dampness in the wood, but it was the same on the dry logs, so I said it wanted sharpening, forgetting that nobody had sharpened a bushman's saw except myself. I took great pains with it & we were overjoyed to find it working well again, for it was torture before, sticking after a blade's depth.

But why be practical in a letter? Because we are all finding our minds confined to practical things only. I was talking to Jim today about my slow mind these days & he was experiencing the same – no thoughts whatever, practically the whole day, not even thoughts of the past. We both agreed that this job, & any physical labour, is slowing us up tremendously. To think a thing out, we both found that we had to do the same, namely, speak to ourselves in order to keep to the point

& Jim says he has even found himself talking aloud to himself to puzzle something out. You may find that hard to believe, but unless we do this, our thought just fritters out & we go on snedding & burning or whatever we are doing.

You must forgive me if I get depressed again sometimes, for even here, when I am living with such a fine lot of fellows, much better than on Exmoor, I have my bad moments, when plain homely comfort, home & friends seem far, far away. But I must dismiss these gloomy thoughts[…]

Summerhill, 26 January 1941

[…] I am like a child these days, the way I look out for your letters, and on a day when I expect there will be one, I am quite eager to get home. I then, with the greatest will power, leave it till after dinner to open & then, leaning back on my chair and smoking, I read the letter and it gives me the greatest pleasure to be thus – reading your letter, smoking, well down in my chair.

The next day I think many times during the day what I am to answer with, if I can think, and then I write it down absolutely unlike what I thought.

After all that, I must thank you very much for 'East Coker', which I shall treasure. I have read it several times by now, which is in itself a feat for Summerhill[…]

> Dawn points, and another day
> Prepares for heat and silence. Out at sea the dawn wind
> Wrinkles and slides. I am here
> Or there, or elsewhere. In my beginning.

Here, where I see every dawn, that sinks deep, for, as you say, while my active mind is practically dormant, my subconscious might be doing goodness knows what and at dawn, one trudges along, not thinking at all, but feeling just like those lines. One does not think or understand, and one need not understand those lines: but both the trudge at dawn and the lines themselves can be felt deeply[…]

I have been rather depressed since about the New Year. It has lifted a great deal by now, especially as one or two good quiet evenings have enabled me to read. On Friday night we finished early, it being pay-day (we are paid at 4.45), and we had a good long evening. To purge myself, I read some modern verse, besides Eliot[…] One piece from [Wilfred] Owen's 'Exposure' suited my mood, after our cold spell.

> The poignant misery of dawn begins to grow…
> We only know war lasts, rain soaks, and clouds sag stormy
> Dawn massing in the east her melancholy army
> Attacks once more in ranks on shivering ranks of gray,
> But nothing happens.

Despite the fact that I have felt nothing of poor Owen's 'Exposure', I have honestly held some of those very impressions. "The misery of dawn" & "dawn massing in the east her melancholy army" to attack us. Our only hope these busy days is that the attack begins before we set out, but it never does, and we go out and stay out and take the attack unresisting. We come home soaked and miserable and I think you will understand why I am depressed sometimes[…]

I read the Coventry article from *NALGO*[13], and was of course, distressed to read of the many casualties and the public services destroyed. Food and water absent in a "civilised" city seems astounding but when you consider the horrible possibilities of modern war, it is not so astounding, only a bitter fact. The figure of 250 killed & 1,200 wounded seemed quite low, thank goodness, when compared with 37,000 homes damaged[…]

[Signed "Affectionately yours, Len".]

Summerhill, 30 January 1941

[…] I seem to have said something wrong when I said I was pampered. But I was thinking today – it's not that I was pampered, but that I was treated as a human being and not as a workman from whom so much output is expected. We are all, in the bothy, very fed up now over this, since we were told that our next pay but once would be full pay, 48/- a week, and the forester now comes daily on to the job to do nothing except stand over us and watch each man carefully to see if he is "proficient". The ganger is also smitten with the same disease, and we all now experience his stare when we rest a little, for rest we must sometimes, even if he does not. Yesterday the forester was on the job twice and we were very tired, trying for some daft reason to look proficient. This morning, imagine our disgust when the ganger says "No slacking today you fellows – most of you were just about marking time at 5 last night. Every minute counts you know." Now none of us likes this and none is used to it either. The contrast makes me wonder if I was pampered, but I was only treated as a man, and I'm grateful for that[…]

Summerhill, 31 January 1941

[…] I saw today two seagulls courting somewhat noisily above the wood today, and their queer cries, & the way one followed the other patiently as they circled around, reminded me of a night when I was listening to Vaughan Williams's setting for orchestra, violin and choir to Walt Whitman's tragic poem of the deserted gull, who is left alone through his mate's disappearance, to care for their young ones. That music haunted me, and even now, in my present dull state, I can recall its mysterious flow[…] Those evenings were delightful, and peace to me is embodied in them. How happy I should be if I could only recommence them, just now, listening in as we used to, or reading poetry, as I did sometimes (I must have had a nerve, with my voice!), or just talking. If I'd been at home, how we should have had rushed to Iona Road to hear as much as we could of *La Traviata*. And then, after that, we should have had supper, always delightful, even in the days when I did not know there was food like that on Exmoor. All that is not indulgence, but just peace, and I cannot tell you how much and how often I long for it[…]

Sunday. It was a glorious dawn today, and as I was up by myself to make breakfast, my mate Jim being at home, I hurried round in order to have a walk up Kenick Hill, behind Summerhill. It is nearly 1,000 ft, not very high, but commanding a magnificent view. The locals call it the Hill of Health. [Long poem written by Len about the experience enclosed][…] That masterpiece was composed (rather concocted) on this delightful walk – most of it. I thoroughly enjoyed it[…]

[Signed "Your affectionate poet, Len".]

Summerhill, 6 February 1941

[…] On Tuesday we had a day at shreefing, the worst job I have ever done in all my life. It consists of making holes for planting trees in heather. You slash at the heather and its roots with a special razor-edge spade, and every blow needs all your strength or the spade just bounces off the tough heather. Try cutting heather the next time you see any at the roots and you'll see. Even the ganger, a tough little stoic, was thoroughly tired and complained of his shoulders. The Summer-hill lads of course were almost prostrated. Imagine our relief, therefore, when we woke next morning to find a fine old blizzard blowing. It was so terrible that work was out of the question, but was it. No we had to grind axes, and again I must ask you to try if possible turning the handle of a grindstone with two axes on it and you realise the full significance of having your nose to the grindstone. When the forester came up to see what we [were] doing, he noticed that while we were not having a turn at the grindstone we were idle, so he made us wash the whole bothy out and saw wood[…] So on the whole, my short-lived happiness at the weekend is about gone. Excuse the writing – a pen is hard to grip after an axe[…]

[Letter unsigned]

Len gamely tried to write again the next day, although he could "hardly hold this pen" after three days of shreefing. "Writing is really a painful process, making my hand ache." The forester had put the men back on summer time so they now started work at 7.30, although it remained dark until about 8 so they stood about wasting time. "A 9 hour day is terribly long, especially when half an hour has to go on top of that for dinner."

Clearly Len went home late in February, apparently having not written to Mona for some time – perhaps due to his writing grip being incapacitated by work. By now the group at Summerhill was beginning to break up, the early idealism worn down by the rigours of the job and the demands of the forester. Len himself had arranged a new job at Horsley much closer to home.

Summerhill, Monday 3 March 1941

I arrived here quite safe & sound, though of course very depressed, last night about 10.30[…]

To return to Summerhill, I found things worse if anything, the boys being very much discouraged. John is leaving on Thursday and has even sent off his trunk off with his clothes, all without giving notice. He has no job to go to either & is very silent & glum about the whole matter.

Jim goes to the other extreme in a fortnight's time and is getting married. He is bringing his bride back to Laurieston where he is renting rooms off the farmer[…]

That means that only 3 will be left at the bothy and poor souls I don't know how they will manage. Probably the unit will be broken up unless 3 more can be found. This latter is improbable as men are very hard to get I'm told & bosses are unwilling to release those who are not COs.

So our poor unit has gone to the dogs all of a sudden. I am coming to the conclusion that the COs are not half so tough as in the last war. We can't stick much you see. I've moved twice already myself & will probably be just as discontented at Horsley. I'm fighting it already but I'm sure it'll be just the same[…]

As I never thank you properly to your face, I really must thank you for the good time I had while at home, having evenings at your home & nice meals & a quite [sic] time (or sleepy time) in an armchair. And also for those beautiful records[…]

[Signed "Yours affectionately, Len".]

Summerhill, 7 March 1941

I have not answered to the delightful parcel of malt etc yet, and tonight I was well in arrears when I received a second letter from you. Thank you very much for the malt & for the papers today[…]

Now as regards the exam. I know you will think I'm just trying to find excuses but I find that after two pages of writing I'm absolutely finished & this is written with numerous interruptions (two on this page). My wrist aches so. So after your kindness in paying the fee, you must think me awfully ungrateful but I really think it's impossible. Please resign yourself to this and don't be vexed with me – circumstances just aren't favourable[…]

[Signed "With my thoughts & love, Len".]

Len now moved to a market gardening job in Horsley, a small village between Hadrian's Wall and the River Tyne some 10 miles from Newcastle. This meant he could see Mona most weekends, yet they continued to exchange letters regularly. Over the following months their relationship began to deepen. In his first letter from his new lodgings he mentioned the visual arts for the first time.

c/o Mrs Henderson, Duke's Cottages, Horsley, Newcastle,
26 March 1941

[…] Your letter was somewhat of a surprise to me, for as far as I knew, I left you in quite good spirits. However, I seem to have upset you somehow. I hope it was not because I declined to come back with you to dinner. If so, you must surely have thought I declined because of being tired of your company or something like that, which of course is absolutely untrue. The truth was that my parents thought it would be a treat for me to go with them in the doctor's car on Sunday afternoon. As it was it was no treat, as I expected, for the car is far too small for long legs like mine and it throbs most violently all the time. The drive proved to be a dreary tour up the North Road to Morpeth, to Mitford & around a little & back down the North Road home. I hated it, but of course did not tell them so, and all this while Beethoven's Fifth was on. No, I would have preferred coming back with you, but as I had to be with my parents some time, especially when they asked, I had little choice in the matter. I hope I have not offended you, but I know what your headaches mean so I must have done. No offence was meant, as I hope I have shown. You really must not get upset like this when I am with my parents or with other friends. You must not take it as a slight to yourself when I go to them, for it is not that I put them before you but because one must not forget parents & friends[…]

I am finding [Bernard] Berenson's *Painters* heavy going but well worth it. Some day perhaps I shall be privileged to visit Venice Florence or Rome and so on, and I shall have a background as I visit the various places of interest. At present I must content myself with reading of the various artists' qualities beauties and characteristics.

[Signed "Yours affectionately, Len".]

Horsley, 2 April 1941

Here's April in and what vile weather. Things are hopelessly behind now and we are anticipating a rush as soon as any fine weather comes along. There are umpteen acres to plough, then to sow or plant out. With a few drying winds that are to be expected in March the plough- ing should have been finished but it rains without ceasing, so here we are, fiddling about with leeks and packing up young cabbage plants into dozens.

This morning I came in wet from digging up old sprouts, but when I saw your parcel I cheered up. Thank you for the nice things[…]

So much for the "jam" – now for the "pill". What the _ do you think I am. *[The Fortunes of] Richard Mahony*[14] is some 980 pages long, [Walter] Pater also attracts me with some long chapters and I have a whole essay of Berenson to finish, and you go and pile it on with Long[15] and the *Age of Wordsworth*[16]. Now please, miss, do you mind. I'm not taking that exam and that's that. Since gentle persuasion does not seem to work I must be firm like the bloke in *Fumed Oak*[17], and yell down your neck that I'm not b--y well taking that exam. How's that now. It does feel good to assert oneself. Not that I can lose my temper these days[…]

Horsley, 9 April 1941

[…] We are, like you!!! very busy, and I've been getting up a real bumper cargo for the market tomorrow. Mordue [the farmer] has been out all day for two days trying to get manure, so left me to it with Mary. 40 dozen cabbage, 30 stone of sprouts, 24 dozen leeks, 80 dozen pickle cabbage plants. They are all packed & I had a good time getting the numerous loads out from the fields to the yard. Anyway, I seem to have done alright in my first job as "foreman" and he meekly thanked me, saying he didn't know how to get Gilroy his order and get the precious manure for the potatoes[…]

Reading is so precious to me now, not only as leisure, but as my chief link between the past & the future, that I am forced to read what interests me deeply only. In other words, I cannot read haphazardly like a librarian, tasting this & that, jumping from one interest to another, but must confine myself to those "must" books we all have, the books "we must read some time"[…]

Your suggestion that access to [Quaker] meeting was making me happier is quite true. Frustration there will always be as long as the war lasts & after, but to be constantly away from like-minded people is the greatest frustration of all. I've not been to meeting for months until a few weeks ago and I know now how valuable it is for us to meet like that[…]

This letter was signed "Affectionately, Len", as was his next one dated 16 April which noted the effect of "war nerves" on his family and the Hendersons, with whom he was lodging: "They are losing so much sleep over raids that take place about 15 mile [sic] away that they are rather crabby."

On 24 April Len thanked Mona for sending him "the expressed soul of Michelangelo all in one parcel". He admitted to only a "slight knowledge of Michelangelo's work", and was impressed by the "exquisite unfinished items in the volume". It seems Mona at least played a part in introducing Len to the world of sculpture.

Horsley, 30 April 1941

[…] I said I might elucidate what I had said about Michelangelo's art, but I have come to the conclusion that it is outside the scope of a letter. That is not an excuse. I have thoughts about the matter, I have compared and contrasted him with others as far as my meagre knowledge permits, and I believe I could express, though probably very obscurely, my conclusions. But there are three reasons for not doing so. One, I would be presuming too much, not having seen an original piece of his art. Secondly, my conclusions would be no doubt very immature, and lastly, they would be influenced, I know by what I have [read] recently concerning him in Pater, Berenson and [Jacob] Burckhardt. You may think I am presuming even to say so, but I have developed, in my own little way, certain theories of art, and by now, they have a background (very small I know) of reading. The chief influence is Roger Fry's *Last Lectures,* particularly the two on 'Sensibility' and 'Technique', which are the culminating point of years of aesthetic experience and speculation as found in *Vision & Design*[…]

I am reading exceptionally well lately and the gradual departure of that living on my reserves which seems to have characterised my life these last few months, has left my mind more retentive than ever before I'm sure. I am laying aside almost everything and reading for my exam, not the text books only but the works themselves, the latter mostly in fact, though I like Herford's *Age of Wordsworth* very much. This is not to say that I have hopes of passing the exam. I am enjoying the poetry, not studying it drily, and I'm afraid those "little people" will finally be my downfall, along with facts, dates etc. I don't mind in the least however, for the poets are fairly fascinating me at present[...]

[Signed "Affectionately yours, Len".]

Horsley, 7 May 1941

Your parcel came to cheer me up, for I have been depressed this week for no definite reason. Probably it's this messing about with the clock – the day seems much longer, working until 6.30. Getting up later does not seem to make any difference[…]

Regarding my own exaggerated sufferings at Devon, they have produced nothing, to my mind, and though you attribute my present more stimulated mind to that I'm sure you're wrong and that it is only lighter work and more outdoor experience that has caused this. The whole thing is negative, and no positive results have accrued from what I felt at either Devon or Laurieston. My mind is not yet up to the pitch it kept while I was in the library, though that of course was never very high. Any elation I might express at increased mental facility must be taken with a pinch of salt. Last week, I think it was I said I was thinking better than ever before, but that's all rot. It only seems so after months of utter torpor of the brain[…]

The time Len and Mona were spending together every weekend was bringing matters to a head. She now wrote to him conveying deeper feelings than ever before – this after one of their difficult meetings. In his reply Len tried to explain himself and clarify her feelings.

Horsley, 13 May 1941

I received your letter (& chocolate etc) this morning and the letter has been with me all day. I am still vague as to how to answer such a letter, but I hope you will believe me when I say I thought that letter the most lovable I've ever received in my life. It is preposterous that I, who can be so cruel, received such words, and they entered deeply (all this sounds like an effusive Frenchman, but I cannot say what I mean properly.)

In my journal, where I am quite honest with myself, I have written for yesterday the following. "I wish I could cure them (the moods), but they seem to wrap themselves around me like a mist that will leave me only at its own pleasure. In the meantime, I may have insulted a friend, and I'm afraid Mona found me too much for her on Sunday."

I quote that because the entry was made spontaneously, without any thought beforehand, and because it is therefore sincere if anything I write is sincere. And thinking today, it suddenly came back to me that I wrote in a similar strain to you once, after my behaviour between leaving Exmoor & going to Laurieston. My mood on Sunday was similar, self-centred as usual and yet somehow beyond me entirely. How many times have you been snarled at in such moments? The best way is not to speak one word. I am making excuses here, but I don't apologise or even wish to excuse myself. It's no use – I can't even talk about such moods. When I'm not in one, they seem as mysterious to me as to you. I'm not trying to simulate some Byronic mood to be exclusively trotted out at irregular intervals. Oh, "words fail me!" We'll let that pass for the present.

It is with the other part of the letter that I am now concerned, where you write how much you care for me, how you would help in anyway [sic] possible and comfort and encourage me. If any friend has ever done all those things and more for another friend, you have done them for me, and I feel always undeserving, ungrateful and even unfriendly. But underneath all you say in this letter and indeed underneath all your letters to me, most of which I have kept, I know there is something deeper, a love which transcends even that of the deepest friendship. Forgive me if I am wrong – it sounds awful to say I hope I am, for if I am unworthy of your friendship, what am I worth to your love. I know such a love is heedless of faults in the object of its love. Again words are difficult. You will wish to know just what you are to me, and since this letter is the frankest I've written, I shall be quite honest, even if I'm "terribly honest" as you write. First I need hardly say you are my best friend, and that if I were to make an inventory of my possessions in this life I should put your friendship at the top along with my family. (Please see through what appears to be flattery.) In my years of youth, i.e. from first meeting you till now, you have been the guiding light in my life. All I have aimed at and attained has been due to you, and you have been a parent to me in guiding me, be it unwittingly at times, to those things which have come to mean life for me. Would I have known Quakerism but for you? Art? Literature? All those other things which have raised me from an ordinary colliery boy to at any rate a more or less emancipated colliery boy? Perhaps rather less than more in ultimates, but that is not your fault.

All that means nothing perhaps to you, if only I return that love that you have for me. And though it must hurt you extremely, I have to say quite honestly that while your love transcends friendship, mine is contained in friendship, even if it is that deep Platonic friendship of Michelangelo for Vittoria Collonna. And God knows how I want that little quality above the deepest friendship that has come to be called love in the sense of that bond between man and woman. I love you as a friend, and whatever I do to discredit that, I still love you, and yet will still be the same awkward duffer as and when I please. It is no fallacy that those we love most we hurt most. Perhaps your love for me is just the same but if I divine rightly it is above that. You would be deeply hurt if I were to form a friendship with another woman. (Forgive me if this sounds harsh.) I am not accusing you of so low a thing as jealousy but, even if you hid your feelings, I know how it would wound you. And yet such a thing could be possible. My love for you could go alongside that different kind of love I might have for another woman, and that would be a cause of distress to you, distress which I pray I shall never give, and yet give at every moment[…]

No, whatever you may think of me, however much you idealize me, I am not worthy of your friendship, much less your love, and it is a great pity that things are as they are. I do not wish to humiliate myself, but this unworthiness, this instability, & even lack of integrity are a source of distress to me, especially with regard to my connections with you & the Friends[…]

Forgive me for what is harsh in this letter & please realize that in spite of everything my affection for you is the same as ever.

[Signed "Affectionately yours, Len".]

This was followed up on the 14th by a short letter flippantly dismissing his previous day's thoughts as "such drivvle". It was signed simply "Yours, Len". He saw Mona the weekend after. His next letter was dated 27 May.

The war is rarely mentioned at length in Len's letters before he joined the army, but occasionally his pacifist instincts were pricked, as in this startling letter.

Horsley, 27 May 1941

I suppose you are experiencing the same feelings as myself just now, after the gory *Hood-Bismarck* affair. Have you ever heard such gloating, such satisfaction at revenge. Humanity has indeed sunk low. I was greeted at tea-time yesterday with the question "Have you heard the good news?" I could not think of what to say. I knew I was expected to be overjoyed like the rest, but like you, I had hoped and hoped the *Bismarck* would get away safely. It's no good hiding the fact. When Englishmen gloat and pray for such sinkings I become naturally sympathetic with the Germans. The worst thing of all is that the *Hood* & its men are almost forgotten, while the sinking of the *Bismarck* is a source of rejoicing less than a week after. And even without the *Hood*, we learn in discreetly placed columns that 2 cruisers & 4 destroyers have gone down off Crete. That's over 20,000 tons, and many hundred men, no doubt. But why worry, we got the *Bismarck*.

It seems to have been like a fox hunt, with plenty in at the kill. But still we boast that we got down the "unsinkable" Nazi battleship. I suppose such things will always be on this earth. Now aren't we a hypocrisy?[…]

Don't think from the rather gray tone of this letter that I am unhappy this week. While not so far gone as to indulge in Lotos-eating, I am quite dull and unconsciously doing my work quite presentably I suppose. I was working in the downpour, alone, cutting and packing 720 head of lettuce, i.e. 60 dozen. Tuesday planting. Today 46 dozen lettuce and 4 and a half cwt of a new I.P.C. manure spread[…]

Mona and Len had another difficult weekend together. She remonstrated with him, and he again tried to apologise. He now set the template for his response to these periodic upheavals; he would blame himself (while yet trying to find an explanation), suggest that Mona might be better off ending contact with him, but leave the decision to her.

Horsley, 12 June 1941

This time last week I was rather tired and did not answer your letter because I did not feel up to it[…] However, the letter has been very much in my mind since I got it and tonight I read it in reference to that other letter which you wrote on 15 May. Talking personally can be quite a difficult medium and that is the prime importance of letters.

Now in each case these two letters followed after one of my stupid tantrums, in which you quite rightly dub me "the spoilt one", and "the only one to be considered", and I'm sure that, despite what you say about my lack of apologies, that I have conveyed to you how sorry I was after them[…]

The important thing is that you consider in each letter breaking off with me and just being a sort of pen-friend as you are with Matt[18]. And here I must make myself as clear as possible. I want you to realize that I am looking at this as detachedly (?) as possible. You are quite at liberty to cease seeing me as you do at present. I don't wish to bind you in any way as regards our friendship, and while this sounds awfully chivalrous etc, I really mean it, because, in the first place, I know we live on different planes, and without flattering, it is I who bring you down from your higher plane to my power. This is constantly in my mind, even if my egotistical and self-centred attitude belies it. And I do so want you to stay where you belong without me in any way spoiling you. That may sound much too 'umble, but we are of different levels, don't you think? Friendship should be mutual in the aspect of the contribution of each friend, but I'm afraid my contribution to our friendship is very meagre when compared with your own. Not only in material things, of course, for there I contribute scarcely anything, but in spiritual values. You have made me what I am, and if I am of any worth it is due to your friendship. And in return – what? Reserved feelings, occasional tempers, ingratitude and in short, absence of any spiritual contribution to our friendship[…] I want you to consider coldly our relations, and not to consider me (I do that) but yourself. If for your own sake it would be better to break off our friendship as it is, you must please do so and I will understand[…] I have always made it clear I hope that you meant much to me, and even though I would go further and say that most of my thoughts centred round you, I should be willing to learn to do without you if I thought it was better for you. Willing, but need I say, sorry too. However you must not think of that and do what you think is best. Your holiday is a good opportunity to think things over, to value things in your own light without any interference[…]

[Signed "Ever yours, Len".]

Mona now wrote a "confession" of her true feelings for Len. He replied with one of his own – the revelation that his mistreatment of her was partly caused by "class feeling" arising from discomfort at being dependent on her as a "parvenu" in the "different world" to which she had introduced him.

Horsley, Wednesday evening (18 June 1941?)

[…] In some parts of your letter, you call it a "confession". Please don't think of your letter, which I shall keep of course, as a confession, but rather as a confirmation once & for all of what you feel regarding me.

You are right, above all, in what you say of Olive & Arthur [Good][19] – we are in harmony as much and more as they are, for very definite reasons. I have always felt they were a nice couple, but that Arthur, who once at any rate looked higher, is dragged back by Olive. With you and I there is nothing of this but on the other hand an increasing desire on my part to come along with you in that higher plane of which I wrote last time.

I know I have been the opposite at times – many times I'm afraid – but we'll not go into that now except to say that you will be quite aware, as I am, of the two facets of myself which have loved you and ignored you in turn[…]

You know how I have snubbed you & hurt you, & I know too, and yet it was not because I hated you ever but, as I said in my last letter, because I resented you. It wanted but the slightest excuse to precipitate this queer aversion, & its usual expression was to ignore you & perhaps flirt with young things or be too effusive to Arthur or Olive or Norman[20] or whoever we were with[…] This resentment – why resent you?

Well, you have always been kind to me, and always I have been dependent upon you, for something or other. And along with your kindness you gave a warmth of affection which in my untrained "Felling" eyes was just the same as familiarity, & therefore enabled me to speak & behave to you as I pleased. This meant I could make little pin-prick raids on your loyalty as my expression of thanks, for when I was so dependent I subconsciously hated it and you suffered.

But we became greater friends than ever, & your hurts more personal & the resentment developed, though here more subconsciously (if there are degrees of the subconscious). The feeling was now what has often been called class feeling. In ourselves it is not so obvious perhaps, though obvious enough. But contrast your father with mine, your family, in fact, your whole upbringing, and even your heritage. God – what a difference! No wonder I have fought with you. I have felt these things so deeply, even though that may sound like the hero in a Communist novel. To touch a different world from what you were brought up for, & yet be a parvenu in it is difficult to describe. And it breeds a kind of psychological distrust of oneself, a disease which expresses itself in such things as hate or resentment of the one who brought [me] to this new world. [W.H.] Auden would know alone what I mean without his having experienced it.

Just lately, however, I have become more aware of the other emotion concerning you. All along I have felt both, but my preoccupation with the resentment has hidden the love. And now it is the opposite and I hope that the resentment will die & disappear, as I feel it is, quickly.

And so you say inevitably "What do you think?" Well, again I am not too sure of myself, in the sense that I know, but do not trust myself. I am still very young and am worried about that "holy grail" of mine, personal integrity.

You say beautifully "When we are together… we are perfectly happy, as we were on Friday evening. And perhaps you love me as much as I love you. That is for you to say." Yes, I feel there is a bond between us that many a couple lack, and it is a bond that is based not

upon worldly desires or passions, but upon a deeper basis – there is a
bond of the spirit if you like, though that is vague[…]

And that is how we are linked. And that is how I love you & you
me. The outward things are all against it, but what of it. You are 37
or something, I 22. You have a middle class family, I a working class
one, but we must ignore these things and many others "And so live
on, or else swoon to death"[21]. In fact, my main fault is that I will think
of them. And I am always left with the thought "What will come of
it all?" I also wonder what your people would think. Mine benefit
much the same as I do from your affection & must hurt you sometimes
as I do, but they will always be like that. I'm young enough to change,
they aren't.

"*Carpe diem*" immediately leaps into our minds. But I feel about that
philosophy as I do about Marius's Epicureanism & about most
philosophies – that it does not hold for every situation & in all, may
fit mighty few. "So what?" you say. Well, I just don't know but could
we leave it at that just now. These would amount to love letters, would-
n't they, & yet we are so matter-of-fact, aren't we, and so careful not
to go too far. We are both shy in that respect[…]

[Signed "With my thoughts and love, Len".]

Horsley, 25 June 1941

I think you will have been disappointed not to see a letter from me
waiting for you when you got home. Unfortunately, it was most difficult to write last night or Monday night. I got a letter from Bill
[Hamilton] sort of asking for advice, as he seemed very upset about
the Russian business[22] & I think he will join up because of it. He
seemed rather depressed & I tried to cheer him up as best I could &
also told him (after giving my point of view for what it was worth) that
I didn't give a damn whether he was a conshie or a soldier, I was
always his friend.

So you won't be cross with me after being so "big-hearted" to
someone else. And it is now impossible to write more than one letter
an evening as my regular starting time is 6.30 until further notice.
Besides this blow, up till now I have worked on until 7.30 every night
this week, so leisure is considerably cut down. Which is all very

mournful. Oh, I forgot, my back is nearly in 2 with three days' planting, so I'm once more in need of what you once called "female adulation"[…]

Matters were coming to a head between Mona and Len. His response reflects the social mores of the time, and also reveals that he had gone to Exmoor the previous autumn because he thought "things weren't correct" between them.

Horsley, 1 July 1941

Somehow your letter was no surprise this morning, in the sense that I expected a letter, but not in the sense of the contents. The contents – well – I don't know, I might have expected even them, and yet I was so moved that I had to give up my breakfast in the middle & just sit & recover.

For you have written what I had myself in mind many a time & yet had never dared develop the thoughts or mention them even to you. So to see my former "renegade" thoughts on paper was a bit of a shock, but as they have been with me all day, and I knew you would expect some word from me, I decided to write, even though this is a mere "put-off" till we see each other again, and I don't really know what to say yet.

I may as well discuss your "several courses" that you suggest we can take.

Your first course was, strange to say, the one in my mind on Sunday. I was in such a puzzle over the whole business, unable to see any end or anything, that I felt like rushing back to Exmoor & just rusticating there, bearing the discomforts & leading a monkish existence. All very romantic, and yet a real idea, for, though you may think I am exaggerating or making up stories, my sudden departure to Exmoor last summer was because of you. I don't mean to blame you or anything by that statement, but you know how my decision was then rather inconsistent with my previous theories and it was made because I thought things weren't correct between you & I and I had better solve it all by acquiescing to what must come sooner or later[…] The idea of leaving each other alone would solve our social difficulties etc but otherwise would only hurt us, & be a sin as you say.

The second course reminds me of the most moving sentence in Virginia Woolf's life of Roger Fry, in which she just mentions that at a certain time Roger had decided to live with Helen Anrep. Virginia, as I said, just mentions it, because any development would only be to satisfy curious minds whose business it was not. But in her mention, she somehow conveys that she approved, even if it was not correct to do so. And for you and I, it would be an easy way out. We already live together in one sense, & in the complete sense, it would seem almost the same to other eyes. But the secrecy involved in even that statement would always torment us I think, and there would be, as you say, always a doubt. And then again, is it right to ignore social standards so fully. But I must discuss this with you & indeed the whole situation.

"Remains friendship (which we have already) or the deeper relationship of marriage". You make what amounts to a proposal to me. It is a strange feeling, being proposed to, and it really did make me just sit back to recover. I may exaggerate the importance of what you say, but I think not, for you even go so far as to mention material details. I know it's all up to me, now, and I cannot say where I stand. That I love you is without question, since it has been questioned so long & stood all tests that I know that by now. But to be practical – and blunt – I couldn't live on you so to speak, though you would do everything possible for us. I might sound proud, but it is not pride. There is a deeper feeling of responsibility, which hitherto has not extended very much beyond contributing a little to the home. It is not security I want or any smug living on the fat of the land before I move, but there is an instinct which is weak in me & which I could easily ignore, the instinct that made the cave-man go out & hunt for his mate & family. But I must obey it and never feel I'm just resting on my oars while you're pulling your weight[…]

So, my dear, I will not, here, at any rate, raise hopes or dash them, but just wait till I see you, when this cursed week of toil is over[…]

[Signed "Love, Len".]

Horsley, 2 July 40 [means 1941]

[…] Your own brief letter this morning came as usual to cheer me up and really, you must not worry about me either. I know you will not worry, but I mean rather upset or something. I'm quite alright, just plodding along, & thinking things out gradually, and can't put it into words what I think of you when you acquiesce so cheerfully to my slowness (for I shall be slow I think) and just wait. And also, too, I'm most grateful for the way you wish to mitigate what you describe as suffering, but I don't suffer anything beyond the usual pain that all people but those like Blake must undergo[…]

[Signed "Love, Len".]

Horsley, 9 July 1941

[…] It seems that we must encounter many obstacles before things will settle down for us. We must never forget that and if ever it really does [seem] to be an impasse for us, as it seemed on Sunday evening, we must apply your late philosophy of "*Carpe diem*"[…]

And your idea, a beautiful idea, you dear woman, is also full of obstacles, and as I say, we shall have obstacles all along. I don't want you to be unhappy over it, but I am pretty positive that there just aren't any houses or cottages for us in the first place.

Oh, how your idea worked out would make me happy! And you, in your fallen state, would be happy, too, I like to think. Beyond getting a house, all you say could come to pass. But there is one remote hope – Mrs H's next door neighbour is away again, and likely to stay as before at Alnmouth or somewhere. Suppose she would let her cottage! I'll discuss with you on Friday whether or not to write her. I'll not be practical any further until then. Also we must discuss your own position, for I cannot ask you to do anything like this for me without the most careful consideration. But how happy I would be, all the same.

You mention doubt as to whether we even decided that marriage was best for us. We have known each other now for several years, from all positions & in all moods. And one thing remains, now that we have admitted our love for each other, i.e. that we do indeed love & care for each other, not in any superficial or infatuous [sic] fashion, but in a way that time & thought have tested. So it seems we ought to marry, though one cannot just marry & say "That's that"[…]

I am sorry to dampen your idea, which is the one to appeal most to me yet, but we shall see on Friday.

Forgive this rather short & blunt letter, but you know why it is so.
[Signed "With my love, Len".]

P.S. I have just read your letter again, and this is in no way what I want to reply. I can only say it makes me love you even more, if that is possible. I shall try to do all I can.

Life was becoming too complicated for Len. As well as the intensity of the relationship with Mona, his employer, Farmer Mordue, was dishonest and exploitative. All this was making Len restless.

Horsley, 15 July 1941

Thank you so much for your surprise letter. It is quite convenient, this finding a letter waiting at breakfast time, because then I find I am most in need of a note of cheer[…]

I am quite depressed, as you will gather, but not in a bad way. Mordue's attitude has unsettled me greatly, despite my efforts not to be upset. I felt at the weekend I wanted to be away – away from the women I work with, from the Hendersons, from Mordue – and go among people like myself – Bill, Jim Kirkup or MacDonald[23]. I was so preoccupied with my own unsettled feelings that I neglected you rather at the weekend. I'm sorry for that, for I know how equable you are so long as I have a mind to be. You are always sane and helpful, & if you did not keep me right so often, I should degenerate into a moody fellow of the worst type I think.

Tonight I stayed behind & approached Mordue. I said I wanted to know what prospects there were of me getting full wages. Mordue has nasty eyes when crossed & they did give me a glare at that. He said in a rather surprised tone that I had only been there 4 months & was not yet a skilled man. I then told him of our agreement, which he had somehow evaded putting into writing, that after 3 months I should come on full pay. He said that was the first he had heard of it, & went on to say how only yesterday he had received a letter from the War Agric. Committee saying a "Mr L Jones" was in his employ – had he any remarks to make as to the work he was doing was he satisfactory etc?? Here Mordue came into his true light[…] If I behaved & did not push my claims, in other words, he would write "Satisfactory &

quite essential". If I insisted he would write "Not too satisfactory in a post not of national importance". So I gathered from the tone of the conversation. However, I am insisting, as I am constantly assured by Mrs Ord & Mary that I work quite normally & Mary thinks I work jolly hard for the long hours[…]

Anyway, Mordue asked if I had another job in view & I said "Yes – two" & outlined them. He dismissed me then by saying, of all things, that he would think it over & tell me tomorrow. This means that I shall get the 50s 6d, but that it is given because he is pushed for labour, & I must never forget I don't deserve it[…]

[Signed "Love, Len".]

Len's final weekend with Mona broke something inside him, and he felt he had to get away quickly.

c/o Mrs Forster, Bedale Lodge, Jervaulx Abbey, Ripon, Yorks
– 23 July 1941

You have no doubt been waiting anxiously for some word from me to explain my disgraceful behaviour last weekend.

It seems strange to me now, having emerged from the terrible emotional crisis I underwent last weekend, that as yet you know nothing about it, except that you can divine that something is wrong.

Well, Mona, to get straight to the point – it couldn't go on any longer. Having gone so far and raised your hopes, I have now dashed everything. I have come to Jervaulx to begin a new life – to forget my rotten youth with its quasi existence – and to prevent my seeing you. And you will wonder why I say all this.

There are many reasons I suppose. One of the main reasons, one which covers many of the others, is that I realized last weekend of all times how terribly shallow and unstable I was. My life had no foundation it seemed. There was never any depth in my inner nature to ensure that I was honest and sincere in my relations with other people. And I can now tell you how I know this.

As you know, I was quite young when I was with Lily, and I can honestly say that I cared for her, and that at times I thought I could not live without her. Yet when I knew she was mine and she made that clear, everything went wrong. My love for what I had desired had developed into indifference for that which was now mine. I left her, and the poor girl was prostrate with grief.

I then became your friend, or rather you became mine, for I know now I was never worthy of the name of friend. For years we were friends, getting closer and closer friends until we professed a love for each other that surpassed friendship. I was quite honest and sincere as far as I am capable of being honest and sincere. And then, again, and in spite of my deeper bond with you than with Lily, when I knew you were mine, the love withered and I could not marry you, Mona. Why must this happen? A fortnight ago I was happy with you & you with me. We both dreamed of a happy future together. But always with me that dream turns into a bitter disillusion. I seemed only to love that which is not mine, and when it is mine I am indifferent.

You must be suffering terribly now in the face of this, and if I could do anything to help you I would. But I cannot think of anything. You must try to forget me. I am not worthy of remembrance. You are not losing anything after all, though that is a hard thing to say.

When I saw you on Saturday, I knew that I was becoming dead. I felt like empty wood. I ought to have told something of what I felt, but I had felt the same feeling before and wanted to fight. And I left you suddenly on Saturday night, hurting you even in my manner of leaving. I was a little insane then I think – from then until well into the night my mind was unbalanced. It certainly hadn't ever been the same before. It was feverish and I couldn't think. I wanted only to be dead. I couldn't be that, but I woke up next morning with the idea of running away. I felt that action should follow quickly or I would just procrastinate as usual. I confided in my Father at about 10 o'clock in the morning and was on my way here at 12.30.

My father I found was unable to understand properly and I got a letter from both parents tonight which has shocked even me. They think you are in the wrong, and I am afraid by now that you will have suffered at their hands on Thursday night. They seem to think that because you were older you are to blame. They cannot seem to think that I loved you as far as I am capable of loving any woman and that because of this love you are suffering after such happiness. Please, if this is not in time, take no notice of them. They cannot understand, and my Father is even harsher than I am, and I'm afraid by now you will have been told off. And we were fools enough to think they, or at least my Father, would approve of our marriage. Believe me, they were both bitterly opposed to it, and would have been even had I been good & true.

This letter is hopelessly inadequate, but I cannot express myself at all. You will realize however that I am here, having come to prevent my seeing you anymore and going on with our plans. Mordue is reporting me to the M of Labour and I am expecting trouble. I hope however that I can stay here; I am in excellent digs with Jim Kirkup as bed-mate. We get on very well, & have very similar tastes. If I can stay on here I might find some happiness. But can you find any? I do hope you get over this and forget me. I cannot think of life without you, and had things not gone beyond me, we should have been friends for ever I think. I wish we could have been. But because of your deep feelings concerning me, I suppose it would be better to try to forget me. I feel an utter rotter now and unless I have somebody with me all the time, like Jim, I think over things and I feel like a murderer after his deed is done. I have spoilt something very beautiful, and in spoiling it have spoilt anything that was good in me. One might blame fate but "Dear Brutus" is too recently seen to think that. The fault lies "in me" not "in the stars".[24]

All this is hopelessly mixed up, but I am not yet quite over the turmoil of last weekend. Please try to forget me. I cannot ask you to forgive me – not after such a cowardly trick, but I do want you to be happy – to be your normal kindly self, that is so pleased to serve others and to live in peace. I have spoilt that peace. I do hope you can find it again.

[Signed "Yours sincerely, Len".]

P.S. Because of what I have done and because of my weakness all round I am severing what connection I had with the Society of Friends. I am not fit to bear the name of "Friend". I shall remain on the land, and be nominally a pacifist, but I now know that conscience means nothing to me. It allows me to do what I want, that's all[…]
P.P.S. If you would like it, I would write later again, when I am not so

fuddled, for I feel this is inadequate. I am always thinking however, that you have been wonderful to me always, never failing me when I failed you and I shall never forget you as the greatest friend, and the most devoted, that I shall ever have.

Jervaulx

Len fled to Jervaulx, at the entrance to Wensleydale in North Yorkshire. Here he joined an old friend from Tyneside and fellow pacifist. James (Jim) Kirkup, the only child of a carpenter in South Shields, was a sensitive young man similarly drawn to the Quakers. He had taken a degree in French and German, and held a teaching post in France before the war. Jim was dedicated to his vocation as a poet and writer. Having been registered as a conscientious objector he was assigned to forestry. Living and working with Jim, Len gradually recovered his equilibrium and began to explore his own creativity, encouraged by his friend. However, the relationship would not prove straightforward.

Jervaulx, 28 July 1941

I was going to write you in [any] case tonight, but as I received a letter from you this is in answer to that one[…]

I know I have hurt people, everybody I knew. Do you think I dare come back now and face them? No, I dare not. That is why or is one reason why I'm leaving the Friends. What roots I had in Newcastle and Felling I have now torn up[…] To some extent I am touched with Bovarism. But while in the past I have always striven to cure this fault & that, trying to attain an impossible perfection, I am now resolved to give in. I am what I am. If I am rotten inside, well, there's nothing to do about it. I am beginning to think I am rotten inside, for what I said was true. I loved you as far as I am capable of love. I said so – that I loved you & honestly thought I did, until we discuss marriage, and after a mere fortnight of dreams & plans, I know that we must not marry. I could never be your husband, because I should never love in that light[…] I thought at last I had become purged of myself and wrapped up in another. All the time I was completely unaware of what would happen to me. It grew quite suddenly on me, however, in the last week, and I knew I did not love you as a prospective husband should[…]

Can I comfort you in any way is all I want to know now. Is there anything I can do, for if it is possible, I'd do it. You know what I am, and that I shall not marry you, but please let me help you, if I can, to get over your unhappiness. I wish you could forget me altogether, forget those qualities you believe in, and just forget me. I know that is impossible. I think continued friendship would only hurt you. I will not trouble you with what I want. I have no rights whatever, but if you would like anything, I would like to help[…]

Jervaulx, ?3 August 1941

[…] This is a holiday for us, and we are just staying in all the time, except for Saturday, when we made a raid on Darlington. Jim has £5 to spend, and I wanted some braces & a few things. The £5 was for a review of 'East Coker' which Jim sent in to *Poetry*. It is an excellent review, the most understanding (& of necessity eulogistic) review I've read of that poem. He has also had 2 poems published in *Poetry* which I shall try to remember to enclose. The editor of *The Listener* read them apparently & sent Jim a nice letter of appreciation, asking if he could send him some of his work[…]

Before I came, Jim never did a scrap of work, scarcely even reading. Since I came he has begun in earnest, sent for umpteen books, written 3 poems & generally bucked up. He is pleased that I influence him in this direction, for before he went out every night almost, drinking or dancing or to Gwen's (the lady supervisor of the land girls round here), & was late in returning as a rule. On those few nights he did stay in therefore he just slept. Hence no work[…]

Jim is begging me to begin afresh in water-colours, & I might begin anew, only it is such hard graft before you get anywhere.[1] However, I did buy some pasteless board at Darlington & I don't want to waste it.

As you guess, Jervaulx is a beautiful spot. I love it already. And from the fell, where we work, the view is magnificent. There are many things to interest one, & Jim & I are always exchanging little impressions. At work, we are rescuing rejected 12, 18 & 20 feet props and sawing them into 3 and a half & 4 and a half ft sleepers, which work affords ample opportunity for conversation. We are not required to work hard, so that we usually manage to read something to each other. Just now it is [Thomas] De Quincey's *Confessions*.

We are only 5 minutes from the River Ure, a lovely stream, and nearby is an excellent, deep, but safe stretch for swimming. The bottom is clear gravel, not the usual mud of rivers.

At work, we are very popular, strange to say, Jim always having been, so we have plenty of friends. Gwen, the women's supervisor, lives in a caravan, & we go there occasionally, & have a haircut, for she is a good amateur, & listen to the gramophone, as the records are quite good. Things like Sibelius *Valse Triste*, *Swan Lake* Ballet, & Mozart concerto & the like.

My digs are excellent after Henderson's & I feel much fitter already. She is a chatterbox but that does not worry us a great deal. There is always something nice to eat & her Yorkshire puddings are beyond description. They almost inspire poetry!

Mordue & the M of L might rudely disturb me but I must just wait, & I have a good case against Mordue, which makes me think he may not cause any trouble.[2] And Mr Tarran, the boss, is definitely with me, and in fact we are good pals. He told Gwen he liked me the first time he saw me, so I think he would help all he could[…]

[Signed "Affectionately, Len".]

Len now received a letter from Mona which suggested to him that she was "not changed in the least. Still disinterested in the best sense", "still loving". He went on: "I could ask you to forgive what I did. But I cannot ask you to forgive what I am." Len had made two "abortive attempts" at water-colours and been so discouraged he was now ready to sell his materials. Jim was urging him to "get down to something" so now he was writing "very bad poetry".

Nothing, however, tests a friendship so much as prolonged time spent together. Len began to realise this with Jim, even though they had so much in common. Jim's "Bohemianism" sat uneasily with Len's more moral approach to life, and he had become aware of a central trait of Jim's at which he could only hint – his homosexuality. Len's initial reaction was conventional: he found it hateful.

Jervaulx, Wednesday [13 August 1941?]

[…] Your letter was very interesting and as full of the hum-drum as ever. Jam-jars of all things are now news. How I should know a letter from you if it were read among 100 others. You have the same style, or lack of it, & the same interest in mundanities. You are like Breughel for detail, especially in the sense that the details seem too characteristic to omit.

As for my letters, you must find them terribly morbid just now, but you will know by now that this morbid self-analysis is a habit of mine, my particular form of neurosis. And I do believe that something accomplished, something done, would help me. But when I say that, I did not expect bibliography driving down like rain upon me. Yes, such rain that I must seek shelter, but don't be cross, & I in turn will not be cross with you. I know you mean it all for the best, & perhaps I shall try it some day – but not just now thank you[…]

I try occasionally to write verse, goaded by Jim, who makes me work hard, & tells me faults and so on. I only try a little objective writing – you know, trying to impress upon another mind the exact image I myself have in mind. It takes quite an effort to keep the image before you objectively, & not veer off with another word, not so exact. For instance, writing once on light rain, I wanted to give in a line or two, that picture of the damp streaks on stone walls that it leaves you know. One might do so in a single sentence or so, but in a poem, in a particular context it is extraordinarily difficult. I failed miserably of course, but did not worry, for it was a good exercise[…]

And the forest is from today going to be more absorbing for me, as Jim & I went on piecework, cutting trees into props etc… just like Exmoor. Jim is a very bad mate, being weak & slow, so will not make much unless he bucks up, but even so it's terribly absorbing, & you can rest when you like, go home when you like & so on, you are your own boss[…]

Your remarks about the Friends interested me very much. I am still very attracted by all that Friends mean and are, but I still think I should be better to be out of the Society, or rather the Society would be better without me. It is no good hanging on and never overcoming the feeling of incompleteness & unworthiness. In fact when I came here, I set out deliberately to throw the whole business overboard, in the hope that I would thus find satisfaction. But naturally it just could not be done, and after a fortnight Jim['s] Bohemianism etc seemed terribly inadequate after my craving for the spirit that exists among

James Kirkup

friends. Jim, in fact, though a good friend, is very biased & incomplete. And for a certain reason which I may be able to tell you later, I hate him, but otherwise we live, work & enjoy ourselves together. And he at least is a great enthusiast over many of the things that interest me & helps me therefore in furthering those interests. But he just couldn't understand your kind of friendship – would in fact call it a sentimental nothing. Do not infer from this that I am crying out now that I need you again. I want you to look after yourself more, as I said[…] And when I seem depressed, don't take any notice, as you know it will pass. Every day has its long depressions & nights too, but they pass, and I live on a sort of Stoicism which regards them as all part of the day. I do not expect too much from life, so cannot be disappointed too much[…]

[Signed "Yours ever, Len".]

"Yours ever" – yes John Gillie is right.[3] Whatever happens, I shall always claim some part in your mind & you in mine, as long as we live, & maybe after.

Len's introversion, and his worrying about Mona's peace of mind, continued in his next letter (21 August 1941?) She had been trying her hand at poetry, of which he wrote: "Your poems are wonderful, & one is too personal of course to criticize from an academical point of view. Jim would massacre both, but he does not understand certain viewpoints. Jim was a great help to me technically, in my feeble efforts until our friendship was marred by something rather horrible. Since then I have been very unsettled again, horribly depressed[…]"

Len was troubled by the thought of Mona bearing "the constant recurring pain of remembering me". Even though he desperately wanted to alleviate this, he could "only make it worse, for I shall not come back – I cannot". He added: "I know now that I shall never again know such union with another mind & personality as I have had with yours. That is a sad thought for both of us – and yet such is not enough for marriage – I cannot explain why because I don't know[…] It seems a barren life, & sometimes I have felt it is not worth living – have even thought how easy to go round the chemist's shops & buy the necessary quantity of something (aspirins I suppose) to put me to sleep for ever. But that is only when I [am] really bad." He had tried everything to get away from this mood except getting drunk; "I went out for one or two evenings with a pretty land girl, and was the worse for it, of course, for it seems an awful strain trying to clown for a whole evening to entertain an empty girl." Len then again urged Mona to break off contact with him, "for nothing can ever come of our friendship". His next letter was only a little less low in mood.

Jervaulx [no date/day – late August 1941?]

[…] My reading is as haphazard as usual – a book of criticism *Enemies of Promise* by Cyril Connolly, & some of [Ronald] Firbank's novels, which I think are brilliant. Jim is Firbank mad, but I'm not so dotty as that. I notice Connolly remarks that Firbank was homosexual! Connolly himself certainly is, which might explain a lot[…]

Your "book of members" was a thoughtful addition, but honestly, I feel quite unable to come into contact with Friends, & round here, without posing, I have become known as an ordinary workman who is not averse to going into a pub, & who is really anything but the sociable yet ascetic Friend. I'm too ordinary perhaps they would think, to be a Friend. Not that appearances matter, & not that I'm afraid of spoiling the picture of the hard-drinking propper etc. No, I'm not of the Society of Friends now, because of reasons which to me are obvious, but seem incommunicable to you.

In fact my whole mood seems utterly incommunicable – just like De Quincey, who found his reasons for running away from school "incommunicable". At least my letters to you seem to be misunderstood or something. There was no "*j'accuse*" in my last letter, no ridicule of your "*Carpe diem*" motto, in fact, there was no telling you what to do. No, I only wanted to help you, for in doing so I would be quite selfish & be helping myself; the less I hurt you, the less I hurt myself[…]

Jervaulx, Thursday [28 August/4 September 1941?]

Thank you so much for your parcel, baccy, letter & everything. I believe Jim himself has written to thank you for France etc…

My weekend [at home] seemed very brief indeed and I don't think I shall try it again until Xmas perhaps, when I can have a day off above the normal holiday.

The weather is very hot these last few days and quite impossible for working too hard, so we are taking things easy. Jim raised a universal laugh today by appearing in very short brick-red shorts with a white belt and a vivid blue shirt. He loves notoriety however, so he didn't mind, in fact was quite pleased with himself. No resin had to soil the shorts, however, so no props were handled all day by him. Honestly, he's nothing but a conceited fop at bottom, and I saw through him after a fortnight of blind happiness at finding a friend with tastes like mine.

So either Jim or I goes shortly, for we must separate I'm afraid, for other reasons too[…]

Finally Len plucked up the courage to explain what had come between Jim and him – homosexual advances which he had rejected with horror. His remark about class background is also indicative of his state of mind at this time.

Jervaulx, Wednesday [3/10 September 1941?]

[…] Your letter was read in a more open-minded manner this time, for I am brightening up, now I'm on my own. I still sleep & work with

[Jim], but hardly a word passes between us. I try once or twice to make overtures, but the university student & poet is careful to ignore the mundane remarks of a mere librarian cum navvy[…] Shall I tell you. Jim hates me because I resisted, on three occasions, the last time with angry words & a little force, his attempts at homosexual intercourse with me. I hate such unhealthy filth, particularly as I think this is just one more thing to make him feel exotic, different, Bohemian, poetical etc etc… As I said, Firbank & Connolly are homosexual, so I suppose Jim wanted to be as well. And there was nothing worse for what friendship existed between us. For weeks it has been a strain sleeping with [Jim], as on each occasion I was not sure what to do. I did not want to hurt him yet the thing revolted me. The last time he was so persistent I lost my temper & did hurt him, both ways. And it worked. I sleep in peace now, whereas before every move was enough to worry me. You've no idea what a strain it was. I can tell you this because you are never likely to meet him.[4]

Without him I am getting along better. I read a lot & [am] beginning to take interest. I am still bad inside I think but will always be, so why worry. I am now content to be what I am – of the lower class & the middle class can take me or leave me. Class is still a very real thing you know, & breeding is a real thing. I lack it, but it doesn't worry me now[…]

The two roommates finally managed to discuss their differences frankly and reasonably calmly. When Len realised that Jim's homosexuality was not a pose, his response was humane, even if he continued to find the idea of taking part in gay sex himself repulsive. In the aftermath, Len decided he was "not an artist".

Jervaulx, Monday [8/15 September 1941?]

[…] I'm sorry for the continued morbid analyses of my letters and really since coming here I've been more self-centred than ever, sometimes completely abandoning myself to it. Jim only unsettled things more, and honestly, his attitude has sometimes made me very unhappy. But I've got over that.

For over a week he never spoke to me – would not even acknowledge the casual remarks that are often necessary.

So one night I set out to pick my bone with him.

"Jim" I said "just why won't you speak to me?"

No answer – sulks!

So rising temper on my part.

"Now don't be so bloody childish & tell a man, can't you!"

Still no answer.

By now I'm fit to kill him but by amazing self-control I don't.

"Listen! I work, live, sleep with you. For nearly 24 hours I'm with you. And for a whole week you've never spoken to me. Now I'm not going to stand for that. Tomorrow I'm asking for a go at felling and you can work with who the hell you like – but I warn you – there's no other fool on that fell that will stack all day for you, so you'd better learn to stack & eat more for breakfast or you'll faint."

But to this vehement outburst, obviously self-righteous I expect a scornful look and shut up – resolved nevertheless to leave him to it.

He does, however, move, and finally speaks though very haltingly.

"Actually, I know I'm completely in the wrong, and I'm sorry, but somehow – well, there just wasn't anything to talk about – oh – talk seemed so futile and barren – I just couldn't bear to speak."

And on, quicker and quicker, opening out, until I explain that I'd often done that to you & understood, but I couldn't understand doing it to a man – no, only a woman warranted such silences. To which he replied that I didn't understand him.

Why did we hate each other.

"Let's be frank with each other."

And so. Oh, how we analysed each other, picked our brains. But we never got to the final point until once again I pluck up courage to mention the unmentionable.

"You know, the real reason we hate each other is this homosexual business," I say. "You are hurt because I resist your advances, and honestly, I'm so normal & healthy in that respect at least, that it's just horrible for me – that's why I resisted you & hurt you. I didn't have the courage to talk to you about [it], & I didn't know what to do really, and I just lost my temper."

"Yes" he answered "I wanted so much to talk about it. You see, you think it is a pose and so on. But really I am homosexual and have always been. It makes me terribly lonely, and when Bill [Hamilton] told me so much about you and your habit of thought which he so much noticed for some reason, I thought you were a – I thought you were like me. I got you here – or at least you came without any pressure – and when you came you told me in our first quick flow of friendship about your treatment of your two women friends. You were puzzled. I wasn't, or I thought I wasn't. It only confirmed, as I thought, what I guessed at first.

"I thought you repressed what was natural, found my first advances strange, but I kept on trying, thinking you shy maybe, until you finally showed me you were, after all, quite normal."

All of which somewhat stunned me. I knew he was being honest. I knew now that he was really a homosexual, and when I talked of the strain for me, I now realized the awful strain for him. I did feel for him at that moment.

But the things he said about me. They sounded so terribly plausible! Were they true? I tell you, honestly, I did not know. He was right. In warm, almost adolescent youth I had left a girl almost broken-hearted. Now when not much older in years, but I believe much more mature, & more conscious of each, I had found it necessary to do the same to yet another. Something was wrong, I knew myself, and Jim had supplied the answer so adequately.

It was only after some consideration that I realized he was wrong. No, it was absolutely unnatural, in fact, highly repulsive to me to have any part in homosexual intercourse, and that was enough. If unnatural – if it needed to fight something back to do it – then it was wrong for me where it was right for him. In sex, physically at any rate, I was quite normal, I thought. And explained it to him. He understood, said I was right, even apologized.

Next day, we did talk. We seemed friends again. We talked about living. He picked all my faults. He seemed to think I was a born artist and all that, who had just let his mind get constipated. He urged me to live more intensely – go for every experience hell for leather – without thinking of the consequences. We discussed Baudelaire's utter self-abandonment to evil and utter depravity. It was the artistic life worked out to its logical, or final conclusion. Jim said if he was told he had some fatal disease like syphilis, he would enjoy it, would go around announcing it, and abandoning himself to the uttermost depths of depravity. It was the real life for him – life lived intensely, touching depths unknown except to the artist, to whom this intense form of living was natural.

I argued, but was bottled up every time, for all along I was conscious that he was more than half-right in a way I would never finally understand. I knew at that moment, whatever pretensions I may or may not have had that I was not an artist.

And yet – since – I have found holes in his argument. I agree about the utter abandonment – the intensity he sought after, but need the intensity find its expression in depravity? I don't really know, I suspect I have missed the point and want him to be wrong because my old moral self wants him to be wrong. Nor do I say this because I still want to be an artist. It does seem to me that the artist lives the fullest life – as E.M. Forster says – the business man thinks life is everything & the mystic thinks it's nothing, both are extreme, and it seems one must connect the two. "Only connect."[5] And I think the artist might. I cannot be an artist, but I don't really mind. Living is an art, and as you know has also interested me in many ways, morbid & happy, religious & political and so on. And we must let that do.

All this must read queer. Anyway Jim & I have gradually relapsed into a half-silence, at any rate, but I know how to go on now, and I know how we stand, so its allright [sic][…]

I still think he is mostly pose, is very conceited & unsociable to the workmen & our landlady and so on (he despises my being so sociable & tolerant, but I think I'm right there). His remarks thrown off in front of girls (whom he professes to despise and calls "bitches in heat") are quite conceited for instance. Tries to be very witty, oh terribly witty & surrealist[…]

You are leaving me your superannuation eh! You know, I don't know what to do about you. In your absence I revere you and in your presence hurt you – come to love, then must leave you, always this ambivalence. It does frighten me, and the consciousness that it all applies, not only to me, but to a mature person with a precious personality of her own, is quite terrifying at times[…]

In his next letter Len expressed his wish not to be like his parents. His mother had turned away an insurance agent who was trying to collect a sum owed by Len; the man turned up at Felling library and Mona paid a portion of the debt on Len's behalf. Complaining about his mother's way with money, he went on: "My parents distress me sometimes more than myself. I don't want to be like them. They seemed to have frittered life away doing absolutely nothing, though of course strikes, unemployment have prevented them from ever taking root anywhere. It seems to have been a second-best life all the time for them and they are to be pitied, but certain things could be avoided, such as this insurance business."

A few days later Len wrote again about his relations with Jim.

Jervaulx, Tuesday [23 September 1941?]

[…] Jim and I are queer these days, or shall I say these hours, for we live by hours, some hours quite, but not over, friendly, others just as hostile as ever. But tonight we are friendly & are comparing our relative merits as spendthrifts. Out of our pay of over £8 last fortnight, I have precisely £1, and Jim 5s. I thought I was bad, but 5s! And I had a weekend at Harrogate & bought a 30/- pair of pants. The trouble is when he goes into a pub it is 2s straightaway for a double gin, and then for bravado perhaps a thimbleful of advocat.

That is going all out for any experience which apparently I shun. He is right, but not in practice I think. It needs a genius as terrible as Byron's, Marlowe's or Baudelaire's to indulge like that. Or Gauguin's, or Raphael's (surprising eh?) or even Wagner's. All indulged in Satanism, as Eliot calls it. Not indulged, but just lived Satanism, because they had to. But I'm [sure] Jim hasn't got to any more than I have to[…]

Jervaulx, Friday [26 Sept 1941?]

Your letter was very soothing somehow tonight, for it conveyed so well the lovely atmosphere at Alston. It all seems very beautiful[…] I was very happy and at peace in a week alone in the Lakes. It is like a dream all the time.

And always when you are like that you think the native or the forester, shepherd or whatnot must be the luckiest person on earth. It is a delusion of course, for to him it is his work and everyday and his whole life cannot very well be lived at the state of supreme happiness which marks a townsman's presence there. You see, our forest was once beautiful, unmarred by the axe: then men came, laid it bare, burnt the lovely fronds, scattered bits and pieces all over, dug up the ground to put out the fires, exposing the naked clay, and left the place a veritable desert for dust & dirt. At night my whole body has this thin film of dust all over & I must bathe somehow[…]

No, the forester is a destroyer of the best parts of the land, and is really a nuisance, but can't help it, because it's his work. On our job, about 2 acres fall each week when felling is in full swing and the bareness afterwards is appalling. As a job though it is good, so he must not worry[…]

Jervaulx, 1 October 1941

[…] Today is the first anniversary "by date" of my days as a forester. I can hardly imagine what I was like when I started, but I can vividly remember Bernard, Myrddin and I rejoicing because we had cut up 11 trees as a team. Now 2 of us think nothing of cutting up 70 trees, and the same size too.

12 months today I walked about 5 miles to the forest, worked till I was almost sick, had dry bread and water for lunch (yes, honestly) and took 2 hours to walk home because we had to rest and pick the huge blackberries to pacify our empty bellies. Then the foulest dinner, followed by the awfullest homesickness, and bed, dreading tomorrow[…]

Now, work is drab and monotonous like most work, but is not painful and in fact is, well, "all in the day's work". I believe I was often more tired when I was a library assistant. – (joke!)[…]

Len's old friend and library colleague Arthur Good became restive in his steady job, envying the independence of comrades who had got away. This prompted Len (writing on 3 October) to tell Mona some of the advantages of his job, along with its drawbacks. The latter included winter ("hellish for outdoor workers") and "the brainless monotony of forestry in certain jobs". On the positive side Arthur's life experience would be broadened. "And being a navvy does make you somehow independent – career doesn't matter, promotion is absent & all that worry about pushing for it. In the library you are all mapped out & each step so carefully planned etc. As a navvy you don't give a hang[…] Then if you want to shift, it's not like tearing up your roots, you can easily go, and are welcome anywhere." Len thought Arthur might benefit from joining him, but in the end he stayed put.

Briefly Len had the chance once more to work with another old friend – Bill Hamilton. He had stayed on in Devon until mid-1941, when he was fired for being a troublemaker. He had arrived in Wensleydale sometime after Len, who wrote: "This morning Jim felt unwell, so did not work. Bill's partner the same, so I have had a grand day felling with Bill. Stripped to the waist in good DH Lawrence male exhibitionism, it's grand. I've enjoyed it, the weather so warm & nice. Bill & I work superbly against Jim & I. I've persuaded Jim to take tomorrow off too, so will have another half-day." [6]

In his next two letters Len wrote about his reading (Rilke, Isherwood, various French poets) and thanked Mona for her parcel of tobacco, socks and books. He wrote again (13 October 1941?) after a weekend trip home, which as too often had not been a complete success. "You so obviously wanted to see me again after Saturday, and you must have thought me very unkind to prevent this." Trying to be fair to his parents, Len had spent Sunday alone with them after Saturday with Mona.

Len's attempt to explain his conduct on his weekend at home, perhaps inevitably, led to another misunderstanding. Mona wrote back in an aggrieved vein, and he in return (17 October 1941?) once again suggested that they break off contact for her sake. He added: "As for me, I am reforming, having thrown over Jim's rather bad influence, & am once more just reading & spending quiet nights & weekends. I shall go on as my normal self, and shall no doubt get back into the library profession somehow when the war is over[…]". Len's next letter continued the dispute.

Jervaulx, 22 October 1941

[…] Do you really mean all the bitterness that is behind such a remark as "Your love lasted about ten days, didn't it?" If I could repair the damage done in those ten days, I would give anything to do so, but it did not last ten days. What I felt those ten days was what I had felt for a long time concerning you, as I once explained, but that it was always an ambivalent emotion I felt for you was my way of putting it. For ten days this was mistaken, as you put it, for another emotion, & when faced with the reality, I then knew the truth.

If you wish to drop me, do so – if not then we shall be friends as ever – the queerest friends ever surely, or should I say that only of myself?[…]

Len's next letter (28 October 1941?) is notable chiefly for his postscript – his revelling in the pleasures of tree felling. "Felling is so grand, I'm almost persuaded to save up and go west to Canada after the war & fell there, where there is more doing than in England in peace-time. I feel so strong & fit these days, as though I could bend iron bars etc etc etc. I must be sickening for something or other." His remark was of course flippant, but clearly he was enjoying his work – and it contrasts with the absence of any sense of a vocation for the visual arts at this stage. It raises the image of Len the lumberjack, rather than Jonah the sculptor.

While Len's expectations for himself were still modest, he was reading voraciously and dabbling with writing. Mona fed his interests with a steady stream of books lent from the library, and tried her own hand at writing.

The relationship between Len and Mona had settled down again, and he even managed a weekend at home without setting off the previous tension between them. His letters over this period are mainly about literature and work. He read the life of Eric Gill "in one reading on Sunday" and "found it fascinating in its intimacy & frankness" (4 November 1941?). This must have stayed with him, for Gill's legacy would be hugely important when he embarked on his career as a sculptor and letter cutter. He enthused over Hemingway's For Whom the Bell Tolls, *which brought about a rare mention of the supposed Welsh connection in the Jones family: "Thank you for allowing me such books to read. I count it as a great privilege & always the best books it is. (Welsh inversion – unconscious, suppose its ancestor worship coming out, indeed!) Do you remember David Jones book* In Parenthesis. *It is one of my favourites[…]" (15 November 1941?)*

Clearly Len found genuine fulfilment in his work at this time. His letters reveal lively interest in the lore of forestry and pride in his acquisition of the skills needed.

Jervaulx, Wednesday [26 November 1941?]

Thank you so much for the parcel. The books were marvellous[…]

The forestry extract from *Uncle Vanya* is very interesting, but do you know that in England, conifers present the sorriest picture after 60 or 70 years. Our wood is about 30 years in parts, & is quite lovely. A neighbouring wood, (a private estate) of about 70 years is simply disgusting. The larch, having reached the end of their lives (in England only this seems to apply) are rotting & losing not only their beauty but their commercial value. We look at them, noting the 80 feet length & monstrous girth & feel a genuine sorrow that such trees are rotting & wasting[…]

You will think, to return to forestry, that I am taking an almost improper pride in forestry now, and will think "What a change!" I do take a pride in my work now however, though one doesn't flaunt it here. Felling has given me a happiness that many other things have been unable to give. It has somehow loosed my hands, let free something suppressed, and I suppose that is why the workman who uses his hands finds little need for creative work or creative thinking. He is sometimes scorned for his "Work, eat, sleep" life; and to one who has tried at times to do other things besides "work, eat, sleep" it might seem disgusting & animal. But it is not. Having had certain interests (mainly in books) in the past, these still hold me, and prevent me from becoming wholly a workman. But if these interests were to slip away, I could still be happy, I believe, in my work alone, because it is creative, problematic, & needs skill of hand. I say creative because from the growing tree we produce a dressed piece of timber with a neat butt. And the skill of hand is an amazing factor in happiness. That is why men play outdoor games like golf & tennis, & derive great satisfaction from a correct stroke. Why should they? I don't know – but I'm gaining the same satisfaction all day[…]

Jervaulx, Monday [1 December 1941?]

[…] My friend Macdonald (of Grasmere) has got himself married to a girl called Louie. He was only engaged about a fortnight, so he was quick off the mark. Which makes me bring up a dreaded subject. How are you now? Are you still deeply hurt by my inexplicable actions of the past? I ask because almost every day I wonder, about you now, & about myself in the past. And when I think of course, I often feel very wretched, but don't want you to give me sympathy for that. Please tell me, and I still think, by the way, that you ought to finish altogether with me & try to forget me. Forgive me for bringing up the tabooed subject.

The reason is probably because I've been on the theme all weekend, having spent it with rather a lovely girl, Kate O'Neill, an Irish lass who is in charge of the measuring. And you might think I want you to finish with me so that I'll be free in all ways (conscience, I suppose) to carry on these affairs in comfort. But that's no reason, for where do they get me? My relations with women seem to be absolutely warped. I can only get along so far, and yet I seem always to need a woman friend, for I am not a success with men. Sometimes, therefore, I feel very mournful down here, because with the estrangement between Jim & I, I have no friends whatever. Bill is seeing another nice girl just now & I hope it goes on, because she really is nice. George [Peacock], my working mate, is grand as such, but otherwise our ideas of life are at variance.

To get back to women, you know what I am & what I think, so just do what you think best[…]

Living together with Jim had finally become unsustainable for Len, so when the opportunity to move arose he took it.

Jervaulx, Friday [5 December 1941?]

[…] I'm sorry I disappointed you over the weekend, and I'm sure I don't know when I'll have another at home besides Xmas. I'll let you know however if I have time to write. Unless I have time off on Saturday, it is a hopeless journey of course.

There is quite an upheaval at my digs tonight. Bill has been called up, & to get away from Jim I have arranged to go into his digs. Despite the fact that Mrs Foster has known I was going to do this for several weeks, she is in tears tonight, and I can't make out whether she's only sorry to lose me (for we got on well) or whether she thinks I'm doing a dirty trick on her. I am inclined to think the latter[…]

Ah well, I suppose she's right, but you know why I must leave Jim. We have not spoken a single word to each other for weeks now & Mrs Foster knows quite well that we can't bear each other. I tell her we just can't live together & she blames Jim for his sulky ways. He has sulked with both me & the family for weeks now. Tonight she "boned" about it, & said it was through him I was leaving. But as per usual, Jimmy was quite imperturbed. It ran off him like water off a duck's back[...]

First Months in East Witton

Len would be happier in East Witton than anywhere else during his time working on the land, although the emotional and psychological upheavals would keep recurring. He got on well with the Dinsdale family with whom he was lodging and with his workmates. For the next six months his main intellectual preoccupation continued to be serious reading.

23 East Witton, Leyburn, Yorks – Tuesday, 9 December 1941

[…] Please do not think of me as carrying a burden, for heaven's sake. If anybody needs help in carrying a burden, it is surely not I who live in comfort & have a good job[…]

I did not want you to know I was home a week gone Saturday, but apparently someone has told you. I did not want you to know because as you will now know I was accompanied by the measurer Kate, who had wanted to see *The Swan Lake* for a long time. How well I keep up the reputation "men were deceivers ever". But truth will out, so I shouldn't try to deceive in the first place[…]

East Witton, Saturday [13/20 December 1941?]

Thank you for your letter which got to me on Thursday. I have not been able to answer because I have been out Thursday & Friday nights – Thursday to see *The Mortal Storm* [a film] with Amos[1], and last night to East Witton's big annual "do" – a fancy dress ball[…]

The fancy dress ball was a hilarious affair, with village lads very self-consciously parading before Lady Jane Scroop, who was the Judge. The most beautiful girl (1st prize) was a Mary Queen of Scots and I agree she was quite becoming. These village girls are not so clog footed as folks think.

I was "half-dressed" – not exactly fancy that is – I borrowed a kilt, a sporran & a dirk & went as a Scotsman. My leg was admired much to my satisfaction. The prize-winner was a very funny Zulu – a Dane dressed up. He wore funny tights, white ones with a up-turned tail sticking from his behind. A little leather apron carefully concealed the fact that the tights were what I later found out to be an old pair of linens! (or linings?) – you know[…]

My new digs are very comfortable & the food is excellent, as they have 3 milch cows, hens & have just killed a 20 stone pig. The food is plainer than at Foster's which is better really, because I had too mixed a diet there. Mrs Foster was a good landlady & I'll never forget her kindness. It was a pity I had to leave her, but it was for the best. As I said she got catty & spiteful when I first told her I was leaving. On Sunday however when I left, she was like a mother losing her son & wept & kissed me & I was quite overcome & felt like weeping myself. She sent a letter to Mrs Dinsdale saying I was "a canny lad" & all sorts of things I didn't deserve.

It has been a queer week at work. On Tuesday we finished our patch of spruce, and as the Danes were also nearly finished, we were ordered on to the very top of the mountain to fell some giants left from the last war. That means they are 30 years older than any of the others. It is on a high plateau (1,200 feet high) – a sort of "blasted heath" with these giants withstanding the constant winds that sweep across. Other giants lie in peace on the ground, their roots torn away & standing high above the ground. The general landscape of dead stumps, fallen trees & wind-blasted live trees resembles a battle-field)[…]

Naturally, as the trees are big, the price goes down, because there are so many cube at one fall. But the price dropped from 2d a cube to 1¼d. We appealed for 1½d & he[2] said he couldn't give us 1½d (which is usually considered the lowest price even for the biggest trees). He asked us to try it & we did, but found we had to eat our hearts out to make over the day rate even. We went again – "no but he would come up and see what the conditions were like." He came. We showed him the huge heels on most of them, grown by the trees to withstand the wind. Sometimes we had to start axing roots as far as 3 feet off the tree. He fooled around and then decided he couldn't do anything as the Divisional Inspector & not he had fixed the price. We tried another day & then gave up & sent in the usual ultimatum – "1½d or we go on day-work". So today we started on day-work - taking it easy & felling about 8s worth of trees & receive 10s for it. This does not pay them & if we stick out & they cannot find men to fell them at that price, the 1½d will come. We even detected signs of weakening this morning. The Danes are not allowed to fell them as the trees are too precious to be split. We two have to fell several acres of this big stuff & what with wind & cold, we wish it was finished. But we are going to stick out for the price, as it is principle with fellers not to accept below 1½d. Four men in a wood at Harmby stood out for the same price for 3 weeks and won, so we must be prepared for the same.

The trees are grand of course[…] It is very interesting indeed, & very satisfying to hear [the] huge crash when they finally topple over[…]

Sorry to talk so much shop again. Forgot all about Russia, Japan, Libya, America, Pacific, Mediterranean!!! etc etc etc etc…

East Witton, Monday [15/22 December 1941?]

[…] George described the job as "absolutely buggered" tonight, for we are to be kept on day-work for the felling of the big stuff. The 1½d has therefore been denied us, & they are prepared to lose by putting us on day-work. They know the 1¼d is unacceptable to us because we would not only be blacklegging our own job but others in the district, for 1½d is the lowest for miles round. So be it[…]

Mona and Len could not stop themselves worrying at each other about their relationship. This round would continue for over a month.

East Witton, Wednesday [31 December 1941?]

[…] I cannot adequately answer your letter – but, I will say this: that all that the letter conveys has been hidden in your letters recently (or openly expressed) and I suppose that without reading mine you too will have a general idea of how I stand[…]

Your letter does give me the truth, I think. (I don't mean in the sense that you may be hiding something, of course, but that you express yourself clearly.) For me to do the same would probably hurt. You must know by now, however, that I shall not "come back to you". You once said in a rather bitter mood that my love lasted "exactly ten days". How true, in every way, not only because the heights seemed to last ten days, but also because I do believe I did love you then. And as I have said before 24 hours seemed to, did, in fact, destroy what I valued most. In those 10 days, I was happy in every little thought of the present & the future. In the 24 hours I knew all was wrong. And the 24 hours were to be right in the long run, much to your dismay & grief. I would have it otherwise myself, but it is not so[…]

Like you, the last six months have been a deep experience for me. I have been in several different positions, flying as it were from pillar to post. First I recover, then I settle to literary pursuits, find preoccupation with Jim, become capricious, frivolous & devil-may-care, look slightly towards Satanism, repent, become estranged from Jim, settle down again & now I am at the settle down stage, in which I often reflect of course, and think round in circles.

Do not worry about me in the least. I fare very well and do not suffer like the conventional person who cannot love one who loves passionately in return. I am interested and content with my work, and as a result am in good health. I get on extremely well with the men & if you saw 4 of us today round a huge fire at dinner, yarning & enjoying a smoke, you would not worry about me at all. In the evenings I read or write. I was seeing Kate once a week, but I've stopped that too and was quite happy in the house all over the weekend just passed[…]

East Witton, Monday [5 January 1942?]

[…] We went back to our mountain top, in quite deep snow with drift behind the trees. It was not particularly cold however, and we had a good rosy fire all day. I got the shock on returning to find that we had been blacklegged by two men who had accepted the $1\frac{1}{4}$d. All the Danes took their stand with us, I hear, so Tarran looked elsewhere, and a tractor driver & a propper, who are not even proper fellers, are now doing Loftus plantation. Being put on the plantation was rather unfair I think, because we weren't allowed Loftus until we'd finished the rotten stuff we're in at present. The Union is taking up the matter, but as the Government is in an independent position for timber now, on account of Russian supplies, I'm rather pessimistic – but not worried![…]

Regarding the important part of your last letter, I think after our talk (rather meagre on my part I'm afraid), that you know how things are[3]. Perhaps "the gentleman doth protest too much", but please read me aright. I protest once more that either I made a mistake, or am deeply unstable in my emotional life. I know where I stand now, and if I make enquiries about yourself, it is probably to satisfy my conscience. You persuade me yourself not to suffer these pangs of conscience, and I do see that nothing else could have happened, that it was "fate" and not all myself to blame. It seemed inevitable when I look back, that the whole affair, so painful to you, should have happened as it did. But I must not seek to exonerate myself thus. I know one thing however, and that is the seriousness of the whole matter, and I never dismiss it as something light & frivolous. I know, or I can imagine how it affected you[…]

East Witton, Sunday [11 January 1942?]
I think, after reading your last letter (of Thursday), that it would be better to finish everything.

East Witton, Friday [16 January 1942?]
I had an idea that in spite of the impertinent finality of my note you would still write, and in such a tone. I don't know how to answer, and find already that the first two sentences begin with "I", which is unfortunate.

Much you have said in your recent letters is untrue surely, but if I were to go into what I think, you would no doubt interpret it as self-analysis etc… After all, "I am what I am" and cannot change into another being. If I displease you as I am then you must resign yourself to the displeasure, because I cannot just say, "I'll be so and so this time" and write like someone else. And that, I suppose, is "the domineering tone". How the devil is one to write? This is distressing, getting worser and worser I am[…]

Len's next letter is notable as the one in the whole correspondence with the most quotations of Mona's own words, giving at least a hint of her style and mood, which here is bitter and sarcastic.

East Witton, Thursday [22 January 1942?]

[…] Apparently what you now call a female "tantrum" has blown over, but I don't think so. From the tone of your recent "strong" letters, certain things are in your mind – things which, I think, prove that we aren't friends at all. That was why I wrote that it was better to finish altogether. You disagree, but do you still think certain things, or look at certain incidents in a certain light?

"You were all the time trying to placate your conscience one way or another."

"Why couldn't you have put it crudely and bluntly in the first place and have finished with it e.g. you could have told me that I am a woman of 37 and have not the qualities which appeal to you who are a young man."

I couldn't have told you that because it wouldn't have been the truth. Again:-

"You have spent 6 months trying to tell me that in rather ambiguous terms and trying to soothe my vanity, I suppose, etc etc…"

If I was ambiguous, it was because I was, well – inarticulate, if you like, but certainly not in order to soothe your vanity.

The word "useful" cropped up again, even against your will. It is so forceful that it must crop up even if only in parenthesis. It is easy to think therefore that the word is constantly in your mind in connection with our relations. Granted, you are "useful", and it is stressed by a lack of response from me[…] But if the fact that you are "useful" to me, & that that fact is important to a great extent in our relations, keeps recurring then wouldn't it be better if they ceased?

"You want me to find nice things to say to you to help you through your time of inward searching, but you quite forget that in friendship there are two sides, and that I should be helped by you too." If I remember rightly, the tabooed subject was brought up again because I was genuinely concerned about your welfare after what I had done, and couldn't gather from your letters whether you were still terribly upset or had perhaps recovered a little. The enquiry, I now realize, would do little to help, but it was because I was concerned about you[…]

The phrase "led up the garden path" hurts, because I feel after that that I have been gulling a poor girl of 16 like some experienced married man. Again, if that occupies your mind a lot, we really ought to "finish".

"Drop that awful soul-searching etc, and think of my feelings as well as your own."

My soul is the most interesting in the universe to me, and I count it as a duty to enquire into & examine it as far as I am able. "Know thyself" is an old adage… but that does not mean I'm not concerned about you or others. Soul searching is only a sort of hobby, because in approach & materials it is much simpler than fretwork etc, if the results are feeble. But I am really concerned about you and my family in particular. For you I seem unable to do anything to show it, for my family, I know that money is a constant worry for unknown reasons and I try to be realist enough to send them as much as I can. You cannot know my daily life sufficiently to judge my actions & say so often that I am self-centred & self-absorbed[…]

"The present individual seems a far worse stranger than the one who came to us from Exmoor" would provoke anything because of the phrase "far worse stranger". It seems to incriminate so, and the following parenthesis was worst of all:-

"(Don't think I am flippant, but however did you manage so much to avoid catching my eye…??? I quite chuckled about it afterwards)" I do think that's flippant, because when one begins to observe other people's eyes, one sees that they look very little at one, eye to eye – only when one's eyes are averted does the other look, as a rule. And it was rather a shock to find I had been invited to be observed in such detail. No, that's bitter – rather I was shocked at being so observed after being invited.

But worst of all, and this hurt more than anything, was this:-

"You are feeling, I expect, that mine is another scalp added to the collection" and more…

Now the tone of this letter is terribly self-righteous, and instead of being a sort of apologia, has turned into a sort of counter-attack, which I didn't at all intend. I know too that facts seem to refute the words as soon as I write them. It depends how you take the facts. It is natural for you to take them as any normal person would, and the "six months of ambiguous remarks" have failed because – well – because they were ambiguous, I suppose. And now, where are we?

After six months, the position is that you are in love with me, and I find myself unable to return that love. I am sorry to repeat that, but it is the prelude to what I want to say now. If you are in love, it is natural to desire to be with the loved one, to keep contact with him, to show that love as far as is discreet & possible, and generally to love without response, a thankless and hurtful affair. The loved one, on the other hand, benefits from these attentions, is perhaps embarrassed by them and in a different way hurt because he cannot return them. Now I don't want you to be carrying the burden of the first one, if, as I say, it is a thankless and hurtful task[…] I hope you don't mind me recounting here a conversation I had with Kate (whom I don't see now). She thought a man, finding his love not being returned would try to get right out of it, run away from it all and blot the loved one from his life. But a woman, she thought, was entirely different, and could carry on just as though nothing had happened, even after a confession. She even thought she could lavish all her love upon the man without asking for any return[…] Kate and I don't see each other now, by the way, because we found we did not really believe in platonic friendship, and thought it rather silly to try to form a friendship, and because I realized that I prevented her from being with Joan & Jennica her pals, whom she would rather see at nights I think.

But to get back to the point, think for and of yourself, and I think you should decide whether to remain friends or not[…]

East Witton, Wednesday [28 January 1942?]

[…] I learnt recently that a close school-mate of mine, George White, was killed. He was a pilot. When it's a pal it makes you think all day[…]

East Witton, Sunday [1 February 1942?]

[…] We seem to be trying to take each other down a peg or two in our letters[…] You are not, as you say, "a dreadful prig", and I didn't mean to give you what you "deserved". It's a battle of words, isn't it. Who can be bitterest? We are so bitter that you are led to think our friendship is nearly defunct.

I now realize that I am to blame for that, because although I wasn't prepared to admit it, I have been high-handed, too concerned with myself to the exclusion of others. Perhaps I am much the same with the people around me at present as I used to be before, but to you, & even my people & Arthur, I have appeared different, proud and stupidly arrogant. Well, my relations have been spoilt with you, because past behaviour has made me somehow nervous, unnatural, too effusive or too dull as it suited me. But I hope you can see it as unnatural[…]

So if, besides our love, our friendship too is to go, it is my fault, and if I can repair the damage I would do so willingly. But can I? Would I not be the same again after a week or two? I don't know, but I'll try not to be.

You somehow deride me for declaring that damned "soul-searching to be easier than – painting". Yes I did ask for that. But really my present life is quite incompatible with artistic attempts, as Jim Kirkup will even assert. You can understand that, though. I sometimes scribble bits of things now & again.

But of course, my hobby is what has always been my hobby, reading, & I read as much as ever[…]

This would be the last letter in which Len worried about relations with Mona until late June at least. He visited home the first weekend in February apparently without anything untoward ensuing. For the next five months the main preoccupation discussed in his letters was literature and his desultory attempts at writing. Len read Henry James, H.E. Bates, Aldous Huxley, Joseph Conrad, E.M. Forster, Turgenev… He described some experiments with short stories:

East Witton, Thursday [12 February 1942?]

[…]You ask what I write. Well, I write mostly to you. I suppose you mean in a creative line. Very little I'm afraid. Each attempt produces even more dismal failure, and days after a "good idea" pales into laughable insignificance. I got so interested in the short story a bit back that I began to read a lot of them & then tried my hand. I read a [H.E.] Bates volume, and all other books of stories I could find or borrow[…]

Virginia Woolf, with a phrase somewhere or other on the love one can have for inanimate objects set me off on one such a story. A man is found outside a big city railway station talking to a bus – a description of his love for such inanimate life (buses, monuments, car mascots), a mere suggestion that this was caused through a motor crash before which he had been a respectable though rather reckless chauffeur. A car drives up, disturbs him with the movements around it. Offers his services carrying luggage, but is subconsciously disturbed by the orders & general attitude of the owner, a wealthy lady, apparently. She is a former employer who recognizes him, but he does not remember her, just obeys her orders so automatically & so by habit, that her last order, a normal dismissal sends him to the car, not realizing what he is doing before he's off with it. Off, as reckless as ever, & not being able to realize what he's there for. All the time he is disturbed – more and more as he goes, & cannot tell what it is. Whatever it is must command his attention but cannot yet, until late in the evening, the sun low in the sky he turns eastward after a bend, the sun flashes in a mirror just above his eyes & he sees, when he looks up, the thing that requires his attention, indeed more – a gollywog dangling in the back window – he begins to talk to it – & – 1.2.3 he's gone.

But that was an utter failure. Then an experiment with a man's mind before he's asleep, after some trying experience, in which the physical agitation of pillows & bedclothes mixes with his mental agitation. Again utter failure. Not a subject for short story or even anything except chapter in a novel.

Mrs Foster once began one night when we were alone, to talk about Mr F's neglect of the stock & his laziness at home, & got from one thing to another, telling how he joined up in the last war and she was left alone to look after two children and a farm or smallholding (cows, calves, bullocks, pigs, hens & so on). She told of how the farmers around never helped her in any way, her struggle with a thankless task. She lived for only one thing, like most women, the return of her husband. How she longed, and struggled on, and what's more brought the two children on, & kept the stock going somehow. He came back 18 months after the war had ended (he was in the army of occupation). He was a changed man – swore to her and had no interest in the stock. Since then he had done no more than his work – she carried on with the stock, brought up the children, losing the elder at the age of 6 or 7.

The situation (her sitting before me with some mending was so typical) and her pathetic story, which though full of a sort of tragedy, is the fate of many women & sometimes men, worked in my mind but again I could not express myself adequately.

These were my 3 most ambitious attempts, but were so far below what I wanted, so devoid of life, so dull in my hands that I could not let you see them[...]

East Witton, Thursday [19 February 1942?]

[...] Jimmy [Kirkup] has got away at last. His policy of ca' canny[4] has worked so effectively that Tarran was sick of him and gave him his release after all. He is going to an agricultural hostel at Thirsk, which I think he'll not like any better than this but he's got himself to please. I can imagine him finding a job like spreading manure both back-breaking and distasteful[...]

Occasionally the war obtruded into the correspondence. Mona's concern for her brother Tony, stationed in the Netherlands Antilles, elicited a calmly logical response from Len. In a subsequent letter, his thought on the Thirty Years' War arising from reading Aldous Huxley's Grey Eminence *seems a little ironic in view of what he would later see in the Low Countries and Germany at his own war's end.*

East Witton, Sunday [22 February 1942?]

Dear Mona,

[...] Your alarm about Tony [Mona's brother] is quite unwarranted, so you must keep calm. This sounds domineering but is the reaction to female alarm which misplaces the facts & takes too much notice of the press. Now was it a Japanese submarine that attacked the Standard

Co's island?[5] I think not. It was a German, and the same day another German sub commander boasted of gazing through his periscope at New York's skyscrapers and even distinguishing the movements on Long Island. You say "What's the difference, German or Jap." Well this. That Jap action seems a prelude to invasion. Now Tony has South America and the Pacific between him & those swarming armies. And I think even Japan must find South America, to put it mildly, out of reach. And as for Germany, always remember that outside of Europe, we are the most vulnerable country, and South America is again, I think, out of reach. It is even less vulnerable than USA, except for an occasional far reaching sub, which is much less harmful than an occasional bomber over Tyneside[…] So don't worry unduly about Tony, because so long as he's at Curacao he [is] as safe as you are, indeed much safer, if not so comfortable. Forgive me if this sounds complacent, written as it is from comfortable quarters in Yorkshire, but I don't want you to worry until there's something to worry about.

One of our land girls has just lost her husband. He was killed in action over Germany – a rear gunner. It is a tragedy because they were very much attached to each other & were a nice couple. I only saw him once, but liked him[…]

East Witton, Sunday [1 March 1942?]

[…] Here is the Huxley and Miriam [protagonist of Pilgrimage novels by Dorothy Richardson] […] I wasn't in the correct mood for such a book.

The Huxley, on the other hand, suited me tremendously. Fr Joseph [Francois Leclerc du Tremblay, adviser to Cardinal Richelieu] is revealed in his true light. At least I felt so all the time. The subject was not simplified – he was treated as a human being who is capable of the usual failures, despite his austere asceticism, masochistic practices and mystic experiences[…] Father Joseph shines through, one of the most remarkable figures in history surely. The horror of the 30 years war seems to have been far worse than anything we can imagine nowadays. The present German occupation of the Continent cannot result in such horrors surely – rape, yes – looting, yes – individual & collective atrocities, yes – but it cannot result in the conquered people being reduced to such depths that they will dig out the newly buried to eat, kill young, sick & aged[…]

East Witton, Wednesday [4 March 1942?]

[…] Thank you for these books and for the other things. The paragraph or two on Stefan Zweig[6] was very sad. I could understand every word for once. One of the Danes here once talked to me of his nostalgia for his home country, which he hasn't seen for over two years. It was really sad to listen to him. Then I talked to one of the new land girls who are French. She too seemed lost here, where there is no sun. They come from Bordeaux, leaving on the last ship before the Germans arrived. Their mother who is English was interned, but has now been released. The pathetic way in which she asked "Do you never have any sunshine here." Last week, before they came, it happens we had some, but the last few days have been raw & misty. I think it would be awful not to see England for 6 months. We seem to gather the exiles here, for we have about 10 Danes, 2 French girls, 1 Dutch girl, 1 Italian (a former mosaic worker), and about half dozen from the Irish Free State[…]

Len/Jonah could never bear the idea of boredom (a condition he was incapable of experiencing himself). He felt the need to rouse from torpor the forestry workers at the camp near East Witton with literature. Mona characteristically responded with alacrity to his request for books for the men, who were "very grateful". Len/Jonah's urge to educate (a trait he shared with her) would re-emerge in 1946-47 and much later in his artistic career.

East Witton, Sunday [15 March 1942?]

[…] We are trying hard to educate or at least interest the camp men, & quite a number of my books are out now. I don't think Dr Cockcroft[7] should be asked to come unless we are sure about support. I haven't yet written an appeal to the newspapers for books and am wondering whether I ought. If however you have any books you really don't want, of neither sentimental or intrinsic value to you, I'd be glad to pass them on, and put the postage in your fund. The men have little to occupy them, and I feel that everyman reading, even trash, would bring a more complete rest than the perpetual yarning and dozing that goes on. They are bored stiff, & as only a few bother about getting access to books, those few find it difficult to read in the talk of the others[…]

During these years of enforced service − first on the land, later in the army − Len became preoccupied with the "death or sleep of the spirit" that could flow from having life planned out with all possibility of following a vocation suspended, even if one could feel a contentment in the circumstances. This was a thought to which he often returned.

East Witton, Saturday [28 March 1942?]

[…] I was very much impressed by an article in the Library Assistant this month. It was by a young poet-librarian (not well-known) serving in the forces, and faced with problems which have concerned me more & more as time goes on. I like his division of librarians into librarian-as-artist and "businessman" librarian − quite arbitrary I know, but one which I make myself, probably fancying myself as the former. Lewis Halsey is very patriotic, apparently, but he says much that I like, because it is so pertinent today, and is almost identical with my own thoughts. He quotes from Spender, and the poem quoted is so beautiful in its suggestion that I'll give the whole version.[8]

> He will watch the hawk with an indifferent eye
>   Or pitifully;
> Nor on those eagles that so feared him, now
> Will strain his brow;
> Weapons men use, stone, sling and strong-thewed bow
> He will not know.
> This aristocrat, superb of all instinct,
>   With death close linked
> Had paced the enormous cloud, almost had won
>   War on the sun;
> Till now, like Icarus mid-ocean-drowned,
>   Hands, wings are found.

The reference to Icarus is extremely lovely, I think, and in 1930 odd, when it was written, was not so hackneyed as it is now. But the poem is in the spirit of Halsey and, I venture to add, myself – all of us, in some way or other, the "aristocrat, superb of all instinct". The airman is "with death close linked" while I am probably "with earth close linked", and I am as spiritually flat as the airman or Halsey. And yet we are happy with it, if questioned point blank, but what does it mean? The worst part is that happiness in the services or in "war work" comes with a cloying of the senses and a death or sleep of the spirit. So long as I was unhappy, in a temporal sense, my senses & spirit remained unimpaired, but this queer earthy contentment, pleasant (even making me hate to journey home) kills them, if they were ever there. "Passivity" is a good word, one often with me[…]

East Witton, Wednesday, April Fool's Day

[…] I thought my remarks on Halsey's article in the *Assistant* would provoke some comments from you. I didn't mean to suggest I was a caged lark & even went out of my way to say I was happy. I wasn't even complaining. What I wanted was to say how I appreciated & agreed with Halsey on most points, so read it and see. He doesn't complain either – he just states a fact – that it is new life he is leading, a new experience altogether, that though beneficial in the long run, he is not the same man & tends to seek distraction & entertainment where once he wrote poetry, that he feels he could not or should not write now, believing in a sort of emotion recollected in tranquillity. But he's quite happy – only realizing like most serious people that happiness (of the temporal kind) isn't all. But I presume in identifying myself with him. I ought to say that much he says appeals to me as true of all who are in new surroundings, among different people at different work because of the war[…]

Len went home twice during April. The first time he met the wife of his old friend Jimmy Gale, who had aspirations to be a painter and had been sent to prison for his conscientious objection. A fortnight later Len saw his library colleague Norman, who was willing to suffer the same fate as Gale for his beliefs. He also met Miss Pumphrey, a member of Mona's Quaker circle. She was probably the inspiration for the character Miss Pomfret, the steely Quaker guardian of the main protagonist in Jonah's first novel, A Tree May Fall *(published in 1980). Miss Pumphrey took an absolutist view of pacifism; all COs should be ready to go to prison, for any kind of work which in any way contributed to the war effort was an unacceptable compromise. This set Len thinking about his position and the principles of conscientious objection. Shortly after Mona informed him that Jimmy Gale's appeal against his imprisonment was under way.*

East Witton, Tuesday [7 April 1942?]

[…] I enjoyed my weekend very much and am very glad I came, despite the rotten journey. I'm glad I went to the Friends, and the Carrs, and glad too to have met Florence and been accepted more or less as a friend. I'm afraid she must have found me somewhat untouched by what has happened to Jimmy, and I thought you might have found that too, but really his case has moved me more than anyone's, and I really felt for Florence and Jimmy, without being able to do anything about it. It woke me up to reality somehow, made me feel terribly for the persons involved, enter them somehow, a thing which doesn't often happen to people like me. I could only say I hoped all went well for them both and it seems horribly futile that that is about all I can do. If it was Florence in jail & Jimmy at "liberty" I might have helped occasionally with my company, but even that would be doubtful[…]

East Witton, Wednesday [22 April 1942?]

[…] I found Norman quite unchanged, but felt sometimes I could charge him with a word he liked very much in describing me once – "truculent" – but I think it is a natural sort of mischief in him, and not of a bad nature. It was Miss Pumphrey strange to say, with whom I felt quite out of harmony at the weekend, and though she's getting old, I was a little shocked at her intolerance. She made a remark referring to Norman and I being free while Jimmy [Gale] was in jail. I ignored it as far as possible and went on to say how sorry I was about poor Jimmy having to suffer at such length, but this she resented, quite surprisingly, saying there was no pity in it since there was every reason to be pleased when a young man is willing to suffer – it was us, in other words, that were a matter for regret, who weren't willing to sacrifice & suffer for our conscience. She implied much I'm afraid, without saying a lot, but the freedom of Norman & I set her off. I think she was a bit too bad, particularly about Norman, for after all, Norman has offered to do what Jimmy has done and it is not Norman's fault if the Min of Labour has not yet brought things to a head. He is quite willing to go to prison as we all know. For myself, I have been inquiring into the whole business again, arguing to myself[…] I still arrive at my phrase in my tribunal statement nearly 2 years [ago] – "latent evil" – and my conclusion is that since by living we are helping the war effort, existence requiring food etc, we must as far as possible find not the implied evil but the latent evil in the things to which we are put, and I can't for the life of me find latent evil in land work. There is the implied evil of helping the war effort, releasing others & so on, but no latent evil. To be absolutist is, in other words, to commit suicide. Therefore to me there is no great distinction between Jimmy and I, since even Jimmy cannot be an absolutist (he must help, even if he only pays some tax or other), but only a difference in degree. Please don't think I'm trying to be an apologist for my own devious ways. But when Miss Pumphrey and others imply that we who don't finish up in prison are evading our consciences, it is rather irritating, especially when one has frequent taunts from the other side about evading our responsibilities & not joining the army[…]

On 25-26 April, Mona's home city of Bath was bombed in the Baedeker raids; her parents were made homeless, although they escaped unhurt. Len expressed his concern when writing on 29 April and in his following letters.

East Witton, Wednesday [6 May 1942?]

[…] I suppose you have had many expressions of sympathy over the misfortune of you and your family and I don't quite know what to say to you. I only know that the thought of my own home being wrecked fills me with horror, and I can imagine what you feel. It is not the material loss, but the fact that your family place has gone, with its own peculiar emotions, comforts and treasures. Why, the thought of all the books going west is too much. My little collection (about 2 small shelves) is coveted too much to lose without feeling that something had gone that was part of life. So what must your family feel. I can only say that I sympathise with you and them[…]

During the spring Len became very keen on fishing. On 14 May he described in loving detail how he had caught "a lovely pike", "the biggest fish of my life, nearly 3 lbs" which Mrs Dinsdale cooked for dinner. Angling was an excuse for doing nothing else – he was in a blank phase of mind.

East Witton, Sunday [17 May 1942?]

You are on the warpath about Fellingism, but after this week you'll be on to me about Oblomovism. For strange to say, after reading that magnificent novel[9], I had the worst attack of Oblomovism I've had for a long time. In me, of course, it does not mean staying in bed, but in leaving till tomorrow what can be done today, taking the easy way & even being very sleepy. Thursday, Friday & Saturday I was quite unconscious the whole 24 hours of each I'm sure, and my mind was in such a state that I began to get worried. Today I feel I've recovered and this is my fourth letter[…]

My Oblomovism, by the way, took this form. "I don't feel in the mood for reading or writing – anyway I'm too tired – I'll go fishing – it's a nice, quiet, pleasant, sleepy occupation. Zahar! Zahar!"

"Yes, Leonard Normanovitch."

"Bring me my fishing rod, Zahar."

And so I spent about 20 hours this week, just dozing and hauling in my line a little, waking up for a few moments when a pike was in sight and then dozing off again when he refused my panicking minnows[…]

I had a letter from Jim Kirkup, saying he had already a copy of Janus of his own, but that your copy was being read by a friend. His egoism seems worse than ever, and apparently has plenty to feed upon in the people he is living with & meeting. He says among other exploits that he is "negotiating with Faber for the publication of my semi-autobiography 'Adolescences' (in verse) though I am regretfully having to translate its 10,000 lines from the original French"[…]

Describing his attempt to analyse the poetry of William Collins (1721-59), Len
expressed his longing for the rigours of a university education, of which his family
circumstances had deprived him. This wish was never fulfilled, but his voracious
reading and discussions with Mona, together with his later learning in the Army
Education Corps, would equip him for a rich creative and intellectual life.

East Witton, Tuesday [26 May 1942?]

[…] You appear (I don't know whether you are) to be cross with me
for something – "Yah!" you yell and then repeat it & go on "Don't get
uppish with me" "fussy" "– I might produce some really juicy sentiments."

Please don't torment me. I want you to promise me you'll send me
some "juicy sentiments" – now will you promise me, please! You're
good when you produce them, much better than if they seethe
unexpressed in your brain and make you dream those funny dreams
of yours. Which reminds me, I had a very bad dream the other night,
in which I had "to retire from public life" with the most morbid
disease, called either Peebles or Dunstable strange to say. I suppose
some recent gnat bites had led me through Measles to Peebles and my
concern about some recent lazy spells through Constipation to
Dunstable (I defy any man to find a nearer town than Dunstable to
Constipation!)[…]

Perhaps I have verged a little too near purism, but I've lately been
forcing myself (against Oblomovism) to study words through studying
Collins[…] I really got down to brass tacks using him (awful phrase)
as a basis for some close reading instead of skimming. I felt if I
imposed upon myself some task such as might be set at a university (o
ambition!) it would be a sort of discipline over my unruly habits of
reading & thinking[…] I was quite pleased because, though I had
found some slight evidences of original poetical genius in at least two
of Collins's poems, I was rather bewildered about the rest & in fact
could not lay my finger on that general something that vaguely reveals
itself in his Poetry. Then that something came at the weekend – that
strange diction peculiar to himself, was it not parallel to that other
strangeness & peculiarity – his madness? – no, he was not ill till age
29 & the Odes were out at 24. But again, I looked more closely and
found a gradual change from the Eclogues, through the lines to Sir

Thomas Hanmer, to the Odes, which marks a change of mind. The happy objective approach of the Eclogues (even with their hints of sadness) are healthy & so too are the lines to Hanmer, but in the Odes there is something already creeping in, which come with this involved diction. And I traced, like a good student, my theory, and yesterday formed the embryo of a grand little thesis. I believe I am unjustly proud of my little piece of critical analysis, and am quite certain the weekend will bring the usual disgust, & reveal its pettiness. However, as I've chosen you as my Professor I should like you to mark it when it is finally completed – if ever[…]

It is a great exercise & I feel it has been good for me. It made me read all his works thoroughly and repeatedly (thank goodness their quantity is meagre)[…] I am sure it is better than this one or two works business, & I'll try it elsewhere & try thus to extend my reading instead of skipping here & there. That is what I value or admire about a University Education – it appears to me they make you stick to one or two things at a time, & then leave you to explore. My lack of that education has allowed me to wander haphazardly all over the place. You won't realize how much this sort of thing means to me – I must sound gushing with boyish enthusiasm & ambition. I'm sorry if I do – but it is real for me. I do wish I could have had a University Education, even though I know that at 16 & 17 (& even now) I was incorrigibly lazy & ignorant & couldn't have got on ever. I once spent a whole week discussing the question with Jim Kirkup who of course said University Education was nothing! Perhaps, but it made him stick to his languages & equipped him with something real, while I was wandering all over the place[…]

The exchange of letters continued as regularly as ever, but Len found himself in a mental rut at the beginning of June. Fortunately a chance encounter while travelling back from Tyneside offered a new stimulus.

East Witton, Monday [15 June 1942?]

[…] It is curious that all day I have been saying "It is time [I] wrote a proper letter to Mona" & thinking of all I wanted to write and now my mind is quite blank. That keeps happening to me these last few

weeks & it has got me worried – only a little[…] What worries me
most is because this strange disease or whatever it is, is not like the
absent-minded professor's, whose poor memory I would willingly have
with the rest – he has a poor memory because his mind is preoccupied
– but mine is unoccupied. I can't get things to come forward as I used
to, I can't hold things. Consecutive thought is quite impossible. Why?
Is it a disease or what & will it last?

Unfortunately I am tabooed from certain former friends here
through a row with a sergeant-major who had a dirty mind, & though
I don't mind being alone, it is hopeless when your mind won't work.
Next week, however, one of the Castle Bolton Group of artists,
George Jackson, has invited me to his home for the weekend so I
should be alright because one doesn't need to "think consecutively"
to look at pictures. He has been accepted by the RA [Royal Academy]
3 times but the hanging committee ploughed him, which is most
unlucky. He wants to "draw me", which is a new experience, excepting
the childhood efforts of Gladys & Betty[10] who wanted to "draw
me"[…]

East Witton, Wednesday [17 June 1942?]

[…] The first part of my journey home on Saturday night was
extremely interesting, and I made a new friend – one of the Castle
Bolton artists. He seems very interested in me for some reason and
invited me up to Castle Bolton for the weekend coming. I received a
very nice letter from him today & I'll enclose it, because it is so like
him. He is a typical Dalesman & speaks good Yorkshire, much to my
comfort, since most people who are interested in art flaunt a terrific
accent which confuses me. I feel like a monkey chattering to a
Pekingese or something[…]

I've often told you I think, of alarming coincidences in what I
sometimes write. Recently I tried to write some symbolist verse in an
arid despairing manner in which I got my atmosphere in the first two
lines "I am old man's bacca/Captive in a shock of poppies". You
know – the colloquial expression for that weed that waves drily &
aimlessly in meadows – "old man's bacca". The association with the
scarlet vividness of poppies expressed just what I wanted – the word

"shock" was exactly what I wanted. Last night I read for the first time some of DH Lawrence's poetry & came across the following – in quite a different music of course. The poem 'Twofold':-

> How gorgeous that shock of red lilies, and larkspur cleaving
> All with a flash of blue…

Strange, isn't it. But I leave it to DHL. He is a true poet and last night I thought he was beautiful[…]

East Witton, Friday [19 June 1942?]

[…] I'm a little chary about making new friends like George Jackson (oh very chary!) but this weekend should prove to be very pleasant for me don't you think & I consider myself very lucky. I could have blessed him when he just took me up – I was feeling awful when he just "capped" me as they say here[…]

Your remarks on Jimmy's artistic adventures please me, and I wrote a letter just like Caesar exhorting his troops[…] I think that composition being all with Jimmy he may, like Stanley Spencer or even John Nash use literal truth in nature to convey certain visions of form. That's how I should paint I think – quite literally but using visionary forms, even exotic ones[…]

Actually I'm sure I see lovely pictures in new compositions and all sorts, with every transition & nuance quite fixed, every mass arranged and so on, but I know it's not mine to convey. My ambition would be to have the same vision in poetry – to have my visions (for what they're worth) transmuted in word symbols and write them down warm from the heart. But I can do neither – that makes me unhappy sometimes & can lead me on to awful depths of depression, which is silly. On the other hand I am sometimes happy to just range in someone else's genius – You know I was happy at Whit paddling about in Collins's work. Why should one wish to be an artist? – if I were, I should cry to be a genius, and if I were a genius I'd want to be greater than Shakespeare or Leonardo. No – I don't think I would – no – I'd be quite content if my personality were just a little greater & could convey the visions (again, such as they are)[…]

You ask me "Why are you shutting affection out of your life – your parents' friends as well as mine? How can we reach out to you? What hinders you from reaching out too?" I only vaguely gather your meaning. Actually your affection & that of my parents for me is a very real thing to me – I appreciate you all so much but seem unable to say so properly. I take so much & give so little[...]

But as for our mutual reaching out – we do connect you know and I hope, if my weekends are most infrequent, that letters are only a little less effective in keeping the bond between us. Personally I like letter relationships – they often are the result of a whole days reflection on & off & that reflection is being with your correspondent don't you think[...]

East Witton:
Beginnings of an Artist

The meeting with George Jackson was a signal moment in Len's life, for it would lead him into the company of the Castle Bolton Group. Before, he had had an undefined urge towards creativity, as shown by his attempts at writing in various forms. He had an interest in the visual arts, but no true aspiration to practice them, judging by the letters to Mona. Now he would develop for the first time a craving to master the technique of watercolour painting. It would bring a measure of satis-faction, but far more frustration at his limitations in the medium.

Witton Fell, at work, Wednesday [24 June 1942?]

[…] I was out last night sketching – a lovely subject of a lonely farmhouse set in a hollow on the moors. The result was so bad that I'm afraid I obeyed the old impulse to tear it up. Another impulse follows that – to never think about painting again – but I'm going to fight it, though if things go on like last night I don't think I'll be able to stand it. In fact I'm amazed at myself going out tonight again. I have such a lovely vision of this farm setting that if ever I do paint presentably I'll come back & get it down[…]

I had a thrilling weekend with George Jackson – so thrilling that I'm afraid we were so intense (in Keats's sense) all the time that we exhausted each other. We were quite prostrated with nerves all the time & it's one of the few occasions when I've lived through the artist's intensity. He has a little cottage (resurrected from a derelict state) in much the same style as TE Lawrence's Clouds Hill. It was so charm-ing, with just enough room for two queer fellows to bore into each other. On Sunday morning we got up fairly early & after breakfast I posed for a quick portrait. It was an awful strain posing but he was terribly interest [sic] & so utterly absorbed that I became entranced too & before we knew where we were it was dinner time & we both emerged into a flat spin. He works very quickly & nervously & in rough washes. I think you may see it. I'm fond of it already as a painting – it is marvellous when you've seen it done or tried to mix wash colours yourself. As a likeness I'm not at all sure – nor is he. He has captured what he calls my "earnestness" which since I posed as naturally as possible, must be, for him, at any rate, a characteristic attitude. He says there are parts of me like Lawrence for some reason & somebody else famous whom I've forgotten which I take with modesty or conceit. In fact, he would have interested you in his sort of analysis of me as he went on. The weekend was hopelessly bachelor with a very sympathetic married man popping in so often – Fred Lawson – one of the most lovable men I've ever met. He likes me too – I'm quite a success for once & felt so obviously at home, as though I'd been in the circle for years. Conversation, usually so difficult with me, was difficult to keep down, and there was no redundant or "phatic communication".

I'm going to have the portrait (or rather sketch) all next week so that my parents may see it. If they like it, I shall save up or draw from your bank & buy it for their joint birthday present. I am inordinately proud of it because I can see (as a painting) that it is one of his best creations & though there are faults I can't help liking it. He paints so quickly that it is either success or failure. I'm sure I can't judge it at all and I must let you see it[…]

Evening […] I've been out & done quite a presentable sketch of last night's torn-up subject – I got a sky effect for once – my first. It's so pleasing to get even one item. It encouraged me. I'll answer your letter at the weekend – but I hope you'll excuse me if you are sometimes neglected. You are never so in my thoughts & if I'm sketching, the good ones are for your eyes – if I'm fishing, a big one is all but wished on to your plate, & if I'm swimming I think wouldn't it be nice if you had seen me do that trick etc… Swimming & fishing will not prevent me from writing to you but sketching might[…]

East Witton, Thursday [25 June 1942?]

I'm writing to you between sketches so to speak – my sketch of Sowden Beck [south of East Witton] turned out to be awful again –

so I left it at that & even managed to refrain from tearing it up. It seems to give Mrs Dinsdale & daughter pleasure so I have already an appreciative public for the early Leonardos. But I'm bloody bold & resolute. Tomorrow I'm out for another subject – perhaps the tragedy of fallen trees if I can make a picture of it from a nearby wood[…]

My reading is sadly neglected now & it is sad to throw over an old love with such nonchalance as I do at present, flippantly departing to fishing, swim or sketch. But there's the winter & I'll always be a reader so why worry if a few summer weeks find me prone to temporal distractions[…]

George has brought my portrait which at the first renewed glance I couldn't resist so bought on the spot. It is an equivocal me; it might not be me, but in one mood it quite definitely is. Anyhow the earnest, rather affectionate look, a sort of superb benevolence that assails me when I'm so fully alive as when I posed, is just what I should like my parents to have with them. George's medium is Conté pencil (red chalk) rather than water colours, but as the former is practically unobtainable, I think the most difficult of all mediums for portraits is, in this case, a very suitable alternative[…]

George has left me with a lot of old sketches to paint on the back. "Posterity" will puzzle over early Jacksons & early Joneses all mixed up. So don't trouble too much about paper for me. It is kind of you to think of getting it for me. I should like some cakes or preferably tubes of Raw and Burnt Sienna & Aurelian but in the Students Class – the other class is too dear[…]

East Witton, Wednesday [1 July 1942?]

[…] My parents seem to be only partially enjoying their stay here. I feel they find it a poor substitute for Warkworth or Alston & I suppose they're right after all. And three or four days with my parents has shown me terribly clearly how far apart I am from them & they from me – we live in different worlds. I must have changed drastically since I left home. It is very depressing when one can't bear one's own parents, & I am so temperamental that I just had to refuse to go out with them tonight or I'd have snapped them up or something. I felt such a pang of utter despair when my father came for me tonight &

I just said I wasn't going out. He looked so disappointed, & I feel so terribly wrong about it all, such a pig. It is an awful feeling, just as though you had murdered the dearest person in your life in mere temper[…]

You ask me about George Jackson. He is 43, son of an old established draper [in Ripon]. At an early age he showed artistic inclinations, following a rather eccentric grandfather. When still young went to Harrogate School of Art, but on last war breaking out had to help in father's business. Joined up 1917-1919 – had hard time of it but adventures vague & probably exaggerated. On returning was still compelled to help failing father, whose business he took over when he died. He only gained release from it (for he hated it) when this war forced him out of business.

Actually he had contemplated going out of business before that, having built up quite a reputation for himself. His interest in drama was at the time bringing him in about £100 a year, for dramatic classes in Ripon & district, with extras in various branches of art.

His artist career has thus been confined to a place behind business, but that hasn't prevented him from getting on. He became friendly with the Yorkshire artist Fred Lawson in early 1920s & after a time spent with him they formed the now celebrated (in Yorkshire) Castle Bolton Group. George, after spending his spare moments at Lawson's house, acquired the derelict cottage for his studio at Bolton. His main interest is figure drawing & he has gradually developed a flair for portraits, culminating recently in the delightful equivocal picture of his celebrated friend, the artist Jones, who shows every sign of being the greatest of the Castle Bolton Group yet (if he ever begins to paint which is as doubtful as ever it was). To continue, George is very interested in drama, & has written & produced local folk dramas based on past characters & events in Wensleydale. His whole life is confined to Wensleydale – he wants nothing more & is not himself when he is away from his beloved cottage. He is at present forced to work for money (& compulsion of course) & can only visit Bolton at weekends[1]. His present occupation is as a measurer for a Ripon firm of timber contractors.

He seems extremely interested in me – too interested almost, but so far I have had no reason to be wary of this for we have come to a very strict understanding that if ever I pose in the nude for him, which I have offered to do, he is on no account to touch me. He was perhaps a shade caressing at odd moments on my weekend with him, when he was overcome somehow by what I'd said or something, & I'm terrified of being touched at all now, even to shaking hands. So I've told him & he was so grateful for my frankness as he calls it. In fact, our friendship seems to have bloomed most naturally & is already of value to me. I have had every chance with him you see, benefiting from past experience, & we are already quite natural & at ease with each other[…]

I've decided I've no talent whatever for painting. That's tonight's opinion. Tomorrow I may find I'm too ambitious & must creep before I can walk. Looking at it impartially I think the first opinion is right, & if it is I think I ought to commit suicide, because if I don't create something I'll have little to live for. Other things seem to count for so little. That aggravates you, doesn't it? Suicide would be easy I think if one wasn't afraid of one's parents suffering too much. Though we are worlds apart, still I'm attached by my umbilical cord[…]

East Witton, Saturday [4 July 1942?]

[…] My parents have gone home by now – I hope they've enjoyed themselves, but I think their enjoyment wasn't complete. Their son is getting very difficult to understand & seems to be miles away – which must mar their holidays I think. Anyway, we had a pleasant evening on Friday which sort of made up for my neglect. Of course we've never had words – no, not one wrong word. But there seemed a sort of film between us all the time – it was so difficult & sometimes a strain to talk on their queer trivialities, with me wondering all the time what high & mighty thoughts would float upon the air if they would incline that way – yes, what, if their talk is barren would I have? I'm blowed if I know. So I can only hope I did not hurt them in any way[…] I should like them to know or rather feel more – to live things more vividly, to be either thrilled or denunciatory about my portrait (despite its faults it thrills me), to see the beauty of these dales as I see it[…] And I wanted them to be simply enraptured with my thought of getting that portrait for them. And now the thing's been left behind, due partly to me not taking it to them.

But why should I want them otherwise? I'm wrong quite. I would put it all better if I said I was disappointed that they didn't enjoy themselves more than they did[…]

At night, after seeing my parents off, I was with George, & we got all het-up about the war almost immediately so that I thought our vastly different views would keep us apart for ever[2]. I was quite prepared never to see him again his views seemed so bitter, until we suddenly realized that we were being crackers & were 'artists' for the rest of the time. But I mean to have understanding on that too, in case we break out again. Friday morning I got up early with George & after he had gone to work, the people in the house were so awful that I went out & appreciated the serenity & devotion of the people at Holy Communion at 8 o'clock. I felt like a heathen, & remembered the Quaker warning not to let art (among other things) take your eyes from the true vision of life or something like that. But with some people it must be otherwise – don't let anything detract from the living intensity of art. It is an accident (or rather coincidence) if an artist, like Michelangelo or Eric Gill, finds his art in his religion. But what about poor Baudelaire at the opposite end of the scale, or a blunt personality like Augustus John or a Bohemian like Sickert. To them religion is dead, not because they wish it dead, but because it just is dead for them.

And then I came home again, & sketched East Witton Church, & the result was a little more pleasing, because every failure gives me valuable experience. I am a hopeless failure – but as George says, if it was easy, everybody would be artists – and the harder it is the rarer & more beautiful the end. So if I can hold on to my present frame of mind, I'll be content if it takes 6 years before I paint a picture. But the 6 years will be nothing but pain, and yet joy. I love painting those failures & hate the results the day after. I could tear them up violently & curse my mind that it should ever have been even content with it. But if only I can be patient for the years after, when technique has come & I can fuse it with vision in an occasional picture. That probably will never happen, but I mustn't let that deter me. I must forget that people like me usually get stuck at a certain phase & stay there for life[…]

East Witton, Monday [6 July 1942?]

[…] I sketched an old crumbling plaster cottage on Sunday with moderate success. My distances are falling into place, especially distant (or rather middle distant) trees which I have contrived to suggest in a manner like John Nash, rather than in the normal method of Jimmy [Gale] & George (I can't do it in their way probably but I like my way best anyway). My subjects (I mean the actual objects in the foreground on which the eye is supposed to be focused) are hopelessly weak.

Tuesday […] To return to my plaster cottage; Jock, our foreman, having seen it half way through on Sunday expressed a desire to see the complete thing last night, when I was passing his house on my way to sketch somewhere. I thought I'd let him see it, but wondered how to make my foreground live more. I found with a few discreet darks that I could achieve it to a certain degree, & made a more presentable picture (if such it can be called) than my feeble Witton Church effort. And then I took it round tonight and it was encouraging to see him & his wee wifie so pleased about it, & I couldn't refrain from giving it to them. Jock wanted to pay for it, because as he put it, I must have a lot of customers for it. I discreetly said I didn't give them away as a rule (pardon the immodesty – business you know) as it was a very expensive hobby & that there was a sort of agreement between artists not to make their work cheap. He had been good to me on the Fell & as he was leaving I could give him Twemlow's Cottage (ahem!) In addition to the feeling of grand beneficence & generosity, it was an introduction and in short I was commissioned to paint their cottage, so how's that – a fortnight's sketching & I'm commissioned! It means this to me – that even if I haven't by any means started to wield the artist's touch, I do get a picture to suit ordinary folks who want it to be "like" the subject. It's all tremendously interesting of course. And I now have a little more confidence before a subject. I'm not afraid, so to speak, of my commission, knowing somehow that even if I'm dreadfully dissatisfied with my sketch as a work of art, I shall still get it to satisfy the Jocks, who want the sketch of their cottage because it is the place where they "started life together"[…]

East Witton, Thurs [9 July 1942?]

[…][M]y remarks on DHL, whom I revere, as you know seem to have gone astray, and I'm often capable of crooked thinking. I knew what I was after however when I quoted that sex was a crucifixion – it is – but I quoted it in a bad argument. I mean this – that sex, as signified in a sort of "vegetable love" (as distinct from spiritual love – a vague difference I admit) is strong & inexorable enough to tear a man or woman from his ultimate end & direction in life. It not only tears him away, but can deaden or cancel out a former instinct which arose from something outside the body – as an artistic or poetic instinct in particular, which two, though very small in the whole measure of man are the strongest & purest in an individual, as compared with say a business or even religious instinct. By instinct I mean that slight determinism in a man's life which seems to lead him to a certain interest – art, poetry, religion, business, politics etc – & which can develop, if great enough, into creative directions. Well, I say sex, where a man has a body normal, can destroy those instincts, and art in particular, so that the victim, or shall I say the subject can never look in the former direction his life took. Perhaps more potential artists have perished on this quicksand[…] But I repeat, sex must weed out the most, being a strong and lasting, universal impulse. And your example, Rousseau, is an excellent example of the destroyer placated. So the animal instincts, in so far as they destroy art are to be regretted; in so far as they surpass being "of promise" and indeed contribute to art they are fine and noble. In a person like me who cannot fight great battles like an artist, they could destroy what I now value, if, as I say, the love was only "vegetable" as it might easily be[…]

Sunday evening: It is bright and sunny, and across the road the good people are worshipping God in the Chapel. I can hear them singing and the hushed music sounds beautiful.

Yesterday I painted a very poor sketch of the Church tower, but I do not weep over failures now, and went to Jock's today to paint his cottage. As a picture I wouldn't have it on my walls, but I think it will please the Jocks as the actual cottage is quite pleasing, and I managed to produce the crumbling plaster effect. It is the foreground of vegetable garden that troubles me, so I have washed it out a bit so as to focus the eyes on the actual house. They haven't seen it yet and they may be horrified (though they won't admit it & just say "Yes it's very nice" etc…)[…]

Jock has seen the sketch – is over the moon with it but Mrs Jock wasn't in so final decision is deferred. Anyway while I was round there who should roll up on a bike but George Jackson – in he comes & boosts my sketch up tremendously – oh I don't know what it wasn't – it was so excellent.

So I dare ask for my 10/- now – I daren't ask for more. But George outside said the praise was for "trade purposes" as he knew what was on. He did go on to say I had advanced considerably & said I must go on. Furthermore, I ought to make a start & send something into the Northern Counties Artists' Exhibition. It might look bad among the rest, will in fact, but we must start so I'm getting a form. And my portrait, bad though it is, is going in for George's exhibit, because though nobody else likes it, George and I do[…]

East Witton, Tuesday [14 July 1942?]

[…] Your letter gave me great pleasure – I hope this does for you. I'm very depressed and sort of rankling inside me at the moment. The policeman from Middleham is on my tracks – he came to Dinsdales today and all the village simply had to know. Apparently he knows practically every place I've been to lately, knows even that my parents have been & even knows they took some of my work home. He asked Mrs D. which sketch or sketches they took, asked to see my work (Mrs D. wisely refused) and asked them specially not to tell me he'd been as he wants to catch me red-handed, having lost one or two cases recently.

It has shaken me so much that I could weep with ease (I speak the absolute truth there) and though I know I shouldn't be so touchy about it, seeing that I have little to sacrifice if I gave it all up, I can't help it. It is what was in my dreams I suppose, that make it so for me. I was full of this and that and oh I wanted to do so much. But this eternal shadow snooping around after me, informing the police of my every movement is a bit thick and I certainly can't paint tonight and I think it will be a while before I venture out if ever. It's not that I'm afraid, but I don't think I'll be able to work properly with something else at the bottom of my mind. In fact I know I can't, so my ambition to send a picture to this year's Laing Gallery exhibition is squashed. In fact painting is off the map if I'm being sneaked upon & snooped at every turn, I just can't paint with that eternal presence, knowing it will phone as soon as I've started, for the policeman to come and pluck me up by the scruff of the neck – and then to unfold work, however bad, to such revolting Philistines is quite beyond me[…]

East Witton, Friday [17 July 1942?]

[…] I'm afraid I've gone right back to where I started again, and I don't know why, unless I've been under a delusion, and George too, that I had advanced[...]

Painting has gone right into the background and I shall have a struggle to start again. I tried composition but it was so hopeless, not in conception so much as the most hopeless inability to get near what I was after. It was a lovely picture in my head of foxgloves & willow, the former on a bank sloping down to a boggy area. But if my mind picture was good how despairingly poor the result on paper – so obviously an amateur.

There is hardly time to produce anything decent enough for the Exhibition now and I'm afraid ambition must wait. I'll have to be content with the doubtful glory of my portrait, since the people who see a likeness in it are few.

I have permission from the superintendent of Leyburn Police to paint East Witton camp, & have been given quite a free hand in fact, so I can ward off the local policeman. I have also got the War Office artists' permit thing which has a list of prohibited objects – things obviously military like barracks, docks, the coast, railways, army etc[…]

Len was by now well settled into a psychological pattern that would keep reappearing periodically all his life as an artist. The joy and fulfilment of creating was balanced by intense frustration, depression even, over his shortcomings and his failure to measure up to his high ambitions. As an old man Jonah was making similar comments (rather more succinctly) fifty years later in his journal or letters.

East Witton, Tuesday [28 July 1942?]

[...] I've decided I don't like going home for the weekend at all, so journeys in future will be only out of a sense of duty, a sense which sometimes emerges from its dormant state.

The company on Saturday night was most interesting from an objective point of view – I mean to stand out of it all, & view the creatures objectively, study their habits, expressions & various modes of making themselves understood[...] But such studied observations are bound to strain my nerves, & consequently I was in a very bad mood, and I do wish you would let me be alone then, please – which means you shall see less & less of me because weekends at home never fail now to ruffle me right up to the neck. And painting is a very bad thing for frustrating all of me – bless me – the only possible way to say anything I might wish to say & it won't let me even whisper. I wasted a lovely clean sheet of David Cox paper last night because – well, I wasn't interested, to tell you the truth and now one must confront a new enemy besides lack of ability to do anything – lack of desire. Of course, all the time there is an insatiable hunger but before an actual sketch is commenced one just feels bored stiff at the thought that another mess is about to be produced – that what you want must inevitably go by the board – and that hurts, the latter. It goes on sometimes until you begin to muse and reflect that you'll never be a painter, that at 23 you ought to have had all the graft passed by of life-drawing, techniques etc... Plenty of work & money could just save me, but I'll never have money & don't want it, because I can't work hard like that, as you know. The ambition is always strong in people like me – a little talent must go a long way, and naturally it can't spin out for ever. What worse source of depression, or rather, what better? So if I continue to daub about, you must see these things, & of course I know you do – and if I cease to daub which is quite probable (since I don't see why one should be unhappy about a "mere hobby") then you'll see that too, & then you must let me go and be the mere nothing that I am.

Then at other times, a mere word from George or Fred is enough to keep my 'revs' up a little longer. "You've advanced as much as is good for you" one says – and that paradox is a power of good to me.

But it's mostly a miserable business at present, and from even my slight experience I can see visions of a terrible veil of suffering that must pall a great artist as he sets out – as though he had not enough to endure[…]

It is always in my mind, art, and I shall talk about it all the time knowing that this desire & propensity to circle round the actual thing is very dangerous – I may be talking about pictures, dancing & drinking at Xmas. I think art is a bad thing for people, particularly the artist's friends & people – I know for instance that if I were painting well, I should do the most unforgivable things to them for little reason. An artist must be forgiven in his best pictures, however bad he has been, look at his best, enjoy it to the full & forgive him there & then if you can – he has done it for you – it's his own little crucifixion, and however vile he is to you, if he paints well, bless him as you drink in the beauty of his art. Hope too that he need not be so vile to do such things. I hope whatever little I may create & however poorly, I may not be any more vile than I am now at times[…]

East Witton, Sunday [early August 1942?]

Your big oblong parcel gave me quite a shock yesterday, for when I came in and saw it lying there, with my address on it, I felt sure my poor little picture had been chucked out of the exhibition & you'd been kind enough to send it, all packed & padded. I don't know yet whether they've accepted it, but they may. One thing is absent which these committees (following the Royal Academy) are hot on – draughtsmanship – but they should realize, I think, that more draughtsmanship would have put too much "edge" on the whole thing, & would have spoilt the soft neutral effect of line, tone & colour that is there. I quite like my Cover Bridge picture on looking back, mainly because absence makes the heart grow fonder, because a picture always seems better when you just vaguely re-image it, and because I've gone back disgracefully since I painted it.

I painted a lovely scene yesterday – all hard rough stone cottages, with hump-backed bridge against a very green hill slope with stone walls behind, but the result was such a hopeless mess (I'm trying not to be modest) that something drastic will have to turn up soon to save what little art there may be in me[…]

You ask me about painting indoors – no, I can't do much – if I want to paint with any enthusiasm I must have my model, so indoor polishings of landscape are quite beyond me – I haven't tried any still-life yet, but usually when there is bad weather, I sneak a drawing of my own face on paper and shove it away so that no one can see it. I have done several self-portraits but they are all so funny, with screwy mouths, black gipsy eyes, or long sallow cheeks etc… that they would raise nothing but guffaws – and needless to say, nobody would dream they were me[…]

Fred Lawson (1888-1968) was the member of the Castle Bolton group who had most influence on Len, by a fair margin. Born near Leeds, he studied at the Leeds and Kensington Colleges of Art. He was both deeply rooted in Yorkshire and keenly aware of the work of the Impressionists and Post-Impressionists. Settling in Wensleydale in his Twenties, he became well known for his paintings of Dales landscapes and life, and his images were frequently printed in The Dalesman. *He also captured the industrial cities of the West Riding.*

East Witton, Monday [early August 1942?]

[…] I have had a full look at some of Lawson's work and it left me astounded – it seems impossible to handle paint like it. He is taking me into hand and I may start some proper lessons next week. And if that does me no good then we can safely pack up because I'm not content to paint finicky little cottages with roses round the door, like typical amateurs. Bedtime!

East Witton, Tues [early-mid August 1942?]

It seems ages since I last wrote to you, but I suppose in all it only amounts to about 4 or 5 days. I was very busy over the weekend – did a picture for Fred to pull to bits next week[…]

The picture I did for Fred was a set view & I should think it is as good as anything I've done considering it was quite difficult – looking over the roofs of Castle Bolton to the distant hills. Even so the result is by no means a picture, though I'm determined to paint at least one this month to be framed.

Painting is rather a rush job at nights now – putting the clocks different was rather a blow for me, if for no one else. Soon I shall have to adjust myself and find some drawing or still life exercises for nights & paint from nature at weekends.

I have had a good look at Fred Lawson's work. It is so beautiful – effortless, yet always with that salient effect possible with water-colours. The pace seems too great for me, but I'm committed now and I'm going on to the bitter end. Fred's work really is magnificent and it is no exaggeration to say he is one of the best water-colour painters in England. He is quite neglected and he doesn't seem to mind it – he just goes on in his own quiet way, domestically unhappy, artistically a happy master of his medium. "Quiet way" – "quiet" is one of his favourite words. "Just go on quietly," he'll say, "draw any old object quietly and take no notice of anybody. Go to as many galleries & exhibitions as you can & go round them quietly – take it all in quietly."[…]

Everything I do is a sort of experience in something or other – a sky, trees, houses, foregrounds, distance, composition, contrast, tones, colours, drawing, general handling (very bad as yet), all sorts of problems – and each attempt has a grave fault that even I can spot at first sight. The handling can be excused for sheer lack of practice, but all the same it is rather appalling and when my work is compared (even in my mind's eye) with a competent water-colourist, I feel ashamed that I consider & describe my work to people as adult work. However we must try hard to make a picture shortly[…]

I was out last night painting on the summit of Witton Fell, but was so windswept & dithery that the failure was worse than usual, so I came down much disheartened to be met at the bottom by the police-man who demanded me to show him what I'd done, despite my protests that it was unfinished & incomprehensible to anybody but myself. Out it came, and his sort of grin of pity for me, as much as to say I was a poor dabbling simpleton, nearly made me crash board and picture down on his head. So tonight I've stayed in to be a decent citizen, and write to you[…]

Fred Lawson soon became Len's favourite among the Castle Bolton group. His unassuming manner and quiet way of teaching endeared him to the young aspirant. Painting had become such an obsession that it was taking over Len's life. At the same time, James Kirkup resumed contact after several months of estrangement between the two friends.

Castle Bolton, Saturday [mid-August 1942?]

I'm so sorry I neglected you last weekend. I know how disappointing it is to expect a letter and not get one – not even one late. I just seemed unable to crush one in anywhere, though I did want to write. I think what you have said (in warning) about me living on my nerves lately has been very wise, because I think I have really been in a queer nervous state, unable to eat for days on end, and feeling almost prostrate at work. I thought this was going to be another weekend of nerves, but as I walked up from Redmire to Castle Bolton I suddenly felt I was better as soon as I saw the Castle and I'm going to try my best to have a quiet time, see what it does.

I came on the early bus, have been here nearly 3 hours – George will be here in about an hour. Fred has been in and we've had a quiet chat about painting. He is kind about mine, but I've learnt with him how to find grave faults. He won't hurt you by saying so and so is bad until you yourself say you are weak on skies, say. Then he takes you up – "Yes, that one's very bad, it wants so and so" – as long as he knows you are not going to weep because he criticizes. I'm sure he must have had some such students, for he is always the same – he won't point out faults, you've got to draw them out of him and I suppose that is his method of fostering self-criticism[…]

I may get a letter off to Arthur [Good?] some time next week – I feel terribly remiss about it all. In fact lately I've lived quite selfishly, partly because interest in art (even mine such as it is) seems to wash all else out, partly because a straight selfish assertive attitude to life seems necessary to keep your revs up. George isn't selfish in the ordinary way, but he tends to assert himself that way, egotistically, his every emotion of more importance than the greatest outside events. It seems the necessary counterpart to his art. Jimmy Kirkup, much in my mind lately, was even worse.

I had a delightful letter from him this weekend – it enclosed this most beautiful of poems.

Noon on the Farm

Now the horses gently
Sway and enter golden stables.
Men like sacks lean
In holy straw-light.
In the enclosed noon
A swollen kitten and two
Hens in white bloomers under
uncle horses wander.
The blue-slotted whitewash and
The tiles' rococo gloom
Recall the cooling summer, the tiny
Reapers in the sun and dead
Abandoned jackets under
Dark steps of corn.

He is exquisite when he writes a pastoral – he seems to emerge, like
Collins, from mere conceits to depths of feeling and vision peculiar
to himself[…]

P.S. I have had a quiet weekend – a grand lesson with Fred, a painting of my own which made me want to weep with despair. When I
brought it in disgusted, George liked it rather more than usual, put it
[in] a lovely mount & frame and it looks quite good so I'm not so
miserable about [it]. It is a miserable affair, on the whole, this learning
and I wish I wasn't quite so raw. Fred gave me his sketch of this
morning – it is little more than sky but oh what a sky – it is racing
beautifully, departing in wisps into the blue. He is a sheer joy to watch
as he paints – a marvellous craftsman as well as an artist. His eyes too
are wonderful – they simplify so – he doesn't see half so much as I do
& has the advantage of me there, until I learn to simplify by practice.

East Witton, Friday [mid-August 1942?]

Thank you for the nice batch of things you sent me tonight – I do
hope I can put something worthy of your diligence on to the paper
before I waste all the Permanent Blue. In fact I had a grand mail
altogether & felt the centre of the universe. George was being very
nice about a recent effort: "It certainly struck me as being very individ-

ual and un-Lawson-Jacksonish. I do look forward to seeing how your style develops." Poor soul, he'll have to look forward a hell of a long time – still, his words make me feel very bucked and the effort is safely stuck away in a drawer so all's well.

And Jim Kirkup sent me a whole sheaf of poems, bless him – the most beautiful stuff – and he's in an awful plight as his employers haven't paid him for 5 weeks – & could I lend him a quid. I think he is the most lonely, precious poet in the world – too lonely & precious to be published ever. He is an absolute misfit in society and I think suicide must enter his mind quite often. But when it does there is always a highlight to follow – such is Jim[…]

Event – I painted a sort of picture yesterday. It will frame anyhow & could be called "In gay gangs they throng" if I had more mastery with skies. It is a [Gerald Manley] Hopkins sky travelling over a field of stooked corn, or it's supposed to be. Anyhow it will not disgrace a wall, so I've got something. My sky pleases me – it is hot where there is blue and heat comes down (just between showers – so hot) on to the stooks, which travel in rows across the warm field until they are arrested by three very badly painted trees. The whole thing is very amateurish but is about the best my stage can produce so why worry[…]

Have you been to the exhibition [of Northern artists at Laing Art Gallery in Newcastle]? If you have please tell me all about it. I'm beginning to be ashamed about my contribution but that is natural if I'm to advance at all[…]

And now, another book – can you get me [Eric?] Kennington enclosed? Request after request – I'm so selfish – you shall have something from me. Yes, here is an 'Epithalamion' by Jim

> Under the dome of home
> subtle my lover wakened
> alone, and wakened me,
> calling my soul his own,
> calling the dim bone
> mine and his own, bone
> born of his bone.
> He leads himself and me
> to the brief balustrades
> of his second smile,

his colossal ramparts
I dreaming climb, he climbs to be
the sleeper on the heart, awakening
the heart of hearts, awakens him and me.

And this extraordinarily beautiful thing. If it is addressed to anybody who lives it is the loveliest thing, but I think it is addressed to Jim's invisible ideal companion.

You are the consolation of my amber age,
the past concert of my voices, and my involved failure.
In the bolt-upright poorish churches
the crimson motors of the choir-fed organs still
emerge, like wedding-monsters,
electrocuting no one. You for a while
cover a whole book with your hair.
The ugly cataract
bombs the revolving ravens of the precipice.
Some have believed perhaps
in something more than me,
or after all in nothing,
shattering too the vast dong-bell of beauty.
And even you, prophetic miracle,
over the marvellous remnants of the world's collapse
for a wonder hold only rival sway,
knowing the awful end, integrating ruin,
must loosen all
and he come with nothing,
voiceless, lover of none.

He being "integrating ruin". I remember when he wrote that - we were hysterically happy for a few weeks – I even remember suggesting "revolving". Perhaps the poem is to me, but I don't think so. He did write one for me, but only let me read it once and won't let me have it now. And yet there is a sort of malice between us, which at one time became quite overpowering – letters are becoming more loving however and the malice, "integrating ruin – voiceless, lover of none" is bound to depart. He even calls me "My dear" so we are good friends again, who have learnt that two queer 'uns, especially with Jim as one, should never live together for more than 3 days[…]

East Witton, Wednesday [19 August 1942?]

I've worked my hardest day for a jolly long time – Tom [Allen] and I have been given about 2 acres of Japanese larch to fell. It is not too good, being rather dirty and the price small, but we are glad to be on the job, even if it doesn't pay us. I think felling is about 400% heavier than other work and your heart fairly pumps all day, until a few days settle it a bit. Sweat has almost blinded me all day, and I drank 4 pints of water at work[…]

Your art man seems most obliging – I'll collect the mounts on 5 Sept if they're done. The charge is a bit stiff, I think, but then these things are dear so why worry. How I long to paint something respectable enough to go into the mounts – I have a man who will make me frames – however, I seem utterly incapable of producing anything decent, not even my *Cover Bridge* standard, if that has any value. Apparently the Laing Art Gallery think it's good enough to go into the exhibition, as I've had word it's been accepted & an invitation to a private view on Saturday [22 August]. I'll try to remember to enclose it[…]

Of course, both George & Fred know I'm a CO. I've learnt to announce the fact before beginning friendly relations so to speak. It only leads to subsequent embarrassment if one doesn't. And they appreciate the fact that I was a librarian because I keep the queer Mrs Lawson going with books. She is very well read from what I hear. They don't approve of pacifism, being very like Eric Canning[3], afraid of Germans trampling on what they cherish[…]

East Witton, Thursday [27 August 1942?]

Late again this week – out painting "rain stopped play". However it was nice to fondle all the nice pads & papers you sent me – the people are very kind. If I don't send them a letter just now – I'll send them a linocut sometime – but I'm sure I can crush in a letter for each this weekend as I'm not going away from Witton.

Your comments on the exhibition were grand – I feel quite bucked to think I'm not tucked away on a screen. I think my poor picture would have deserved it, but I couldn't bear to think of it on a screen. It must look frightfully feeble beside Fred Lawson & somebody's 10 guinea effort.

Painting has gone badly this week and I think that bloke in charge of weather is grossly unfair to send this tropical climate when I've started felling. This stifling thundery weather simply brings gallons of sweat from one – it stands on my body in great beads and blinds me, & tickles my nose, then tastes salty as it enters my mouth. It is quite exhausting & makes me swing the axe lazily & carelessly with the result I cut clean into my boot toe, through the sock & left the toe itself untouched[…]

East Witton, Sunday [30 August 1942?]

I am very busy just now, trying to sort out the chaos of our saw-mill, which is to be demolished. If I could make a decent picture of it, I have a ready customer in the boss Jarrett, who has kindly suspended demolition operations for a fortnight to allow me to paint. It is in an awful mess and it is a strain trying to fit in details from memory & placing figures of men working.

I wasn't going away from Witton this weekend, but I got an urgent note from George last night to say [Jacob] Kramer was coming up & if I would like to meet him I must come up today. He also said Kramer planned to stay the week, but George had to scotch this as he had somebody coming. It looked like your name, but I think he must have got mixed up. I'm very anxious to see, as I don't want Kramer to be sent away because he's got your dates mixed up. I would like to see more of Kramer anyhow, he seems so brilliant to me – the Jewish complement in painting to Epstein's sculpture. He is a typical Ghetto character I believe, & has illustrated Ghetto life profusely. Of course he is absolutely outside RA tradition[4] […]

East Witton, Monday [31 August 1942?]

[…] Painting is very mediocre these days – I show no improvement on the *Cover Bridge* sketch (which by the way would lose its neutrality of tone & colour if more detail were put in). It was not an "exhibition" picture, & its lack of finish, though regrettable to some, is very dear to me. I love to see how a picture has been painted, and finish almost always destroys sensibility. There is a kind of finish which is lovely in

a picture – the finish that sunshine puts on things, but even there elimination is the great factor. Detail I often see but ignore, if it suits my
purpose. But of course, I have no real style yet, if ever, so I can't say
how my art will develop, again if ever[…]

Regarding Jimmy's poetry, I'm rather sorry I sent you 'Epithalamion' which is his most androgynous poem. He asked me later to keep
it for myself and not let anyone else see it. I don't know what experience or dream has engendered it – it is the truth, that's all I know. He
has of course his personal god, personal enough to make "concrete"
dream poems.

"I badly need someone who will look after me," he says: "I cannot
stand alone without feeling defenceless & in constant danger. I must
have someone stronger than myself who will protect & worship me,
not unquestioningly, but devotedly & sanely. When I am so much
alone, my own sanity comes so close to falling apart. My strength as
a writer is in my weakness, my huge sentimentality (a perfect basis of
elimination & purification, from which I extract everything) and my
constant adolescence. Find me someone with a will stronger than my
own, a heart more passionate, and a soul more prophetic; someone
who, when I'm hysterical will

> lay a finger on my lips,
> and gather up the hours in his hand.

"Find someone whose talent is greater than mine, whose imagination is more varied and intense, whose speech is god-like, whose
beauty becomes hourly more and more that incessant haunt, perfect
love. Find the angel and the devil who will out-do me in everything,
and I will live subdued and happy. Until then, it is no use. I am born
to be mad, melancholy, sexually insatiable, a monster fairy, alone,
tragic, a perpetual boy with a chosen instrument.

"With all this, how can I be calm and good? Oh my beating, torn,
flower-like face fountains me into every brief brilliant hole, the
backless mirrors of my ancestry. There is too much frenzy, torment
and scepticism in me – I could never, never, never, never be more than
lovely imperfection.

> Lover & poet, the rectifiers,

Man prone to lovely fault, outdistances.
They, dishonoured and alone, to the wall
Shot-at must go, and love humanity."

How can I help worshipping him. I wish I could fulfil him – be
perhaps the complement in painting to his poetry – a futile wish, but
a dream I cherish. To build up a new psychological aura like the
Sitwells' would make me happy. Alas, I am so horribly deficient in
those essentials that could build it up.

*At the beginning of September Len paid another visit home, which to his surprise
he enjoyed. Writing to thank Mona, he had to add "[I] hope my voracious appetite
did not eat your pantry empty. How did it look – I bet you got a shock to see anybody
eat so much. Felling does that – every weekend alike – I could eat all day, if I'm
well." Not long afterwards, Mona paid her first visit to Wensleydale, staying at
George Jackson's cottage during the week.*

[No address] Tuesday [15 September 1942?]
I hope you have enjoyed your holiday and are feeling better by now.
That means too that I hope my nervous state did not affect you. I'm
always high-pitched when I'm painting, even if the results are feeble.
You will have found after seeing Lawson's stuff that I'm still at a very
feeble stage, and when I'm talking all that nonsense about the qualities
in my work, my genius etc it is – well, just nonsense, meant not to
impress but to amuse. But sometimes people are impressed and it is
such fun to go on impressing them – I couldn't make out whether you
were impressed or amused. I hope the latter[…]
   Tell me what you thought of Lawson's work – adverse and other
criticism is good from you and puts things into perspective. I worship
him unstintedly, for his imagination, strength and craftsmanship. But
I wish I knew just how I stood with him, for though we are such good
friends, I wouldn't be surprised if he was just egging me on to procure
the lesson money. But I think he is genuine with me, and in any case
I do learn a lot when we go out together. Then one can't blame him
for not giving me a whole treatise on painting in one lesson – last time
he did a sky and little else – this time some water and half-hearted
foliage – I suppose he reckons on one going back to him for my trees.

Mona with Fred Lawson

He's right and I can't blame him – but you can see how expensive this hobby of mine is. I often wonder if it is worth it – I have literally spent pounds on it already and made about £2 out of it. It ought to pay, or I'll always be smashed, but I'm not worried, only it seems daft to spend so much on almost worthless efforts. I take it too seriously to think of just frigging on and having a few little sketches at home like the usual amateurs – but that's all I'll manage, I think. And then conceit and modesty are always butting in – you don't know where you are. The best thing to do is just paint and care about nothing[…]

When the prospect arose of being moved to another area, Len realised how much he had come to love Wensleydale. Although he would always remain appreciative of typically English "gentle" landscape, his preference later in life was for the wilder forms of North Wales. Len was also beginning to appreciate that Fred Lawson's wife, Muriel Metcalfe, was just as fine an artist as her husband.

East Witton, Tuesday [22 September 1942?]

I'm quite flat tonight, because I'm beginning to think I'm hopeless as a painter. I have 2 pictures to paint for people and I can't succeed at all. I would like the money to buy a picture of Lawson's I have my eye on, but no – I've failed so disgustingly, so dismally that I'll have to swallow pride and tell them I can't do it.

I think it may be a bit of a shock I had at the weekend – that I may be shifted from Wensleydale altogether, to near Thirsk. I didn't realize how much I loved Wensleydale until a shift is in the offing. I've rooted myself here quite forcibly, and leaving will be quite horrible for me. Thirsk seems a big distasteful desert after Wensleydale. It isn't a desert of course, and I ought to be thankful that I'm not being sent to a real desert like Libya. I am, yes I am, but I still don't want to leave here. Wensleydale is not an obvious beauty spot – I'm not surprised for instance that Swaledale appealed to you as a visitor more than dear Wensleydale – but I couldn't get "ha'nted" to Swaledale – it is too deep, not intimate like Wensleydale, it hasn't the same lovely gentle forms – no there's no dale like Wensleydale for living in: Teesdale, Weardale, Swaledale are all very beautiful, each with a characteristic wildness and spirit, but Wensleydale is for people to live in. The people are the best I've met yet.

Both Exmoor and the Southern Uplands are more beautiful, especially the latter with its bare Kenick Hill rolling down to the loch which reflected always the exquisite skies there. But Wensleydale has kept me satisfied – I never sicken of looking at its greenness, its squares of fields and elms along the roads. I'll have the most painful nostalgia if I do leave, so pray for me because I don't want to leave[…]

I saw some of Muriel's more precious work on Sunday – a special privilege, and I think poor Fred was on the point of tears as he confided one or two things to me – her sheer indifference to what appears to me to be one of the most original imaginations alive – she is straight & warm from Blake, full of his same "fine madness", his childlike simplicity of line, and his wistfulness[5] […]

[No address] Wednesday [23 September 1942?]

[…] I'm so glad that your holiday has made such an impression on you. I think Wensleydale must have caught hold of you, even in 4 days – can you imagine how much I love it? I love it, I love it, oh I love it – I'll come back if I must go and come back again and again – I can't, daren't think of having to leave, I'm breathing as much of it into me as I can in case I must go. Now I know why weekends at Tyneside pall, why I must get back quickly[…]

I think Castle Bolton liked you tremendously and you have captivated several people already. Fred keeps referring to you as a "nice little person" and "a really fine friend to have" and so on and I can tell beneath his veiled words that you impressed him[…]

And now I've come to an idea – I want Muriel to paint something for me and though I think it's just about impossible, I think if you'll help with one thing, I might have just the teeniest weeniest chance of something from her. Can you send me *Green Mansions*. I'm hoping she hasn't read it, for I think the poetic suggestion of Rima may move her as it moved Epstein. It is a remote chance, but I am so anxious to try[6]. Do you think our sort of mutual affection for poetry can break her indifference. She was so enthusiastic a fortnight [ago] walking round the road from Redmire – it was very dark and Fred and George loitered behind to enable us to have our talk in peace. She seemed bursting, as though nobody had helped her for a long time, as though even a splendid, talented husband could not relieve her of her burden of poetry. For in such people it is a burden often[…]

George has been bullied by me to send me the completed ms. of his book *Bolton Castle* by Xmas (I hope) which is progress I think. He is determined to allow no setbacks to prevent and if it can be placed with a Yorkshire publisher he'll feel less of that frustration that seems to bury him all the time[…]

East Witton, Monday [28 September 1942?]

[…] I've had a good weekend painting, you'll be glad to hear, and I've got a nice picture of the Castle for Arthur's wedding present (unless you want it). It is looking up, across pasture, from down below to the S.W., further away than that other one. The sky is a success this time – my first successful blue sky – it is hot with a white wisp across (done

Len's sketch of Castle Bolton in his letter of 28 September 1942

properly this time) and a few clouds piling vaguely behind the tree
and the castle. The composition is very simple – the pasture forms the
whole foreground and the castle is breaking a line of trees on the
horizon.

I also did a sketch with a very fantastic sky which nobody likes but
which I like myself very much[…]

I'm sending you some of George's plays. Lend them to anyone who
promises to return them – especially *Eva St Claire*, of which there are
only 4 copies. The others can be bought I believe. *Swan Inn* needs
dalesmen to act it I think, & his best play *Madeleine Clement* is only in
typescript, unfortunately[…]

East Witton, Wednesday [30 September 1942?]

Still here, you see – I'm beginning to hope they've got other men for
Thirsk. Wensleydale is friendly and isn't going to part with me so
readily as at first appeared[…]

A man has been to Dinsdale's to see if he could buy my *Sawmill* –
Mr Durrant the vicar. I didn't know he was interested except that he
asked me to paint his church. He told Mrs Dinsdale that if I took it
down he would buy it if we could come to an agreement. After
Jarrett's refusal to buy the same picture, I'm sure I can't make my
mind up, but as it is a copy and the Vicar didn't actually commission
it I shall probably let it go for 10/-[…]

East Witton, Wednesday [7 October 1942?]

I think it must be nearly a week since I last wrote to you – I'm so sorry. The weekend was spent trying once again to paint pictures for various people – once again failure. So I went dashing up to Castle Bolton to weep in my master's lap, went out for just under an hour and got bitter cold doing a bitter cold evening sky. That redeemed the weekend somewhat despite the rapidness of execution & black masses.

Fred is very kind to me at such moments and George too, who, despite his being full to the brim with his book, found time to console me. I know you'll be laughing at such swings of the pendulum, but I find that, however much I persuade myself that I shall paint something decent again, a bad stretch always affects me the same. Still, decent efforts keep coming and I now have about 5 or 6 that I dare show to people.

Monday night I went to an art class at Middleham – I am friendly with the teacher and we feel we can help each other. You may wonder how I can help him – but his knowledge of water-colours is old and rickety and my very broad haphazard method seems to appeal to him very much. He paints very slowly and carefully, striving after detail, and I can't bear that. He doesn't like it either, but can't seem to think in other terms. Anyway, I joined in the class and painted a sunflower very badly, but very differently to everybody else, which was surprising[…]

Jimmy Kirkup has disappeared I'm afraid – I haven't had word since I sent Burckhardt's book, and I'm beginning to think I'll have to pay for it. Fortunately it can be replaced because there have been recent impressions of it. I rather think he has moved [from Thirsk][7] […]

We shall finish the new woods on Witton Fell shortly – a fence is being made now, but Tom and I are still propping, and we are being constantly harangued to hurry up in case we are fenced in. We should finish tomorrow – then what I don't know. Probably a shift to Ellington again, either to fell hardwoods or fiddle about – or perhaps Thirsk.

In mid-October Mona entertained Len and James Kirkup at her home. It was the first meeting between Mona and Jim. While on Tyneside the two young men talked about how alienated they felt from their backgrounds. This had become a major preoccupation of Len's. Although he later regained a fondness for the North East, he never lost his sense of distance from the place and its people.

East Witton, Tuesday [20 October 1942?]

[…] I may be seeing Jim [Kirkup] again this weekend at George's – he aims a weekend with us anyway. We had a marvellous weekend, strangely enough, and though we are still agreed that about 3 days is the limit for us to be together, we make the best of those days. The Ballet was extraordinarily lovely, specially for us I wonder. And you entertained us as we would have it, and we hope, as you would have it. The only blot on the scutcheon was my home, which was terrible, so we both rushed off to Newcastle and as Boris[8] was out, we went to the Tatler and had coffee and something or other and talked about all sorts and everything, analysing each other's sex complexes, and our homes and all sorts of naughty things.

Don't you think what Jim called "the furious domestic miasma" of home quite terrifying. I found it so before I saw Jim – my pictures, such as they are, weren't worth firespills in my home – they seemed utterly futile and stagnant and I couldn't be bothered with them after I showed them at your house. In fact I hated them. So I shall be very careful about anything good I may do – it may not be shown at home. I am skipping all the respect due to my people etc of course, but I don't forget it.

Poor souls, a son who has got mixed up with folk above his original (?) class has dragged them into a terribly maladjusted life. They never saw people like you or Norman, or Jimmy K. or Florence before I did. I can look at it impersonally because I seem to be outside class now, and I can see how vastly different you & others are from poor colliery folk like my parents[…] I've got over most of the hurdles now, because I rush them and inferiority complex in that line has died away and given way to new growths which are becoming more of me than my upbringing, which acted as a slough so long. Only a complete divorce from all that can save me – George at 43 is held down & stultified by it, and he must lead a chameleon life between Ripon [his family home] and [Castle] Bolton – I don't want to be at his stage at 43 – if I'm still nowhere I don't want to be stuck at his stage[…]

Yes, home was a bellyful on Sunday and we were glad to extricate ourselves.

Once, I told Mother (heartless I know) that I would never live at home again – poor angel, it nearly brought me to my knees in tears, when I realized just what that meant to her – it was one of the cruellest things I'd ever done (I know I specialise in cruelty). Father understands I think – he is liked by all these people I bring to them, and he is so lovable really – but poor Mother – oh, how much I could tell you, how terribly, desperately unhappy she has often been – she has experienced far greater depths than most people are capable of, because she has never had the escapes of drink, nonchalance and face to bear her along. You would revere her if I told you some things but then telling them would sound trite beside the real experience.

Jim is wrapped up in so much of my own thought that being with him brought out certain things more forcibly than ever.

He liked you and your home extremely, even liked your own "tittle-tattle", to which he is usually so intolerant.

And from his talk he even liked my *Cover Bridge*. That means much to me. It confirmed me that I was on a particular line – you will notice few of my subsequent pictures have it – they are exercises in technical difficulties, because technical faults spoil *Cover Bridge*. So, though I didn't offer you any of those pictures, don't think I overlooked you – I want you to have something which fairly satisfies myself, and none of those did[…]

I don't want Welsh books 'on or about'. Reading is feeble when it is on such a matter. So many people who want to go to the North Pole read about it to satisfy their craving, but I don't see how it can – books shouldn't be read in that spirit[…]

East Witton, Friday [23 October 1942?]

[…] I'm inclined to agree with Hope Dodds[9] in what she says of George's plays – George has never had a chance as an artist, and he has had a sensitive spirit strangled. So his plays are only part of him, that part which rushes up to Bolton at weekends, and is too maladjusted to the rest of him to fulfil his art. They are small and cannot live outside Wensleydale. A pity, because I believe George, if he'd been given the chance, or allowed to take it, would have been as good for Wensleydale as Hardy for Wessex. As it is, he doesn't even count as literature, though I don't say as much to him, but encourage him even. George is one of those tragedies, especially modern, that often waylay potential artists. *All the Conspirators*[10] puts it admirably on paper. That novel applies exactly to George. Buried alive! It's an awful choice – Bury yourself or bury your mother – and there is rarely a way out – usually the exception brings a great artist – Augustus John pushing his mother where he wanted without burying her[…]

It's a fortnight since I held a brush to paper, with only a few scribbles crushed in now and again with pen or pencil. I am taking a quarter off tomorrow to try my hand at a lovely view of Witton Fell that I have been worshipping this week. I am back again at Ellington, and taking a walk to the very west end of the wood to look up the dale, there was the old fell, from an entirely new angle, looking very fresh & charming with only a stretch of fields & woods between us. So I'll take my things on the lorry to work tomorrow, & try it, though my ideas of treatment are rather ambitious. I am wanting to leave the brighter greens of my recent stuff and try to capture in a more mature (?) style the tonal & colour neutrality of *Cover Bridge*, which seems to be my vein. These fields of stubble & fading trees should help me[...]

Did Jim turn up at Felling. I suppose not. Isn't his taste in piano-playing dreadful! I wish my technique was up to his (in our respective arts I mean), because over the weekend we talked wonderful things which I just can't do for lack of experience & models. How does a fellow who clamours for nudes ever get them? I feel like marrying the first figure I see that is suitable and telling her to undress immediately whilst I draw her – poor girl! One can't marry men so easily & though I prefer their figures to women's, I suppose my chances will be few. Jimmy would pose, but then we aren't together & would soon separate if we were. George is willing, but looks a trifle emaciated to suit me[...]

East Witton, Wednesday [28 October 1942?]

[…] You mention somewhere that I appear to have been bored with you all, these last few visits. I wasn't bored of course. But I don't seem to take you in – I haven't time in the first place, because I usually go somewhere or see somebody and if I didn't I'd be in such a rage to get back to Wensleydale that approach would be even more difficult.

First, in spite of all, I do realize what a lovely place I'm in, and through everything in me there is a love for it and a wonder in me too, that it can mean so much. Even the people, the most sordid & mundane appeal to me far more than any townsfolk, and that is a source of regret to me. Tyneside gets further & further away from me and I seem quite incapable of the slightest feeling and understanding & pity when I come home[…]

You make me say one thing however. It affects your own puzzle – you've felt you never wanted to see me again. I don't want to appear to be chucking valuable things overboard with ease, but I think you would do well to chuck me overboard. And I don't want sympathy in the midst of this. I know by experience that I am a poor friend, a very poor one indeed, and nothing you say will make me think different. Apparently friendship is not a thing I need a great deal – nothing much beyond acquaintanceship. I don't know what I need – I should have thought love, but I send it packing when it comes. I have a hopeless job persuading myself I don't love a girl now[11], yet if she took the bait, to put it bluntly, I know what would happen. It would seem so lovely to be loved and love, but it is not for me. I could understand so much if I were like Jimmy or George[12], but I know I worship women really and men leave me cold – that is, certain women, because a whole class is too broad to worship & there are so many empty ones.

But amidst the "I's" my parents have disappeared. I am not much to be proud of as a son, and if I could only please them & be happy with them & they with me, it would be good. But we seem to live in such different worlds. At least I have a companion in this in Jimmy, who is distressed at his parents being so kind and tender. He just doesn't know what to do. Sons like us should be disowned I think, because I think, if I had a son like myself, I'd disown him completely – but that's me, and it is an example of my parents' tolerance & kindness that they accept me always the same[…]

East Witton, Friday [30 October 1942?]

[…] All news of leaving Wensleydale has faded I think and as I'm on a solid 2 years job in a splendid wood of big ash, elm and oak, I think any discontent is quite unforgivable – but such outer content cannot always allay what goes on inside, I find and if I'm the most awful person you know and you find me ungrateful, and harsh to parents and you, and so on, and an incorrigible swine altogether, well, I just can't help it – I'm just made like that, it seems, and as I said before, "there is no health in us", no sweetness in my nature. Sometimes I'm very happy, often very unhappy, and it is unfortunate that the former mood seems the most unreal, unfounded & elusive, and the unhappiness very real, bitterly tenacious & personal. So don't worry about me – I'll work out alright I hope. I'll try so hard to be good.

Len was becoming introverted, given to solitude – but that would remain a tendency all his life (while yet, in maturity, being also the most sociable of men). The following letter describes his state of mind, and also has one of the most substantial references to Wales. He was in love with Wensleydale, but the idea of Wales as a spiritual home lurked in the back of his mind too. Len believed that his ancestors were Welsh, and a few days later he mentioned his "desire to be a Welshman again".

East Witton, Tuesday [3 November 1942?]

[…] What you say of friendship is so true, but I don't know whether Hudson's concept[13] was quite complete. The subject is so elusive that I can't say what is the final quality. An almost ideal affinity of minds is something but other qualities (probably sex) can make people friends who are intellectually unlike. I'm not well qualified to talk about it – as I've said, I consider myself a poor friend, and I'm gradually drawing in my antennae like a snail and keeping myself to myself. I never open up towards anyone between weekends except perhaps Tom [Allen], and there it is comradeship more than friendship – beyond work we couldn't aspire to actual friendship. I think it's best to do so when one's warmth is so limited. Perhaps I'm going through a strange period but I think that's how I stand really and I've always had a yearning for loneliness or oneness, and an aversion for society.

If I had a cottage like George's I could be quite content to be alone with some work and books, though of course I'd welcome friends who came. George is quite unlike me there, and is lost now if I don't go at weekends. If I'm not going I have to warn so that he can get someone else till my return – if only because he abhors sleeping alone. That suits me, and his cottage is resolving into a home from home for me. I go every weekend now.

I do hope some day to be able to tear myself away from here and see what Wales is like. George Graham[14], Lawson's contemporary in our Group, invited me to see his work on Sunday (considered an honour!) and he has painted much in Wales. It made me very nostalgic though I've never been – isn't that queer. When I looked at those landscapes they seemed to be just what I'd want. Graham was very enthusiastic about Wales and hopes to have a cottage to which he and his satellites (not a few) can retire some times to paint. He invited me poor soul, and I hoped so hard for him – he is 63 I think, though looking much younger. Will his dream of a cottage in Wales ever come true? "After the war" as usual. It's a sad uncertain phrase, and I often find myself using it. But I'm trying to persuade myself that this is the life, that if I'm to do anything, it must be done now, not left till "after the war"[…]

On 5 November Len wrote about the difficulty of working in the winter evenings. "I had planned to do lino-cuts or something & have all the materials but as we all live in the same room, Mrs Dinsdale objects to the mess & uproar I create when I start getting out materials. Art needs so much paraphernalia I want a studio now. But I can't find one I'm afraid."

He continued to wax effusive about Muriel Metcalfe's artwork. He had fallen in love with a line drawing of hers, "a Madonna and Child (I think)", which Fred Lawson had given him with typical generosity. "I worshipped it so unstintedly that Lawson just could not bear to do anything but give it to me, as a gift for spiritual acceptance of such beauty, his wife's. Or so it seemed for money never entered our heads – we tacitly understood that it was above that if it passed between us, and altogether this single act bound me to Lawson for life it seems."

When he next wrote, Len had heard some vivid tales of his grandfather John Jones from his roommate Amos.

East Witton, Thursday [12 November 1942?]

I wish I could have another good spell at painting. Perhaps one good thing at Thirsk if I were moving would be more laxity about time off. There are still some units where there is little discipline over long weekends etc. At present I'm painting mediocre water-colours at weekends and doing absolutely nothing in between – not because of laziness, but because any kind of drawing is impossible in our digs since we all live together and I can't have a lamp in our bedroom[...]

I have received the copies of Poetry Folios – delicate hand-produced things as you see, reminding me of 18th century production. It is good I think, though the cover is dreadful. Alex Comfort's poem is a gem and Jimmy's too. John Bayliss with Wordsworth & Prior appeals to me. Vernon Watkins is one of the best of the young writers and being Welsh just overwhelms.

I've never talked much about my desire to be a Welshman again – I think my forbears were Welsh, & only beyond my Grandfather – and it's time we went back, because after reading De Quincey last year I think it must be wonderful – and Lawrence (TE) was there – and Myrrdin [sic] filled me full. David Cox loved it as an Englishman, but I want to be [a] Welshman. The Ministry of Labour would not let me go when I asked.

By the way Amos came in last night full of legends about my Grandfather Jones – somebody at Harmby [in Wensleydale] knew him and was telling Amos about his very powerful epics – preaching with shirt sleeves rolled up, sweating and weeping, moved himself & moving the people – beating his sons, tyrannising his daughters, a huge big-voiced man, holding a prayer meeting in the pits when a man swore, & commanding fear & respect not contempt. He rescued one son from some telegraph wires – he had touched & couldn't leave go so old Jones got two rubber balls, cut them up to fit his hands & with this home made insulation rescued his son & no doubt beat him righteously. Then he descended an old pit shaft to effect some pit rescue or other – but all the time a real live big fellow – what a wonderful grandfather to have and his epic sung in Yorkshire & coming back to a grandson, who has probably inherited nothing but his big voice[…]

East Witton, Wednesday [18 November 1942?]

[…] Mr Durrant, our vicar, is a regular old boy and simply raves about my pictures. My last effort was of his church, and he paid me on Saturday. Yesterday however, he approached Mrs Dinsdale very anxiously to see if I could do anything about the weathervane on the church – I'd omitted it in my picture – would I go down to the vicarage, especially as Mrs Durrant wanted to talk to me. I went, and placed his blessed weathervane with a thin brush stroke or two (unsightly thing) and then Mrs D played the piano, very sweetly – Chopin and hosts of things I liked, & we talked art (I very professional of course – painter to patron style you know). But Mr D was itching to ask his painter a very important question and after a decent stretch of art, pipped in "Do you play chess" – Ah hah very difficult – yes and no – no – no well yes I did really, don't be modest, it's only conceit – but he'll be terribly good – oh it'll please him – quite panicky & leaving it to my tongue finally, it said "Yes". He brilliant, I Lovellish – walloped of course – Would I like another game – panicky again Ye-No! – it was rather a strain for me – oh yes, I understand. Shall we have coffee Mrs Durrant – Er – of course – er do you take sugar – no – milk – no – what relief – and I thought it tasted rather good myself despite the fact that I like both – Back to art – and me – oh my – skies so beautiful (hasn't seen Lawson) and atmosphere superb – had I showed, sorry shown, at the RA yet – oh I should, oh yes you're quite good enough you know, some more coffee, no thank you, as a matter of fact I think it better to test the provincial galleries like Newcastle, where I had a picture of Cover Bridge – oh how beautiful, we simply must see it, – what! 9 o'clock already, oh I must be going, along a passage into colder air, guided by his torch, out into the damp cold air, and black as – "Goodnight" – pitch, lost in the garden, 'Todt und das Mädchen'[15], oh fearful, groping into hedges, damply, stiffly, nervously, the gate, oh where tell me where, and got home damp to the wrists but feeling very proud of my enthusiastic patron[…]

Lawson & George seem amazed at my progress & selling pictures occasionally already, but I'm very dissatisfied myself with what I've done, and don't think they are real water-colours, except for one tipsy effort or two – that view of the railway bridge in Wensleydale is decent but that's all. I'd love a real smasher of my own to look at, but I'll have to wait now. I itch to paint but am constantly frustrated, like most people these days[…]

And all over the wood is air, frost laden, pregnant with noise of spiders and ladybirds, and the tissue of trees beneath axes, resisting, strong, and I leaning, wondering, on a pitch-fork, watching lecherous starlings alight on still tree-tops, breaking the frost-coat with their greedy claws and gorging elderberries, flying drunk away in one stupid, nervous cluster as I move my stiffening torso. Autumn is so beautiful. Every morning, rosy cloud break, horizontal beauty quivering into light and warmth, trees streaked and silhouetted in rose and gold, with sheep chewing silently beneath them, the last attended ewe quivering ecstatically beside the bluff male ram, while all the time the biting breeze in the wagon brings tears to my eyes and a dribble on my nose as we go to work. Then from yesterday's charcoal, a little rosy fire, bigger and bigger, until we are burning the rubbish and making way for tractors and steam winch, and the wood rings with spasmodic laughter from unseen girls and all is a wonderful Champs Elysées. All the time thunder and fighting, far away[…]

East Witton, Wednesday [25 November 1942?]

[…] I've also had a letter from Jimmy, including his long poem 'The

A marginal drawing of berries

Sound of Fountains: an Adolescence'. It is a very lovely poem but is a trifle wild and unbridled in form – it seems to me to lack the ultimate unity that one expects after reading a long poem. This may have been my faulty reading, particularly as the emotive sequence of Jim's imagery needs a fine dream-world appreciation, a sort of extra finely tuned ear, of which I am often incapable. It is impossible to read him after dinner, or between times, as one can often do with others' lyrics. He needs a careful, attentive, full and appreciative reading and his music is exquisite when it has been read often enough to be known by heart[…]

Enclosed a proof from a book-plate linocut I tried. No good, but here's the print, very dirty, and printed beneath *Polish Painting* and *Seven Pillars of Wisdom*[16] as printing press. In case the subject is too vague & blurred, it is meant to be Calvary.

East Witton, Monday [30 November 1942?]

[…] I seem quite dried up for letter-writing, but I must remember to thank you for having George [Jackson] & I – he was very keen to meet you, so keen that he went as far as disappointing the Donaldsons[17] to come and see you – so you see what beauteous impressions of you I give to my friends – Jimmy [Kirkup] was just as keen to meet you[...] But as you seem to think I did not do justice to George, I must say he annoys me at times, particularly in his narrow mindedness, little things which betray a terribly small mind sometimes[…] George is often smugly complacent & self-satisfied about his own work, and I feel that if it could be knocked out of him he would go forward again & do something fine – for he really has a most sensitive spirit. And once started I could go on, but I mustn't or you'll [think?] I'm very catty – but Fred is my man really, because sex will always come between George and I. I love Fred because of his wisdom and happiness – he gives little away in his friendship, somehow, but he compels me inevitably, and his exceeding singleness of mind will always be a shining example to me. He is the most single-minded person I know[…] But singleness of mind is not usually a natural attribute & even in a man like Fred is a matter of interest, discipline & finally habit. So interest & discipline are essential & if they are enough the habit will come. Fred won't even read books or write letters if it's keeping him from work, or rather using his mental faculties unduly – for he is not a prodigious worker, but when he does relax it is mundane things like domestic jobs and a quiet gossip over a pipe that occupy him, as the natural opposite & counterpart to his art[...]

East Witton, Thursday [3 December 1942?]

[...] I am busy working out a three colour linocut now I've finished *Tess*[18]. It will probably come to nought, but I'm going to take great care with the cutting & see what arrives. I'm held up for a ruler of all things but will get one tomorrow.

At work I have a new interesting job as driver's mate in the articulated wagon. We load all the big hardwood timber with a jib and take it to a sawmill at Masham. It is quite heavy work and seems to have brought unused muscles into play – but I like it, and though we are on the worst lead, only two miles (making 4 loads possible) we may have longer leads from places like Thirsk etc... when I may drive the wagon sometimes too. We are at present dealing with big pieces of timber ranging from 30 to 80 cubic ft (there are about 25 cubic feet in 1 ton) so they are pretty heavy to deal with. The average is from 180 to 220 cubic feet.

I found *Tess* almost unbearable in its tragedy. Hardy had built her up so personally for me that she dogged my footsteps & almost talked to me – she was so pure, so fresh and lovely that you couldn't help but love her. And on Exmoor I knew a girl who was very much like Tess and her vision was therefore more real. This girl (whom Bill [Hamilton] ensnared I'm afraid) was pure like Tess and trusting, and earth bound and one of nature's creatures, almost unknown to civilisation & not knowing it herself. Tragic in her parental shackles, for her parents were gormless like Tess's. I remember most vividly how I left Ivy and Exmoor. She stood in the porch with her arms on the stair rail that ran up from the hall. I was shaking hands all round and came to Ivy and kissed her very tenderly, before everybody, because as I now see it, she was like Tess and I loved her in a lovely dispassionate manner.

Her story was quite tragic (I can recount little details which illustrate the essential hardness, selfishness & cruelty of men, among whom I number). She fell in love with Bill, and Bill, having absolutely nothing to do, played with her and she was so happy with him when I left. At night, after dinner, Bill and I went to her to help wash dishes & then I left and they did goodness knows what. She did all sorts for us, and when Bill was leaving, they had become so intimate (without sex of course) that she built up all her hopes in Bill & longed & looked for their wedding day, for it had got as far as that with Ivy. But Bill got home & was alright until she reminded him of his off-hand invitation to her (and her mother) to go to Durham for a holiday any time they wanted. And Ivy came sure enough –and went away heart-broken. Such things make you see Hardy in his proper light because they are always happening. But I'll say no more. I believe in Hardy – he experienced life and was not melancholy, nor morbid, but truthful and lovable[…]

East Witton, Wednesday [9 December 1942?]

[…] I am very interested in this linocut business. The technique is so absorbing and it is so satisfying, so intensely satisfying to be doing something with my hands. The present one was a rather ambitious idea, but like the rest I think it is a failure – mainly in design. But the only way to get a good one is to gain the necessary experience through bad ones, I suppose. So as soon as a new design evolves I'll try again. Anyway, I've finished the three blocks and will print some on Sunday, just to see. It helps to analyse faults, when they're printed. Lawson is so kind to me – he just gives me his studio keys and lets me potter about on my own[…]

East Witton, Friday [11 December 1942?]

[…] My new linocut is not so good after all – I'm sorry – but it's not an easy medium. I've almost run out of lino now so will have to vamp the library staff again, though I rather think there is some at home[...]

I'm at a loose end, all ways somehow – is it the constant stream of lovely girls that seem to cross my trail lately, so persistently hammering at my poor bewildered sexual centre? Anyway I'll stop.

*Sometimes Len could show searing honesty, as in this confession of the withering
of his pacifist beliefs. While it was true that the credo had ceased to be central to
his life, he never entirely disowned it. Rather his ideas and priorities were evolving.*

East Witton, Tuesday [15 December 1942?]

[…] Being a CO is a barometrical affair. The slightest clash sends you
right up, & then you come down & are as much the other way. You'll
be cross to think of all my ideals gone with the wind, but they have.
A man like Jim [Kirkup] has more power to sustain me than Amos,
say, the most fluent, lucid and clear pacifist I know or Arthur
Raistrick[19] for instance. The latter I could worship once, now he would
make me curl my lips. But it is true of me that if a greater force like
artistic emotion (arriving perhaps with technical facility quite
suddenly) or physical love (however elusive, still possible, oh horribly
possible) if such a force came along & commanded me to be a soldier,
I'd go in all humility. And in my weakness and pride, I'd have to forego
all you good people & even my parents – what a terrifying thought.
But it's just possible.

A young artist asked me on Sunday if I painted – I said "No not
yet, but I live to paint". It seemed so true then, and as far as pacifism
goes I do live to paint, whether I fight or forgive. In other words
pacifism as a force has gone – once it could rule my life, now it hardly
matters. But please don't think I'm feeling superior or anything,
because I know it was hardly the truth "I live to paint". That was
presumptuous, the fool walking in. And more and so on.

My linocut was a failure as I thought, though Fred was very pleased
about it as a first attempt. I only feel now, what a waste of good lino,
and I hate the sight of it. But the technique satisfies me, so I'll go on.

East Witton, Friday [18 December 1942?]

[…] I find myself unable to sit still now when I have leisure – once I
revelled in it, sat down and read and read and read without cease,
now I have to be doing something, and between reading today, I've
fiddled with linocuts – I have two tiny efforts this week, which show
improvement – black & white. They are all immature and I don't like
showing them to people, except a critic like Fred who can help. I sent

you one murderous attempt & you showed it to Eric Canning you bad woman. He is a perfectionist.

There is one thing – I can get them printed almost perfectly on Fred's press, so anything you get now will be decently printed. Unfortunately, my lino being from a small roll, my blocks have a tendency to warp, making it difficult to print the middle without overprinting the edges. But anything good I may do can be pressed for a week to bring it flat.

And between times I'm trying to become familiar with human anatomy – the digitations of the Serratus Magnus, the Pectoralis major, the Sartorius, the Gluteus Maximus or bum, and fancy names for common objects. It's surprising what queer things muscles do though, & Lawson insists on theoretical knowledge so that I haven't to think it out in practice. Drawing from the nude is full of subtle hints & suggestions which can't be appreciated & recorded unless you know what they hint & suggest. But it's not learning the names so much as knowing they are there – to many people the digitations are ribs sticking out, but they are not, they are muscles and would appear wrong if you suggested the hard structure of bone. Elementary[20] […]

I'd like to try my hand at all sorts of mediums that need slow patient labour, because these evenings are made for it while I wait for summer again. Etchings, woodcuts and wood engravings, mezzotints & aquatints & such like. They seem, as mediums, to have been a lovely sidewalk for artists in the past when they couldn't get to greater work – I imagine Rembrandt on a wet day, kept indoors without a model perhaps, working away on *The Blind Tobit, The Supper at Emmaus* and so on. Whistler the same, Dürer, Cotman, Van Eyck. It is fascinating & satisfying to work somewhat laboriously on the varying surfaces – of course sometimes it is easier than pencil on paper, like etching, where you merely scratch a wax surface, & there the finest sensibility of line & treatment is needed[…]

I had a loving letter & a poem from Jim [Kirkup] last week[…] "Leo darling, I'm so bored. Can't you do something about it? When tomorrow comes I shall have been here a week, one whole week among nice dull people. Don't you feel my screams… Stephen (a name which always fills me with the most excruciating urges) – 21, dark, good-looking, reads Cocteau & Joyce and seems to have a soul singularly unstained by sin, and I'm not going to the trouble of making myself 'pleasant' to someone so elementary & toneless… I called in on Staples when I was in London and chivvied them until they promised to bring out 'Sound of Fountains' & twelve short poems in January. They want (having seen me) a portrait of me for the frontispiece. Can you have a crack at me from memory? If not, I shall go and ask Augustus John to do me…"

I give way to John, but so reluctantly, even if it were never published. He has a heavenly face, dear boy. And now, goodnight.

East Witton, Tuesday [22 December 1942?]

[…] George's carbuncle has made him horrible – Fred and I were heartily fed up of him at the weekend. There was a furious scene on Sunday when Fred, making a humorous comment on "the book", which George had handed him after dinner, put George in a rage. He snatched the book from Fred, & Fred & I hoped it was going on the fire, but unfortunately & purposely it fell on the hearth with a resounding crash & George went raging upstairs. Poor Fred was upset, & George too I suppose, but I'm afraid Fred I accepted & George I couldn't bear, so I'm not going up this weekend.

Honestly – that bloody book is too exasperating for words – George has no imagination for writing, yet treats a mere guide book as his "Odyssey" and as a work of art. He has quite lost his sense of values. In fact, he's just about finished as an artist if he continues as he is, and the Group will be petering out with Muriel, George & Henri Lister[21] painting nothing. But summer may be different and "the book" will then have been forgotten for the most. I thought it was to be a good guide book or something, something anyone could have written in a month. He's been on 3 months and the result is too feeble for words. It will never be published as it is – it contains his worst writing, his worst style & mannerisms, the most dribbling, silliest sentiments, that are too utterly conventional & out of place. George needs his best writing, like *Madeleine Clement* to pull through at all. This book has made him silly.

But then I'm gloomy & morose at present to an even worse extent than before, & we are up to the thighs in the worst mud I've ever known. It makes you wretched. And accidents seem so frequent and possible that I'm nervous as hell, and nearly lost a finger yesterday. A 2 ton log lost its grip & pulled my fingers rapidly into the pulley wheels of the jib. And the driver of the other wagon slipped from the top of his load and had to be taken to hospital – concussion I should think. A boy of 16 also fell from a wagon, & was unconscious for an hour but is only suffering from a cut face & arm. Joe Hird got his fingers crushed in a chain, a boy was burnt badly filling petrol, and so on. It's the mud a sea of mud 200 yards by 50 & the logs are rolled & dragged through that. When they get to the wagon they aren't fit to handle. Amid all this, I still feel so sheltered beside the poor bored, wretched, fighting soldiers, that I'm ashamed often[…]

P.S. […] Enclosed a little book-plate I tried last weekend. It was meant for you, but is a little deficient in design. How do you like it. Show it through a mirror & it is our living room.

East Witton, Wednesday [23 December 1942?]

[…] George has had a letter from Jim [Kirkup], to whom he'd written an offhand letter. Jim may spend Xmas with George, before trying to return to forestry in the district. My friends seem to be intermingling strangely and I feel like God bringing people from all over into otherwise improbable contact.

I am so weary with myself that I shan't go to Bolton this weekend, but on the other hand I am looking forward to having tea on Sunday with Muriel at her mother's, all being well. She seems to have reached out to me, finding sympathy and understanding I hope, and that has not happened for years. Fred is pleased, and if only we could go further, heaven knows, she might revive, might even draw & paint again, but I doubt it. Fred has begun to exhibit her work again (she still has several drawings left) and there was a good notice in the Saturday paper about her[…]

East Witton:
An Unforeseen Crisis

At the beginning of 1943 Len was reasonably content with life. In the spring, however, he would find himself embroiled in emotional and mental turmoil once more. His solution this time was drastic.

East Witton, Friday [1 January 1943]

[…] Work has been a bit of a trial too here, but a few days of cold dry wind & snow were such relief from seething mud that I enjoyed those days. Today it has thawed and it is mud again, but I was considering today that taken all round this is the best job I had in forestry and I'm grateful for that. And I seem to be doing it well enough to please, because the other day, the foreman offered me his bacca pouch to fill my pipe, an unknown gesture. That was an honour. Not that I'm living only to load timber in order to please, but while I'm on I like to keep going & do it as well as I can[…]

I find these [land] girls amazingly interested in all sorts of things. They borrow my books and *Madame Bovary* has been read and appreciated by all of them (there are 6 or 7) and two have ventured into the art class. My linocut of Ulshaw Bridge also hangs in the cabin and they are too too keen for words – I answer questions all day and the main thing is that they like things spontaneously without reference to facts & dates etc… They often see things in a new light, noticing details I'd perhaps missed. They vary from hard-boiled to quite innocently feminine[…]

East Witton, Wednesday [6 January 1943]

[...] I had a pleasant weekend at CB. George was very amiable and teased a religious fellow he had up there. The chap took it all in good part & the weekend was good. But I made sure I had a few hours with Fred.

G wasn't too grand mind you, but on getting up at dinner time, Sunday, he was in good form, and seemed to revel in his "old age" – for he seems to think of himself as being very very old.

We have had snow here today, and we had to turn back with the articulated wagon, which began to run back on Jervaulx bank until I ran with ashes to help it on. We took out a Ford Thames wagon and went to Leyburn for 2.5 tons of coal, so we were kept warm, with work, not with burning coals[…]

Len was enjoying the cold winter, but an incident at George Jackson's house got him thinking again about homosexuality. His comments reveal the prevailing attitude at this time, that this was "a grave underlying problem" for society, a "sure sign of decadence and weakness". Len himself had become sympathetic to gay men, understanding their position as "tragic", but wanted nothing to do with homosexuality.

East Witton, Saturday [9 January 1943]

Pardon my ditheriness. I have just been out doing a rapid pencil sketch of Cover Bridge from a different angle – for a proposed linocut. It is the first time I've got down to things since before Xmas, and as Wain[1] will want my explanation for the [art] class shortly, I must try a new cut & incidentally spend a lot of time & thought over it & try to do a real smasher. I had noticed the Cover winding its way between lumps of ice and snow and it looked so beautiful, as though direct from Abelard's world, that I felt, if I couldn't paint a water-colour I could at least try a linocut to show the Bridge in snow[…]

It is strange, but all these intensely cold days I have worked without gloves (simply because the mud finished a new pair I had) and yet, except for this morning I have borne it easily. This morning however those props, covered with frozen snow, were terrible and after handling a score or so, I felt a fainting feeling pass over me and only then realized what I was doing. The pain of the cold was too much for a weak fellow like me, but I soon got over it and was soon warm.

So life is good when times are bad and so often bad when times are good[...]

I am spending this weekend at home, instead of going to Bolton. I still love to go up there of course, but am spending this weekend away. Last weekend, George had Bob up for the weekend & also a young religious CO who lives with him, Douglas by name. Douglas & I happened to sleep together at Betsy's, and apparently my charm & beauty prevailed, because a third time I was groped stealthily and had a bad time[2]. I told George, who knew D was a queer lad, but who had found G unattractive I suppose. This was so shocking to me, especially since the fellow professes the strongest Christian principles. I can forgive all, but the frequency of this business is becoming a terror to me, and this lad with his awful problem of an inverted sex complex contesting Xtian beliefs was too much. I felt exceedingly sorry for the poor fellow, for he began to sob, and about 5 am he had a terrible shivering fit which must have lasted half an hour.

Apparently he told George, who was all ears, and the latter wrote to me a letter beginning "You have a lover". I could bear it no longer, and wrote rather a sober note to George saying how this business affected me, how I could not bear to be touched, in fact I was quite mopy and complained of this male persistence while all I wanted was female love and friendship. Which was quite unnecessary, but it had the desired effect, & the flippant note was followed by a sober & sympathetic letter, promising to close the subject & to keep me from Douglas, or vice versa at all costs.

Is my experience strange? I think it is, and feel such a veteran in such matters now. But from all I realize there is a grave underlying problem, which Lawson suggests is racial, running through society as a whole at present. It is common knowledge that one of Hitler's main problems after Jews was homosexuality, which was rampant. You remember the hints in Isherwood's work – *Mr Norris*[3] in particular, and the story (I don't know how true) that Roehm (the famous SS leader Hitler had killed) was found in bed with a youth when arrested[4]. Then Von Kramm the famous German tennis player was imprisoned for improper conduct. Hitler's aim to restore the vitality & virility of the German race was perhaps engendered in part by experiences like mine. He may have been aware how such a hidden secret thing was the sure sign of decadence and weakness, and his desire would be to restore the old vigour and wholesomeness. His approach was racially, in the mass, his programme general fitness and discipline etc… but as a personal problem it is tragic, especially since outward help is impossible, there being ostracism, stigma, almost mental leprosy & perhaps imprisonment to face. That is why a person like myself who has learned to know & tolerate such things has to be careful of being overloaded with secrets and confessions, and the general overwhelming, gushing conversation of these poor repressed individuals. Sometimes I am utterly weary of George at weekends, just through that. All talk of art & life in general, such a valuable & entertaining mine, must be foregone & the unwholesome chatter allowed full stretch.

But these letters have put things right I'm sure, and I can go back to George with confidence, good friends, for despite faults, he has wisdom and experience, and extraordinary sympathy, so that he can be a most lovable friend. He has done so much for me too[…]

[Between letters – print of what must be linocut by L, with paint colours listed on back]

'Gate', an early linocut by Len

East Witton, Wednesday [13 January 1943]

[…] The weather? – well, a desirable thaw, I suppose, leaving the most undesirable mud, so that I'm left designing roughly some sort of mud proof costume for outdoor workers. My mind can only conceive of something approximating to a diving suit, quite impossible to work in – or otherwise working in the nude with a warm hose playing on to you all the while. Alternatively, an anti-mud solution for soil. But then, we can wash & disrobe at 5 o'clock, dine vigorously & settle down clean & comfortable till 9 am, a decent stretch of immunity from mud. So don't feel terribly sorry for me – I have short periods of mud-caked wretchedness, despondent, weary, but they are short & I'm quite cheerful outwardly, where the mud belies it, while inwardly I might be teeming with problematic thoughts, happy or unhappy as the case may be, but thoughts that would come were there mud or none. Happiness is relative, elusive, perhaps unrecognisable, and certainly not to be found in consciousness, so I can't say whether the mud makes me happy or unhappy – I feel it wouldn't matter either way, being only mud, and I can't take sympathy if I don't deserve it, nor will I be envied[…]

Mona responded to Len's throwaway remarks about getting cold hands handling timber in the snow by buying him strong industrial gloves. She also anticipated his painting needs, sending some David Cox paper. He wrote on 19 January: "Really, Madame, you overwhelm me! What am I to do! Gloves, books, paper, picture, all in one blinding rush. I feel so indebted to you, and I'm blowed if I know how to repay you." While thanking her he offered to pay her back. He reported that George Jackson had done another portrait of him in Conté crayon, "100% more vivid & sensitive than the other". Len added: "How I long to paint outdoors again", looking forward to "improving perhaps & mastering technique a little more". He wrote again two days later:

East Witton, Thursday [21 Jan 1943]

I have finished the blocks of *Cover Bridge in Snow*, but haven't the foggiest idea whether they will make a decent print or not. I'll see on Sunday. Anyway, I can turn to other things & the result is I've almost finished the Pre-Raphaelites book[…]

And now, thank you for attending to all my various wants. The colours are valuable, & the David Cox paper too as I said before. And the little frames are no doubt just what I want. When you get them please take one for yourself, and I'll send the first thing good enough to go in. If not one of Fred's might fit in in the meantime[…]

East Witton, Friday [22 January 1943]

[…] You must wonder what I'm doing with all these art materials & books etc… Like Jimmy Kirkup, I must plead that you consider all my work up to now as mere exercises. But all the time lately, I have felt a terrible urge to paint, and you've no idea how I'm longing for more warmth & light – I want so to paint the things I'm seeing all day, odd bits of the landscape all round – even individual trees are singled out, bits of road – I say to myself "I must come to grips with trees this year, and study them anatomically so that knowing them, I shall feel them too, and not paint meaningless washes"[…]

Something unpleasant came up for me today. I'm to be taken from my job I like so much and put back on my old job, felling. Apparently the country is in a desperate plight for pit props & we are going all out for a while producing prop wood. They are short of fellers and though I had been prepared for this, it was rather unpleasant. After what has happened to George and Tom my two former mates, I had set my mind against felling. And despite mud, I did like my present job very much and was quite happy, because the work was steady and interesting[…]

East Witton, Tuesday [26 January 1943]

[…] Here are the linocuts – I hope you like them – several were special reprints for you, those of Muriel's were[…]

Perhaps I could say how much we need David Cox now though, because all the alternatives [water-colour paper] being manufactured are quite hopeless.

Arthur Good, Len's old library colleague and friend, was becoming restless at home; he was considering renouncing his conscientious objector status and joining up (a step he did take). This led Len too to muse on his own ambivalence about his

position, and the psychological effect the war was having on society with so many
people having their lives changed utterly.

East Witton, Thursday [28 January 1943]

Dear Mona,

[…] The thing that came most out of your letter strange to say was the comparison of Arthur [Good] & myself. I am so perpetually reminded of others who have joined up & suffered accordingly – like Tom Emerson, George White, George's friend Tom Peacock and others that I am always reconsidering my position, lately particularly. I wrote to George recently a letter which as far as was possible told what my thoughts were, tho' I'm almost inarticulate on pacifism at present.

But I've never been seriously confronted with the position of the bloke who has been left behind altogether. I must say first however that with all the youth & even middle aged going here & there & everywhere the poor bloke who is left behind must feel like Cinderella. When the world of so many people is changing, I suppose it is natural that Arthur should feel restless, whatever the change might be. I say it is quite natural – natural too that once the change has been effected he should wish to be back, like most soldiers etc… that's how it is, we can't know one feeling without the other. Quite mad I suppose.

But if I'm always finding myself compared with the poor soldier, how much more Arthur, still in his peacetime niche. It's not what people say, or even think – it's just the facts that will strike – to read poor Tom Emerson's letter, to hear a quite irrelevant detail about some far off relative, to read the news even, will all sink in, and no doubt hurt. To be American "it makes you think!"[…]

I also realize that you two [Mona and Arthur] are left behind – only you are so different, and I can't think of you as "left behind", but rather as "business as usual". Not that the war leaves you unaffected, but the almost trivial, restless romanticism that makes people leave everything must mean little to you. And I admire you for that – without flattering you. People like George Carr[5], Gladys and yourself who seem to transcend the ordinary fluid longings of restless people are the leaven to the lump[…]

Work is not too good. I miss my old friends at Ellington, and the trees are so stunted & small on Bardon Moor[6] that they barely pay us, so we have to work like the devil all day. Why they ever bought the wood beats me. The people are strange, but on the whole I like them, all except the measurers, who are upstarts.

I work next to two other fellers called Fletcher – father & son – father knows my father well, coming from Washington – he thinks I've got my voice straight from my grandfather. Both are among the nicest men I've known, friendly and helpful. I'll be alright soon, only my wind, hands & heart were in poor fettle for starting so vigorously on felling. I've been quite exhausted at nights but feel more cheerful tonight. Tell Arthur he's best where he is though. Aren't young men foolish!

East Witton, Tuesday [2 February 1943]

[…] I'm getting on fine with the felling by the way, and find that breaking in in winter is far easier than in summer when sweat brings blisters galore. This time I have no blisters, and I feel quite normal already, though after mealtimes I still feel queer and fainty. My main trouble now is a bad cough, which usually awakes me at 3 am and keeps me hacking and sweating for ages it seems. It seems so utterly exhausting and long, coughing in the night, though I imagine it isn't for long really.

Ellington Firth has been finally disintegrated, and many good pals have separated. Two proppers and a measurer went with me to Bardon – the measurer was Josie, a lieutenant's wife, & not really my friend like Kate, Joan and Jeneke. Poor girls, they have been quite dispersed – Kate to Boltby near Thirsk, Joan to Sutton (?Penn), Josie to Bardon, and poor Jeneke's case is a real tragedy, rather like Camille. She was to return to us about now, after six months' rest. She was married at the beginning to my only enemy, Serg.-Major Bull, but all the time the dear girl was racked with coughing. Lately she has had an operation for rupture and the coughing has so wrecked her body that she is now too weak to raise her hand[…]

Which reminds me – two good old pals were at Bardon when I got there – George [Peacock] (hale and hearty) and Tom [Allen], who is looking very thin and weak, and has a bleeding lung. He is not the same lad that I first knew, though we still rag each other severely, calling each other Pussyfoot and Bones. He is a great chap, Tom, and the best mate I ever had. And George was good to me too, showing me many tips in felling that I am now able to pass on like a veteran. Neither George nor Tom will fell again, & they are now pottering about laying a railway. We enjoy their chatter about the opening day & Stalin coming over to open it etc...

George wasn't so nice this weekend again, but I think he has lost sleep fire-watching. Despite a rather despairing letter to him about my pacifism last week, he had to answer, concerning Germany, "What I saw and experienced there is indelibly impressed on my mind to their eternal, as far as I am concerned, detriment. When such a time arrives as they cease to worship FORCE, I will bend all my energies to forgive them." Then he asked casually on Sunday how many Germans I had known, I had [to] confess but few, if any, but he had known thousands, seen them there, so to speak, which went to prove... all tacitly expressed, the latter. Then after he went to Peacock's for bread and returned gloating, yes gloating, about the Berlin bombing. Why should he do it? It seemed so deliberately cruel and yet I suppose it was a passing mood, for he's usually very sympathetic, and it [has] become a tacit agreement that if I tolerate his complex, he'll tolerate my pacifism. But tolerance consists of listening all weekend to his sexual life etc... & I daren't mention pacifism. Fred & I give him up sometimes[...]

East Witton, Friday[-Sunday] [5-7 February 1943]

The David Cox paper arrived yesterday, thank you. It is a grand standby, and as Lawson says, whatever paper or board you use, you always return to David Cox. It is certainly the water-colour paper with the most qualities. I painted a rather rough sketch last Sunday of Bolton Village, on Whatman paper, and though it has a lovely texture, it did not take the paint like David Cox. So the picture is overloaded in some parts, but you can have [it] till I paint a better picture of Bolton. It is this year's first, painted from Betsy's window.

I shall let Lawson have some of the Cox paper for conscience sake, since he is short.

Jim [Kirkup] seems to get his friends mixed up, because as you will now know, I knew about the poem in *The Listener*. Perhaps the enthusiasm appears quite unnecessary, but actually of course it is one of the very best publications that a poet can appear in. It is not exclusively for the poetry-reading public, in fact, [it] is as wide in scope and demand as any journal could be. So it is a good sign, and is the culminating point of a long interest taken by the editor in Jim's work. He was asking for Jim's work when I was at Jervaulx, and the editor seems to have the pick of the land, with Spender, MacNeice, Auden, Treece, Scarfe and such first-rate poets[…]

It is very nice of you to admire my fells picture. I think it is one of my best, possessing atmosphere to some extent, and is about my best sky[…]

Saturday night

I've tried a water-colour – always terribly unsatisfactory indoors and it makes you feel so conscience–stricken to have used up such a lovely piece of paper. So I shan't do it again. Then I studied some marvellous reproductions of the Farnley Hall collection of water-colours by Turner. They are in colour and are really exquisite. Every one is a masterpiece in technique, and strange to say, almost every one seems to be inspired, possessing its own peculiar mood and atmosphere[...]

The Listener arrived to day from you – this week's though, not next week's, you eager woman. I found it very interesting though, for it's a good magazine. Perhaps like *Punch* it is "Middle Class", & therefore deplorable, so Arthur will be cross with me. But tell me where, in a typical workers' magazine like *Highway*, I am to find reading for apparently unworkmanlike tastes like my own. In vain, I search in *Highway*, among articles on Beveridge Plans, social systems, educational systems, army educational systems, economic systems, anti-semitism, for a little flutter of sparkling, living, iridescent, inspiring, breath-giving poetry. But no, it's not only absent, it is not wanted. The workers, amid a general prosperity still grieve and plan and discourse and chatter, because their leaders do so. All sense and no sensibility. So I have to go to "middle class" & "upper class" journals if I'm to read journals at all. Because you see, while I'm confused and benumbed as to what one can do about the rest, just as other young men are, Spender,

Lehmann, Auden, Isherwood, I must gain spiritual sustenance from above, stealing perhaps what is given unwillingly. (?Men) nowadays have no voices like Carlyle and Ruskin, because with the gradual dissemination of culture, each drowns the other and anyway there has been a gradual and general dissemination so why worry if the voices are small. Conclusion – culture spreads or contracts of its own accord – and perhaps mere indigestion at an overdose in the 20s & 30s helped on the war. But I don't really think so. No, I'm definitely an exception, and if I'm a pacifist, it's for that very exception more than anything else, and if I wanted everybody to be a pacifist it would be to share & make me the rule. Then perhaps I'd be a Hercules and fight snakes for spite. So often it impinges upon me that I am the exception, when I feel terribly lonely, with no one to talk to about the things I love. Culture is quite tabooed at George's strange to say, for to talk so is to lose grips with humanity – but that is wrong I think. So the residue of my repressed thoughts goes into your letters, but it is necessarily only a residue, since conversation follows the will far more easily, the mood and the atmosphere. How I longed for Jim, and stepped on hot bricks![...]

[Signed "Yours, Hookie"]

James Kirkup now came back to the fore of Len's life. At the same time, Len was finding George Jackson more and more difficult to deal with.

Castle Bolton, Sunday [14 February 1943]

Would you believe it – Jim [Kirkup] is really here – and is more charming than ever – I simply adore the dear boy, though we haven't talked much with each other since George was here too, of course.

I thought they would find each other too awful for words after an hour or two, and when George just went out to Redmire last night (a thing he never does), I was sure he was just getting out to be rid of Jim for a while. They slept together though Jim was rather terrified of George last night and would have given everything to have slept away from him. But apparently each slept undisturbed, for which I was thankful, for a pleasant tranquillity reigns now, and George is just drawing the first lines of a head of Jim[7].

Jim is proposing to stay a week, though how I don't know. Food worries him very little thank goodness, and only coals are the problem. He is longing for the week alone, for he seems terribly eager to write, is full somehow. His latest poetry is quite enchanting – his imagery is perfect now and the slow musical rhythm is ever better. But most of all, his vision of life seems to have enlarged and matured, and his poetry is full of life. George was out a while this morning and Jim recited some of the latest poems to me. It made me very sad, I wished to be alone with him for most of these days, for we seemed so utterly in sympathy with each other, our friendship had transcended the terrors of sex and flowered unseen. At least that was how I felt, and perhaps Jim felt it in part too, though his range of friends is larger and his recent contact with a beautiful personality called Angela[8], and with l'Anson Fausset[9] & his son Shelley has meant much to him and when I mentioned the broader vision of life, he suggested that they had much to do with it[…]

East Witton, Thursday [25 February 1943]

[…] I am going to Castle Bolton at the weekend, though goodness knows whether I'll be really welcome. I found too [sic] very stinging & hurtful letters from George. He implies that I have been wantonly maligning England. "I do wish you would be a little kinder to your native land. The flagrant way you despise it, particularly when it is giving you such a good time compared with Tom & thousands of others… I can only put it down to you being sadly over-read in a particularly biased type of literature. Etc…" Lots in the same strain, all very distressing to me. I questioned very much whether we could be friends, but after refuting much of his over-statement, & being quite cheerful, a letter eased my mind somewhat. I am wrong, I think you had not better pepper George with pacifist comments to help me out. He is quite put out about you, I think, & begs me not to send the letters on to you. Perhaps he detests us both for our views, & he certainly suspects a mutual conspiracy against him. So I'm resolved to be silent from now on, though I assure you that George has always started this & I have only made provocative comments in self-defence, which, alone, seem all that George says they mean. I'm rather tired of his ways, but can't forget his better part, & the way he made me paint. I want to be his friend, but such bitterness is outside friendship, if it persists, but I don't think it will. He has enlarged little phrases to alarming proportions & made himself ill. I have very little patience with him sometimes, & yet I like him & want always to be his friend. But there is a devil in his face, which I saw the first time I ever met him, & which fascinated me, but it sometimes whips its tail in my face[…]

I enjoyed my weekend immensely, & it didn't make me tired. So thank you once again. I'll close as the table is wanted for supper.

East Witton, Saturday [27 February 1943]

[…] George's letters have made me very depressed in spite of myself, and I wouldn't go this weekend were it not that Jim has asked me to go up as he too is very depressed, & also wants to read to me the newly written 'Ten Pure Sonnets', a desire for "essential poetry". George wrote me a warning note that a Corporal Green & Bob would be coming, & if I cared to be in "such a sad lot" I was welcome. I realize, in fact, I was told by George himself that he was going to cut intellectuals altogether (that's me of course) & confine himself to ordinary people. "After Sunday night I decided I would cut all intellectuals & just surround myself with nice, & if possible attractive, ordinary folk".

So I don't know how I'll be received, & if I'm not wanted, I know what to do, & though it will make me sad, I shall feel somewhat relieved, because George is very one-sided & difficult sometimes. I know I am myself sometimes, but not so constantly & endlessly as George is I hope, & I feel he ought to have grown out of stupid ways at his age. He is quite unassailable & impregnable in his philosophy of life, won't be & can't be disturbed, so it's no use talking.

But I still think he wants me to go to Castle Bolton. For once I feel so innocent about hurting a friend – I'm sure it is George who has been cruel, and not I. But you don't know George's side, so I won't prejudice you. He doesn't like you to throw international affairs at him, & apparently you did, so remember – you are an intellectual & taboo if you continue.

It is strange what an effect this little upheaval can have. Before this, I was so tired with work, & yet always happy with the things around me, the form & colour of everything, hedges & grass, clouds & the sun's rays slanting through on to the distant hills, walls and houses and everything seemed to live as they hadn't done before. It was always so thrilling to look "Look, look up at the skies" as [Gerard Manley] Hopkins says[10]. And the same things, so continually thrilling, mean nothing for these last few days, & no effort can make them. I noticed it this morning, how I'd draw in my antennae like a disturbed snail. Of course, I don't want to exaggerate what had happened – this was all real but small I know. It just struck me forcibly. So this weekend, if I can see in the crowd, will tell. And if George is cool, I'll have Jim, who seems to want me to go very much[…]

East Witton, Monday [1 March 1943]

I have had such a pleasant weekend with Jim. There was a crowd but we managed fine – Bob, Jim & I slept at Betsy's, & a Corporal Green & George at the cottage. On Sunday morning I made 3 prints of Cover Bridge, which I now detest, but here's one for you and one for my parents or Miss Mudd, until something better rolls up. The prints are a bit out of place, but I'm just a learner, after all.

Sunday afternoon, George wanted to draw this corporal bloke, who had a nose exactly like my father's & therefore presented a problem, requiring peace, quietness and patient skill. So we were unceremoniously kicked out, & we went through the village, past the castle & being already tired, turned downhill & thrilled to the scene & walked, over the railway, on to a road, off the road, through a big farm, with quaint clean ducks, quacking mordantly. Then down, and oh, a river, even a joining of two rivers, and we hadn't known. "Surprised by joy, impatient as the wind"[11] we turned downstream, abandoned our weakness & turned upstream, requiring strength, through meadows, with bushes and barbed wire fences, and heard the roar, the core of distant water-music and saw below the white tilt of water stepping coolly down slow symmetrical steps. No man was ever there before, only a lonely dinosaur, come to drink, and left its spoor in the livid rock. We both swooned for the sheer beauty of it all, the silver lipping over the steps into the black pool beneath, with no nightmare of long sheer tippling waterfall. We were there so long, but heard some strange clock strike "quarter to", and not knowing what hour, we said "quarter to six", and turned away to hurry home another way, mostly along a railway, and arrived home before half past five. The drawing had been a success, full of strength & muscle, and we had all done well, to draw and go for a walk. Bob went "a 'coorten'".

Jim has '10 Pure Sonnets', a strange fantastic sequence, some of which are very beautiful, a few of which are involved and defeat me for the first time, which is a bad move. But these last are made up more than enough by the simpler sonnets.

> The sad foreigners have come to stay
> The summerhouses & the birdcage trees
> Are darkened with their visitors. The shy
> Pilgrims memorize the land's open screen
> Mysteriously and are kind to me.

Every thought here is a new angle on an old thought. Trees usually darken visitors – here the opposite. "I" am usually kind to the pilgrims – here the other side is given[…]

[Signed "Yours, Amadeus"]

East Witton, Thursday [4 March 1943]

I had quite a fan mail tonight – one from Mother, one from you, one from Jim & one from George.

The one from George was an apology for kicking us out last Sunday (for which we were grateful) and it was very friendly, so everything is alright.

The letter from Jim [is] in verse, and such beautiful affectionate verse that I shall copy it out for you. I hope you don't think I'm conceited, copying it out, but it is so lovely for its own sake that I'm sure Eric Canning would admit its merits. Besides being a lovely poem, it is full of real feeling, for we were so happy together at the weekend, and George's friendship paled I'm afraid, because Jim understood me & George just doesn't. I'm not worried about George now so much – either he accepts me as I am, or he shuns me. So much of George goes into the first few strange meetings, when the mystery & the pose adopted means so much. He was far more attached to his corporal last weekend because he was new. And I think of George that our friendship could never go through the vicissitudes & delights of my attachment to you or Jim[…]

As I thought, Jim and I are to be good friends after all, and we understand each other to a large extent. To have gone to Aysgarth Falls all unbeknown, and with Jim was all anybody could have wished. After all these months, there was every chance that it would be George or Fred to show them to me, & reveal his own particular viewpoint, which might not have been mine. And not knowing I was going to Aysgarth, thinking we were miles away, made it so wonderful, so surprising, with only this distant water-music to warn us. Our ears were charmed, and we had no choice but to press on, and the sheer beauty of those lovely silver steps of water was almost unbelievable. I really think it is one of the loveliest & most impressive sights I've ever seen. Lawson was enthusiastic over the falls in flood, but it is not sheer size weight & power that would impress me, but the endless tippling over these steps, which gave such a flashing illusion of a wonderful fairy-land fountain, that a near view spoiled for a minute. So actually, I regard Lawson's picture now as rather unsympathetic and insensitive, which you will say is hard, after all my worship. I must say this, however, in justice to him, that I could not paint what I saw on Sunday in 20 years. I shall try, but at present I feel I shall go defeated at the start[12].

We were so filled with the beauty of this single fall that we felt afterwards so incurious of the others that we didn't proceed further upstream, or answer the beckoning peal of the church behind the trees. But we, or I alone, shall go to see the other falls, which I'm sure can be no less beautiful, since the whole land round there seems so magic, almost like a stretch of Keats's poem in actuality, shapely meadows, streams, bushes & trees, & a beautiful river running through it all. While I was there, I thought of you, & wondered if this would convert you to the north, for you are a southerner you know, & still can't take the north fully to heart, for which I don't blame you. But you must have realized how this dale captivates me & holds me so that I don't want ever to leave it. But you say, you must live in other parts before you can say that. I suppose so, but I love this so. This evening has given me a glimpse of those exquisite summer evenings when all is green and peaceful, pregnant with birds' songs. Mrs Dinsdale is even gardening tonight, and has just ceased (7.30). When it is like this, or like last Sunday, I long to just live on my senses, without a mind to worry me inside with the perpetual questions & unfinished reasonings. And I do live now far more on my senses, and as long as I can I am living fully; I feel I have reached atonement with something beyond & around me, and it was this I suppose that helped me with Jim, who declares I have turned my "face towards the full sun". But underneath there is the other, the ego to the id, to disturb and sometimes, but rarely, enhance the sensual fulfilment. But since you ask me about Proust, is there any greater proof of him than all the above, which is quite unnecessary but as Proustian as I could be without realizing it[...]

[Jim Kirkup's poem for Len]

Castle Bolton, 3 March 1943

A LETTER TO LEO
These stones have been moved into the shape
of castles, endless walls; bridges and a cottage
where the whole day passes like a fire
in a single room.
Here I wander all day long, alone,
watching the formal outline
of a window that cannot follow the birds, but holds
the rising statue of the hill.
And here, between the passing of a man
and the ascension of a cloud, I write
to you, hidden in the hill, among the forest
of another fell.
To reach you is beyond
my power, or the range
of any window, yet you are not far.
Separation is not measurable.
The mosses on the wall
begin to flower now for your return.
A train in the woods
drenches opening buds with green.
Tomorrow you will walk
across the footbridge of the stream
and hear the waterfall's continuous applause.
These stones will wait for you if I am gone.

J.

East Witton, Monday [8 March 1943]

[…] I had another very pleasant weekend up at Castle Bolton, with Jim & George – no others this time. The weather was marvellous, and on Sunday, when I awoke at 9, there was a frost and mist that filled the village with ghostly shapes. Then the sun rose higher, the frost gave, but the mist turned only to a drowsy haze that lasted till sunset, when the sun showed as a dull bronze orb. It was very warm, and Jim & I went to Aysgarth in the afternoon to explore the river again. We had to see those first (or rather last) exquisite steps of shining water, and as we climbed past them, by the very side of those long steps of rushing water, I did not forget to look back and gaze at that lovely downward stretch below the falls. You liked that – I did too, there was a wonderful bend that went unbroken along the base of the cliff and then the water, broken here & there with white races. Then we went on till we came to Aysgarth bridge, which has a most graceful arch I think & is very interesting. The vista from below & through the bridge of those other falls, broken & irregular against the architectural simplicity of the others, was very romantic. But what I like best of the walk was when we had walked a little higher, above those falls, to where a low weir caught the river and diverted water into the mill race. The water slipped easily & transparently over the weir, so that no motion was visible – no break, no foam, just an easy smooth & even spill over. But behind was the most beautiful pool I've ever seen. When I looked across the smooth placid pool, I saw high cliffs rising steeply out of it, from which ivy, moss and bleached dead boughs of exhausted trees, tired at last of clinging to so precarious a roothold, formed a delicate hanging tracery that was reflected in the pool. Jim & I sat with pencils & paper & drew a sketch of it. Being Jim's first attempt since school, my sketch was the better of the two, but later, when we went back to the bridge to draw there, Jim's attempt was much better than mine, tho' he spent an hour & I spent about 10 mins. I didn't like drawing the bridge. The result of our sketching expedition is that Jim is absolutely devoured with a passion to paint. He wants to come back to Witton & work near me, so that we can go out sketching together. He has very little chance of getting back though, after leaving as he did. However, I promised him I would ask Tarran, though I wasn't too keen about it I must confess. I love Jim, but I don't want his constant presence to make either of us unhappy, and that is quite possible. You see, Amos is leaving shortly for a job near Durham, & Jim will expect me to have him with me at Dinsdale so that he would not have to suffer in the camp[…]

He was very depressed on Sunday night, because this week he must leave the cottage for somewhere or other, & Castle Bolton has been such a wonderful inspiration to him. He has quite fallen in love with the oldness & greyness of the place, and the foreign beauty of Aysgarth just over the fields. And Witton is his destination if he can get the job, because Wensleydale has compelled him, as it has me.

So I'll go round to see Tarran tonight, now in fact.

Later. Tarran said the most obstinate "No", and I knew I should never persuade him. His memories of Jim's last 3 months at Witton are too vivid to allow him to say "Yes" I suppose. I'm terribly sorry for Jim's sake, & in many ways I should like to be with him, but underneath I know it is all for the best really. But Jim will be very downcast I'm afraid, because he was so eager to come. These few weekends together have brought us together till we are the greatest of friends.

But now I must write of [sic] Jim.

P.S. I did a "decent" water-colour on Saturday, which you can have when I have something else to put in my frame.

East Witton, Wednesday [10 March 1943]

I have written umpteen letters this week already, and you Miss are going to be cut short. I was Amadeus in the last letter [in fact letter of 1 March], for no reason at all, except that I remember now signing myself Wolfgang or something in a teasing letter to Jim. Otherwise there was no reason for Amadeus, why should there be – I like it – but I like Antaeus even better.

I wonder how poor Jim is faring. I am quite concerned about the poor boy, who so wanted to come back to me. It is all so ironical[…]

How it thrills me to read of your spontaneous appreciation of a Welsh choir. Now don't you agree that my voice, my father's & my grandfather's (had you known it) are neglected by not being the spine of the bass section in a Welsh choir. Surely you must agree that if we are Welsh in no other way, we are Welshmen in our voices. Even in

Wensleydale, it is said of my voice in any singing that it just "caps things". For I like to put in that bass line which "caps things" – it enriches, even in a second-rate effort like mine, the dull unison of songs set to harmony.

I met a Welshman in Middleham recently, a soldier, who had a lovely Welsh face, I imagine, it was broad & frank, and his eyes were very expressive, while his voice, tenor, was most vivacious & crowned all the talk[…]

May I call myself then,

Antaeus

East Witton, Friday [12 March 1943]

[…] I remember three things from your last letter. One, that the sickle moon with its independent little star was also noticed by me[…] They hung over the west, over Castle Bolton, over Jim, whom I had failed. He is dreadfully disappointed, dear boy, but he smiled in his letter & sent me some pencil drawings of which the still life ones are excellent & show remarkable strength & vision in a beginner. I think we might have been happy together, painting (both of us), he writing & I listening, and he posing for me, for he would have been a great model after George. I don't know, of course, but he was so enthusiastic that I know things would have been different this time. I feel as though I have sent him away, even though I know it is not my fault that Tarran remembers his past misdeeds.

The second thing I remember is that your family is brightening up, if only a little, after the trying times they've had. I hope your parents find happiness in a new home, and I hope too that your brother [in law] & sister in Africa will soon get over the shock of [daughter] Naomi's death[13] […]

The third thing is the holiday suggestion – I shall be glad to spend Easter with you at Castle Bolton, because I wanted to stay in Wensleydale for Easter instead of going home. Actually, however, I would like to stay at Witton, and if you would like to see Witton in its surroundings, I might be able to get you put up[…]

Sunday morning […] I was disappointed with "results" yesterday. In the afternoon I tried to paint a subject not unlike that water-colour of foliage over a pool that you have. But I got little more than a drawing done, for filling in the background got me mixed up immediately and I had to stop and watch trout swimming in case I began to weep. In the evening I climbed the heights, hoping to gain consolation in a fell picture – fool, I tried to paint the sky as the sun was losing its final glow behind the hills – the result was just funny, though 3 crosses would make it into a tortured Calvary. So I'll try again today. Last week's picture was pronounced by Amos to be my best so far, and he asked if he could buy it, but I was so grateful for praise from him that I said he could have whichever he liked best when he leaves in a fortnight's time[…]

East Witton, Wednesday [17 March 1943]

You seem very sure about my qualities as an illustrator already – very kind of you, but of course I haven't done much black & white work yet, & for figures I'd be very weak. But evenings this year are going to be much occupied with pencil & pen-work, leaving water-colours for longer periods at weekends. I'm finding already this year that I have more to say in my pictures, and at the weekend (Sunday) I was 4 hours at a picture and hardly realized it. That is a long time for me, and I had cramp several times, especially as I had to sit on a headstone, in a very uncomfortable position. In the morning I broke my sketching stool, falling flat with brushes, board & paints all over. I must get one soon and I wonder if you could see what there is in Newcastle – something portable, but not of fragile wood or wire.

This year I'm going to send you any money I get for my pictures. That will pay for art with art & will see if a living can be made from it. If I make £5, I can live a year on that (free of tax). I painted Spennithorne Church on Sunday for Nurse Macfarlane with a remarkable success for me. I'd like you to see it – it's my very best yet, though it is an architectural subject, not the church from a distance in its setting, but a close-up of the lovely tower. It is not on a hill as I have mistakenly shown it here, but it is a long picture. The church is the most beautiful in Wensleydale that I've seen, rather quaint & keep-like in structure, with strange rococo finials which I couldn't make out distinctly. Even though my picture is quite good, quite accurate too, I

The sketch of Spennithorne Church

haven't done justice to the church. But I'm sure Nurse will have it, though, being loath to let it go, I haven't taken it to her yet. That will be 10/- to start living on. I gave her two pictures last year at 10/- each, so I daren't ask more[...]

I'm very sorry to hear about the terrible air-raids you're having – I knew something was up on Thursday, because we can see flares about Middlesbrough & the Tees & there were many, with thuds too, & the pheasants squawking wildly. They are our sure sign of a raid on the North East. I'm relieved to have news from all of you this week, all being quite cheerful it seems[…]

Len had been in quite good spirits for several weeks, but on 23 March he wrote: "I was thinking today it seems a long time since I was really mournful & depressed[…]] But since last night, I have had an awful job with myself – despite consoling, reasoning, I cannot get away from thinking painting is futile (my painting I mean), that there can never be any place for any art in the future as it looms through the war, and that even if there were, it would be such a minor, foolish and barely suffer-able place that the artist could hardly exist or be justified in existing." He realised that he was also downcast because working long summer hours from 7.45 am to 6 pm would curtail his painting over the summer and he would anyway be "too tired to do anything". Len finished by dismissing his painting as "horrible", "so far far below what I'm after".

A weekend on Tyneside, when Mona and he heard a concert featuring the Polish Jewish violinist Ida Haendel, raised his spirits a little. Len was greatly moved, and a few days later at work he found himself resisting "anti-Semitic tendencies". Sympathy for the Jews would become a marked aspect of his world view.

East Witton, Wednesday [31 March 1943]

[…] I do want especially to thank you for the concert afternoon. I was enraptured by Ida Haendel. To me she was so romantic, almost unbelievably a spirit of sheer music. She did not "aspire to a state of music", she was music. To hear a Jewess play with such sympathy & feeling the work of a Jew was such a deep & memorable experience that I cannot bear any of the slightest anti Semitic tendencies that are abroad now. On Monday at work strange to say we came on the subject in the cabin whilst sheltering from a heavy storm – I found myself almost alone, against Englishmen, Irishmen & Danes alike. But the Mendelssohn concerto was my standby, my touchstone, retaining my vision in philistine surroundings[…]

East Witton, Sunday [4 April 1943]

It is a glorious day, and this afternoon I shall try to paint, though I find myself quite unable to paint since these longer hours came in. I tried yesterday but gave up half way through, I was so tired and uninspired for some reason[…]

I walked about yesterday and found several places that I'm sure you will like when you come – though this place is not wild and virginal like Alston. Only, I assure [you] it is very, very beautiful, even amid my moods of weariness & despair. And at least I have something to turn to when I feel unhappy and you have so little. I am sorry you cannot stay longer here and gain full benefit from the contrast with the town. You seem very tired and war-weary, and I think a longer holiday would help you, though I don't know what Mrs Dinsdale thinks. She is rather chary of having people, after finding Amos so difficult to please[…]

P.S. I clean forgot about these pictures. Choose one please and send the rest back as soon as you can. The one with the magnificent cloud study over moorland has one on the back which you can ignore. Choose in your own time & put each in the frame if you like, to see it on the wall. Whichever you choose, it is for your birthday & in gratitude for all the kindness you show to me.

P.P.S. I have been out sketching and I think I really must give up. This afternoon's effort was ghastly. I am at the stage I was after a week's painting – i.e. far behind *Cover Bridge*. When I'm painting I notice that I work without knowing what I'm doing – I just proceed and get the desired effect as far as I'm able, & when it is good I don't know how it is done. It is the same now, only I don't know how I am not doing it. Apparently some sort of equilibrium is needed which is quite absent now. Anyway, with the same materials as last year, I cannot paint anything like last year.

So I think I shall give up, and try to sublimate my disappointment & depression in Proust or something. I'm sorry you haven't got one picture of any I did, but I wanted you to have something specially good, something that was to result from this year's added practice & experience. But it is no good living on hopes and I must let you have one from home – perhaps the afterglow picture that you like. I looked at Cover Bridge this morning (it hangs above my bed), and despite all its faults & immaturity & muddiness I wondered how I had done it, where even that bit of talent had gone.

Art and creation open up such a vast idea of life that to go back on your vows to create for ever is like shutting off the light. I do want so to paint, but I cannot go on like this; besides the horrible mercenary fact that I owe you a good sum of money for materials & George several pounds for clothes etc… I must economise & painting has cost me quite a lot, all for no result. Oh, this afternoon – what a wonder that rucksack, sketching stool, paper, paints & the lot did not go into the Cover.

L

East Witton, Sunday morning [11 April 1943]

I was up early, with the prospect of the whole long day before me. I burn to paint, but I hardly dare. I think another weekend like last would make me weep for ever[…]

'The Glass Fable' thrills me. I adore and revere the whole exquisite poem. The Miltonic description of the faery palace, taken from its context as say 'Fragment from The Glass Fable' is surely true poetry, surely with the best I know, even with Milton himself, with the Keats of 'Hyperion', with the Shelley of Prometheus [Unbound]. Not in theme I know, but in language, imagery, movement, thought and feeling. It is as fantastically real and genuine as 'Kubla Khan', as truly a work of sheer poetic character, of genius[…]

I love Jim for the tribute of this poem "for Leonard Jones". It is a very kind and affectionate tribute. It is very kind too that you should type it out for him, and forget all his lightness of heart and frivolity in taking so much and returning so little. I'm sure Jim & I are parasites. By the way, the poem means nothing more than it says – it is itself[…]

East Witton, Wednesday [14 April 1943]

[…] [O]n Saturday – no Sunday – I painted my best yet. I do like it. A lovely cold sky of cloud layers, with a tiny white cloud just peeping over the distant shoulder of Penn Hill. The sky is cut short by a mass of dark trees – larch, Scots pine and budding hardwoods, in the middle distance. All in cold dark tones, in my best colour & brushwork yet. You will see it when you come here. I'm so encouraged by it, because it appeals to me tremendously, and shows promise once again[…]

East Witton, Tuesday [27 April 1943]

[…] Now tell me – are you better for your little holiday? I think you may not be, because it is never very restful being caged up with me for 3 days. I have decided not to have any more friends or relatives here because I simply can't entertain them. Probably I'll change my mind, but really, when I am finally released from work I am so utterly charming to myself, by myself, that the contrast with my impatience before friends is too obvious. I am so so charming alone that I ought to be alone as often as possible. So charming – "Will you not have tea now Jones?" "No, really I won't old boy – this picture is coming off something marvellous – I really shouldn't let tea stop me." "Oh that's all right, Jones, go ahead & finish it – it is good though – your best up till now – (I always say that, but I mean it this time)", "Oh I know it's my best – actually, I'm beginning to think that I'm leaving Lawson behind now, never mind Jackson", "Decidedly – look at those trees, what exquisite restraint in colour, what a lovely cool atmosphere over it all – you are advancing tremendously."

For hours on end, oh so charming to myself. But let a friend utter it – & it's spoilt & the friend is dishonest, too anxious to please, or just being a sheep. So though I'm all to blame, it does seem a pity to spoil the other, doesn't it.

Otherwise I did find you a little tearful & depressed & abstracted & so on. Somebody's pinched your gusto – you are out of your humour (in Jonson's sense). Probably bombed out. Coming to peaceful green (so green) Witton, you seemed hopelessly worried about life by contrast, and it is so hard for me to really understand, particularly as I'm deliberately adopting a carefree attitude to life & am feeling better for it and, apparently, suiting people better. I get on with everybody & am accepted, whereas being worried you unconsciously dig a moat round yourself. I know there is much to worry about – but worrying is quite useless & negative, and if it doesn't lead to action is quite suicidal, & if it does lead to action, action is best without it, so why worry [...]

I see you didn't take the "pictures" after all. I can't tell why you should want them, or I either, but I didn't want poor Aunt Phoebe to have such rubbish foisted on her, as a nice gesture from me, when I'd never thought of her. You were in a temper over them, weren't you. And such cutting things to say "An 'artist' should keep all his work to watch progress." You flash like steel in a temper, are a little scorpion in fact – I love to tickle it & provoke it to greater fire, to see the tail lash in scorpion fury & listen to the ingratiating sarcasms of "Artist" – "Progress". It thrills me & relieves you[...]

I see too that you are giving the appropriate messages to my family – I suppose that's right, but I didn't give the message & despite George & diplomacy, in such cases it is insincere. I do send my love, & my greetings, in all sincerity, when I write. The thought of them comes at strange unexpected times, love too, & sometimes dissatisfaction, & if I love once in a lifetime it is sufficient, if it is there, and not bundled off in little parcels through friends & letters. I am half death, like all life, the seeds of negation are within me – if life wins & love, then let it blossom freely and surprise the death into its grave. But if death is there, still there, as it must be always, evil & negative, it creeps into life, and love, & mars their positive beauty, so that love is so often insufficient, and only an overdose of death, like serum, will make life possible, so that we may live, warped and strained, crooked and sorrowful, but always with that tiny blossom breaking through, at lovable moments when it is most precious. Let it find the light, it is love, natural, passionate, striving love, the enemy & victim of death – but do not force it, or it may die if it has no strength. However weak, it is precious, because the weaker it is, the greater its struggle with death.

"Active evil is better than passive good." I long to probe into the truth of that.

Previous crises had built up gradually for Len; now he was hit as if by a dam bursting. The intensity of his rekindled friendship with James Kirkup had made life seem more vibrant than ever, even if his painting still gave him as much frustration as satisfaction. The realisation that both Mona and Jim were in love with him was too much for Len to cope with. Once again his solution was to remove himself from the scene – but this time into the armed forces.

East Witton, Saturday night [1 May 1943?]

I found your letter deeply moving, and have been unable to think of anything else these last few hours. I have tried to think consecutively around the problem, and I feel, after a long time of unbroken thought (or so it seems) that I have reached a decision.

This letter will be necessarily inadequate & crude in expressing my thoughts, & all my thoughts cannot enter here, since many came & went in a flash.

I know however that you have loved me all along, and though you have tried to deny it, & I myself have deliberately blinded myself to it, I have known all along. I am so sorry about it all, and above all, feel most unworthy of your love. That statement seems cold and heartless – believe me it is not meant to be, and my unworthiness in forcing me to change somewhere & somehow. I must also tell you, though this information is only for you, that Jim too is in love with me, and quite badly apparently. For a long time he has been writing me love letters, and our few meetings lately have been most affectionate. He is unsettled at Cornwall only because of me – I feel so dreadful about it all, especially since I have tried to love him & find I cannot. Sooner or later my own shallowness and coldness will be exposed. But I want Jim to know from me, so will you please not mention anything to him – please don't, though I'm ashamed to ask.

But Jim's affair can be no comfort to you. I only want you to know this because it shows that I must go round the world being loved & unable to love. Wherever I go, I must leave sorrow, and my last cruel meetings with Lily, who must have loved me for months after she last saw me, often return with endless pangs of conscience. Somewhere in me, though I cannot find it, is some quality or charm (?) that makes quite different people love me. I succumb & then find myself unable to carry on, & am left with the nauseating conscience-stricken thoughts of having left some great sincere friend stranded & even heart-broken. So somehow, for your sakes, for others' & for my own vanity & pride, I must hide this apparent light under a bushel. I think the best way is to seek some sort of anonymity & levelling with my fellows – I can join the army, to put it short.

I have thought about it long enough and the solution came with such relief and ease that I'm sure it will help all ways. Your letter, and your recent visit, have both shown me what is happening to you and I am deeply concerned for you. I suppose being loved by a person, & feeling powerless to return it, is an unnatural, if common relationship. For us it has gone on too long, and I don't want you to feel that you're to blame for my decision by your avowal in the letter. I have known the situation all along, I suppose, & I am grateful for your courage in bringing it to a head.

I do wish to release you, to let you go completely. It is the only thing for you, your only salvation, & though we have often considered it before, this time we must be certain, and you shall be released, even if my final cruel act is to bully you into it.

It is difficult for me really to imagine what amount of suffering I cause you – I only know it is great & that it is deep-seated, of that kind for which there is no ease. Don't you think it best to uproot it, to grasp hold of it & pluck out its cause. This is a dreadful thing I suggest – to deliberately deny friendship of many years standing, but it is for the best.

There are several reasons why I should move & not you. The main reason, after the above, is that I need some outside discipline if I am to have any character at all. At present I feel I am doing nobody any good, that I am outside any movement or spiritual society to help in any way – in other words, I am leading a hopeless, selfish existence, & as I'm no help to anyone or anything, I can at least help my country. It has been kind to me, like my friends, but I can help it by merely saying Yes, however uncertain, while I am quite unable to serve my friends, you, my parents & Jim in particular, & dare I add, even the ghost of poor Lily, which always dogs my footsteps. I need the proverbial kick in the pants & am of course too charming to myself to administer it myself. This decision is in the direction of that kick, anyway.

I know all this sounds precipitate, dramatic & characteristically selfish of me. I know however that beneath all the blare of trumpets & flags it is best.

And what of your pacifism? you ask. It is still there, but like my whole life, tainted & probably insincere. I don't know – it hardly seems to count against the intensity of suffering I cause you, and against my own problems of pride and selfishness. That is the only answer – it hardly counts.

This joining up is surely a solution, if an unhappy one, of our relationship & myself. I shall feel happier if I have not to cause you any more hardship by making you uproot & fly goodness knows where. Please let me do this last thing towards helping you. And so that there shall be no hedging, no persuasion & kind offers (I know you will sacrifice yourself even at the last) I have written the letter & it will be posted with this. So it is done & there's no mending it. In a few months I shall be called up & then I shall disappear into oblivion from you & all my friends. I shall start afresh if possible and try to solve my own problems – if I could, I should solve yours too, but I am powerless there. I long to help you, but am quite unable & this step is only a partial help. Please take it that I am trying to help you with my better self[…]

Sunday Morning

[…] It is done – I am throwing the past of aimless individual to the winds & trying to assume a temporary future of anonymous submersion in a collective life with other young men. Without being self-praising, I know that, even if I have never expressed it, I have been an individual among the crowd – almost above the crowd – I have groped after art, and love has come to me with tragedy for other people, mainly yourself. And the individualism is at present draining my life and yours too, and temporary burial, especially when the whole of my contemporaries is doing likewise, is surely the best thing.

All this is about me – but I never forget you, and I do want to help you, for your own sake, and for the gracious & loving way in which you have helped to mould my being these growing years. I can never forget that – how, despite all my tantrums & selfishness, you have never failed to help me in practical & spiritual ways. Your letter, though moving so deeply & urging me to action, also leaves me with the desire to correct certain things which don't matter much really, but which are best refuted. After saying we can never be natural with each other, which is perfectly true, you go on to suggest we are hardly even friends, since I do not send you pictures & poems as I do to Jim. Jim has only one thing, a little anaemic thing done in boredom, which is of my bedroom. And since he wishes to paint, I sent him a copy of my last water-colour to show him how I sorted out trees, since it seemed easier to send that than try to express it in a letter. In other words, he has not got any serious attempt, even like your picture of the Cover which I sent with Fred's. Please believe me when I say that a really good picture was always in my mind for you, & that I did not want to send one less than that. That is quite true, partly because of vanity (I did not want our mutual friends to gaze upon one of my many mediocre attempts), and partly because I felt that you must have only my best, for some vague indefinable reason. The best, of course, has not arrived, so I feel that you can have which of my pictures you like best, out of all those you have seen & which are not burnt. *Cover Bridge*? the picture you have, which is yours in any case? the afterglow on Bolton Moors? my bank of trees at Witton? Being in the forces will stop my painting, but I feel will be a purifying touch for any future expression, if any. So it must be a past picture since the future holds none – and being a past one, it is far below what I wanted to paint for you – that is quite sincere.

As for poems, I am almost inarticulate and Jim has only one, which is a silly attempt to love him and express that in lover's words. Being a sincere attempt to love, it is not such an insincere poem as it may read, especially since I think of Jim at a distance with a loving heart. Now since there is no real reason for withholding it from you, you may have it if you want to read it, & I shall send it if you write. I have also, during the night, tried to empty my thoughts into a sort of poor dirge for you, & that too you can have, in all its imperfection, & for what it is worth. It may hurt you, & I shall only send it if you ask for it – it is only a very few lines of death-like cadence.

Beyond that, I don't send poetry or pictures to any friend, & Mrs Dinsdale only resurrects what pictures are ready for the fire. You don't really want such horrors as she keeps, do you?

You also deplore that you haven't the youth & beauty of the land-girls – please don't worry over such a triviality – all Hollywood could measure our timber & they would no doubt amuse and divert me – but where is the depth & reality of it all. Our land girls are nothing more than empty little females who at best can only raise a somewhat distorted Proustian vision of female vivacity & charm. For the most part, it cannot raise such pleasure as the perfection of a flower or a lamb.

And then this "poetic & artistic feeling & sensitivity of Jim & other artists" with whom I mix. Jim is his own precious self, & you are your precious self – of the two you have loomed larger & still do in my life. George is a horrible coarse individual whose underlying kindness has helped my [sic] considerably – I regret to say that is all I feel about him. Fred too is kind but quite incapable of friendship – I don't know why & I shan't miss him a lot. [George] Graham needs only a patro-nising adoration for his work – I admire his work, the man is too cold & bleak for friendship. Muriel I rarely see & is really no friend of mine. There, I have dismantled the tinselled fabric which you have imagined around me.

This constant repulse & rebuff of mine – I'm terribly sorry about it all, I know it is true, except that you often took jest for truth & seemed to encourage it. But really, I suppose, it is all part of the unnatural relationship between us.

Oh how dreadfully foolish & unnecessary this all sounds – I only want to do what you want to do always, "the decent, honourable, loving thing". Please tell me the truth, is what I'm doing of any help to you. I do want to release you, sincerely; I know it should be one thing or the other. I value your friendship so highly & have come so to depend on it that I could let it go on dishonourably for ever & hurt you & give you nothing but sorrow. If I could, I should have asked nothing more than to share that life you so lovingly wish to share. I know what a sad cry in the wilderness that is, & long to help you, but I cannot now. It would be wrong, dishonest & impossible for me.

So I pray that my submission to national service will help you, and if you feel you are the cause, please remember that I am doing it to help myself[…]

[Signed "Sincerely, Len"]

P.S. Not knowing which force to volunteer for I put Navy, Army & Air Force in my swan ornament on little papers and drew forth Air Force. I had a leaning towards the Army but RAF it will be, if they will have me.

Len had made clear in his long letter that his decision to join up was rooted in a number of problems – but chief was the need to "release" Mona from her love for him. Ironically, she responded with sympathy and understanding, but nothing fundamentally changed in their relationship. Yet Len was now plunged into a spell of mental torment, for he felt his old pacifist friends and his parents would think he had betrayed them. The reality was that he had taken his life as a conscientious objector and aspirant artist as far as he could. He was tired of unremitting hard physical labour, and of his isolation. "I wanted to be with men, to flow with them in the same stream, to touch back to my own generation." He would now endure a month of inner struggle to settle his confusion and resolve where his future would be.

East Witton, Tuesday [4 May 1943?]

Thank you for the two marvellous parcels[…]

But all the time, behind my gratitude I am wondering what you are thinking of me, what will be in your letter tomorrow. I feel you will be disgusted with me, and say I'm too foolish for words.

Needless to say, I am terribly upset & anxious over what I've done. I'm quite frightened too, but I want to conquer that – I'm going on now, to the bitter end, and I imagine rather a friendless existence at first, for I cannot see my old world following me in my shame. The Carrs, the Quakers, Jimmy Gale, Florence [Gale], Mr Acum, all sorts of people come before my eyes in silent reproach and I know I have rejected them and can never face them again. All this is inevitable I know, but so intense and terrifying while it lasts. I cannot help wondering what they will think of me – and the new "friends" ready with praise on my conversion to "common sense", how unwelcome they seem. But it is all what [TS] Eliot called so aptly "the refining fire" ['Little Gidding']. I must endure something to live, and all this seemed to come so readily & upset me so suddenly that it is so natural as almost to appear the culminating point of a long prelude to torment, which I was delaying shapelessly & idly.

And all the time too, I know it is going to help you, because I shall be so different, so submerged & above all, away, whatever that may mean. But the submersion will help me too, for it is what I need. My pacifism was always in danger, because it had no roots in religion or politics, but in a vague individualism which I was always endeavouring to assert, & which thereby strained me & impoverished me. I was not great enough to transcend the struggle and live in grace & exact poise like Jim or Firbank[14] or D.H. Lawrence, whose individualism wins them through. Now the prospect of a level existence, unapologetic & ordinary, among other ordinary beings is such release for me that you need never worry & think you caused all this, for it came so readily.

All I know is that I am always weak, always have been & always will be. Will the army help me there? How I hope so.

East Witton, Wednesday [5 May 1943?]

Your letter was most comforting – you, at least, are not harsh with me. I hardly know what to read between the lines – but the lines themselves are gentle, & I do not deserve them.

Also you have given me courage to write to my parents – they will, as you say, be very hurt by my shameful action, and their reproach will be the worst. They must think me the queerest son to be blessed with. Anyway, I have written "tactfully", as far as I'm able. I told them much that I told you, but tried to be more simple & graphic, though it was hard. I cited married men who have left their homes, wives & children & young boys of 18 having to join up – I suppose that sounds sentimental, but it is real & touching the human heart when it is a lad like Jim Peacock of Bolton, who had to leave his wife & 2 children & is already going abroad – he is a very devoted husband & father. That explains a lot to my parents.

But otherwise I am rather stunned yet – waves of shame and relief come in turn. Your letter came with a sense of relief too, though as I say, it was quite undeserved. I am glad you are more your normal self. I hope I shall never make you suffer unduly again. I feel, though I am probably wrong, that my action has already done a little bit of good.

You may have *Cover Bridge* when I collect it from George. It is quite unworthy of dispatch to S. Africa but you think it good enough & that is sufficient[15.] Needless to say, I can neither read nor paint just now – nor even write properly. When things like this happen, I only long for peace again, when I can love what I have always loved, paint without distraction, read with quietness & understanding, content with life[...]

East Witton, Thursday [6 May 1943?]

Thank you for your kindly letter of tonight. You are obviously very concerned about me and I know you think the best thing I can do is give it all up. You take it that I have made a decision, & that I should consider the whole question & its consequences thoroughly. I know I ought to, but, though I called this wholesale retreat a "decision" it really was no such thing. It seemed to come of itself, and is not the result of thought I suppose. It came just as a spontaneous release from myself, release from the strenuous job of always trying to justify my existence before other people. Why I should always want to do that I don't know, though being a CO would help that I suppose. But without being a lone CO among the rest I should still be trying to justify my existence. Lately it has strained me, sapped my spirit, drained me of any good that was in me, and I think you have found me a much changed individual, a worse & more regrettable character than usual. Now it is I who am full of self-deprecation – but your weekend letter brought me to my senses, & though somehow I think its importance has perhaps faded a little for you, it has not for me.

I wish too that I had never started to paint, or to try. I could never be content with amateurish dabblings done in the nature of a hobby on holidays etc… it was all very real for me, but has often made me very unhappy. Now it is all finished, for now at any rate, though the old urge will try me for a long time, since painting gives you new eyes and vision, & creation is often thrust upon you against your will.

Just at present of course I am in a terrible plight – writing letters to everybody has been a pleasant diversion, except for the few that hurt[…] Hardy is quite impossible & I think I shall send that & [Charles] Ricketts tonight or weekend. Thank you for them both, particularly for Ricketts. He & [Charles] Shannon seem to have been an ideal pair (see portrait of both in Jacques Emile Blanche[16]) & I wish Jim & I could have lived together so. To me that, or living quite alone is the ideal existence, but partnership is horrible if you are not meant for each other.

I am still rather puzzled about you – from your weekend letter, I saw you were in a bad way, through me, and I had meant, as you wished, to release you from all the suffering caused through our continued & apparently unbreakable friendship, which seems to survive all. I wanted to help the break, to complete it, by somehow becoming altogether different, by disappearing into comparative oblivion & shifting anchor from Witton, where my final retrogression had set in, despite my apparent happiness & contentment here. Now please consider yourself in this – shall I just leave Witton finally & not give you my subsequent address; will that help you or do you want it otherwise? From your weekend letter I am sure you wish for the latter, after all you have suffered. Please think that over carefully. For my part, I shall say nothing, so as not to influence you.

This will have cut off so many of my "lesser" friends, that many of them keep appearing to me, as tho' I were a condemned man. I certainly am a new man – the old self is peeling off, & I cannot say whether the new is to be for better or for worse.

There is one thing which you may be able to help me in – you may ease my poor parents a little. I shall have disappointed them & hurt them deeply & I'm sure you can comfort them. I am completely unworthy of them, & the only comfort I can get is in other stupid sons who even came to be disowned or almost, like Baudelaire or Jim. [Siegfried] Sassoon too was a great comfort to me, for he too was troubled with this dual personality, the sportsman & the striving artist, in me, the ordinary cussed workman & the striving artist. In S's case, the war came as a turmoil inside him & he enlisted, & became the Sassoon we know, the poet & memoir-writer. In my case I'm too dumb to learn anything from experience & I certainly lack his spiritual integrity.

Now I join the ranks of the disgraced – Arthur [Good], Bertie Douglas – and in such cold blood.

But it's going on.

East Witton, Sunday [9 May 1943?]

I've just seen my father off from Leyburn, and got a very welcome lift back to Cover Bridge with Dick Stott. As I expected, my father made the most pathetic pleas to me, which I was quite unable to resist – indeed I did not wish to, really. After talking last night, he left me to myself, and I think I wept myself to sleep. After that I just went backwards to last weekend, and wrote to the MoL as soon as I got up, before breakfast. I hardly knew I was doing it, and it was posted and we were getting the bus to Leyburn before I merely mentioned it casually to my father.

However, I remember trying to be gentle & pleading with the MoL, after all my trouble to them, and asked "if possible" to have my name restored to the CO register. Since I had already had notice that I was off it, I asked, if that were impossible, to have my name put down for non-combatant duties, and if neither was possible, just to let me know. It is pleasant to think it is out of my hands, though actually it is not. Having sought to go back on the CO register I realize now I just wanted to go into the forces, just wanted to, for no apparent reason, and trying to explain was merely exhausting me. More has happened to me in a week than in a year. So actually, I suppose, the position is as equivocal as ever. I might as well tell you. I awaited my father in fear and trembling, and am looking forward to tea with pleasure after a two-days' fast. I have hardly been able to eat, which is strange for me. However, he was as lovable and affectionate, as natural and whimsical as only my dear father can be. I loved him from the very bottom of my heart, I revere him, worship him and adore his simple, open-hearted philosophy of life. And, he never tried to browbeat me, though I never thought he would – hasn't it in him. If he had, I'd have stubbornly refused to budge, I know.

So, however equivocal the position may still be, I feel I have not wasted his time, and at least have promised that I shall try, if the worst comes to the worst, to get pushed into N-C [non-combatant] duties. And that wretched, belated statement is the only result of his journey to me. I feel dreadfully stupid & foolish about the whole business. There is nothing to do except wait for the Ministry's reply – in the meantime Tarran is casting around somewhat despondently for another feller to take my place[…]

I have never had a week like this past one – I hope it all settles down to some happy solution. I've spoilt Witton & Wensleydale for myself & got myself into a real plight – the forces seem the only release yet, but I'll accept whatever the MoL gives me & if I stay on the CO register, I stay at Witton, but differently, certainly not with the serenity and calm which I have known, the only desire to live here always. Now the pool of contentment has been disturbed and unless I can paint, it cannot settle[…] So I have wantonly spoiled my existence here, in a passionate bid to escape from life, or so it seemed. As I say, if at last I began to paint, my desire would leap once more, and to take me from here would be to uproot me. That is the state I like, when you love a place till it hurts to think of leaving it. Now, I have no will to paint, none whatever, & only a strong act of discipline will open the way – now it is too easy to think it's not worth a bean. Nor have I any will to stay here – I almost want to leave immediately and would rush at the first opportunity[…] I wanted, now I know, to be with men, to flow with them in the same stream, to touch back to my own generation, from which I stand apart in apathy. But that is something which nobody else can understand, and to have achieved it, while so easy, would have hurt so many others that now I am trying to go back, almost against my will, but compelled by older instincts & loyalties which had wrongly become fogged within me. My father brought them out all too clearly, almost as perfectly and patiently as a god, and though the old desire remains, to go, I cannot say I have sent the letter to merely placate him.

In the midst of my despair & anxiety waiting for him there came a telegram which tore at my heart and seemed to enter deeply like a dart – "Reconsider – forget not yet – I am shattered – writing – Corydon." From Jim who is always Corydon[17]. "Forget not yet", an exquisite love lyric by Sir Thomas Wyatt[18]. I know talking about Jim will only hurt you, but you are the only one to whom I set this down. No one can imagine the pang of grief & despair that came with that telegram. There were many moments too when my father had the same effect on me, until I felt I could bear it no longer. I know too that it is not yet finished, that my letter this morning is a shot in the dark which merely prolongs the situation. If they consent, everything is well at that end, at home; if I am on the military register beyond recall, they will be as disconsolate as ever. And the result is unknown as yet. I have two humours – one turned to others, & one to myself – one is to be satisfied and I can honestly say that the better part of me does long to satisfy the former. So you see it is hardly a question of pacifism at all, so please don't send me tracts about this retreat for "unworthy" people, who only want to mope together about their "unworthiness". Confession and Repentance are to me the most private of spiritual processes, and it is for the individual himself, for his priest or for his friend. But to take it to any assembly, however sympathetic, is to exhaust its ultimate beauty and honesty in the effort to transmute it into fellowship[…][19]

It is cool and comforting to talk about myself at will and I am not going to make the slightest effort to talk about others at all, so that this letter will empty me and perhaps help me, as you so kindly wish. I may as well say that many people already know that I'm to be called up, and some have been nasty enough to congratulate me. There the pride comes in – but I'm glad to say it no longer counts as much as it did. My father seemed to disperse it. Some were quite relieved to hear (for it seemed to spread like wildfire – I presume from a measurer who was in the office when I told Tarran – the bitch!) I have made friends easily down here, but always, of course, there was the slight stigma, the ultimate reservation in their friendship which held them back. As I say, their renewed sting hardly counts now, except collectively, and if it is more than I have felt in the past it will be hard to bear, for I detected it everywhere, this slightest recoil from real friendship which sends you back into yourself. Some COs will feel it more than others, but I love people so much that I long to break this little, last barrier and be released into the absolute jollity, fun, conversation & intimacy that is now denied me by that last little drop. But believe me when I say this has become quite a minor consideration with me, for which I am thankful, since it is an opportunity to preen myself upon integrity & sincerity, usually so rare.

I repeat amidst all this that I have not forgotten about you (or Jim), and I still want to help you with your problem. Please forget me for a moment & tell me about your feelings in the matter and how best I can help you[…]

East Witton, Wednesday [12 May 1943?]

I have had two rather admonitory letters from Jim, and it seems our state is reduced to a bare minimum of friendship, for which I am all to blame. There are so many things to weigh & consider and I'm sure I don't know what to do there. To protest seems to encourage what I cannot fulfil – to give in is to exclude friendship, almost. He is very hurt by my ways, however, and obviously thinks I'm a very weak sort of individual. But he doesn't know all – above all, he can never know what it is to almost throw one's body at heavy [work?] for months on end – its queer effects[…]

East Witton, Monday [18 May 1943?]

[…] I think sometimes I must exasperate you, especially since my determination to keep off the Right Path, which you faithfully explore, is so obvious. I am sorry to hear about Mother, and tiny glimpses of the sadness I have caused at home send me almost weeping from people's faces. It is a great pity that so many human hearts are so deeply concerned about my destiny, that I almost represent for them their own resistance to war, when I am so completely numb and apathetic. I can't abide the name of "pacifism" just now, not only because I have failed it and have consistently sullied its central truth, but because my general demeanour is away from it all. I am beach-combing, far more fascinated in the beachwrack than in the promontory of pacifism & Quakerism behind me, or the headland of heaven before me. And that, honestly, is how I want to live, if people, the dearest in my life, would not cry in grief from the promontory over my downfall. A beachcomber is usually a very happy man. So there are the two views, the one back, the other down on the edge of waves which always move and toss up something fresh. And I think the one back is the truth, but the one down the more attractive and breathing with life & interest. When you wrote your first despairing letter, I knew what it was – and I think I took the right step, to help you, and to lead myself where I had always been going. But it is not to be, and I might almost be petulant and cry "Why can't you leave me alone, forget me and concern yourselves less?" But that is wrong – I know it is, even if I did cry out aloud. Forgive if I pour these criti-cisms on to you, but you realize that I cannot write so to my parents, though I could cry to them even more – you can see both sides, they not so easily, and you can digest what they cannot even savour. But I know you are right, & I wrong, and when I whimper I am ready for the rap over the knuckles[…]

East Witton, Tuesday [26 May 1943?]

Thank you for your parcel – you never forget. But when I am in the army, I want you to give up sending me tobacco & chocolate, because then I shall be paid my library wage. And then again, once in the army, shall I hide behind my uniform & break everything off, not writing to you, & you not writing to me. If that will help you, please carry it out, because it is important. I shall not say what I want, because it is you who must be helped – and I don't want you to think I am being mock heroic or anything – I am trying to be practical, &

if this will help you then it can be done, & I for my part will carry it out. Please say what you think. I know the gnawing anxiety of loving, the eternal bitterness of the dead response, the positive meeting always the negative, the long dying hope that is only fulfilled in daydreams. Love, however abortive, is a beautiful thing – merely to love is so vivid and lovely – but it hurts, and hurts long and continually.

I did not intend writing tonight – I was going out to paint, for the first evening this summer. The weather is perfect, the place as lovely as ever – I was ready before 7 to go out – but no, I couldn't face it. I just didn't know where to go or what to do; I hadn't it in me. Oh how I wanted to paint – and could not. Where is the old will, which forced me through innumerable failures? It makes me horribly depressed, especially when I think it may mean I shall never paint again. It takes such pain and effort to merely start. Muriel, so gifted & brilliant, is in the same plight, only far far worse. It must torture her.

Not so long ago my life was almost based on the hope that I should some day paint. Everything was orientated to that single hope – what leisure would I have in so and so job, would I be able to paint as a librarian, will overtime prevent it this summer & such questions. I myself was the answer of course – and now the will to answer has gone. Now this very minute I could be painting, but no – it cannot be. Don't ask me why. To tell you the truth, I am in a sorry plight – all of me goes into these letters, believe me, and if they are too self-centred, bear up. I'll change some day. In the meantime, I fail to paint, I read fitfully & a letter forms in my mind, mostly to you, for Jim [Kirkup], who might be my other friend to write to, is too quick to pile on the agony if I write in despair to him. Should ever a young man be so gormless & hopeless as I? I only pray that in the army will come relief and consolation, the death of the intolerable burden of "what I might have been". Perhaps there I shall learn to be nothing – or shall I say learn to want nothing, for I never was anything.

There is no need to answer these letters. Just let me write them – I might almost say they were meant to be written not read. Just let me indulge in my last sad months in Wensleydale – if I want to cover these pages with tears, just let me and don't take much notice. You see, something is dying, something precious and peaceful – that tranquil contentment and atonement with this dale. That which I felt once was to be my making has now been damaged and I am packing my trunk again. Nobody can know what it means to me, how sad it makes me. But I do not ask for sympathy.

Now that it is definitely the Army, I have told Mrs D. I did not know she was so attached to me, and I was quite touched by the outpour of her affection for me, which seemed so kind and motherly. She was almost in tears, and I can see a tearful departure when it comes. I hope she lives for a lot of years to come, so that I can visit her in after years and live, if only for a few days, in this my home from home. People are so kind to me, and I so cool to respond that I wonder however the affection arises.

I had better stop, because, I am not ashamed to say it, tears are welling up in my eyes at my own waywardness & stupidity, that I should so foolishly bring about my own destruction, and deprive myself of all this around me.

P.S. Please don't let my parents know any of this.

East Witton, Sunday [30 May 1943?]

Yours to hand yesterday, as they say – thank you. I hope you don't think it an unkind & ungrateful action if I return the quid. Whichever picture it is you speak of, it is yours to do with what you please. There is nothing nearly good enough to send to S. Africa, but then you promised & I know you don't want to let them down. I have tried again to paint, was out last night, but the promise is dying a natural death, I suppose – it was never in me, I know now, and early promise and a few, very few sales, such as they were, kept me going for the first enthusiastic year. Your request for one for your brother & sister has always been in my mind. I wanted a good one for them in particular, naturally, but if it is not there, I cannot produce it. It is one of those impossible things. After all my hopes and promises, it is hard to come to this, and I shall put my things aside most unwillingly, for I did believe, from the slight beginnings of last year, that I would paint ultimately. I knew, & still know, I had the vision – but it needs the craftsman to translate it. I was attempting poetry before I had learnt my grammar – indeed, I was incapable of learning.

So, looking at it in cold blood and honestly, there is nothing I have done which is worth a £1, and under that it is worth nothing except the giving. The picture is given in gratitude for the help you have given in trying to make me paint. Without you, I could never even have tried, and though the experience has often made me unhappy, it has been of infinite value to me[...]

I do hope I don't overwhelm you with my small griefs – unbridled indulgence seems to unchain one – it does me – and if only one friend can bear it without kicking, it is a little selfish way that I somehow like. For after writing in deep, tearful despair, I felt better and went to work somewhat lighter in spirit. And I could then reflect that I was a bit daft, not knowing what I wanted. I wept if I had to stay, I wept if I had to leave – I was being a child. I didn't mind being a child in the least, except for my parents. They are the ones to suffer – I don't know what to do about them. Talking to someone at work about them, he said "Oh, it's surprising how soon the first shock will be over; they'll soon forget and they'll accept you afterwards as though nothing had happened. That's how parents are with sons." I thought it quite wise. It may not be all the truth, but I may as well tell you that before the war, and conscription was introduced, in my young pacifist enthusiasm, I announced to my father that I was going to be a conscientious objector. He will not remember I suppose, but I do – he called me a fool, though he knew what my views were & was himself already taking them in. But he seemed to think a public exhibition of what were only private views was a foolish thing to do – living on theories etc... When he saw I was in earnest, he came round & more than accepted me, he supported me and followed me. It is awful to trade on this acceptance – but after all, I am 24, a man by age at least, and I feel they must leave me to it more, say as it were "It's his own life, it's time he could live, & if he's making a mess of it, well, we've done our best." They are bound to be distressed, I know, & I am wrong to make them unhappy, but I think they are distressed about the wrong thing. They are sad about my chucking in the sponge of course, but I know too that they are afraid of the army. My father has always had a hatred of it when he thought of his own son in it, not because of its own means & end, but because of its degrading corruptive influence on a man. He is afraid that I shall learn all the bad things army life can teach a man – drinking, women, crown & anchor – even if these leave me untouched, they is [sic] the general lowering influence of living with the common herd. That is what my parents fear, I know it is. They are wrong, forgivably wrong of course, but wrong to wish me out of the army for that. For that is their chief regret – they cannot be so distressed about my position as a CO. I have had word from the MoL that I am still on the CO register on condition that I do n-c duties[…] I have a statutory guarantee that I shall never be called upon for combatant duties & where once I distrusted that, I don't now[…] What then am I to do? Like all the others, not what I want to do. But here again, there is surely nothing to regret in my move, for what I have done in the last 3 years has been pretty useless. I have been fulfilling nothing more than a condition of the tribunal, and though I have easily found excuses for doing it, particularly at those times when I have enjoyed it, it has been essentially negative. What I shall do in the army will perhaps be as negative, but no more. If, as I hope, it is the RAMC [Royal Army Medical Corps], I may have the chance to be positive, if I can help to save lives or heal wounds. That is an ideal to live for, and I reject the old idea that it is patching soldiers up to send them back into the front line. If that is so, are we to leave them to die? Don't you think that perhaps my former contempt for FAU[20], & RAMC, was a blind dismissal of something that was good & practical compared with forestry?

The main thing is, I'll be among young men. It is strange, that. Here, & for a long time, I have been among men mostly of my father's generation – young ones have been isolated, like Bill [Hamilton], Amos, Jim [Kirkup], Myrddin and the bothy lads. They [were] among a crowd of older men. Bill, Myrddin and I are frankly baling out. Amos has shifted rather aimlessly. Jim is ever on the move for nothing in particular as you know. We are too restless & "mobile" to settle with older men, especially when our own generation is herded on the other side so to speak, beckoning to us. So a stronger instinct than our former bold ideas leads us over the gulf inevitably, a gulf that war has made, but is there nevertheless[…] I cannot do worse than I am here. But my parents should discount the army influence, considering that the best & the worst are all together now, and I have no right for shelter more than the rest. And they should realize I am still a CO, still on the register, changed only in degree, and that I am damn lucky not to be off it & in the infantry. And forestry, if they are tenderly wishing me well, is not a heaven as I have sometimes described it. Perhaps overwork itself has brought me to this[…]

East Witton, Monday [31 May 1943?]

[…] I went to see Lawson yesterday – without me ever saying I was a little miserable about things, he cheered me up & I enjoyed his company. George is awful, as ever[…]

It seems that Jim & I have finished with each other. We are still friends – but "nobbut just" I suppose. It is one more little heaviness for me. He was always an ideal for me, and I love his sweet gentle nature[…]

Last Months in Wensleydale

After his month of anguish, Len calmed down and settled into a state of mind that was by turns morose, contented, rudderless and purposeful – his usual pattern of conditions, in other words. He was waiting to be called up, but did not know how long this would take, or even if it would happen at all, for the authorities often took surprisingly long over such matters, given that there was a world war to be won.

East Witton, Thursday [early June 1943?]

[…] I have already had a notice to attend a med. exam at Darlington on Monday, when I shall be at Seatoller [in the Lake District]. That made me think - & rage at their impatience but I decided even His Majesty could not claim me from my holiday so I wrote & told them[…] My week off is causing tremendous upheavals in the wood where they are going all out & being promised bonuses & such like. There is not even a man who can wield an axe, much less fell with John while I'm away[…]

Tarran is wild because I dared to go over his head & approach Anderson about an increased price for felling, which just wasn't paying as it was. Believe it or not, though I went by myself representing the others, we got a rise – from 1¾d to 2d. We are bucked & are working with a will, sure now of some reward for very hard work – for believe me, it is very strenuous work. The firm has exploited the fellers who for the most part are good simple men, easily cowed by blokes like Tarran Hutton & Anderson. Such as I are upstarts in the country but we can do a power of good for these simple inarticulate chaps who plod on unquestioningly. I think I am looked on as a nuisance – perhaps this is blowing my own trumpet but I'm very, very pleased about this, for all this year & before that the fellers have toiled on at the hardest & most skilled work without any reward. The firm trades on these simple hard-working men – and really, they are almost

One of Len's pen sketches in the Lake District

irreplaceable now. It is a fact that there is not only no feller to fill my place, but not even a potential feller[…]

The holiday in the Lake District was spoilt by bad weather. Len did some pen sketches and one "muddy water-colour". Later in the month he visited Tyneside again. On his return he wrote of his mental and physical weariness and emptiness.

East Witton, Tuesday [late June 1943?]
[…] Forgive me for shallow aims – but it fills me with enthusiasm that my next job, whatever it is, & however boring sordid or unnecessary, will not mean weariness from morn till night. If you haven't worked till you were really exhausted, you cannot know what that means – it is not the tiredness of being on your feet all day, or doing one solid filing job or something for too long, or the usual long day – no it is a sheer end of your actual physical resource & energy, the end, so to speak, of what your breakfast & lunch put into you. Sometimes I have thought, in self-pity, that not many people reach a limit of human endurance, & I have thought that I must have sometimes, the limit of what human energy can perform for one day, one week even. But that is exaggeration[…]

Can you remember how I wanted to paint; can you imagine that fellow letting anything stop him from painting. Yet he has stopped, for want of will-power. Even the reader, who rushed in at nights & got to his books as quick as possibly is dying. Blimey, I'll soon be illiterate. Do you think I'm destined for manual work all my life? My mind is twice as mushy as it was 4 years ago. It can't think – & is increasingly concerned with trivialities that once were beneath it. And yet other young people seemed only to start thinking & feeling when war came. Altogether, I wouldn't raise much at an auction – though I'm A1 & am used to heavy work & that means most I suppose[…]

Sunday […] I am glad to say I have had a short letter, & an exquisite little poem 'Lament for Victory' from Jim. We are after all, as he says, comrades for life & I do not think we shall fall away from each other because of my recent doings. Indeed, he asks for every detail about the medical exam. "I'm so curious" he says "and "who knows? I might have to go through it myself soon, and it would be nice to know just what's coming." He asks how one can have one's condition of exemption changed. And now the tables are turned and it is I persuading him against the army, since he will be hopeless there. But I have advised him, if he must, to go the whole way, & not confine himself to the CO units, since they mean work I know. He would never fight but he might get in the Intelligence Corps with his languages[…]

East Witton, Wednesday [late June 1943?]

[…] I am working harder than I ever worked in my life – to finish the wood, have a good fortnight & give John the full benefit of my strength these last weeks of work. You will be disgusted to hear that this fortnight we are breaking all records and our figures for the respective days so far are 321, 250, 200, 336, 341 cu. feet. It is 2d a cu. foot between us so work it out & you will see how mercenary I am. I need not say that normally I never do this, and my chief aim in getting a price raised is to make the job easier & not to make more money. So this is exceptional – indeed incredible to me, because I thought 240 was about our outside limit & 200 was a normal average. John is keen as mustard, because he likes money. But it can't last more than a few days – the pace is too big[…]

East Witton, Saturday morning [late June 1943?]

I am taking this morning off to recover from the shock tactics which didn't last long. We had to go to the top of the hill where the trees are scrubby little things & the steep slope is all loose scree – the wind was stiffly against us – so flop went the fortnight, as usual. Two days like Thursday & Friday soon made me thankful that it will soon be over. I know that will perhaps hurt you, but it is the truth, I can't help it. I am really pleased, relieved I should say, that it will be over soon. For me this is the war ending – a selfish choice, but now that I'm leaving, I often feel I could not have gone on a month longer.

Reflecting too, I see what a horrible effect it has had on me – especially this last six months of flogging. What have I done except work eat & sleep? Why is it that painting, instead of advancing, has gone back to nothing. It is not only the energy that is missing – the will for living has almost gone. I got to the stage where I did not care if I could not read with intelligence and alertness, or could not paint – even some nights, could not be bothered to change. I am a different person from last year and before – & I have not grown – I have almost withered up inside. If my father & mother knew what had happened inside me through incessant slogging, they would not only forgive, but approve of my step. The army declares I'm A1 – I am, for their requirements – but they do not need your silent part. That is what has suffered. If I had gone to prison, I might have stored up amazing energy, internal I mean, and been the CO I pretended to be. All that has been (brayed?) out of me – to carry on would have required the very stuff that has been knocked out of me. What made me read enthusiastically, paint and so [on] was the same energy that made me an unrelenting CO. And it has been knocked out [of] me – physically, literally knocked out of me. To nobody will that seem suffering. I don't claim it to be. Suffering is passive and therefore beautiful in itself. My penance (I begin to look back on it so) was active – I was chosen for a job, after that I had to wilfully, forcefully carry it out. There seemed no other choice. These last six months have been dreadful. Of course the reason for the first impulsive decision was quite valid – but it only precipitated what was steadily gathering. So what the army will do to me I don't know. It can't do worse, I'm sure. To be bored is to confess to an overflow of the very energy I lack. I almost feel that, given the energy, I could slay boredom if I had a little book in my pocket, Shakespeare or the Bible say[…]

East Witton, Thursday [early July 1943?]

[…] And now here is a poem from Louis MacNeice. I like it, because it expresses a rare sentiment & is me, except for the "ascetic profile".

Bottleneck

Never to fight unless from a pure motive
And for a clear end was his unwritten rule
Who had been in books and visions to a progressive school
And dreamt of barricades, yet being observant
Knew that that was not the way things are:
This man would never make a soldier or a servant.
When I saw him last, carving the longshore mist
With an ascetic profile, he was standing
Watching the troopship leave, he did not speak
But from his eyes there peered a furtive footsore envy
Of these who sailed away to make an opposed landing –
So calm because so young, so lethal because so meek.
Where he is now I could not say; he will,
The odds are, always be non-combatant
Being too violent in soul to kill
Anyone but himself, yet in his mind
A crowd of odd components mutter & press
For compromise with fact, longing to be combined
Into a working whole but cannot jostle through
The permanent bottleneck of his highmindedness.

In the future, I shall carry that poem with me and read it often – and hope all the time to meet the man. I am going to where he is I'm sure. And in case you think the poem too parallel to my own thoughts lately & that I read the poem before the thoughts came – it only appeared in yesterday's *Poetry (London)*[…]

Len had been through a low spell, but during July his mood improved as he made good progress with his painting. This coincided with another short visit by Mona – this seems to have passed peacefully – and Len working in upper Wensleydale,

Mona in North Yorkshire

which he took the opportunity to explore. Fred, who contrary to Len's harsh assessment on 1 May he now realised was a good friend and a "genuine sensitive spirit", pointed out that he had a real feel for his subject material.

East Witton, Thursday [mid-late July 1943?]

What a day! I wish you could see the rivers now. Where there was a gentle stream on Monday there is now a seething torrent overflowing its banks in parts. The waterfall at [West] Burton[1] is most impressive – a great thundering cascade of water crashing down and plunging over the weir at the foot of the pool. The draught is quite perceptible 20 yards away of the air pushed out by the crashing water as it plunges into the pool.

So my forecast of a change was wrong – it has got worse except for the wind thank goodness.

Therefore my half-finished water-colour must wait until the water goes down. A few days with the other have caused me growing dissatisfaction with it. The top is almost wholly devoid of interest & yet the lines of the trunks bear away from the interesting ground. I cannot improve on the ground which I like very much, but the top is feeble by comparison. But I won't touch it, if at all, until I am certain what it needs. The new one will not be so good I think, unless it improves greatly, but I have greatly enjoyed painting both & they are a definite advance, opening out a new territory almost. It is the most pleasing weekend of painting I've had this year, & you must have inspired me.

Anyway we enjoyed having you here & I'm glad you enjoyed yourself too. The weather was not too good though & you have yet to see these parts in warm sunshine with luscious golden evenings.

Today it has "bucketed". I went to work but did not start. We sheltered & I found a quiet spot where I read Proust. The rest played cards till 3 when it faired up & then we went walling – John & I with 8 others fetching stones for us. We had about 5 yards built in the two hours, because we had no stones to seek.

This spell from felling is such sweet relief for me that I would dread the army papers just now & hope I can be here for Jimmy coming – in fact always if I hadn't to fell. But as soon as felling starts again, I'll be the old weary irritated individual & then the army will be sweet relief[…]

East Witton, Sunday [mid-late July 1943?]

[…] I think you have been too concerned over Jim's typewriter, & I suspect you have just taken [it] to please him, without really wanting it. You mustn't let Jim's affairs, or mine, make you do things you don't wish. He was, as usual, quite unconcerned about it himself, so long as you attended to things for him. He is so lovable and so intensely alive that one can forgive him anything, but still £12 is so much & I don't like to think you took it to satisfy his wants. The whole transaction was done without my knowledge, though I know you could not have let me know in time. Otherwise I should have warned you against doing business with Jim, for his attitude to money is worse than mine[…][2]

I had a grand day yesterday. I took lunch & art materials to work & stayed at [West] Burton, climbing higher up Pen Hill after work. I walked mostly though & only got a small sketch of a bit of "scar" (rocky scarp) which is very strange. It was hot sunlight on the bleached rock and I have a hot blue (very deep) sky at the top with the bleached white rock breaking against it with deep blue-black shadows. A foreground rising, intensely green, rising up to the rock shadows on the left. It is bold & stark & rapidly done, but it is quite pleasing if you like strength of form & colour. It has no subtlety of course, just hot Mediterranean sunlight on white rocks.

The Cover Stream picture I finished on Friday night, & I am being congratulated all round so it must be alright. A wife of a fisherman airman staying at Cover Bridge Inn had apparently been trying to paint water-colours during her week's stay, & apparently water had defeated her completely. So she seem [sic] interested to watch me finish the stream & it turned out quite effective, with a dull olive-green limpidness about it. The reflections repeat the drooping form of the overhanging tree and I suppose the line which keeps coming to my mind is quite natural – "And peace comes dropping slow."[3]

But all that is self-praise & you must judge for yourself when you see it. Though I must say I have enjoyed this week's painting & the three pictures, including yesterday's little effort are my three best water-colours[…]

East Witton, Saturday night [late July 1943?]

I have just got back from a good day up-dale. I am working at Askrigg, and it being Saturday, I took some lunch to work & walked after work to Bainbridge[…][4] As I lunched at a most delightful spot I stayed there, & just drew the scene immediately before me – a pool & a shillet with a bank of stones dividing them[…] I'm quite pleased with it, and it is all done with strong brush sweeps, except for the stones which are broken in texture[…]

Thank you for sending Jim's short stories. The first is a trifle uncertain, but the second is really a superb exploration of child memories. They are revealed quite clearly & childishly, without a smattering of adult motive anywhere, so that all the universe seems to hinge on a game of "(uggers?)". Both reveal the rather terrifying childhood Jim must have suffered, for what an adult can hide by inverted complexes & bravado a child can't. And the stories, if nothing ever came of them, would be most helpful in one respect – that in them Jim is writing off & finally dispelling a bad period of his life. Dylan Thomas is the main influence – have you read his child reminiscences? They are the most subtle searchings into childhood possible[…]

[No address], Wednesday [late July-early August 1943?]

[…] I had a splendid Sunday afternoon with Fred. We are really great friends and seem to understand each other. A gentle feeling of complete repose comes when I'm with Fred. I feel so confident of him, & trust his judgment in almost everything. And beneath all that bluff exterior of the village guv'nor is a genuine sensitive spirit. Then, too, in my complete loneliness at Witton, it is with a sense of release that I go to him & discuss art – he never frowns, like George, at art in conversation – instead he joins in and even provokes it. "Now look at that foreground" he'll say "see how the dark under the hedge there brings out the highlights on those thistles" – all as you're walking along.

I took my latest paintings i.e. since your inspiring visit. The stream below Cover Bridge with the overhanging tree was highly praised I'm glad to say. He recommends me to try Newcastle again with [sic] if there's an exhibition this year. For convenience we'll call that the *Trout Pool.* My latest, *Pool, Rocks and Shille*t he also liked and admired the colour, and that may go to Ncle too, if I send 2. He seemed highly pleased with the sudden progress, and what I liked most was that criticism was purely technical & not aesthetic. He said my approach was beautifully sensitive etc… & that I was on the right line[…]

And yet, as I say, I'm not nearly good yet. I still go out & paint the most miserable failures. And good ones (for me) come of their own free will. A snatch after lunch last Saturday & one came. A long evening last night & tonight – & nothing[…]

East Witton, Saturday night [mid-August 1943?]

I have been out all day – I stayed up dale after work and walked to Semerwater. The weather was against me, raining several big showers, but I managed to paint quite a passable sketch of the lake between showers. I sheltered under the bridge at the foot of the lake.

Semerwater is in a lovely valley all [on] its own, quite cut off from Wensleydale & the world. There are hills all round with little valleys & runnels sloping towards the lake, which is in the almost round hollow formed. Even here, as in Wensleydale itself, there are trees. The head of the lake is clustered with trees which rise in strips into

A view of Semerwater, from Len's letter

the hills beyond[...] Even in the rain it was wonderful – great clouds stampeding over the shoulders of the western hills and lashing rain down upon the valley[...]

East Witton, Wednesday [late August-early September 1943?]

[...][T]hank you very much for the apples – apples are gold to me, and I have just been reflecting that the reason why I've lost so many teeth since the war began was because part of my former diet has just been cut off (I believe apples are good for teeth – do they contain calcium?)[...]

I am felling now for a long stretch without hope of respite, but I am putting other things out of my mind so that I shan't eat my heart out wanting to sketch, read & so on. It is only for the war and I must resign myself. It is not so much the physical strain – it is the mental nothingness that kills me, but if I can sort of deliberately negate that by not reaching for the impossible then I should be alright[...]

Len's respite from felling, and fulfilment in painting, had ended. Out of sorts, he was immersing himself in Proust, and in this letter he offers some interesting thoughts on the condition so central to the great Frenchman's nature, homosexuality. The sympathetic tone is notable.

East Witton, Saturday [early September 1943?]

Thank you for your letter yesterday and for the *TLS*. The review of *Indications* was pleasing, to say the least, and even considering that [Hugh l'Anson] Fausset is a friend of Jim's, and my estimation, too, of his work is high, I think it was a just & unbiased review. I do think the phrases describing the poems, particularly 'The Drowned Sailor' were deserved, and I hope it encourages publishers to consider Jim in a better light. Among the young poets he is or was quite neglected and yet I'm sure his poetry is as rich, púre, prophetic and original as any other more successful poet you see boosted these days[…]

This afternoon I have finished Vol I of *Sodome [et Gomorrhe]*. Proust is the only person I know in my own peculiar position of confidant to "Citizens of the Plain". Somehow he has, like myself, become initiated, first unwillingly, then more wisely and sympathetically as knowledge & confession increased, to the most secret & guarded freemasonry in mankind. So much in the book coincides with my own observations, the conclusions are so analogous to my own (I don't claim wisdom – the conclusions fall inevitably upon the confessions and confidences of these unhappy people) that I am wild with anger when I hear an obvious outsider talk about psychoanalysis and such. The book is invaluable as any that will ever be written I'm sure, in that it is an intimate, revealing & sympathetic story of real people, not mere patients to a psychiatrist. Their world is so enclosed and tabooed that only a very few can ever be aware of it without becoming involved. I have often reflected what a strange world, a secret passionate hidden world, has been revealed to me by mere chance. Like any freemasonry, and as Proust observes, there are signs only among themselves, scarcely visible, which I have come to know, and which, I was told afterwards, made George, for instance, introduce himself to me after so many weeks of gazing. He was sure, you see, and waiting patiently, became finally assured that "I knew", and yet I didn't – but somehow Jim has instilled into me a new awareness of men, something I didn't realize myself. Before Jim told me so much, with such agonising desire to pour himself out to me, I could never think a man could look in a certain way. After, there was a whole world of passing looks which I could not help perusing, not through idle curiosity or mere caprice, but merely because knowledge made it inevitable, as a man, having learnt that all bridges are supported by some simple geometric formula, cannot help passing over one without considering that this one is a cantilever, the other a suspension and so on. (How Proustian my language! How infectious the man is!)[…]

East Witton, Friday [mid-September 1943?]

[…] I was going to tell you about my problem […] I have to join the RN [Royal Navy] or Marines or go down pit (the first as non-com. of course) & I have to go for an interview shortly to the Admiralty. Now my thoughts on the subject are rather feeble, & though I couldn't advance one argument against peeling taters for sailors or being on a hospital ship or something, I don't want to go. I think the only reason is because of all you good people behind me – I have a constant feeling I'm letting you down & now two more grand fellows turn up & we are great friends – they encourage me in what I'm doing & I can imagine how down in the mouth they will feel if they learnt I had joined up[…]

East Witton, Monday [mid-late September 1943?]

I hope you will forgive my long silence last week – it is not that I did not wish to write – I just couldn't. But now I feel a ton better[…]

Once my cold lifted the "problem" was so easy as to solve itself, as far as it could be solved satisfactory [sic]. I realize I made a mistake, but one which I can't regret for it was the result of many things that influenced me. Even as things were I hadn't enough life in me to think I'd ever made a mistake. But Nick [Scorer] & Harold [Marsh][5] in their short stay had a tremendous influence, particularly Nick. They made me realize my obligations to others – to those others who are trying to be peace-makers while I, in my fall from "intelligence", just let things slide[…] I suddenly felt I hadn't done justice to myself (to be egotistic), that I could do & be more than I have, that I had rarely used my time intelligently here. I have had many excuses & they are justified often – it is quite true that when I'm felling I am little good for anything else. Yet I can remember when I took a sort of joy in it, merely, I suppose, because it was the most skilled, most manly job. A little more intelligence and I might have foreseen what it would do to me in the long run[…]

These few quiet days in the mist, when work has been slower than usual I have thought over a lot – the past, the present, the future – probably stimulated by Nick. So that is how this letter is going.

The problem, as I say, was easily solved – the forces was the wrong place, & though I can find no concrete objection, I think if I was to be left to face it quietly & calmly, the same objections would come as I had as [sic] the beginning of the war. In any case, if I can't think, status quo is best. So I stay at this work making pit-timber, or if they call me, I go to the other end & use pit-timber, & go down pit, which is only different in kind from my present job. It is an awful job, but why should I sniff at it more than others?

The solution came quite readily & seemed quite logical – as it is, I may not be called up, despite the repeated notices, but if, as they wrote, they call me up for an interview with the Admiralty, I shall then volunteer for pit-work. I think as a CO my lot has been mainly hard work, & I see now, after Nick's visit, that my place is not to give in but to endure till the end of the war. But if, as I have often thought it was becoming, it becomes unendurable, my plan is just to disappear for about a month & have a holiday, & then, if it is gaol, that will be sweet release. So that is off my mind.

The past – wasted as usual, with its little rewards – the present, our problem solved – so I began to think about the future, because I have constantly put it off, thinking I should no doubt fall back into librarianship. But art, once having touched, has nagged at me, and I saw Griffiths[6] last night & found he too had the gnawing feeling that his vision was years ahead of his hands – there is no expression, because of outward circumstances, and my problem in the future is to overcome the obstacles, if I can. Or else leave it alone completely. Art tends to make one grieve over the unexpressed – all the time it is still-born children for people like Griffiths & I – because we cannot get nourishment. Painting, above all, demands your hands – not clean, immaculate rested hands, but hands lent to itself & worked with the brush & palette or box, in such a harmony with your brain that the first lovely vision can be registered. Michaelangelo's hands were gnarled with the chisel work, but he could immediately transmute his brain into those hands. But our hands are on axes, shovels, saws etc all day long, & so we wimper [sic] […]

East Witton, Saturday night [mid-late Sep 1943?]

[…] I don't know what is the matter with me lately, but I am becoming more & more dissatisfied with people & life. I feel – I must say it, even [if] it sounds silly – lonely, lonely in the sense that I feel there is no one near me. I work & live with good kind people (& bad ones) who are leagues apart from me. Month after month of it gets like imprisonment. It goes on so long that when finally release is possible in some friend, I can't avail myself of the opportunity. Oh, I can't explain it all – but there is only one thing that has pulsed through my brain all week as I worked – 'The Glass Fable' – the most exquisite expression of one who is permanently as lonely as I am only for now. And to read behind that fairy tale the underlying pathos of the always-denied, the will-o' wisp nature of the dream of true, consummate friendship – all that helps one to bear a much smaller burden. 'The Glass Fable' is a continuation of the first theme – "There is but one loneliness, and it is hard to bear" – with the utter loneliness, oh *absolute* loneliness of 'The Drowned Sailor'.

I often wonder what it is I want – if I am gradually becoming more lonely, what kind of friend or companion or occupation is it I want to take it away? And it changes so strangely. What I want one day is useless another. But I am steadily settling too into something, & perhaps in the end I shall know what I want. All at present is an increasing willingness to acquiesce, to give in and do what I'm told. I become less talkative than ever, & I'm glad of [it], since I'm left to myself then, & the girls in particular won't go near a man who won't talk much so I'm spared much. You've no idea what horrors we have.

I think people are born apart & though by birth I might be poorer than some of them, I know that I am so utterly different as never to be able to bend down to them – why need we hide our superiority or snobbishness when ordinariness seeks to bury us? One must stoop to

be with them, & it is not worth the trouble. But perhaps I'm sufficiently buried now not to bother about [it?]. Not yet however, or I
should live in stolid contentment – when all the time I could rave
about the torn finger-nails, perpetually dirty, the black hands, the
constant unkempt appearance. All temporary, easily washed, but
indicative of the navvy whom nobody would address more intelligently than to talk about the weather or today's horse-racing. The
attitude is always downwards towards the navvy, bless him. Thank
God I'm not a real navvy, or they would suffer greater burdens than
I've ever known, since even a navvy is blessed in wartime, but is scum
in the slumps[…]

YMCA Hostel, Gt Russell Street, London – Wednesday [6 October
1943?]
I went for an interview yesterday for the Navy. It was most harrowing
& I was practically hounded out of the place, & I was mostly on the
verge of tears coming back from Middlesbrough until my train,
instead of dropping me off at Northallerton, went straight on to York.
I was too [word missing?] to get the last train or bus to Leyburn, so in
capricious mood just came on here[…][7]

East Witton (at long last!), Monday [11 October 1943?]
I owe you a long letter & many apologies for not writing. I felt too
tired to do anything before I went away & while away, I was in such a
delicious whirl, a flat spin, that again I couldn't write. I'll not answer
all your letters unless I find time tonight, but just tell you what I've
been doing[…]
    First, I had a notice to attend the Admiralty at Middlesbrough for
interview. Now up till then, I had become firmly resolved to go down
pit, thinking it was the right way. But after I'd written a letter saying
so to the MoL & another to my father, I had an awful night in which
my imagination got right on top of me, until I went all tearful &
thought how often I straightened my back & looked at the sky – down
pit I would be in the worst prison of all, since not even a door or
window could show me the sky. I got quite worked up, & as you know,

I rushed home to see my father, feeling that if he seemed too distressed if I went into the Navy, then I would have to make the sacrifice & go down pit. It turned out the other way – he almost bullied me not to give in to pit-work, even if they tried compulsion. So my poor imagination was sufficiently endorsed by my father's wishes & I went off to Middlesbrough. I had a terrible interview lasting nearly 4 hours. First it was alright – a very affable & kindly Wren asked me all sorts about my life in general – & how I'd passed school certificate & with what credits – my library exams too (& she kept bursting out with "Good – oh marvellous" & she was very interested so that I waxed bravely & boastingly & told her all sorts of things). Then she asked me what I read. "Oh, how marvellous – good! – good!" Then my hobbies? (I blush) "Art – oil (!!) painting & water-colours." "Oh really, you are talented." "Mm." "And do you take lessons." "Yes, with Fred Lawson" – "Oh yes I know his work" (all this was in genuine interest & she wrote it all down) "I don't suppose you've exhibited your work yet in public?" "Oh yes." "Oh good! – good!" And altogether I was having a charming time – then she saw my card & saw I was a CO. "You're rather peculiar aren't you" – her kind opinion – not a question – given with a frank look & a gentle smile, for which I blessed her, who from her official military post could gently classify me as "rather peculiar" – with almost sympathy, & a lovely tolerance – so that I looked vaguely & almost lovingly at her two glittering rings & thought what a lovely wife she must be.

And then my dream ended – my sudden conversion to women was confirmed with each horrible petty officer in turn. They got worse until I came before the final one – an admiral or a sea-lord or something – he laughed me out sarcastically so that I boiled with rage – he didn't want such as me on a ship at sea – there wasn't a single job he considered me fit for;- I said sick-berth attendants were forbidden by the Geneva convention to carry arms & that I would do that – but no – he wouldn't have me on a ship. I hated him, not because he refused to have me in the Navy (I'd do badly there I'm sure) but because of his overlording sarcasm.

I felt a bit of a fool too I must confess, for I'm beginning to see it's a queer place for a CO. In or out – not because of principle, but for convenience; the CO is not wanted in military circles, a natural thing,

I suppose, & if he can't fulfil his condition as a land-worker through health or strength or incapacity or incompatibility etc he should join up altogether or go to prison. I haven't the faintest idea how to set about the latter, except stay off work for a few months & I haven't the money to do that. And anyway, it seems a vague kind of masochism that I dislike now, going to prison. So I'm still in a whirling uncertain miasma of ways & means. Anyway, the position now is – I'm not to be allowed in the Navy, the Army is full up & the RAF wants only air crews. So I expect a call-up for pit-work, but I shan't do it because it isn't my fault if the services won't have me, & I couldn't last for more than a month in the pits, & would only give trouble. I think I'll be left here, & I'll be quite content if only I can stick out at felling[…]

What a holiday – I enjoyed every minute of it – even the first night, arriving late, YMCA full up, nowhere to go, lost in London blackout. I picked up about midnight with two drunk RAF lads (tight I should say) trying to find the Salvation Army Red Shield Club, where they had two beds booked. We found it, but again, that was full, so I settled down in a dark corner of the lounge where many lads were trying to sleep on chairs sofas & the floor. I got a sofa, with a Polish soldier, head to feet fashion. About 1 o'clock a.m. the S.A. captain came round to sweep up. We were disturbed – the Pole said "Ach, dis de tord time I wake up!" We settled down, after helping a little, somewhat sleepily, but two Canadian airmen had apparently met after years apart – "Do you remember Wacky?" "Old Wacky – I'll say I do, the guy 'at used to knock around with Flossy – say, did he ever marry her?" – for hours on end it seemed, but I got to sleep. Next morning, I got a wash in a public lavatory, a breakfast somewhere, & got booked up at the YMCA for 3 nights, hired a towel, bought toothbrush & dentifrice, & settled in. I could have a bath every day with liquid soap provided. Boot polish & brushes there for me too, & most important, a good menu & cheap. I was happy as a king & work was far enough off – it never even entered my head. The next few days was usually morning constitutional in the parks etc… feeding birds & listening to the starlings' music under the porch at St Martin's. Afternoons, National Gallery or bookshop, & evenings shows. Ballet twice, Priestley's *They Came to a City* & *Heartbreak House*. I also went to the Studio I & saw a grand French film about the Russian Empress Catherine with

Danielle Darrieux as "Katia". In the grand tradition, I liked it very much.

The ballet was marvellous[...] Between the acts I went into the vestibule for a quiet smoke, feeling extremely happy, when this man looked at me, & I made the mistake of looking twice, then realized that standing alone as I was, with nothing to do, was apparently the sign of the few – I was waiting for anything that might turn up it seemed. I tried to look as though I'd never noticed anything, though the recognition of what I'd done unconsciously sent me vibrating with blushes. He passed once, back again, then over the gents' toilet, back again, & with one fearful blush from me (how much it would assure him, that blush) he spoke – something trivial like "Good show isn't it." He was a charming man, immaculately dressed in a lounge suit & well-groomed indeed. We talked trivialities & I began to be more at ease, but poor soul, he had to ask me, since he saw I was a Northerner, how long I was staying in London, & where. Exactly like the Baron[8]; that is, without appearing concerned in the least. Thank goodness I knew what was up – I said that was my last night, & I was getting a train North after the show, & looked appropriately crestfallen (it was better to lie because I knew he was edging round by now). And so, after a few more words, we went back to our seats, after he'd invited me to have a drink with him next interval. He was a fine fellow, but the other was obvious. I shall never stand so invitingly alone in vestibules again. Like all Sodomites, he took delight in shaking hands & bid me goodnight most effusively & hoped we should meet again – he was always at the ballet he said. And back in my room I breathed again. It is so hard to hurt these people, whose kindness & charm is no less sincere for its being the prelude to advances. I felt rather clever & socially accomplished in cooking up my immediate departure story[...]

East Witton, Monday [18 October 1943?]

[...] What with slyly taken days and pinched weeks and quite pleasant industrial complaints like tenosynovitis or something, I am having all the leisure I envied other people. My wrist is in the desirable position of not being able to do any heavy work, but it must be moved. All movement is desirable except that which aggravates it[…][9]

East Witton, Tuesday [26 October 1943?]

[…] If I don't get something done for Newcastle or Bradford this week, I'm doomed. Though it appears Ncle is not to have a Northern exhibition this year since on enquiry I found the next exh. on 15th is a Norwegian one.

Although I thought my wrist was quite better, the doctor made me grip his hand firmly and move my wrist, & it was far from well, so I have another week of grace – therefore content[…]

Your ideas over the weekend were more helpful than anyone's in conforming with my own. George [Jackson] is an optimist – I can go into the world as soon as war is over and just paint – I'll be a success & art school is unnecessary. Fred thinks an art school most helpful, almost essential, but his ideas on going to one are 1910 ideas. I've never asked Graham about it – he just presumes that Griffiths & I as landscape painters (to be) will just start (again 1910, less competition, or should I say, lower standard would do). Jimmy [Gale] thinks art school essential – ideas of getting into one include degrees, certificates etc with study of Latin (ye Gods!) subsidiary subjects like English & History etc… As I want mainly practical training, especially drawing, that put me in despair.

You were simple, to the point; more than the others, you grasped my ideas immediately & showed me even a prospectus. Anyway, seeing that my ideas can possibly be worked out, I'm determined now to carry them out somehow, by saving up for one thing, & working when possible. I must go to an art school – particularly life-drawing, painting & wood-engraving, because I should like in time to be an illustrator, with cross references in Felling Public Library catalogue. Another thing is that, being with mature artists as I now am, I am inevitably trying to start at the end instead of at the beginning. Coming back to Witton, I looked at a water-colour I was on with & realized that its complications were beyond me & I was trying too much. In an art school my correct pace would be set, I think. So an art school, probably King's, if they'll have me, it will be, for one to three years. Then I aim to take up work seriously if I'm any good, and there is always one outlet for work if sales are infrequent, as they must be at first, & that is the dealer. That is how Fred existed at first, at 5s a picture! Exhibitions, commissions, woodcuts & engravings and if I'm lucky, illustration, should help, and an artist, if [he] can exist, is content. He hasn't to depend on counting his money in thousands to be happy. There is, of course, one way in which an income is almost guaranteed – portrait painting, and we must see how that develops. At present, both interest & talent for it are non-existent, but it cannot be ignored. I don't think a portrait-painter has the pleasant easy, un-social life of the landscape-painter – he is more harassed, allowed little scope, & must compromise more – his income is the advantage. Landscape painting is freer, more soul-kindling if you like.

So there are my ambitions – do you think they are too big. The main thing is absolute singleness of mind – art as a career is so rare and precarious that a strong purpose & resolution must guide you, you mustn't take half-measures to save say, trouble or expense. That is why, if I obeyed my father's wishes & got my FLA[10], I should never get to the end of it. That is the world's idea of security & if an artist is troubled about security he'd better not start. Being an artist is like taking up a religious order – security must go overboard, poverty withstood if necessary. It is no good my crying out that my father should have been richer, that I should have been left some money etc… It would have made things easier, but their poverty & mine is perhaps an advantage. The harder a thing is to attain, the better it is, & the main thing is to attain it in spite of all[…]

East Witton, Thursday [28 October 1943?]

[…] I have a water-colour for Newcastle thank goodness which Fred likes & which Muriel described as having a "strange personality about it". Whatever that may mean. An old spreading beech of pale green, against the dark background of foliage, & with rich brown earth, covered with dead leaves. Supposed to be decent. I think I will soon hate it though, because I missed so much I wanted[…]

Fred & I talked about taking up art as a career. He seems to think it a step that's well worth it, but like me, he said it was like taking up a religious order. No Marriage or anything. He said he wanted to marry when he was 20 but couldn't till he was well over 40. And lots of other things which I must consider. But I want to do it, & probably shall[…]

East Witton, Wednesday [3 November 1943?]

[…] I have tried another lino-cut, black & white, but don't know what it prints like yet. They usually look marvellous as blocks & feeble as prints.

I have also painted a very grey autumnal water-colour of Coverham Bridge, but from an interesting point of view. You may like it, despite its greyness. It was on the dull misty day you mention, Friday.

My little oil of the moors is "coming" slowly, but without all the effect I wanted. In oils, I can see, strength of design is essential. The colour is decent, the brushwork too, but the design slightly weak I think[…]

East Witton, Monday [8 November 1943?]

I've been to Bolton for the weekend, so that is why I never got a letter written to you. I had a pleasant dreamy weekend, talking about Proust with Muriel & with George too, and on Sunday morning printing a lino-cut (more in the nature of an engraving though). You will be glad to hear (I hope) that Fred is most encouraging these days & everything I take to him he seems to like. He thinks my Coverham Bridge on a grey day "my high-water mark" so far. And I have to do more lino-blocks like this one, & so on & so on. Then George (who has your bad habit of passing on to me the nice things people say about me & withholding the nasty) said that Fred was sure I'd go further than Jim. He said that Jim had matured quickly as far as he could see, while I would mature more slowly & last longer. Yes, he really said that, so I'm quite bucked, & not so nervous about the future.

And yet, without false modesty, I think Coverham Bridge rather anaemic now. I don't think you would like it much either. In fact, though I had a fortnight off, I have very little to show for it, but if in that little Fred sees an improvement well & good[…]

Work is not so bad these days. I'm on a tractor & making the most of my "bad wrist" when felling is mentioned. I feel like a naughty child who refuses to eat porridge. I take up an axe & chop a little on the left hand, then start on the right as though with enthusiasm, groan suddenly & declare it's no good yet, & put the axe down as though in pain. So far it's working, but soon it'll be harder than felling. If it wasn't for John I'd never give in, but poor soul he is so hard-up, & he can't find another mate. Tom Allen took up with him but soon crocked & is off for a month. I feel rather selfish & yet I know what felling would do to me & it's got to stop, some time, so it must be now, if possible.

I'll send you a copy of the lino print when "it's published", in other word, "dry". It's very old-fashioned & Bewickish.

East Witton, Sunday [14 November 1943?]

[...] Tomorrow I may have to return to piece-work, since John is still without a mate, but I'm proving very awkward. If I'm told to prop on day-work, of course, I can't refuse, but it's the thin end of the wedge & piece work will follow. But it might turn out better, for so far the awkwardness is working quite well, & I find on reflection that the awkward ones get what they want in this firm, & I must try to keep it up, though it's hard to keep up being somewhat childish. And if it's otherwise, & I return to hard work, as I've said before, I realize that that is what I've to do for the duration & I shouldn't grumble because there's worse[...]

I think before I let you see my new lino print I'll try it in Indian Red. It's just an old hollow elm bole with fungoid growths & holes all over. Quite simply done, in the Bewick tradition. (Ahem.)[…]

Wensleydale was a haven of peace during Len's sojourn there. One night in Novem-ber 1943, however, the cost of war was brought home to him dramatically.

East Witton, Tuesday [23 November 1943]

[…] I have been to Bolton this weekend[…] I found Fred rather low, not having got any work done (?though) Muriel being there a week (don't ask me why not) [sic]. She had departed on Saturday morning,

Pen and ink sketch of a dead elm

and as he himself proceeded to Redmire for some provisions, he found he had a halfpenny in his pocket. So he had to get his art things out & paint a cottage in Redmire (commissioned) before he could buy any food. But still he couldn't get rations, so I found him eating boiled rice. You never saw such an improvident pair in your life. By now he'll have his rations, however, & alone he can spin them out. He never has either money or food for a rainy day, just lives from day to day & is quite content. When I say he was low, that was my reaction. He certainly didn't look low or under-nourished, but a vision of boiled rice was too much. But he was his old cheerful self and we laughed over it for hours. Can you imagine such a life though?[…]

Wednesday Last night was terrifying. I was awakened by an agonising roar in the sky, & yet when I woke, I realized it was not the power of the sound so much as its strangeness and agony. In less than a second it seemed, I was wide awake & listened anxiously to the steadingly [sic] increasing groan in the sky, growing louder & louder, until it grew into a terrifying moan, a big aeroplane diving helplessly in the night. It rapidly approached the fells and after a last loud roar of agony there was silence & I saw, behind Sowden Beck [beyond

Witton Fell, due south of East Witton] it seemed, flames leaping furiously, lighting the billowing smoke which seemed alarmingly near. One of our bombers, which I had seen going out at 4.30 from Leeming for 3 nights, had crashed, and I lay awake for hours wondering & feeling, as we only can in the night, the tragedy of those men, probably unable to leave the plane in its dive from a great height. I can never describe the sound, its note of agony, the strange silence and the tragic leaping of the flames. I lay awake for hours, & had just dozed off when it was time to get up. I learnt from someone else who had heard it that it was about 1.15 am, and yet so few heard or saw it that I must sleep more lightly than I'd supposed. I wanted to get up & go to the place, even though it was stormy outside, but I reflected that special constables & home guards would probably be there & my help unnecessary if any were possible at all. I was wrong, no one went up & so far mystery surrounds the whole affair. Nobody knows if the men were killed, if it was English or German even; only a plane crashed on the moors between Sowden Beck & Colsterdale.[11]

So I am tired, but that is trivial compared with the fate of those men, whether they lived or died, for it was a foul night.

[On reverse of sheet] P.S. Learnt that it was a Halifax bomber. The crew of eight were all killed[...]

[Main letter continues] I was glad to have your letter, more cheerful than the last; & also Jim's new poem. It has some great passages, some of his most mature work, which taken separately are most beautiful, the highest poetry, surely. As a whole, it is a loose, disconnected work, but a rhapsodic flow holds it together. If I had my way, though, I would omit certain passages, & ensure, or rather confirm the sincerity of the whole thing – for some of it is already mine. I am mostly unworthy, as far as Jim goes, of dedicated poetry, but whoever H.R. is, it is not for the best to give him what has already been given to me. Please don't say this to Jim – I shall perhaps mention it myself. It is not an aesthetic criticism, only it seems for me (if for no one else) that one of the loveliest passages of this work is quite insincere. Of course, one of Jim's methods is to incorporate small fragmentary pieces into a subsequent long poem – thus there are pieces written at Jervaulx which I recognise in 'The Drowned Sailor'. But this was a personal poem – a 'Letter to Leo'.

Perhaps I am jealous of something which I never deserved in the first place, but for me, little pieces like that letter & a poem like 'The Glass Fable' are treasures.

But the poem is charming altogether & enhances all that he has written. It will surely be published[…]

Len was fascinated by James Kirkup's poetry; he had been present at the drafting of some of the verses, and his feelings about them were bound up in his complex relationship with Kirkup. During November he did an analysis of the poems which, as he readily admitted, was subjective. The essay does not appear to have survived.

East Witton, Sunday [28 November 1943]

I have finished my essay on Jim's poetry at last, starting afresh and writing in one almost unbroken spell yesterday afternoon & evening. That is the way I should like to write, if I were a writer, for the other straining painful method of bits & pieces is not for me. I am too indolent for that. So the essay is complete, though rather inadequate, because words cannot express what I feel about some aspects of Jim, & in order the [sic] make up for the inadequacy I have enlarged on things where I might perhaps have been more (?sure). Indeed, I know I am biased – my knowledge is too small for me to pronounce judgment; my praise is endless & biased, because that is how he affects me, but by ultimate judgment I may be far from the truth. So if I appear to have presumed in comparing Jim with Rilke, it is because I felt the deep parallel between them, & lack of knowledge makes me see similarities which may not exist[…] And the prospect of writing so thrills & fascinates me that the day must come when I must deliberately strike out the incentives (like reading & even serious letter-writing) and devote myself singly to graphic art if I'm to do anything, for I'm not a writer by a long chalk – it only tempts me like Eve's apple, & would lead me nowhere.[12]

So the essay, more than a critical judgment, is rather a personal interpretation, & may be entirely arbitrary. Everybody so far who has read Jim's work has apparently failed (or not wished) to get beyond the brilliance & beauty and strangeness of his language & imagery, and at most have only got glimpses of the whole truth. What is needed is a complete ed. of his poems to date with an introductory interpretation & criticism on the lines I've set out by some authority like [Hugh l'Anson] Fausset[...]

The whole thing lacks the precision & tightness of prose that I like, but as I say I'm not a writer. I hope anyway that it helps any who may read Jim's work, & you are free to lend out typescripts if you think they'll be appreciated. Because I don't think it will be published anywhere. The magazine Jim mentioned sounded terribly mythical & impossible. If you can find time to type out a few copies, I'd be pleased to have one, & you can send one direct to Jim? Why don't you start a typing agency?

I got your letter on Friday but strange to say didn't open until Saturday morning. On Friday I was trying to fell trees with a boy (John is ill), helping the only girl left to measure (2 ill), loading timber on to waiting wagons with far too few men, & what with shouting instructions (the foreman is ill) to the rather stupid crew, I just about collapsed on Friday afternoon, & never felt so ill in my life[...]

I was the last of the timber-fellers, & fell myself (but I feel still victorious in recovering so quickly, for I was absolutely prostrate for a few awful hours). The last measurer fell with me. It has had this advantage – that these last few days I've worked like a hero & kept things going (since those left were what might be called the "incompetents") & I think I have been largely reinstated in the bosses' favour even though I wasn't bothered. There has been a slight cloud over me at work which isn't serious but is uncomfortable[...]

East Witton, Sunday [5 December 1943]

[...] After giving you the essay on Jim, I'm beginning to think it is rather vague and ambiguous and I hardly think Jim himself will approve. I have missed various points. I might have explained more why he individually, & the poet generally, is so lonely in the world today, and in addition, not have developed [sic] along such apparently despairing & pessimistic lines. There is no emptiness & pessimism about the modern (or it is sufficiently transcended to be merely a starting point) but people tend only to regard the poet as a despairing, intolerant cynic, and actually he is nothing of the sort[...]

What you say of Jim personally is quite typical I'm afraid, and if you're to be Jim's friend, you must be prepared to be "used". You may be cross with me, so improvident myself, but I have given Jim money from time to time, "lent" it I should say, but I know I'll never have it returned. But I understand that, and it never crops up in our minds – nor does the fact (it does hurt sometimes) that he only writes to me when he is in a loving mood, or wanting something, or merely feeling dutiful. One just has to accept – and I know that once you've offered to type for him he'll always "use" you. But behind all his frequent distractions, his neglect & fragmentary allegiance, he still is a friend sincerely – it is only because he [is] so open to every new attraction, so wholeheartedly involved in the most transient affair, that old friends are momentarily forgotten. He can't help [it], and at least one is not wholly forgotten, so I accept the rest.

All the men round here who were interviewed with me for the Navy have got their papers. All but me – so I'm probably for the mines. That too I'm beginning to accept, and I shall go meekly, and lose the last of [Théophile] Gautier's riches "*le beau soleil*".[13] In some respects, if it comes, I see it as a sort of punishment for weakness & broken vows. And perhaps too, I may get more money, because I'm beginning to realize that here, if I'm to clothe myself decently and live, it is quite impossible to save for all those dreams after the war. In fact, I'll have to accept that too, for I see now it is all but impossible to live on nothing for two years after the war, and I shall humbly return to librarianship, which beside art, cannot interest me much. I'm at least fortunate in having such a good job to fall back to. It is a pity librarianship & painting are so incompatible. Even here in the ideal country, how little I get done – so how much would I do in Durham, from which it would take hours to escape?[…]

Len went home twice in December, including for Christmas. Mona fed him "lavishly", somehow managing to present him with goose on the second visit. Back in Wensleydale, Len began 1944 attempting to work in linocut.

East Witton, Sunday [2 January 1944?]

[…] I've been on all day with a lino-cut of Honesty. But I cannot

Len and Mona relax in the park

convey, in such a hard strict medium, the delicate transparent beauty
of the stuff and only a Japanese artist could do what I've tried I think.
So it's a failure, but it was good trying it out and, like any attempt in
Art, it made me gaze at and analyse and finally almost worship the
object until I'm mad about Honesty[…]

*All too predictably, Len was dissatisfied with his linocut of Honesty when he printed
it out – "It was awful," he wrote to Mona on 4 January. He was rather happier
with three prints he did of a "Hollow Elm", "perfect prints in the correct colour
this time". He felt he should draw at nights, but found it too hard "beneath Mrs
D's curious eye", and once more he found himself wishing for a place where he
could work on his own. "What I want to do, by the way, is wood-engraving, but
the materials are unobtainable. If you ever come across anybody who has any, let
me know please," he requested. In mid-month Len visited Tyneside again.*

East Witton, Monday [24 January 1944?]

[…] I found my weekend at home most valuable, and I enjoyed being
there[…] All the same (since I tell you almost everything) I must tell
you that weekends at home do "put on me" to some extent. I'm terribly hard up, but I don't want you to take this as a hint, or I can't tell

you anything. I must get pulled round somehow, and of course I'm inevitably rash at weekends at home. They are worth it, but I must get pulled together, or I shan't come home till March. Please understand – I want to come home, and I can come home, but I can't go on like this, and I find that a few quiet weekends at Witton are all I need to rake a few pounds together[…]

The only alternative is piece-work and I don't want to ask for it. It just about kills me, and if I'm asked I may even refuse – but I certainly shan't ask.

The difficulty of course is sending in to Newcastle exhibition. Coming back in train & bus with eyes shut against the painful half-lights, I thought & thought & came round to Griffiths' point of view that I'm too eager, & haven't yet painted anything worth exhibiting – it's not false modesty – after looking at such things as I've seen this weekend, I realize how far, far behind I am, how trivial, drab and uninteresting, how far even from being myself yet, or as they say in text books, from "finding myself". So I'm not bothered about exhibitions much, for this year anyway, and if nothing goes in, I don't mind. Fred says I must, that's all, if only to keep my name in the catalogue. So if you think it's worth it, I leave you to be my agent to send in (via my Father) what you like[…]

Len had long settled into the comfortable assumption that he would not be called up. He had come to the conclusion that he would stay in Wensleydale for the rest of the war, and that he would probably be able to have another try at painting in the summer. So it was "a great shock" to receive his call-up notice.

East Witton, Wednesday [26 January 1944?]

I had a rude awakening tonight – I hope I don't upset you as I was. My calling-up notice was here for me to enter the Pioneer Corps, for non-combatant duties. I have to appear at some Hotel in Buxton, wherever that is, next Thursday, 3 Feb.

I am still too numb to feel or think anything, but underneath there is a bit of shame I think. I'm not at all proud of it, and I know how much I am disappointing you. But as I say, I am too numb to go into excuses and apologies.

It is a great shock to me, needless to say, because I'd quite presumed I was to be left alone. You know what I was expecting to do this summer – it was to be an industrious summer here, with lots of painting if I went on as I am without piece-work.

Well, I've asked for it – I can't grumble – and if you and my parents aren't more overwrought than myself, I should manage to change over quietly without any fuss.

I'll be home sometime next week, unless anything prevents me.

From Non-Combatant Corps to 224 PFA

The great divide in Len's war years is clearly the point where he joined the army. Beforehand he had felt his life to be aimless, individualistic and even selfish. He had too much time to think and he suffered for it. In the army the ordinary soldier's life was organised for him and introspection was discouraged, although that did not stop Len's moody ruminating in idle moments. The main gain for him was that his exile from his own generation came to an end, yet he only found true companionship when he met a kindred spirit at one of the camps to which he was posted. One thing in Len's life remained constant – the regular flow of letters between Mona and himself.

> 97007375 Pte Jones L, Holding Wing, Lismore Camp,
> Buxton, Derbyshire [No date – 9 February 1944]

My second day has ended better than the first, and I'm writing this in a pleasant mood of weariness in the WVS [Women's Voluntary Service?] Canteen. It's a big hall used as a canteen, with tables all over, & a serve yourself bar, where you can get tea without sugar (I loathe the Army sweetened stuff.)

I hardly know where to start this letter – there are so many little details which would interest you. I feel comfortable at last in khaki – I felt terribly clumsy & conspicuous yesterday & this morning, but lots of marching & drilling have made my battledress less stiff. I found the forage cap most difficult to wear – but that too has found its place.

The first day was spent in getting fitted, waiting about a lot and finally being billeted in an empty house about 200 yds from the camp. The camp is Nissen huts, & we drill & eat there. The billets seemed awful at first. Empty rooms, with torn wall-paper, bare floor and so on, and bunks with steel bands criss-crossed for mattress. We filled our palliasses with straw, & after an evening in the canteen, slept rather fitfully – the palliasse was neither long enough or [sic] broad enough. I used my kit-bag for a pillow, but today I got a pillow of straw fixed upon 4 blankets.

This morning the game started – reveille 6.30 – dress in denhams [sic], wash & shave, strip bed, fold blankets neatly in one certain way, fold palliasse, tidy kit bag up, put everything in one bag or other & leave everything piled neatly on your bed beside the blankets. There's a row if any single article is left lying about. The floor must be kept clean too.

The billet – two adjoining 4 storey houses of the boarding-house type, are occupied by 2 squads of NCC [Non-Combatant Corps] men – about 60 men or more. A sergeant & corporal in charge of each squad. The sergeant is noisy & a stickler for discipline and I've been in trouble a few times – the main thing was that I didn't report to him when I was sent of [sic] the billet. I was sent there with two others – we found nobody & just found ourselves a room. At night he hounded us out and gave a terrific lecture. And I had no buttons on the pockets of my denhams – they are different to battledress buttons & I hadn't been issued with enough. In 24 hrs, I was supposed to know exactly how to obtain things.

Then I couldn't get anybody to tell me where to obtain brown paper to send my clothes home – everybody said the army did it for you, & yet nobody did & nobody knew where to get paper. So I ventured to speak to the sergeant – another lecture on my not report-ing to him, & on how he would have seen to it if I'd reported properly – he may get me some paper tomorrow.

All in parenthesis – 7.20 parade & march to camp, breakfast (porridge and bacon) 7.30, Parade 8.30. I had to join the squad as though I'd joined last week with the rest. So – ATT-ENNN-SHUN sounded funny & isn't as easy as it looks. My tummy, hands, head, feet, practically everything had to be adjusted by the sergeant; then marching "Swing those arms JONES" across the parade square - I felt small – the various turns, turning on the march, which is very confusing. It's all very stupid. But I'm quickly getting used to things and learning how to be thick-skinned – the khaki, in a squad of others, seems to eschew all personality, individuality & incredibly, it seems, you become just a mechanical soldier.

10-11 PT in pumps & vests & shorts, in a field. Then cocoa at the camp. Drill & marching till 12.30 dinner 1 (not bad these dinners & PT made me hungry & I got my fill). 2 Parade for PT at a gym across the town – I hated that, we kicked up a dust & played the stupidest team games in which I was bad because I was bored & tired. That hour & a half was rotten, what [with] the noise of the shouting men & instructors – a medicine ball hit me full in the face & I got to swearing point, but after tea (the teas are moderate) & a wash & denhams off, I felt better & here I am.

I shan't go into my thoughts (nil) & reactions – yesterday the morale of my two room mates & myself was below zero, we reckoned, but it's better now.

They are fine lads, both JOHNS – one an old NCC back to centre for re-posting, the other just out of gaol for desertion from the Pioneers proper.

I don't think there'll be an opportunity for either painting or reading (unless there's a change – there's no incentive to stay in that depressing billet, and the various canteens are all noisy.) However we'll see.

All I know is I've been a fool but we'll pass that[…]

There's one thing – there's no time to brood about things here except for physical discomfort & immediate mental reactions to the ruling stupidity. Still the NCOs are quite decent – our corporal is OK. They are all proper Pioneers of course – their feeble jokes are very boring.

The only regiment here really is the Pioneer Corps of which we are a branch, I suppose. There are many continentals, Jews etc & the camp canteen is queer for the different accents[…]

No 1 Squad NCC, Holding & Training Wing, No 6 TCPC,
Lismore Camp, Buxton Sunday [13 February 1944?]

[…]I had a wretched day yesterday after inoculation on Friday, but this morning I felt fit again with just a sore throat. If you want to know my official progress in the army, I was cleaning the sergeants' room & managed to peep in his 'record of progress' book and I found the remarks "Works well. Good, clean." How's that. Other comments were similar, some were rather laughable like "Very awkward" – "Lacks body control." "Feet impede good marching."

His comments on marching are usually sarcastic but often funny. He is worst before breakfast, when he marches us down to camp. "Come on, waken up – yer like a lot of water-lilies" or "Yer like snowflakes fluffin' abart" or "What yer wearin' Gunter – seven-league boots? Smarten your step lad," & so on. But he's a good man for training, being an old soldier, ex Border Regiment (a smart tough lot) and our squad is about twice as smart as No 2 Squad. Not that I care, except that it's better for yourself to please the sergeant. Our corporal is a good sort, and he is the only pipe smoker besides myself, so we help each other out. An ounce of baccy, with your weekly coupon issue, is 1/10d in the NAAFI.

After inoculation, a soldier is CB [confined to barracks] for 48 hours & excused duties, so I haven't been able to use my weekend to see Buxton[…]

Afternoon. Just been for dinner. Excellent, really good, Yorks pudding, potatoes, roast potatoes, cabbage, very tender meat, stew plums & custard, coffee, with bread & cheese if you wanted them. How's that? But I mustn't gloat over food, except that it is good here and well served.

At 3, I'll be a free man again, i.e. able to leave billets. I'll just have time for a walk then tea at the WVS then John and I will have the evening before us – what, I don't know, but being an old soldier, he always knows what to do & where to go. He was in the RASC [Royal Army Service Corps] for 12 months, found he didn't want to fight, deserted & stayed in his house for 14 months before surrendering himself to the Army again. He was sentenced to 18 months but only served 4 months when he was released to join the NCC.

It is glorious to feel fit again after inoculation, which is like a bad dose of flu. Yesterday the Army was like Hell, & I was to be in it forever, it seemed – now it isn't such a bad life, except for the loss of liberty[…]

Being excused of duties saved me from a route march yesterday. It was supposed to be 10 miles & turned out 15. The lads came back mostly crippled with their new boots & one or two had bleeding feet. The squad as a whole was in such a wretched state as it marched back into Buxton that the whole town is talking & the sergeant has been on the mat this morning.

The Army life is such a vast contrast to civilian life, & the change so vigorous that I have been preoccupied with my own little troubles. Reading, thinking, sensible conversation etc are out of the question. In any case, of our squad of 30, 22 are Brethren so I'm taboo, more or less. But I've learnt to eat, sleep & live or exist without thinking or feeling according to Army requirements. Perhaps when I'm posted I can adjust myself more; it depends on whether or not the job is tying [sic] - smoke screen is, others not so. We'll see.

And now to polish my brasses, dubbin my boots, blanco my anklets & haversack etc. What a life[…]

Route march 20 miles on Tuesday – steel helmets, respiration packs – phew! Think of me – or my feet.

Buxton, Friday [18 February 1944?]

I've had hardly any leisure this week. My birthday was spent on fire picquet duty, which meant, besides the ordinary day, peeling spuds from 6-9.30 at night[…]

I finished the route march sans blisters, sores, or aches, but your heart would have gone out to some of the poor lads without my advantages of keeping fit lately. They are so poor in wind and fitness that even I excel and march in the leading rank. So you can tell how bad some are[…]

No 14 Co NCC, Church Farm, Marston Moreteyne [sic], Bedford
Thursday [24 February 1944?]

I don't think I'll ever write an adequate letter to you in the Army – there never seems to be the opportunity. So you'll forgive me, I'm sure, if I write infrequently and not at length. I feel I often forget to answer your letters – little things you ask about & tell me about. If I do, it isn't because I don't appreciate your letters (you cannot measure how valuable letters are in the Army) – it is because my mind doesn't work the same way in the army, or something like that.

Now my "training" is over, in shorter time than usual, & I'm in a proper company, in Section 9 with 13 other men. There are 7 or 8 other sections, and the whole company, or rather its headquarters is established in Nissen Huts round a farm with the officers in a big private house. About 150 men I imagine or perhaps more[...]

The camp is nowhere in particular; just near (¾ mile) from Marston M. a queer village with a WVS canteen run by gossipy (mouths full) women whom I rather like, though not so charming as Buxton's pleasant middle-class women, who on occasion shied away from NCCs.

Today I washed up and cleaned Dining Hall No1 (there are 2). What a nauseating job, cleaning refused porridge, tomato sauce, bacon rind in the mass from plates. 4 of us were on that. Then pulled some iron railings down for some unknown reason. Then dug a hole 6 x 5 by 4 [feet?] deep. Then swept up some refuse & tins and etc & carried it in an old dustbin till our arms ached, to the hole, which we filled, & then we piled the clay back on the top. But what a long afternoon. Dinner 1300 hrs as they call it, Tea not until 17.30 hrs but waiting for various parties to return it was nearly 6 before we started.

The camp is very bored – nearly every man I've met is thoroughly "browned off" and lots are volunteering for the mines. The main job is attending to food dumps, teeming rail trucks & loading lorries with it etc... Perhaps I'll be on that tomorrow. The air of disillusionment, almost despair, is appalling – all humour is ironic, unless, as with some veterans, you have got to the stage when you have ceased to think, hope or feel completely, you can indulge in the normal horse-play & rowdyism.

There is nothing to do at nights – the NAAFI is a long cold place, therefore bleak & unpopular – the WVS is homely, but too popular & the crush is hopeless, [therefore] letters impossible – nowhere else. Bedford is 7 miles away, with no means of communication besides bicycle. The billets consist of beds (palliasses) on the floor, no form, chair or table so again letters are difficult. I am writing this in the NAAFI & am standing the cold better than I'd thought.

I hope I don't appear too depressed – I'm rubbing along pretty well, but not enjoying it one little bit. I only long (in my quiet moments) for a few hours of quiet civilian life, of freedom.

And so many people are the same just now all over the world (&

worse than I am) that I wonder however a war was carried on[…]

There is an Italian POW camp, about 50 yards along the road from us. The Army's method of flocking birds of a feather. A young 2nd lieutenant (Pioneer) in charge of us on our journey warned George Otter & I (we were alone with him & two NCOs in a compartment) warned us [sic] that the Army's deliberate intention was to kill the normal pursuits of an intelligent man, such as reading or even thinking, & that we had to fight that. I thought it good of him. But what can a man do – he can't fight the whole stupid Army. I've stopped reading & I'm sure it's awfully difficult to write a letter[…]

Marston Moretaine, Thursday [2 March 1944?]

Life is becoming increasingly monastic and I feel terribly restless tonight. It is reveille, breakfast, parade, work, dinner, work, tea & evening reading or writing. Incredibly sober – I thought I was to change & really be still inside for a while. But tonight I'm restless – I don't know why[…]

Still, I'm a good boy. I've read two books in a week – less than a week. And I've been appointed to the staff for 10 days. What do you think of my appointment. Don't forget I have no brain! So I'm not pay-clerk, post-clerk, medical orderly, sergeants' mess orderly, officers' mess orderly, leave clerk, joiner, gardener, painter, store clerk or all the other staff jobs like driver or company office clerk. No, I'm company stoker. I rise before the others and get the fires going for all the hot water for cooking, dish-washing, tea & officers' & sergeants' ablutions etc... and keep them going all day & keep the cisterns full & see there's always some water boiling etc... Keep the grates cleaned and remove ashes from all fires including the cookhouse. It's tiring but there are advantages. On the staff, you know how you're on & what job you've got – you are freer, & can use your time better, i.e. shave in Army time, write letters even put your bed down & get dressed ready for evening before you've finished. All that in your "off" moments, when the fires, 7 as a rule, are all burning merrily & cisterns are full. And you don't appear on parades[…]

Today it has been a warm spring day with sunshine all day & planes flying busily off to Europe. We see all these hundreds of planes go off to Berlin – Flying Fortresses mainly – leaving little streams like flares that drop in the blue sky like bent pipe-cleaners, for signals of some description[…]

Oh, when will this war end. I'm so tired, tired waiting, tired of doing nothing. Everybody is, I suppose.

Marston Moretaine, Saturday [4 March 1944?], 3 p.m.

[…] John[1] has seen the psychiatrist & is being transferred to No10 Coy [Company] at Bulford (nr Salisbury) – his old coy. On Monday. I hope to follow him again because the Field Ambulance I'm trying to join is at Bulford.

In your parcel you sent me an interesting article in *Argosy* on the very thing & as you talked about Tony & his parachute jumping in your letter, I wondered if you'd guessed that was what I'd volunteered for, since in [the] article it was an RAMC unit. The Field Ambulances 224 & 227 are airborne & I volunteered 3 weeks ago. I passed the first medical test & am awaiting developments. I am very suspicious of myself however, because the fact that the thought of jumping doesn't scare me much just now makes me think I may be scared all at once & refuse. At first, before I'd volunteered, my imagination worked horrors, & I was scared stiff. But as soon as I'd volunteered, the fear went. I decided to try for Airborne RAMC duties (if I dare) a week or so after joining up, because I could see NCC was going to be useless, boring & a mere waste of time till the war was over. RAMC, however your conscience lies, is undoubtedly useful, however, and humanitarian. It is a bit hollow to talk of patching up soldiers to fight again. I can't argue, but I hope to join RAMC. The chances are pretty thin – medical exams galore, lack of vacancies, and so on. Perhaps I shan't get in. So it's better not to tell my parents until I'm in and got my wings up[2] (if at all). My last night at Buxton was great with an ex-FA 227 man who had had to ask for release for compassionate reasons, because his wife was very ill, & worrying. He was allowed to keep his wings, however, because he'd done all the training, including 12 jumps, 8 in training and 4 on courses. He talked to me all night it seemed (he came to sleep in my room at Buxton) & told me every little detail, the training, personal reactions, the recurring terror of jumping

& the ecstasy after the 'chute opens. So I know all about it & have no delusions.

I'm sick to death of stoking. My hands are black (that's why these sheets are grubby). I never really feel clean. The S-M [sergeant-major?] thinks I'm a real tough navvy, his best navvy – I'm sure that's what he thinks – "no brains, but he'll do any kind of manual work" I can imagine him saying. What am I to do? I suppose that's all I am really, because I seem quite unable to keep up the clean spruce appearance of other office blokes & such like. I'm always more timber-faller & navvy than librarian or artist(!) I wish I wasn't. Life becomes furiously physical – work, eat, football, sing & be cheerful & laugh & joke but for God's sake, don't think. I daren't think, but it is a job not to – I just had to burst into song again – don't think, it's fatal. Because a bloke like me should be very unhappy here – so I don't think or I might be[…]

[No address] Monday [6 March 1944?]

[…]There is one more Private JONES (A.G.) in the company; an unpleasant loud-mouthed Methodist Welshman. Another Welshman Meadows, equally Methodist & noisy. Another, (?Hans) Evans who is the perfect Welshman the intellectual and artist. He is marvellous, something like Myrddin Jones, but less temperamental, I think. We get on well, and he is an authority on Welsh – declares, by the way, that Welsh blood predominates in me (I've never been able to find out where our family came from). Anyway, on the strength of my "Welsh blood", he has invited me to a big St David's Day evening at Bedford Toc H on Wednesday[…]

Marston Moretaine, Monday [13 March 1944?]

I'm a lucky man – I was one of 6 left behind, at 2.0 pm parade to do fatigues in camp. George Otter and I rushed thro' our dishes, sweeping up & spud peeling, & made a successful withdrawal to our huts, where I'm now writing this at 4. Pray the S-M won't come round prowling – tho' we've finished our jobs, he's a genius at making others, such as digging the garden etc.

On Saturday he picked me because it says "Timber-Faller" in the Army Records, to go for the rations with the Quarter-Master's Corporal. It meant hoisting sacks of potatoes, whole sheep etc on to the van, but we had to tour almost the whole of Bedfords. to get them. About 3 hours riding, 20 minutes work, ½ hour in luxury over sugarless tea & buns in Bedford. There are some pleasant parts in Bedfords. after all, and I enjoyed the ride. The reward of being supposed a big strong brute. It's queer – nobody credits me with any brain because my last job was felling. Have I any?[...]

I was at the St David's supper on Wed, on duty Thursday & undergoing a special medical exam in Bedford on Fri evening. So I haven't had much leisure. The exam was preliminary to my application for RAMC. They wouldn't send in the application to War Office unless I was specially fit. Even now, I shall only go on a waiting list pending vacancies in Field Ambulance 224 & 227 (unarmed, ex NCC stretcher-bearers). There is a rigorous medical exam before I can enter, because it's a special unit. So I may never get in. I'm hoping though, because RAMC is the finest unarmed work in the Army & is much superior to the normal NCC drudgery[...]

Marston Moretaine, Sunday [26 March 1944?]

Forgive me for being so long in writing. In the face of your daily letters it seems unforgivable, but if you'd seen how busy we've all been you'd understand.

First 450 trucks to be emptied & so many to be filled – that meant my rest day on Wed was cancelled because the SM couldn't afford a man to replace me. Cancelled for the same reason on Thurs & Fri, and only when the cook-corporal informed him that I hadn't had any time off for a fortnight did he offer me Sunday. I rushed through work Sat morning & by dint of pleading got an after-duty pass to ship off to London, where I'm writing this in the YMCA at 11.30 am.

Second, I've had to shift my things into HQ hut where I now live & sleep. I am definitely in the staff now & have been issued with a lanyard for some vague reason[...]

Bedford, Sunday noon [9 April 1944?]

[…] Tomorrow morning I have an interview with the Major about my application for Airborne RAMC. It's time I was away, but the WO [War Office?] won't take me simply, but only with other 5, from all the NCC in the country. So there can't be many volunteers. I'm hoping the Major can use his influence. After all my keenness I may refuse to jump. Such is life[…]

[No address] Monday [10 April 1944?]

[…] I'm staying in the hut tonight because Joe Barton has scrounged the wireless from the Italians. It is really ours, but theirs is broken, & even POWs come before conchies[…]³

I haven't told you everything about the NCC – there is too much - besides the little discomforts & the autocratic system of the Army, the NCC, the lowest corps of the British A has many little hardships, psychological hardships such as the radio touch. There is an alien (refugee Jew) attached section – they never do picquet duty, which means the onus of guarding the camp is on the remaining 3 NCC sections. The aliens regularly finish work early & are in camp ready, washed & changed & beds down when we come in. That happened last night for instance. Their arrogance is painful – they have the greatest opinion of themselves because of the super class distinction, combatant as against non-combatant.

And with that my mind's an utter blank. Something has to happen shortly or I'm going to be in a pickle – given up painting or even thinking about it, given up writing letters, given up reading, given up everything I lived for and I'm living a mere existence of nothingness. It's no good blaming the war or bad luck & such like – it's something in myself, though perhaps it's in my generation, because other fellows are like that, & if it is then war and its precursors, slumps, booms and upgathering war clouds are partly to blame. We weren't old enough to appreciate fully what peace there was in the years *entre deux guerres*. Our own rise to manhood coincided with the preparation & acceleration of a war so it is perhaps to blame. And after nearly 5 years of conscription we have reached the awful moment of hopelessness – no hope for liberty again, or at least in those precious years of youthful enthusiasm. Therefore no object in life, all the roots gone – it is no use hoping and planning while everything depends upon the abolition of conscription. And we haven't the spirit to fight against it. Oh, when once I stop to think more, I could weep, not for myself alone, but for the others, and I am only glad of this in the NCC; that I am among the very fellows that are indicative of the hopelessness, despair and aimlessness of my generation, and I share in their despondency & in the efforts to alleviate it[…]

We're tired, fogged, incapable of thought & peaceful living, and without hope. After a momentary peep at a better existence after the slump, we've returned quickly to 'The Waste Land', till all we can say as we dazedly look round is

> This is the way the world ends
> This is the way the world ends
> This is the way the world ends
> Not with a bang but a whimper.

I am sorry this letter has gone all screwy, I'd better close and wish you a happy birthday once again and all the best.

Len had settled into a pattern of one letter a week, finding that he had neither time nor energy to write more often in response to Mona's more or less daily missives. Sometimes, his letters took two or three days to write because of noise, interruptions and lack of privacy. Such was the case with his last letter from Marston Moretaine, begun on 17 April. "Sorry about this – I feel awful about your letters and other people's too," he apologised. By the time he next wrote the company had moved to a camp near Rugby.

9 Section, No 14 Coy NCC, Willoughby nr. Rugby
Saturday [22 April 1944?]

What a day! One big hectic struggle with masses of men boarding & alighting trains, corporals shouting & raising the ire of train passengers & making little heroes of us. And when we get here – a big, drab hutment camp with railway sidings, huge sheds for food stores, concrete roads and (I imagine) between them all, acres of potential

mud. 1,000 men, RES[4], RASC [Royal Army Service Corps], Pioneers
& NCC. No village nearby, Rugby 7 miles away, unless you trespass
& flaunt camp regulations by going along the nearby railway into
Rugby 4 mils. 1 rest day a week strictly, i.e. no long weekends from
Sat noon, all day passes from reveille to 23.59 hours, & not from AD
[active duty?] night previous. District as featureless as before. There's
going to be another big rush for the mines, and I'm starting a big new
last offensive on the Major for RAMC, as soon as the company gets
settled in. We are all pining away for our little company camp at
Marston which we thought so horrible[…]

Stalag 29 [sic], Monday [1 May 1944?]

[…] I've been looking through some of your recent letters and found
much I haven't attended to – questions to be answered, comments
invited etc. All sorts of queer questions like "Do I think the same about
women as George Horne!"[5] The truth is I don't know the first thing
about women. If I flirt (rarely, you'll grant) I usually receive a final
rebuff; if I look at a beauty, I find them ordinary, humdrum; if I seek
to level them to the dust, I find strange sparks of beauty & intelligence;
if I return money to one I am rapped on the knuckles gently. Never
mind. I can't answer that question[…]

  For myself & for your information I'm a very chaste soldier – never
look at a woman & can't raise any interest. I think my subconscious
reason for joining the Army was to find a close male friend – I haven't
had one ever, except an exquisite little "Farraj & Daud"[6] friendship
of schooldays. Ask Mother about Robbie Tomlinson. But the Army
yields nothing except a universal brotherhood which I do cherish – a
wonderful brotherly feeling which I yearned for probably in my more
or less solitary existence at Witton[…]

  Stalag 29 (because we call it that). Its real name, but I'm not
supposed to tell you, is SRD 29 Supply Reserve Depot

[No date – 5 May 1944?]
[…] Saturday night (on stand-by duty)
Have just heard that a recent interview with the Major over my trans-

fer has drawn a blank, so I'm taking the law into my own hands & writing personally to the ADMS[7] i/c Airborne RAMC. It's strictly against regulations so I'm risking a court martial but I am banking on the fact that I have a good case.

Also on Orders today is a paragraph from a letter from Eastern Command informing men that it can now be stated that leave is cancelled on account of the coming invasion.[8]

Also on Orders today that men will not wear woollen underwear w.e.f. Sunday[…]

Monday

I am acting St Peter, i.e. acting courier to a sergeant on gate picquet. He must never leave the gate to the depot, while I run any errands he requires. Messages so far include fetching his soap and towel, fetching milk to make tea, fetching "break" and fetching the adjutant for an incoming convoy from the Army Group. (Better be careful!) I am on duty 24 hours ex 9 am this morning, and I have to sleep when I can because I have 2-2 hours guard to do during the night when 4 other men come to help me. So I've already had a doze & now, before dinner, I'll write to you. Nice job![…]

Tuesday morning I was suddenly too busy in the Guard Room to write any more. A poor fellow caught in "unlawful possession of one Army blanket" was given 84 days detention and we had charge of him till the glasshouse van came for him this morning. Worse still, a man from 7th Coy was brought to us awaiting hospital van this morning because he had gone mad & couldn't sleep without a light. We made him comfortable & settled down to watch both in turns. The prisoner, an ordinary political CO, was sadly cut-up and I felt sorry for him – the sergeant did too, because the sentence was hopelessly out of proportion to the crime & was only laid in because he was NCC. The other was a poor Welshman who spoke very little English, had just lost both parents & gone low. He was quite harmless – his one tantrum was to collect bits of bread & tinned pilchard on to his plate in great piles, all mixed up, put them under his bed & then go to sleep on top of his bed with only his boots off, serving us with a horrible odour of pilchards & sweaty feet. He got up at 2 am & had a huge meal of bread & cheese, though we wanted to make him go back to bed[…]

Barby Camp [No date – Friday, 12 May 1944?]

[…] Sunday We've had a hard day today and everybody is "browned off". Working on a Sunday is worse even than working on a Saturday, I think. Tomorrow 80 rail trucks have to be filled with condensed milk, so we'll probably work after tea because 80 is a lot. The normal goods train is usually about 50 or 60 trucks so you can imagine how many trucks these are. How we all hate this place. Yet we cannot analyse why this place, more than any other, is getting us down. It is all wired round like a concentration camp & the discipline is often childish. It is well over a mile to get on to the road, and the RASC officers are swines, though our own are good & as browned off as we are. The RASC is a repository for old-womanish officers – fussy NCOs and its own silly little rules are innumerable – all mistakes (& there are many due to their bad organisation) are blamed on the NCC, & we are often cursed before an officer for an offence which wasn't ours. So there is a state of suppressed rebellion. I'm afraid the food is shocking too, and often not enough. But don't send anything thinking that is a hint, & don't tell Mother, because she'd worry needlessly. I'm becoming a little out-of-hand, & may shortly be on a charge for dumb insolence or something because some of my "Yes Sirs" "No Sirs" etc are deliberately sarcastic.

The leave cancellation hit a few rather badly – those of us who can't go home & back within 24 hours. Several, about half-a-dozen in our company alone have taken French leave & have been punished accordingly. Of course it's worth CB to have a day at home. But I want to keep a clean sheet in the remote hope that I may still be granted a transfer to the RAMC[…]

Barby Camp, Friday [26 May 1944?]

I must write at least a short note to you, or you'll think I'm lost[…] But it's going slowly, & this afternoon I had a good drink of the strongest liquor I've ever tasted, Army rum. We've been unloading it in boxes of 2 x 1 gallon jars – I was with 2 criminal Irishmen - 2 ne'er-do-wells & as soon as the officer's back was turned a crate was dropped "accidentally" from the top of the pile & mugs held under the damage & immediately hidden under the truck. We kept toddling behind the truck for sips when the officer came and was informed that in shunting a crate had been damaged etc... He replied very good humouredly "I see all you men appearing in turn round the truck with red faces & beaming smiles – All right – mark it with chalk & put it aside." Very nice of him[…]

This is a bad place, so I'm not going to hide the fact. Most COs feel demoralised & heartsick here, not because we're ever asked to do anything against our consciences, but because it is virtually a prison, where so-called privileges are spoiled by endless stupidity & red tape. The worst feature is the long queues which we are perpetually making for our food, for NAAFI, for everything. The camp seems to supply for about 200 men while actually there are 800. But those are things which you cannot help – and patience & stoicism are the only remedies, in ourselves. So don't take things to heart if I tell you these things. We are all war-weary – Barby Camp, Felling, everywhere, so I'm only voicing general opinion & perhaps in time that poor belated complaint, universal, will stop the war. How can we be patient with war, or silent, or enduring?[…]

Len and his comrades were in the thick of preparations for D-Day – but it would seem they had little idea it was imminent. To them, the invasion of Europe appeared still distant.

Barby Camp, Sunday [28 May 1944?]

Now what do you think of me? I'm dreadfully (what a word!) sorry. Excuses are hopeless – a week's overwork, tiredness and horrible depression etc – no real excuse. It's been on my conscience, till I got [so?] I didn't care, so that I'd keep going. Friday night I decided to indulge – go to Stratford-on-Avon on my rest day. Part of the depression was probably caused through the new restrictions – no man to go more than 25 miles from camp on his rest day, & prepare to stand-by even – in case 2nd front trains come in for food. Germany is a nuisance – she is calling Britain's bluff and it looks as though we may have to start a 2nd front after all. So here in the middle of the military season, we are beginning to think seriously about it and slowly filling trains & ships & lorries. But we never worry unduly about it – it is a lot of fuss here, more work restrictions in travel etc. We never think or talk about a 2nd front (few soldiers do either) except as a joke or a nuisance. Newspapers, the big "secret" return of Monty, Eisenhower etc from what was an obvious, settled, hard-slogging Italian front, all the big conferences etc & talk have just meant nothing to Germany. So don't worry, everything still in a fog, as far as I can see. I might be wrong, but Britain (from a military point of view) & US are playing a very dirty game on Russia & China – the ancient balance of power game. With a 2nd front last year the war could have been won, but Russia [is] in too good a position still for our designs[…]

I had a perfect day in Stratford yesterday, saw *Midsummer Night's Dream* – a perfect day, absolute idyll[…]

Barby Camp, Saturday night [3 June 1944]

I have just had a letter from Betty, ending on the note that you were ready to blow me up because I hadn't written a letter I'd promised. I'm sorry, & hope I've explained myself, though I fear not. Is it a breach of language if I say that in the Army my "promises" will probably mean "attempts"? That means a promise is nothing, & that's nasty, but it seems to work out that way.

At Marston I was lucky – the Sergeant-Major often gave me congenial work for some reason. Here I'm largely unlucky, & to bear out my reasons for failure to write, shall I tell you the whole truth & describe what I'm doing. Buried in the 800 odd personnel of the camp, good jobs are rare and for over a week I've been engaged on one job alone, off-loading sacks of flour from wagons & stacking them neatly in the sheds. Two nights I've worked till 10 pm & 8 pm respectively. Indiscriminate call-outs in evenings for urgent work caught me twice, that's all. And though I can "take it", you'll realize that things aren't too good for a while, & some poor fellows are worse. For a dreadful thing happened in the hut last night. Two men, one a quite inoffensive, typical CO of the best type, and a Salvation Army Devonshire youth of 19, in their weariness began to quarrel. In two ticks there were blows & Stan Hurrell, the former, fell bleeding furiously, half unconscious. We laid him down & covered him with blankets – he lay groaning & sobbing till taken away on a stretcher. Ray

Greenslade, the other, just sobbed and prayed – the whole thing was distressing to us all, but most of all for the poor victims. Stan, we hear, is recovering, but the scene is an indication of how things can get to us.

But I mustn't give the impression that it's all like that. In the Army, there's no equality really, no sharing from above. Sometimes you're lucky, just picked from the bunch for a decent job, other times unlucky & hounded off to a rotten job for days on end. So if letters are infrequent, you'll know why. And again, even if it were all easy work, there's little time to yourself, so much life to be spent in huts, NAAFIs, canteens etc, that letters are very difficult[…]

Coventry YMCA Sunday Morning –

Came here on a lorry. What a sad sight. Great debris-strewn gaps, no big buildings left to speak of, Woolworth's defying extinction in a tin hut, a little Baby Austin, only a charred shell remaining, resting sadly among the weeds and broken masonry of a former building, and saddest of all, the lovely twin-spired Cathedral with roofless, gaping chapels…]

Your last letter or two concerned me a little, because you didn't seem to be getting on too well at [my] home. You express the desire only to be there with Mother, in peace & quiet. I appreciate that, because our house is so noisy – but it's not that. What have you & Father been discussing? Don't you get on as well as you did? Have you been getting heated in religious discussions, & why are you so depressed at what he & Betty suggest – that Quakers aren't Christians! Have they pressed their arguments too far & hurt you? I'm sorry about all this. When did it start? And is there any tension? Why do you suggest that they think that I'm badly influenced by you? Are you serious, or simply, in depression, exaggerating a little?[…]

Mona and Len had not seen each other since January. They finally met at the house of a friend of Mona's by the Severn on the weekend of 19-20 June. Len wrote to her, "I enjoyed yesterday most of any I've had since joining up. Just simple pleasures, and absolute peace. It was so marvellous to speak to someone from home[…] And of course I enjoyed my meals – no mad scramble for some half baked hash – just gentle, peaceful eating at leisure. The sunshine, the willows, the

*houses in their labyrinthine lanes, the walk to the Severn have all meant something
to me[…]"*

*A week later they attempted to meet at Stratford on Avon to see a performance
of* As You Like It. *Somehow, through confusion over train times, they managed
to miss each other. Len did see the play with his new friend, the artist George Downs,
whom he had met at Barby camp. Downs was the kindred spirit and close companion that Len had been longing for ever since joining the army. On the Monday after
he wrote a long account of how the mishap must have happened, and apologised
again in a short note on 3 July. He next wrote on 15 July.*

Barby Camp, Saturday [15 July 1944?]

[…] Last Sunday I blotted my copy. I'd worked so hard & so long that
when we were asked to do yet another truck I couldn't budge – just
worked to a standstill – so I was put on a charge, tried on Monday,
remanded till Tuesday & sentenced to 14 days CB for non-compliance
with an order. So those nights when I'm not working, I'm bashing
spuds. Fortunately I'm allowed out on rest-day within bounds, but rest-
day doesn't count as a punishment day.

I wish I could write more & get things off my chest. Not that I want
sympathy – I know you sympathise – but I just want to end this vicious
flat spin in my head – just relax a little and pour out my woes. And I
ache all over[…]

Tuesday night

I'm on fire picquet and am the man chosen to stay awake all night
and waken the orderly sergeant at 5.30 in the morning. So here I am,
enjoying a rare phenomenon in the Army, peace & quiet in the CS-
M's office, waiting till 5.30 & hoping to keep awake & write a few
letters[…]

Oh this last fortnight – I seem to have lost touch with you, &
received your letters without the slightest thought of replying – I
simply couldn't. We are really overworked & the RASC which runs
this place is hopelessly disorganised, & quarrels with the RFs, who are
in charge of trucks & in their efforts to "nark" each other we are the
victims, always, in ways difficult to explain to you[…]

I have been engrossed (as far as it was possible) in John Farleigh's
autobiography *Graven Image*, which is more a textbook on wood-
engraving & an account of his more important commissions like

Shaw's [*The Adventures of the] Black Girl [in Her Search for God*][…][9]

George (Downs) was one of his most promising students at the Central School of Arts & Crafts in London. George is like a child & can think like a child – i.e. he delights in nursery rhymes & tales, write rhymes & illus. them with marvellous Learish pen & wash drawings, & has pub. one book, another ready, almost. Is now writing a story of Yanya, the lonely ewe, with the sheepiest of drawings to accompany. In contrast, in more melancholy mood he does more mature drawings in all sorts of mixed mediums, like ink & chalk, in a rather Henry Moore manner which defies description – I love his work, but feel he is too experimental – the Army prevents any style forming, of course. He is a charming friend, & I wish you had met him at Stratford. He has an exquisite taste for old furniture & trinkets etc & prowls in old shops to unearth bargains[…]

P.S. […] Friday […] I saw the principal of Rugby Art School a while back, Mr Hodgkinson, & he invited me to spend any part of Mon. Tues. Wed. or Thursday at the school. Sad to say, I've never had one evening free for it, & of course, the school closes shortly for summer. He is very interested in me, & particularly in George, because Farleigh, George's master, was a colleague of Hodgkinson's at Rugby for 2 years[…]

I'm going to Mr Hodgkinson's house tonight, ostensibly to explain that George can't go since he's working, really to have a quiet evening in the correct atmosphere.

And I hope I've written all I meant to. Goodness knows when I'll be able to write again.

The army's logistical framework was still working flat out to supply the forces in Normandy, which was why camps like Barby were such furious hives of activity. Len was exhausted, as he explained on 23 July.

> Barby Camp, Sunday [23 July 1944 –
> airmail letter date stamped 24 July]

There's a revolution here as well as in Germany. We worked till twenty to two in the morning after being on all day yesterday[…] We haven't a rest day for ages – I only had a day out to the dentist for a filling & managed to hear Moisiewitch[10] as a result. It is awful, & letters are pouring in to MPs & WO etc. But I feel, if we've accepted the Army we mustn't let a stretch of imprisonment & overwork get us down since we are at least safe. It seems so endless & thankless a job – yet if this lasted 6 months it would only be a short spell in life. It is being indoors that I hate – I feel pale & wan. A spot of leave would bring the colour back. I can't think properly of course, & the days are all mixed up with there being no weekends. The time of day, the date etc have never meant so little. It's a queer timeless, aimless affair working all day & evening & thus being too confused & shattered when an hour's leisure comes along, to know what to do with it. The sick parade is increasing, we have 8 absentees, but I'm still a good boy after my lapse[…]

Writing again a couple of days later, Len reported that had suffered a second "tussle" with the dentist which left him unable to eat afterwards. The orderly sergeant insisted he was fit enough to work. Len finally managed to write a proper letter a fortnight later.

Barby Camp, Tuesday [9 August 1944?]

I've wanted to write for a day or two to make a proposition but just haven't had the time – I think you ought now to write twice a week instead of daily. Your amazing constancy in writing to me daily seems to have finally silenced me. How could I work out how to answer them all? How could I write but about myself & work etc? I had begun to think, in London it started, that I wanted to write you the long rather discursive letter I occasionally wrote to you, & just couldn't work out why I wanted to because I had nothing to write about apparently. But when did I have more to write about than now? So I decided there was something wrong with me & if I didn't put it right, I was harming something & someone precious to me & here I am determined to start afresh. After this, you shall write when you feel like it, but not every day[…]

And then I have something to grasp, something to answer, & to ponder over, and since the present balance (or lack) of a daily letter from you & a monthly one from me is so unfair, I think the new idea is better, don't you.

I can't answer yet, except to thank you for the daily letter which has ensured a letter for me every day since I joined up, & for the never failing stream of books & papers & tobacco, etc[…]

The poem 'Implicitly' shows Jim going all loose & emptyish again & I hope he gives his verse more flow again, as in the little pastorals like 'Moonlit Cattle' or 'Moon at the Farm', or his best longer works like 'Glass Fable'. He so easily pours out words & loses the lovely flow & sequence of ideas of which he is so capable if he disciplines himself more. One of the loveliest little gems is an early one 'Moorland', only 12 lines, which I believe took 6 weeks to finally get down. And yet how spontaneous & fresh it still seems. The words of 'Implicitly' are so new & wonderful – pervert Owen & say the poetry is in the wonder – but is it considered, was it all worth writing, was the struggle to express so much in such an angular way worth it – no. I'm sure it wasn't[…][11]

Life is so much easier now, suddenly, though an accumulation of trucks in the marshalling yards threatens us with another rush. But now with 50 reinforcements we are guaranteed our weekly rest day, & I've had two since they began again – last week in London at George's home & today with George at an old friend of his in Bedford – Gretta Fairley. She is a marvellous person, crackers about helping others & doing social work in Bedford for evacuees & refugees. But she is like you in that she believes in her own life too, in the inner life, & seems like a character from Charles Morgan – more nervous & emotional perhaps.

She has a brother, in the FAU [Friends' Ambulance Unit?] at present, in a London Hospital attending to bomb casualties. He is in the operation theatre & when I met him last week he told me some interesting things about nursing & dressing etc. I do wish I'd been accepted for RAMC work, but it seems it wasn't to be, & anyway I might not have met George.

It almost seems as though I joined up to meet George – he was looking for me, & I was looking for him. I knew I wanted to meet George when Tom Cunningham once told me about him at Marston. Tom was an ex-7 Coy man & therefore knew George before we shifted to Barby where we joined with 7 Coy after about a month. I introduced myself to George & he seemed to cotton on at once & all he can say now is "It's so marvellous to be with someone again." I'm honoured, since I'm the first soldier friend he's taken home. His mother is a sweet soul, eternally blithe & merry amid the bombs. She usually shops at Lewisham but one morning decided she'd get fruit better at Lea Green – and the same morning a bomb killed 20 people in Lewisham shopping centre. We got to Blackheath about 11 at night – had a morsel of pork pie & salad & some cider & after a restful chat, went to bed. During the night I was nearly shaken out of bed by a fly bomb – Blackheath is on the path & any dropping short fall there. A number went over & the ominous silence as the taxi cab noise stopped was rather terrifying – but you know all about them. This letter is all about sad things.

I was brought a cup of tea at 8.30 & a white shirt, slippers & dressing gown & I had a bath (how the water rippled from the sides of the bath as a fly bomb dropped!) & went to see George's Henry Moore drawing. He knows Moore & the latter gave George a drawing cheap. We had a nice easy day together & forgot about the Army[…]

Barby Camp, Sunday [13 August 1944?]

I am on Gate Picquet today, so have a few opportunities to write[…]

I have been having more fruit & vegetables lately & am feeling very fit. Also, I usually have supper "as for sergeants" which George brings from their mess & we eat like a *fête champêtre* on the grass near the camp. Vasus (Cypriot) always brings me apples from London & indeed, in this company, to show an artistic disposition seems to command respect and I have many good friends[…]

2.30. Flying Fortresses have just gone over, to liberate Europe. It seems from today's news that the war is coming to an end. I've been often wrong in my opinions of how it would close. I hope I'm wrong in the future in some ways, because I'm pessimistic. I never believed in a really successful 2nd front, which I now see is blindness on my part. What mostly concerns me is peace now. The war goes on relentlessly, claiming its thousands, & nothing can stop it so far. It is certainly victorious in Europe for us & I suppose in time in the East too. But what then? I detest the spirit of Churchill & his like but they seem to

Above, and opposite: drawings made in this period: 'Dejection' and 'Men Resting'

represent the people. The intelligent few are overwhelmed in war, & if in peace too, then we're lost. I only hope a more enlightened world policy from all sides will prevail as the war is gradually forgotten, & peace comes. The main thing is to fight for individualism & particularly our own, not selfishly, but expressively. I think it is true to say, for instance, that the Quakers are doing that and will always do so & it is not aggressively done, thank goodness. And poets, painters, musicians and their true lovers too. But what of the rest? Why are they so ready to merge in a drastic flood & never think or feel but just flow along or be canalised as their leaders dictate? Germany is a tragedy, don't you think, a sort of boil in the whole rottenness of the world & she suffers through her own stupidity, which is only worse in degree than the rest – but she must suffer all, & peace for them will only be an extension of war. If only there were peace for us all, there is so much that is

good & beautiful to turn to – as Jim puts it, we could turn our face to the full sun, all we can do is hope & live our own lives, as an example – that isn't presumption, or self-assurance – we have something to live for that is eternal, while so many don't live at all, I'm sure of that. And all the greatest changes in life, for better or for worse (& surely we will turn, if at all, for the better) are slow & gradual, & the swift revolutions only precipitate present evils, which is negative good & not positive[…]

[Letter unsigned]

In a letter sent about 19 August Len enclosed some sample notes George Downs had sent him, most of them cheery messages about meeting times. One of them advised Len "What ever [sic] you do, don't play 'hookie', because they're sure to get you in the end. What ever we have to bear, the best thing is to become a Stoic and treat the whole routine with indifference." Downs signed himself "Georgius".

The mishap at Stratford had left an imprint in Mona's mind, for she was clearly suspicious of Len's motives and wrote as much to him. It seemed to him that she was jealous of his warm friendship with Downs, as if Len now had less time for her with his new army comrade. He tried to rebut her accusations.

Barby Camp, Wednesday [23 August 1944?]

[…] Wilson came to relieve me for dinner at 10 past 1, embraced me, kissed me once on each cheek & announced Paris was ours. *Vive La France* etc & a lot of clowning. And he brought your letter[…]

I find lots of bitterness in your letter – and, horrible thought, jealousy. I've read it through & through, & one very sarcastic passage about George is sad – because I'm sure you'd like him. I hope I'm never jealous – it is one thing that I'm sure I can claim, that I'm not jealous. And from your letter, I think that's all I'd better claim.

Beneath it all, & between the lines if you like, I think I can detect unbelief. Somehow I find I'm not believed, and movements are mistrusted. So there is little I can do really. You write in a strange tone "I don't think you should bother much about Tchehov, the world & artists, for an artist, like Fred, is blandly indifferent to the world & the world tolerates Fred." Please presume that when I talk of artists that I don't include myself, because I can't claim to be an artist though I try to paint. That sentence is full of mockery, sniggering unbelief. And because I have often been a fool, it hurts. But I won't pray you should-n't hurt me – that would be self-pity and I've often hurt you[…]

"Your Mother has been pining for you for months and… But can the leopard change his spots? You may be an artist, but you are still a man…" & so on. Don't you think that appeal is mean. Do you think my Mother means nothing to me – more than that, do you think I don't love my Mother very dearly! It's obvious you do. I don't appear to, in your reply. How does one appear to them? There are little ways between Mother & I that I wouldn't tell even you. We are undemonstrative & love as colliery families do – but while to some it is almost empty, it isn't in our case. My thoughts have been with her particularly these last few days, thinking of her in her new surroundings, resting & recovering I hope – and I've prayed for the weather to improve & it has. But all that is sentimental to you, rigged up for the occasion. Somehow as I write, the way I write, you disbelieve me[…]

Barby Camp [no date – 23 August 1944?]

I've posted the letter I wrote today & it's irretrievable, so you must take it as you find it. And I wrote two pages before this & had to give up, I got in such a tangle.

I've been thinking of nothing else all day, & after writing so much I think I'm writing the guts out of me. I want to know what is the matter just at present & why the tornado. I'm tired of this trying to write down thoughts & I suppose I'll have to be almost curt. Tell me, how am I to treat you? I'm puzzled. May I not tell you of my activities in my leisure hours? I mean as far as you're concerned. If you'd rather I didn't I'll stop. And do you think I should live in solitary confinement & not make any more friends? Are you trying to reproach me indirectly for writing so infrequently in the past month or two? And trying to imply that in my thrill at new friends, I forget the old ones! Or am I just fuddled? And have you said all you want to say? If not, can I beg of you to get it off your chest? I would count it as a favour, so that there might be no unpleasantness when I come home. And do you think I ought to spend all of my leave at home? To the last I'm afraid my answer is No because I really can't. My home, my own home, is somewhere in Wensleydale & I must go there, so please don't deprive me of that. It isn't just a holiday place for me. But all the time now I feel my sentiments unbelieved, so I'll not bother to explain the impossible.

In any case, there is so much to reproach me for that I know it's presumptuous of me to write this kind of letter to me [sic]. But don't bring Mother, or George & such like into it. Get at me if you like, I'm often at fault, but do you really know what sort of life I'm leading particularly for the 2 months following D-Day? No, you'll never know

– you'll never know, & I don't want you to know, what it has been like, & what it was often like in the woods. And being a man, unable to cry, only able to indulge in a general moan in letters & conversation. And the same old cry to yourself to be a man & not pity yourself. It's not only me, it's other young men, it's yourself, too, to a large extent, though you are still unspoilt by manual or factory work, even if you are overworked.

This all hardly means anything – I only want to say, don't laugh & scoff, leave Mother to me in those things that only she & I understand, & don't be jealous please. And lastly, if these letters hurt, be angry with me, answer my questions if you like, but don't reproach yourself if you think I'm right on some points. I think I should be past that stage now, of making you reproach yourself. We all have faults but if the faults are our own sacred little failures, best let them be.

Please don't be hurt.

Barby Camp, Late Sunday night [27 August 1944?]

Have just got in from Bedford & am writing this in Bed. Your letter was awaiting me & makes me feel a wonderful happiness – so that I almost feel like tears. That is literally true, because my stomach is just a wee bit queer & I don't eat much & therefore feel weak. So it is easy to weep in that state.

Anyway, I'm so happy about it, so childishly grateful to you, that I don't know how to thank you for that letter. I'm sure it will cure my poor stomach[…]

Barby Camp, Thursday [31 August 1944?]

[…] Several big trains have gone out, besides the usual intake, so we've been busy again, & one or two nights. I'm so stupid I find I'm in the flour gang, a gang of 12 men who are assigned to special duties that only the flour gang can do, such as emptying, or filling trucks of flour. They are rather a stupid gang & seem pleased to be imposed upon, in fact honoured to be in *the* flour gang, whose pride it is to handle 5 or 6 tons of flour in a morning. Still we're always chopping & changing – I might as easily find myself out of it.

I got your still life letter just now – you seem to have got completely rid of your cold – isn't it grand to feel your health return. My tummy is much the same – nothing serious – only a semi-permanent unpleasantness so long as I'm in the Army. If I'd got into Airborne RAMC, I'd have got special & more balanced food of course & I heard such tales that I looked forward to that. By the way, a fellow came up to me yesterday, & said he'd just volunteered for Parachute RAMC work, & when I told him it was apparently impossible, he said no – he has a pal in the office at the Hardwick Training Centre who says far from ceasing to train men, they were dropping the medical grade a little to bring more men in. So they still have a long-term policy in view, even if the war in Europe is ending. I think when they turn to Japan, Airborne landings will be their main attack, so the RAMC will have lots of work. So there will be even worse suffering yet, against a more fanatic & mysterious enemy. It's strange, I feel less concerned about the fate of the Japanese than about the Germans, probably because they are more remote & therefore more unreal. I should hate to be a soldier fighting them, all that distance from home, only a far flung ship or air route to keep you in touch with your people, death a steamy horror in the jungle perhaps, & falling prisoner an even remoter exile in the hands of the strangest nation in the civilized world at present[...]

In mid-September Len spent leave visiting both Tyneside and Wensleydale. With the war approaching its end he was beginning to think about demobilization and what came after.

Rugby, [no date – 23 September 1944?]

[…] I rather think everyone will be unsettled by this demob bill. I'm out of that for the present, so I'd better not think of it just now, tho' sometimes I can't help myself, & find myself almost praying for the war to end, however much that may mean to others. And ideas begin to precipitate in spite of my conscience, such as applying for scholarships, grants etc & showing a general (but false) enthusiasm to teach art to the coming generation. Anything to get out. And we'll all be thinking the same, blokes in every unit, home & abroad & most of all poor prisoners. Nothing in life is ever "just so", is it. We frantically bother & worry about life at 25, while Mother, at 50 odd, is doomed to some sort of illness all her life. That's something to worry about, yet she faces it with courage & apparent unconcern.

Never mind; I had a good leave – I got a bit stalled in the second half, but I did enjoy it. And the best thing was to see Mother gradually improve as the days went by.

Thanks for keeping me (sounds bad) for feeding me, bedding & bathing me (sounds worse). Anyway, I enjoyed the fruitarian breakfasts best of all.

Wensleydale was a rather sad little episode – I hardly seemed to see anybody. What made me most sad, perhaps, was the wood job. I came in their bus from Leyburn & it seemed a different crowd altogether. And the job, like so many war jobs, is on the wane. That made me sad for no obvious reason[…]

Just when Len had almost given hope of ever joining the RAMC, he was called for an interview in London. It would be the start of several exciting months for him.

Barby Camp, Wednesday [4 October 1944?]

I wrote you a most depressed letter last Saturday, but it was too bad to send. And, I think, unreasonable. I was bemoaning the fact that now my chance to join the RAMC has come, I can't do it because of Mother. It preyed so much on my mind, & the prospect of finishing my "Army career" in the NCC appalled me now I'd had a chance to do the job I wanted[…]

Friday London

I seem hardly able to catch up with myself. I've been rushed off to London suddenly at a "minute's notice" & here I am, waiting for something I don't know what. I didn't volunteer, but was told by Lieut Blythe that WO had had my name down since 25 Feb 1944 & I had to go willy-nilly. "What will Father & Mother say" I thought, but lo! just as I was changing to come up to London to see somebody or other, a telegram came to ease me. "Volunteer Father love Mother."

Anyway, I rushed up here, & found 22 other volunteers at a house in Eaton Square, Victoria[…]

Last night I got a sleeping out pass & got to Blackheath, where I found Ruth[12] feeling lonely, so my visit was propitious (good word!) Flo was on holiday, George still away of course. A most terrifying fly bomb seemed to knock the chimney pots, & made the house throb as it passed. It was one of those that just wouldn't make up its mind to pass & seemed to come nearer & nearer until it couldn't get closer without touching & blowing us to eternity. It seemed to be falling on us rather than passing by. But it did pass & we never heard it explode. We were flat on the floor involuntarily. Another passed further away & then during the night I kept hearing more as I thought but Ruth says they were planes[…]

Barby Camp, Sunday [8 October 1944?]

What a hectic week it's been. In fact, I've hardly been able to catch up with myself since I returned from leave. I've hardly had a moment to myself. I have stacks of letters to write, but can't get the time. However, my last letter to you must have read so stupid & confused that I must try to write something more considered, if it's possible. Anyway my days with 14 Coy are numbered now and soon I shall be moving to yet another job. I don't know how I'll take to it, but I've known all about it since I met Ted Biles, and I think it is probably nearest to the job I've wanted since the war began. Since it's in the Army, I know now that it's silly to surround it with ideals but in spite of all it's a grand job. Colonel MacEwan was rather a Lawrence figure, unorthodox, without ceremony, & without descending he talked easily, as man to man. Ted always spoke highly of him as apparently he's good as an OC. He spoke of his early doubts of COs as Airborne nursing orderlies etc, but of his ultimate conversion and respect and he spoke very highly of the work they did on D-Day, giving specific examples of where men's lives were saved by their zeal etc etc & lots more, very complimentary really, but he seemed sincere. And he was honest enough to give the disadvantages to us (to belie any suggestions that he was fishing for volunteers) the risks etc. Then he interviewed each of us personally, asked questions about us & why we wanted to join the RAMC.

First we go to Bulford (Salisbury) though I'm not able when I get there to give that name. My address will be 225 Parafield Ambulance [sic], Home Forces, which you can take to mean a self-contained field ambulance of hospital or casualty station, connected by radial paths with a ring of living huts, with balloons & planes in the sky to harass the mind of the poor paratrooper who must needs keep in practice & not lose his nerve or whatever it is that makes him finally commit the quite unnatural act of jumping into mid-air[…]

Len now joined 224 Parachute Field Ambulance, part of the 3rd Parachute Brigade within the 6th Airborne Division.

224 Para[chute] Field Ambulance, APO [Army Post Office]
England, Wednesday [11 October 1944?]

I'm sorry I couldn't warn you of this quick move, but until further notice. I hope I pass my course, because I'm going to like this unit very much, already they have made us so welcome & are so friendly that they almost make up for my separation from George. The course is going to be quicker than I thought, & I must confess that a nasty sinking feeling has taken my stomach at the thought that in less than 3 weeks I shall be facing my jumps at Manchester.

But anyway, they give you every encouragement, and I am now writing to you in the rest [sic] amidst people who never ordinarily hobnob with privates – officers, all of us together in the quiet room, listening to Beethoven's Sonata No 3[…]

I got a letter from you 2 days ago – just a little cross – you seemed to think I'd written to Jim or George before you. Of course that's wrong. I distinctly remember writing 1st to Mother & Father, then to you, the night I returned to Barby & later to Jim & George. Did you get the letter? I'm sorry I haven't written much, but I've hardly written to anyone[…]

So I'll close, & please if I don't write often, understand that it is because I'm busy with PT & such like. But I'll try[…]

224 Parachute Field Ambulance, APO England
[No date – 19 October 1944?]

George has written me rather a strange letter in which I read much between the lines. I'm sorry there is such little opportunity here for writing personal letters, except that once a week we are allowed to send one in an enclosed Army envelope[…]

Friday

I'm leaving here tomorrow morning early & then the fun starts, so probably I'll never get written what I wished. But please, I do want you to think a little before you get cross with me[…] I probably spent more of my leave with you than anyone even my parents. I hate to be writing like this but from George's letter, he mentions that you hadn't heard from me & you couldn't understand it. He seemed concerned about you; he is kinder than I, but I tried to let everybody know I was back. And if I don't write it's not because I'm trying to be deliberately unkind or anything. I have never been all I should or might have been, & I know only too well how much I've failed you. I think you must suffer on my account, in fact, I know you do, & I wish you didn't. You have been more to me than I've deserved, & I do so little in return – but I'm past being so unkind now – it's not neglect either – in my letter-writing you naturally come first; I would answer you first if I were faced with a pile; but I must answer other friends. Goodness only knows how little I write to Jim & Bill & Amos etc & even George, who is neglected like you, though you may not believe it.

So I'm sure I'm not unkind, & the neglect is because I'm busy or tired, or mostly (in the Army) sheer lack of opportunity. The last excuse is hardly understandable to anyone except a soldier. But to search round like a restless dog for a quiet spot, & then to have to share it with a noise lover who switches on the radio – to retire instead to your rather cool & lonely hut (at evenings the desertion [sic] is oppressive) – to try the NAAFI in vain, or any canteen – to do all that, & then end the evening with a hopeless inadequate effort to someone, & others unanswered (or neglected if you like) all that is too common an experience in the Army[…]

Here it has been a holiday, reveille about 7 it appears at least that's when I used to roll out – marvellous after 6 reveille – a forced march i.e. alternate marching & running from 8.30 to 10 – break – gym from

10.30 (always later) to 12, Dinner, Gym from 2 to 4. One day we had a cross country run from about 1.30 to 2.15 & finished for the day. One day a route march from 8.30 to 2, across the plain to Stonehenge stopping at every canteen I'm sure. Stonehenge is incredibly bleak & lonely even when you see it with others[...]

I hope I pass my course – I then hope to get some leave (it's not possible to give us 14 days now unfortunately) but 7 days I hope. Then I return here I think & train for Nursing Orderly 3 exam with jumps every so often, route marches & PT to keep your ankles & feet in trim[...] I'm a bit stiff, & bruised a little, but it's been fun. The sergeant is by far the best I've met & likely to meet; he's one of the lads. And there's another thing – there's no class distinction here – no officers, sergeants & men class. And conchies are very much liked & respected[...]

I'm thrilled with my jumping smock & beret etc. Oh, & the grub is fine here.

139 Course, B Camp, Box 200, GFO, Manchester
Tuesday [24 October 1944?]

Let me just blow the gaff a little, to see if I feel any better. Saturday and its 700 feet approaches rapidly, & I'm wondering all the time why I ever volunteered for this. The nervous tension is terrific & everybody is like myself, very tired. Everything is attended by a little nervous quiver, the instructor shouts "Ready One", a horrible pain in the stomach, "Go!!" he shouts and you find yourself winging off a ledge about the height of your roof above ground, on a swing. Out you swoop, feeling your stomach turn & then you feel fine & wonder what made you nervous. Everything is like that – I do it all & feel fine after each little venture – except for "exits through the aperture".

Wednesday

[...] This morning we have had more aperture exits. I did 3 with a parachute on my back. The actual aperture is difficult to explain. It is about 5 feet across the top but slopes inward so that at the bottom it is much less. You sit on the side thus, &

I [sketch of man sitting] you are supposed to go out at attention thus.

II [second sketch of man vertical] If you don't you hit your head on the other side. So trying to strike the happy medium of preventing your parachute catching the back & your head hitting the front you have a very nervous moment. I haven't yet "rung the bell" (touch wood) but every time I get on the edge of that hole & the instructor shouts "Ready", my heart pounds, my whole body shivers with fright – "Go!" & off I go, fit to faint as I land safely on the mat below. But I'm glad to say the 3 exits this morning made me a little more confident, so I hope to progress with it, until I make a safe exit from a balloon & the Whitley.[12] After that we jump through a door, again in a certain manner, but easier I imagine. We do 2 jumps from the balloon, 1 jump in addition at night, 2 or 3 from a Whitley (same as Wellington) & 2, or 3 from a Douglas Dakota. 8 in all. I've done 4 jump[s] from [a] "fan" as it is called – a leap into space from 40 feet I think. You are suspended in a harness & it looks a terrifying height, but I go somehow, but apparently I'm making bad exits. Still, I do improve, I think. Particular stress is laid on landings, & all day we are swinging & falling & rolling. You must land with both feet together, must fall on to the side of your knee (it would break them probably if you fell forward onto them) then along your hip on to one "cheek" & turn on to your back. But I do that reasonably well where others don't.

So altogether, I'm not normal this fortnight, which you can understand. I'm all pale & washed-out with terror, & can't eat, but if I do everything I'm told, it'll be over in 10 or 12 days from now. By that time, I'll have got no less terrified of jumping, but more inured to the nervous tension between times. It's so difficult to control myself, even relaxing at evenings in the canteen etc, & so common to find myself imagining that balloon & shivering where I sit. It comes in fits, like a fever.

You'll excuse me writing so much about my beastly feelings of terror & so on. I can only write about myself, & haven't much thought about anybody but myself.

[Signed "Yours in terror, Len"]

139 Course, Manchester [no date - 1 November 1944?]
[…] Your letter of yesterday ended on rather an amazing note. In

your own sweet way you were expressing the fact that even if things seem to hang on, time still passes & it's soon enough over. You mustn't talk like that to a parachutist, because if you get your static line through your lift webs, things do hang on & you dangle from the plane in mid-air. One of 224's officers died so. It was his own fault, of course, or the checker's, but don't talk of hanging on. Our poor little superstitious subconsciousnesses are full enough without visions of being dangled along at 150 mph in mid-air. Still, I appreciated the thought.

Where did I last write – after the second balloon jump I think. We then did a Whitley, leaving in slow pairs. I was first of the fifth pair, made a good exit from forward, had an extremely pleasant descent (more your idea I suppose) & a good landing. Tuesday the fog never lifted all day, so after a day of acting the fool & working off surplus energy & nerves in terrific scrimmages & sing songs & laughing, I went to bed at 7 pm & slept soundly, leaving letters unanswered. This morning the fog or ground mist persisted, but at dinner time it lifted & we emplaned at 2, for 2 sticks of five. I was No 1 of the second stick, & I'm afraid this time I was rather shaken. Whether my nerve is going (it has been wonderful for me really) or what I don't know, but being No 1 I had to sit on the edge of that hole & this time I knew the sergeant wasn't going to shout "GO!" & hypnotise me off. No. A red light came on as we circled into the Dropping Zone & I had to go as soon as it changed to green – if I didn't get off in that split second, the whole stick was delayed & every second meant hundreds of yards wasted & the last man in the trees perhaps. I hated it, but somehow I went from aft, was caught in the slip-stream full face, turned somersault & as my chute opened I felt an awful pain in my nose & I was seeing stars. Apparently my chute opening past my face, stunned me a little in passing & a rigging line had burned the under part of my nose. I recovered instantly of course, but felt shaken that I couldn't enjoy the descent as at other times. I made a good "pansie" landing, but blood dripped on to my brand new shute. I thought it was something serious, but it soon stopped & I recovered soon & realized it was all a minor affair. The little marks under my nose are negligible & the stars (I don't know what caused them really) had caused my nose to bleed.

The stick of five is a difficult jump though, & two of our 10 rang the bell, one requiring two stitches in his upper lip, the other having a cut face. Many people fail with it, partly because it is the first time when you go of your own volition – don't have the compelling "GO" yelled in your ear. Believe me, it is very hard to compel yourself to jump into space. But it's probably the worst jump over, & after a few hours I feel no worse. Tomorrow, WP [weather permitting], we do a Dakota stick of 10. Dakotas have doors & you can almost stumble out, tho' it is still best to try to get into a position of attention to prevent twists & somersaults. At night we do our night balloon jump. Then two more Dakota jumps with kit bags strapped to our legs. So WP again I ought to have my wings (how proud I'll be) by the weekend & ought to be home the following weekend, to prowl round Hills as you suggest.

I'm glad to say I feel much better in nerve this week (despite today) than last, when the mock apertures & other things, with the mere thought of the first balloon ahead of me all the time, all made me feel the worst nervous strain I've ever experienced. Then as soon as that first balloon was over, the strain lifted & since then I've ceased to worry; I take things as they come, & only while in the plane or balloon am I nervous. Then it is intense, almost agony, but it is better that way, because it's over in five minutes, & not a long drawn-out misery that I was making it in the first week.

It is never certain, of course, that I shall jump. Each jump, if anything, seems more difficult, & not easier. I don't know why, but it took all of me to get out today. If you hesitate for a split second you're done, & it is that split second which might pip me. So far I've gone out without a pause, so let's hope it continues[…]

139 Course, Manchester – Friday, 3 November 1944

Thank you so much for your letters of today, & everyday for that matter. I'm needing them now, because it gets increasingly harder to jump & until the last two jumps are over, the nerves have returned again. The two balloons, the two Whitleys I went to with spirit, but that 2nd Whitley shook many of us. Poor Jamieson in our stick had 11 stitches in his bottom lip, not 2 as we thought at first. O'Connor too got a bashed face, so I was lucky with a slight stunning & burning with rigging lines. Our next jump was from a Dakota, i.e. out of a door. It was horrible to see the landscape far below through the door & our No 2 jibbed, O'Connor, which shook us all, Thorne after him hesitated & the sergeant half pushed him out & half compelled him with a terrible scream "Go!", then Bristow, OK, then me, in a faint I suppose, but I must say I was comfortably airborne, looked round with relief & made a very comfortable landing. That was at 5 pm after a full day's wait for weather. Bus back, 5 minutes for tea, then away again with another chute to do a night balloon jump. It was pitch black at 7 or 7.30, & again I was terrified but somehow I went into the night. I was fully conscious of the long drop from the balloon, but it opened – I adopted the landing position, & then it is luck. I wasn't very lucky, because I must have landed on the back swing of an oscillation, & next I knew was a terrific blow on the back of the head. I shouted "OK" but it had shaken me. But there have been no after effects so far, though the sergeant says I might have delayed concussion.

Again the weather is bad & it is now dinner-time. This afternoon, since it is clearing up we'll do our 2nd Dakota, & only sheer pig-headedness makes me go. But I find others like me, because there have been some misfortunes with our first Dakota. The least hitch is horribly nerve-racking, & an officer in one stick, instead of jumping through the door, sat on the edge & had to be pushed. Two men jibbed after that, so altogether we are being sorted out, & heaven only knows how I still find myself jumping.

So here I am ready, & I'll leave this open till after the jump, when I'll write more.

Saturday 3 pm I have just posted a letter to you telling you of my ankle. Apparently it was worse than I'd thought, & I can't jump tomorrow & that means end of next week before there are any more Dakota sticks. I'm feeling very fed-up about it, but then I was lucky to get off with a sprain. I have just left the masseur, who is a very nice sergeant. He placed my foot under some sort of lamp for ½ hour & then proceeded to gently massage it with Yardley's Freesia Talcum Powder. Isn't that nice. Next to me, an Irish Padre was enjoying a nap as his leg absorbed the soothing rays of another lamp[…]

139 Course, Manchester [no date – 4 November 1944?]

I've written part of a letter to you, but left it open till I finished my 7th jump. Unfortunately, I've had a slight accident & in the confusion my haversack with writing pad etc is mixed up with piles of others in the Standby Room. I'll get it later, but this is to let you know I have finished my 7th jump intact but had a queer descent, so queer that I tend to become celebrated with people all round me asking me questions "How did it feel? etc." Briefly, I landed with half a "Roman Candle", (a Roman Candle is a chute that doesn't open). And I'm so lucky that all I got was a sprained ankle. I can't explain here how it all happened, but I jumped with a 50 lb kit-bag strapped to my leg. When caught in the slip stream this tends to give you twists. These are easily disentangled by leg movements as you descend, after a special release device gets the kit bag off your leg & leaves it dangling on a 20 foot rope beneath you. So I got out, was spun in the slipstream, "she" opened, I released my kit bag & oh horrors! it formed a noose round my ankle. I just got this out & looked up to see how many twists to get out – I saw my poor little parachute all lightly screwed up like a half open umbrella & twists, right up to the rigging lines. It required say 8 to 10 seconds (which I didn't have) to get these out & get my chute opened when I heard a voice scream "Feet together!" & next thing I'd crashed next to the instructor & his microphone. Putting my feet together took the shock & as I say, all I got was a sprained ankle. Thank goodness that instructor was there. Strange to say I was so preoccupied with the rope & my twists etc that I felt nothing – no terror about the candle etc. Which is a good thing.

You'll read in the other letter that we've had a shaky time but yesterday we had a rest & I was better this morning. I went to M'c [Manchester] with an Intelligence Corps corporal, we dined on grilled sausage, mushrooms & chips, went to the cinema, had 1 half pint (honest!) returned to a camp dance, & generally got jumping out of our minds for 8 hours or so. We spent a lot naturally, but it was good for us. Jumping begins to prey towards the end.

Excuse all my moanings. I asked for this, but even if I volunteered it is still very, very hard, believe me. Every moment in the plane is a nightmare, & whatever makes that final leap, I'm sure I don't know. It all seems outside me, & I'm pleased I go without a pause[…]

Len wrote again on 9 November from SSQ Woodend, Styal, Cheshire to report that he was back again in hospital. The previous day the medical orderly had allowed him to return to the course, but after "an afternoon's steady trundle round for meals, massage, making my bed etc" Len felt unwell, and in the morning he was sent back to the hospital. His ankle had still not healed completely, and he had to lie up. In the meantime, of the 20 COs on his course 14 had "got their wings up"; three had pulled out and three, including himself, were injured. Len recovered quickly, and he wrote again from camp on the 10th.

139 Course, Manchester – Friday 7.30 pm [10 November 1944?]

Just a short note. I'm glad to say I'm feeling much better, and I think I'm prepared for my first balloon jump tomorrow morning at dawn. I feel very, very tired (everybody does) due to the nervous tension. I have improved in the last two days, but it hasn't been an advantage, because the instructor has placed me No 5 in our stick, i.e. last, and I'll have to endure watching the other 4 going out & waiting my turn. I have just fitted my chute on, fondled it tenderly, & wondered how the devil it opens. Of course I know how, but it still seems funny. We have a special rubber helmet too, for the landing, which has occupied most of our training. We've tossed & jumped & tumbled & rolled till we ache all over. But it's for our own good, since the landing is all important, & if you don't land as you've been taught, injuries often occur[...]

After tomorrow I jump every day, weather permitting.

But I'll close this till tomorrow morning, & I'll take it with me to jump & add a note when I've jumped.

Next day

I have been out to the Dropping Zone in a sickening little bus – donned my chute, waited my turn, marched out to the balloon & the rain came – back again – out again, back – so now, I've had dinner back at the drome & the suspense is horrible.

Len did make his eighth jump, and duly got his wings. He next wrote a short note to Mona in mid-November (probably from the family home) while on leave. (True to form, it was a pre-apology for possibly not meeting her in the evening.) From Tyneside he visited Wensleydale, returning to 224 PFA at the end of the month.

He wrote briefly on 30 November suggesting that he might see Mona in London one weekend. His next move was to a camp in Hampshire for medical training, from where he wrote to her around 11 December. He was back at Bulford on the 16th, when he wrote to thank her for two parcels.

War Experience and Aftermath

Unexpectedly Len found himself abroad just before Christmas. On 16 December, German forces under Field Marshal von Rundstedt had launched a surprise offensive through the Ardennes aimed at forcing the Western allies to make a separate peace with Germany. The 6th Airborne Division was among Allied forces rushed to Belgium to halt the attack. Suddenly Len's medical skills would be tested. His letters (all passed by censor while he was on duty) become almost devoid of introspection, with one exception. They give vivid impressions of conditions in Belgium and of some of his experiences. Army rules prevented men on active service from mentioning the places they had passed through until two weeks later, lest such information fall into the hands of the enemy and give clues as to the movement of Allied units.

224 Parachute Field Ambulance, BLA [British Liberation Army] –
23 December 1944

It's a strange life – I never thought I'd be on the Continent before Xmas, but here I am, in a transit camp at the port [Ostend] where we recently disembarked.

We had a calm voyage over, uneventful as far as I know, but I slept most of the time.

Tomorrow we move again, I think, but of course we don't know anything. I'll write when I'm able, but please don't worry if you don't hear for several days or even weeks at a time.

The local men served our meal this evening, all looking a little pinched, perhaps, but very facetious & obviously fluent in the richest English swear words. Even little urchins came into our dining hall with sacks & filled them with cakes or crusts we gave them, & if any fuss arose, they just swore roundly in English. All Esperanto etc might start with swear words, because they appear to be the easiest learnt & most popular words.

I'll write again soon – so greetings for the New Year.

[With his move to active service Len signed his first three letters "Yours ever, Len".]

224 PFA, BLA – Boxing Day [1944]

Perhaps Mother will let you read my letter to her of yesterday. It will tell you what a good Xmas I had here.[1] After only 3 days here, I am quite at home, but unfortunately today we move on. But I had indeed a very happy Xmas with these kind people & they have made [me and?] my friend Halstead very welcome. It didn't matter how much we protested about rations and food difficulties, like our own colliery folk all they cried was "*c'est le Noël*" – "*ce n'est rien*" etc. So we have had some delicious meals – have you had "*chicons*" [chicory] done in butter? Or apple fritters dipped in batter of *farine, bière et oeuf* [flour, beer and egg], & fried. They even brought old red wine from the cellar. Madame is a widow; she owns a clothes factory in a nearby town. She has one daughter, Isabelle 23, two sons, Paul & Hector, at high school. Paul is very good at English but Hector's rapid French leaves me confused. I understand Madame & Isabelle very well however. Perhaps you notice how three days of speaking French make my sentences short & clipped. It's got to be a habit[…]

Best wishes for the New Year.

Len was assigned to the 1st Canadian Parachute Battalion, which was part of the 6th Airborne's 3rd Parachute Brigade. In early January he arrived with the Canadians at Rochefort, at the western tip of the Bulge forced by the attacking Germans.

224 PFA, BLA - 9/10/11? January 1945 (forgotten date)
[envelope postmarked 15 January]

I got a lone letter from you yesterday, for which I was grateful. And now a day or two's rest to bath as best we can, to rest, get warmed, write a few lines, & generally recover. It is very cold, with snow making things difficult[…]

I don't think my parents & friends quite understand the circumstances in which I left England & I think everyone may be a little hurt to think I just didn't bother to let them know. Well, at 6 one morning we learnt we were going, by noon we were gone. It wasn't permitted to write letting people know, & in any case any letter to or from us (like my hurried note to my parents) were "frozen" for a week at the APO. So the first letter I could get to you announcing my embarkation was from this side when we landed at Ostend. It is always difficult for soldiers going abroad to let their people know, & if it is a long journey, as with Tony [Mona's brother], it might take months.

Later

Just had your actual first letter of 3 January, so I can now work out that you heard from me 11 or 12 days after I wrote. But you had conjectured correctly before that I see.

You know I had a good Xmas & even a decent New Year, but I'll not (I can't) say anything about things since. But it is sometimes a source of regret to me that I can speak even a little French, because there is no chance of detaching oneself completely somehow. By some silly chance it makes me more vulnerable to the soul-searchings of pity & remorse. The sufferings in this war (& any I can see) are terrible, but I think it has taken this to really reveal the full picture, to me anyway. To be on the spot to so many things is almost more than I can bear, & yet one must perforce callously ward off the poor clamouring civilians who have perhaps a dear one dying or missing or merely ill. We do what we can, & the MO [medical orderly] is overworked. But we do what we can, though we haven't the supplies.

Atrocities are unbearable, but I can't say any more. I only want to be a blind unthinking soldier but not many of us can be like that. The problem of the homeless here is much worse than that of those bombed out in England & that is bad enough[…]

I hope you're well & happy yourself. My own morale is heightened this evening because for the first time today my feet are warm.

For the sake of narrative coherence it is worth including here a letter Len wrote over a year later from Palestine mentioning an incident while he was in Belgium. While at Rochefort he almost found himself acting as a midwife.

Sarafand, 4 February 1946

Hugh Mowat has just received a letter from Belgium which rather concludes a story I may have started [in] my letters from there last year. I thought I would like to finish it properly, but haven't time, but the letter [hand-copied by Len] explains itself. Forgive another war story. Only now are we beginning to know the end of them, & in this case, & that of Emilie Maîtrejean[2] it is a great pleasure to hear.

Briefly, when at Rochefort, a patrol called out a medics party for a family stranded between the lines and Moruzzi & I went out to get them into our Aid Post. They were in a cellar, here called *caves*, of a big Chateau, badly blasted by shelling. Family well-to-do, husband English-speaking (see from letter), 5 children all tiny, and wife already in labour. I hadn't the foggiest idea what to do except that gentleness was imperative. We got her to a jeep, thence to Aid Post, thence to the MDS[3] behind the lines in an ambulance, where I handed her over to them. Hugh Mowat was the orderly on duty & he escorted her back to Namur & the letter concludes the story. Apparently they had lost a former child and so the name Marie-Ange is given to this child. Isn't it pathetic, the belief in the dead child watching over the unborn one. How pious and believing those dear people were in the Ardennes.

Hugh, with his usual sense of detail, got their address and wrote to them at Xmas.

The birth of the child was delayed even to Louvain, where they went from Namur. And to think Hugh & I were sweating in case it would be born in the ambulance.

The letters from Belgium continue:

224 PFA, BLA – 14 January 1945

[…] I have read an atrocity story in the paper of 9th or 10th. Have you? It's terrible[…]

As for what I'm doing, sometimes I feel at last I'm of some use, especially to civilians, but that is all done on my own, not officially, so I have to be tactful. It is hard for them. It is little enough we can do.

Len's next letter was posted in an "Army privilege envelope" bearing the note:

"Correspondence in this envelope need not be censored regimentally" and a decla-
ration "that the contents[...] refer to nothing but private and family affairs". He
replied to a letter from Mona in which she clearly expressed concern for his safety
and once more poured out her feelings for him. Unlike most of his letters from the
field of action, this one is intensely personal.

224 PFA, BLA – 22 January 1945

[…] Your letter of the 9th concerned me of course, & to tell you the
truth, it never occurs to me here that we may not see each other again.
I merely presume that we shall, & I know inside that we shall. I'm
lucky, I have a guardian angel I'm sure, so as far as I'm concerned
there's little to fear. When I was out with the battalion I was often
scared, especially one night, but as I say, I'm lucky. In my constant
doubting I'm reluctant to speak of the protection of God – there are
so many others in worse circumstances by far – those with more faith
& trust than me, those more innocent, more ignorant, not knowing
the why or wherefore of it all. So I carry on, believing in myself, &
helped by all you good people at home, & probably (who knows)
protected by God of whom I speak so diffidently. But don't fear – and
above all, don't believe all the newspapers say[…]

As to your other, more personal remarks, as usual I am tongue-tied.
I can only repeat what I've said before – that you over-estimate any
qualities I may have & that I am unworthy of what you feel. When I
read your words last night, it was so intensely cold that it was with difficulty that I held the tears back. I'm honest when I say that your letter
brought tears to my eyes, because I felt all at once how much I'd failed
you, and how little you have deserved the suffering I have caused you.
To have felt, in a single moment, how much you have suffered was
hard to bear. Yet as time goes on, I realize more & more what I've
done in the past, how empty of heart I've been, & I'm much the same,
only more careful, I suppose. I'm not very happy about it; of course,
it's no credit to me. But that is no comfort to you, & I think it is comfort
you need. Perhaps if our positions were reversed, you would become
so preoccupied with all the little difficulties & discomforts, how to
overcome them, & with the sufferings of others that you would worry
less about me, & though I certainly don't want you to be out here, I
think it would be good, if only to give you your own burden.

There is so little I can do to comfort you. I should like to be worthy of your friendship forever, & return all that you have done for me. The latter is impossible, but I think the former may be the best we can do for each other. I want to help you, & if my friendship can mean anything (& I believe it does mean something) to you, then I offer it forever in the hope that it will help to give you joy & comfort. I know you have sufficient work & purpose in life to make your life fuller & more beautiful than that of most people. All I want to do is to belong to that life as a friend, & if I'm good enough & don't continue to be as worthless as I have been, then I can help you, I know. But there is so much in life, & you know it, that I hardly need say more. The present seems a suitable arrangement, but I sometimes worry about the future & all it may mean. If, for instance, I might really fall in love and wish to marry. It hardly seems possible, even though I'm speaking as barely 26, but it is possible, I suppose. I wonder how you might react? I can't help thinking that you would suffer intensely and I don't want you to. I suppose the best thing is to say "Come what may – *Carpe diem*" & so on, but I do think of you, now, in the past, in the future – how you will fare[…]

I don't think any friendship has ever gone through the vicissitudes that ours has suffered (all my fault) & yet survived. Can it still survive? I think so, & I hope it gets richer, despite my own failings & neglect and weakness. Beneath, in my true self, you know I value your friend-ship as much as anything life has given me, & it is my loss that I have been unable to return the depth of love with which you regard me.

This is quite a long letter for me – my hands are wrinkling with cold & frost but I hope I've conveyed adequately what I feel. But as I say, it is not yet time to speak of the lovely passage from Turgeniev – perhaps only when I'm on an Airborne operation shall I begin to expect or write what you call the "last letter". Then, there is a good chance for me but not so good as now I must admit when I do at least operate from behind our own lines. But whatever guards me will not fail me, I'm sure, & what I look forward to, like everyone else, is peace & a return to our homes, conversation on our own beloved subjects (not those imposed by the constantly recurring barrack-room arguments), privacy, & all those precious pursuits which war, or the army, interrupted. Is it a dream? Not so long as we cherish it in the spirit & can return with sufficient strength of mind to take up the threads once more.

The short time over here has already been an experience to me. All the time I want to return to England – the worse it is, the more horrible it is, the more intensely I want England – but I feel I have done a little valuable work already. I find myself quickly adaptable, & am a free-lance with my Canadian MO who seems to appreciate one. I do a lot of everything as the need occurs, dressing, bearing, translating, helping civilians (some dates you sent went to a little girl whose eyes would have rewarded you) sawing wood for a fire (there's lots of mundane tasks you know, as important as the actual care of the wounded) & so on. As you know, there are Canadians in the 6th & in action I'm with them. They're good lads, silly sometimes, but full of courage & good spirits[…]

[Signed "Ever yours, Len".]

Len now gave a little more detail of the atrocity he had referred to earlier. At the eastern village of Bande the Germans shot 34 civilians, mostly young men, in retaliation for the killing of one of their men by the Belgian Resistance. Len became friends with a local family called Maîtrejean, whose 18-year-old son was among the victims. A year later he received a letter from the boy's younger sister Emilie, thanking Len "for little bits of things I had done for her & her family, for I never saw such distress as at Bande & the next village where Emilie Maîtrejean was forced to stay". The poor girl was ill with TB. "Without you I would no longer be here," she wrote.

224 PFA, BLA – 27 January 1945

[…] I had another bundle of mail tonight, with letters of the 17, 18, 19 & 21 from you, including a little parcel. Thank you. Your letters are a great source of help & comfort to me, & I'm sure it must be a hard job for you to write to me every day as you do.

I'm afraid you'll be getting my letters in "pending numbers" – according to our mailing list, there are long gaps between dispatches, so you will understand if you don't get a letter for perhaps 2 weeks. After that you ought to get 4 or 5 at once & probably you have, because I've tried to write to my parents & you at least twice a week, if only in a few lines. I shall certainly write home twice a week or more, whatever happens, so you'll be able to find out from them when the gaps occur. I'm sorry you had such a long gap about the 4th[…]

Your words about the poor civilians over here show me that you understand & can imagine some of their misery. The Canadian Padre did much good work at some of the places we went through, and the MO too. At one village, he was much loved by the people though I don't think he realized it. In his broad unassuming & direct style he tended their needs, without the proper medicine often, because naturally we'd not equipped for special sicknesses. But the civilian doctors were mostly miles away & there was no transport & so on. One village was in deeper distress than usual because in addition to shattered homes, the Germans, in taking reprisals against local Maquis activity had killed 37 [sic] young men & hidden them in a cellar & left them. So that, in addition to sickness, semi-starvation & lack of proper shelter, many wept for a loved one who had perhaps suffered before he died. There is no hysteria – only a desperate apathy & an anxious searching for belongings as they come from their cellars or from a few miles back. Once in the back area again they begin to smile even, as the war moves on & they feel safe again – but many have lost what can never be replaced – a loved one, the little priceless possessions of home; one woman had lost a child, & a brother in the atrocity too. Oh there are many things I could tell you about these forward areas, but perhaps I'd better not say more. I feel so terribly sorry for them, & though we did what we could, & even evacuated certain cases, there was little we could do really[…]

In one of his letters from the Low Countries, Len described getting to know John Petts, who was already an established artist in North Wales. Theirs would be an enormously important friendship for Len; Petts was the prime agent of his move to Wales and his embarking on a career in art.

224 PFA, BLA – 30 January 1945

I want to write you a longish letter, because it is several days since [I wrote] to you or to anybody, & though I've wanted to say certain things I just haven't written. The old complaint, depression & *laissez-*

faire, & not pressure of service. It's the first time I've felt really depressed since I came over here, but I think I am a little unwell & haven't been standing the cold so well. And perhaps there is a certain reaction after what I was doing.

But a thaw has come I think & at any rate I'm warmer. And if I can get this letter written as I wish, I shall feel better[…]

Whilst on that night duty I [was] with an artist whom I've tried to contact & have always missed somehow. John Petts, 31 years old, strong & healthy with a manly face & like Johnny Geard[4], full of that character which is strong to give some to other people. Naturally, the war meant little to either of us really; we talked of personal things, starting from books, but I was so suddenly content for an hour to be talking to this "brother in art" that I derived something from our conversation akin to the spirit of some Quaker meeting. And I felt this particularly when we found ourselves discussing friends. Suddenly, as though impetuously, John spurted out "Oh, but there's nothing like a friend you were once in love with & have got over it. You know – beyond sex, & differences and so on. I think that's the greatest friendship of all." I can't convey the spirit & enthusiasm with which he said this. I was just silent, taking it in, & feeling then I must pass on this message to you. I don't know why, because I feel you still regard me in a different light, which you cannot help doing of course. But the words struck home, & I determined to pass them on.

Later, talking about after the war, I said that, barring obstacles, I hoped to take up Art altogether even if it meant poverty. I hoped I wouldn't get married or that would scotch it. "Oh, you mustn't talk of marriage like that. I was married, and I'll marry again – it's wonderful really you know." That was all – no details, but a touch of humour in his eyes prompted me to ask if his wife was still alive. "Yes – she's a poet – perhaps you know of her. Her name's Brenda Chamberlain." Well, as it happened, I did know of her & could even remember a particular long work which she had published in fragments, mostly in *Poetry Quarterly*. One might put her in the same school as Jim. As to her relations with John, I could glean no more, of course, but he is a fine fellow. He is content to live alone & paint in North Wales. His best friend was Alun Lewis, who died recently & John spoke very fondly of him. John designed the book jacket of one of Lewis's books, with Lewis's portrait. Perhaps you can get it for me. And get too, if you can, James Bramwell's *Going West*, please.[5]

Petts was enthusiastic about Welsh arts, shared my enthusiasm for David Jones, & my hatred of Cronin[6] (who merely cropped up somehow), my interest in miners & so on.

It's a pity I see very little of him, because Army life has been rather friendless & lonely without George [Downs][…]

Incidentally, the atrocity I mentioned was in some papers, & some day I must tell you about it. It was a sad affair & consolation was impossible. The MO had to go to see them first, & then I had to tell two sisters. Their mother was terribly ill & yet they had to bear that too. The *curé* spared me the pain of informing the old lady, but she was very courageous. That night we were dive-bombed – it was terrifying of course, & the sisters came downstairs in a panic & asked me to carry the old lady downstairs to the cellar. Some day I can tell you all about these things, but there was one thing, it was always a pleasure to work under Captain Costigan the Canadian MO & I did everything I could for him. But he was grateful, I know, & believe me, Mona, if only there was a little more of his appreciation & gratitude throughout the Army it would be much better.

Anyway, that dear old lady made it her job to tell the Captain what I'd done, & he thanked me very warmly. To find appreciation, though I wanted no thanks, helped me a lot & I tried always to work hard for the Canadians & the civilians.

The Russian news is very stirring, & I wonder what it will mean? The end in Europe soon? – then what? We all think the longer we are here, the less time in Burma, so we mustn't fret for home & you mustn't fret for us. What a position.

Around late January or the beginning of February, 224 PFA were moved from Belgium to the Weert area of the southern Netherlands, facing the Germans across the Maas. The people here were even more starved than the Belgians. Len, constrained by the two-week restriction on divulging where he had been, did not mention any of this in his intermittent letters. He wrote of a chance meeting with Captain Bill Brown, with whom he had shared an art prize at Jarrow County Secondary School ten years earlier, and of finding a "delightful billet" with spring mattress bunks, luxury after the Ardennes cold. He returned to England with the rest of the unit late in the month. A week's leave in the North followed.

224 PFA, APO England – 9 March 1945

I'm sorry I haven't had much time to write yet. But here's a note at any rate. I've had two letters from you already, thank you – both rather sad, I feel. I think you must have found me rather out-of-tune (I confess I was) amidst the quickness and wistfulness of Jim's recent visits. I can feel it in the letters. Perhaps I couldn't help it, because our lives have been such a contrast since Xmas, & leave tends to make one so excitable & talkative – it was such a release after prolonged absence from friends. No leaves, except for the few days alone on the Roman Wall & in the hills etc, last time have brought the peace that I felt for one day as at the Leigh.

Wensleydale, as usual, left me rather sad, & packing things up at Witton was like breaking up a well beloved home. I did enjoy my evening at Boltby, though only Joan was there that I know. And of course I had a good day with George [presumably Jackson] – though I think I made him ill[…]

The 6th Airborne Division would only remain in England for just over a month. It went straight into training for a major operation – the crossing of the Rhine into Germany. Len described the preparations, and calmly considered the possibilities of what could happen in such an engagement.

Monday [12 March 1945? – envelope postmarked 14 March, Salisbury, Wilts]

I did a jump yesterday and it was quite a success. I was no 5, in a stick of 12 and we flew round for a long time before we took action stations. During the flight I nearly went to sleep (I suppose it was nervous exhaustion) though I had perfect control of myself. Usually, to give myself every chance, I don't look out of the plane except for brief glimpses – that was a pity because we flew west and I could have seen Glastonbury etc from the Air. But I'm afraid aesthetic considerations & even curiosity are annulled by my nervousness.

Later in the week

Dear me – what a week! I haven't had a moment's peace till now,

Wednesday, when Petts & I have rushed off without tea to escape for a while. I was going to describe my jump on Sunday, because I was more conscious of the actual jump than ever before. But I must skip the finer feelings. We had two minutes on the red light, standing waiting in the swaying plane. I couldn't avoid seeing the other planes flying tip to tip beside. I never saw the green light – there was a quick movement, I moved up, there was no one before me & I was out before I knew what I was doing & even before my chute opened I was putting my hand up because I'd forgotten to adjust my crash helmet & it was loose. Holding it on, my chute developed perfectly, [John] Dunster was there beside me, swinging in a wide arc & shouting "Good show, Sir". In fact we talked all the way down, our chutes touching & we seemed to swing in huge arcs. I had a perfect landing, but John was "out" for a while, landing in a swing. So altogether it was a good jump, & John, who was soon OK was the only casualty in the unit. It was good to see so many fellows around in mid-air.

Jumping is going on all the time & we can watch them as we go about our daily routine. There was one nasty accident which we, knowing something about it, were horrified to watch. One fellow got caught somehow and was dangling from the plane. It flew round for nearly 2 hours & then disappeared – we don't know what happened but the last time it happened the fellow died as they tried to cut him off above Poole harbour. So much for the jump.

As for my actions in the near future I'm very vague. Everything is veiled in secrecy & we only guess. But I think next week at this time we may be in "concentration", but whether for a big Division scheme or an operation I can't tell. I think the former, but preparations suggest the latter & we have no free time, even on evenings, just lately. We did a vicious route march yesterday at such a pace that we were half dead. But a shower soon pulls one round. Then big signs are being painted urgently on jaconet visible from the air & artillery, with red crosses, directions etc, I am on with Petts painting them & am a sort of protected person – the RSM [Regimental Sergeant Major] nurses us & altogether I am getting on in the unit at last. Our officer seems to rely on me for several things, which I like, but the RSM wants me in a new HQ section with the operation theatre orderlies, with Bramwell, Petts & Mowat, the fellows after my own heart. But, silly fellow, I feel a sort of loyalty to my own officer & against my desires am trying to stay put. Frightfully Quixotic of me, but you understand the feeling. At any rate it's good to feel you're wanted.

Then I have been typing:- a history of the unit in Normandy ed. by Mowat & Bramwell & it had to be finished urgently, having been interrupted by the "Ardennes campaign" as we now call it. You'd have been amazed to see the Quiet Room last midnight, three typewriters typing furiously & three men dictating. So you see how busy I've been. There was the Army to torment us still, of course – blancoing for a CO & inspection today & big preparations for an ADMS inspection on Friday[…]

I must be quick though with these letters. In case next fortnight or so is an operation & anything happens I want you to do one particular thing. That is, if anything should happen to me, there are two bundles of letters in my big box at home where my books are kept – one is of your letters, the other of Jim's. Will you please take yours (the little fat bundle) & also return Jim's to him please. I feel letters are between friends only & I want the lovely personal sacredness of those letters to remain unspoiled by others' reading, even my parents.

Please don't take this as an indication of the future & don't refer to it please in your letters. It may not be an op. & if it is, I may be OK. So beyond just making the mental note about those letters, just forget it.

I must write to George now.

P.S. I am going to post this in Salisbury to avoid censorship. But I must wait for the dark as it's strictly taboo[…]

I agree with you – leaves are a mistake – next time my one object is to "find myself again" & leave people & places out of it. I'll probably go painting in Yorkshire or Northumberland – but all I want is to have myself back for a little while.

[No address], Sunday 1.0 pm [18 March 1945?]

Paper from my empty sketch book.

Once more I've managed to escape & this time good and early and after getting a lift in a Jeep was in Salisbury by 12. I've had dinner &

have walked along the river (the Avon?) till I'm well out of town & can see the Cathedral flanked by a long line of poplars[…]

I'm about to go into concentration, probably during the coming week. There we shall be absolutely cut off from the world and my letters will indicate nothing. They won't tell you I'm in concentration, certainly won't tell you what I'm doing, & most certainly won't tell for when we are jumping. For the sake of the rest, anyway, I'd never put such details in a letter but of course censorship will be very strict, & probably all I'll be able to write about will be to say that I'm well etc etc. So excuse the scrappiness of my letters please – it's so difficult to write sometimes, knowing all is to be read by some officer of your unit before your correspondent does.

Between working time etc I have been training & like the rest am fit to bursting point. We are like prize fighters, ready for the boxing ring, trained to such a key that we can hardly hold ourselves. No wonder the lads go round smashing things up. Soon Salisbury will be out of bounds there has been so much damage done lately. When they get some drink they're fighting mad. I've been working with John Petts, knocking out all sorts of signs & directions on the lovely smooth jaconet. Each sign folds up and takes up hardly any room. We are almost finished and the CO & RSM are highly pleased because it is an innovation in Army signs – Airborne signs as it were. Signs, especially abroad, are very important, and for miles around there will be signs directing stretcher-bearers etc to the dressing-station & operation theatre, resuscitation etc… Slit trenches will be dug for each – one big slit trench for operations & resuscitation which are most important of course. So our first labours as we drop are to dig in & try to provide a MDS. I'll be with the Canadian Battalion of course, & our job is to establish an Advance Dressing Station, where we collect, treat & hold casualties until we can evacuate them to the MDS. All evacuation will be over open country by hand so I'm not looking forward to that, because it's there that mortars begin & I hate them. A sniper can see & respect the Geneva [Red] cross, but a mortar can't. But we should pull through, it's amazing how only mortars scare me, but they do – indeed they terrify me. I think it must be the strange cough, whistle & splutter they make. Perhaps we shall make an unopposed landing. After all, perhaps the Germans are more frightened of parachutists falling than we are of them by then on the ground. If so, they must be mighty scared. In the plane I shall have a terrific load. I have medical equipment in every pouch & pocket on me & my load besides that is a folding stretcher, Thomas Splint (ask Father) & 3 blankets, all wrapped in a ground sheet. It is about 5 feet long & a foot thick and feels mighty heavy. But apparently, when I jump, once I'm in the slipstream, I just ride it like a witch riding her broom until my chute opens. The weight all at the bottom so a somersault is impossible (I hope). We drop on a specified dropping zone (DZ) which may or may not be raked with fire or mined – probably not – then getting our bearings we make for a specified rendezvous (RV) – some wood or landmark etc. Then, all being well, having RVd, the battalions attack their objectives – perhaps a road junction, village etc... & hold it until relieved by the ground forces.

All this is merely to inform & interest you. In concentration, we shall be fully briefed, to the last detail, plans will change every day as the war moves, & it is quite possible we shan't jump at all, because the big-bugs want to be more certain this time & won't make gambles like Arnhem.

John & I have talked quite a lot. He is a charming fellow, but so completely in love that he is really unapproachable at heart. All of him is for her [Kusha Miller], & when I met her by accident last night I realized how very much in love he must be. He had brought back from leave a portrait of her, which he showed me. I was so completely enthralled with it, it was so much in the spirit of Renoir's women, that, not knowing all the details I begged him to sell it to me. But he wouldn't naturally. She is an artist herself, & last night, as I was walking across from our barracks to the road, I met in the corner of the field this girl – I knew her immediately from the portrait; made myself known, if only to let her know that John *was* free & would soon be with her. She was very happy to know that, & that I'd recognized her from the portrait. I hadn't known she was coming right up to Bulford to see John – I thought he was going to Salisbury, but of course, she was saving valuable time, for she'd come a long way to see him.

Why do I tell you all this, I wonder? I suppose because it is such an ideal love affair – they met quite by accident at a mutual friend's house. John might have spent that weekend at 10 other places he says. And the whole business is rather on the same level as Charles Morgan's people.

As to Brenda Chamberlain, that is a sad & strange affair – as John says it is very, very rare; simple because Brenda is as wild & strange as Jim – can you imagine Jim married. John & Brenda were students together, married, lived together – she began to write & one day, just like that, declared she wanted to live alone, seemed final & he had no choice. Either he or she had to leave the house – so being the man he just bundled up as much as he could with a sad heart & left. That was over 3 years ago – now a divorce is on the way – but John hates the word. Because it hardly applies (they left good friends, but as an artist he realized how final she was) & it is hard for his lady. But she understands all, I'm sure, & some day they will marry. John talks for hours to me about it, because I'm the only one who knows a single detail – I told him about Morgan, about *Portrait in a Mirror,* because my own experience of the portrait (I'm in love with it) was so like that. He agreed that the whole affair was like Morgan, their relationship & the inevitability of their meeting. We discussed this inevitability – how all of life falls into a plan it seems – the mistakes, successes, regrets, joys, everything in the past build up into a great I, great Us – was inevitable – the present & the future is beautifully inevitable – for some unknown reason, if we go to Germany, it is inevitable that those who don't return don't. The plan of life has worked out that their lives should end then [so] it will be inevitable – but it is hard to explain. It makes me feel uncomfortable rather, because there are more reasons for me to die than for most people – I hope for instance, that if George More or I had to die that it would be me, because George has a wife & 2 lovely children. But those aren't the reasons. It is a strange thing, something which makes even the minutest details & movements in our lives vastly important. Nothing is too small in this plane of living, & the tiniest movements, the most apparently inconsequential are controlling us all the time. They are controlling you, me – they will control me (in a most consistent line if we could discover it) to or away from the piece of shrapnel or the bullet. It is as intangible, indescribable and far reaching as a radio beam, but as inevitable and controlled too. So it is useless to try to explore it – psychology, the mysticism we are sometimes privileged to possess, religion, philosophy, all merely touch at a tangent, because can't you see how impenetrable a thing it is, how many moments of our lives are spent in darkness, how comparatively little we ourselves control life, how little, for instance, even the best of us thinks, how lost to us so often is the mere turning of our eye or opening of our lips so often (but how important is this controlling spirit)[…]

Some have been making out wills – I haven't. Because I don't presume we are going to be cut down – I think we may not go, & if we do, may have an easier time than we expect. I have told you only what to do with the letters because of their personal preciousness, because something may happen – but please don't take that as a premonition. Above all (I need hardly beg this) don't take it as a rather dramatic sentimentalism. Probably I shall return alive & well, & the whole thing, this letter, will appear in retrospect rather silly. That is why, as you know, though there are many things I might say about us in particular, I am not saying them. All has been said, & I prefer, if anything should happen, that the thread should go on as though it had never been cut by death or by last words in a letter. Let life continue, let death, if it chooses to come, be merely what it is, a part of that uncontrollable spirit in those still living. I might, if I think of better, & if I have time & opportunity to get an uncensored letter to you, let you know how to dispose of my few possessions, my books, but in general they are for friends & I make you a sort of executor (all just in case)[…]

I hope this letter doesn't disconcert you – it's a mood, if you like – things exist, if you like, in a "shrill stem of laughter", and only after a month, or perhaps 2, will you get a normal letter. In the meantime, I have enjoyed writing this – you know how much I like to write a long discursive letter to you & how little opportunity I have now.

[Signed "With my thoughts, Len".]

Before troops went into battle they were meant to write a "last letter" to their nearest and dearest in case the worst happened. But Len had already said everything he wanted to say to Mona, so he used his last letter (dated 22 March) merely to enthuse about some sonnets by Rainer Maria Rilke. The crossing over the Rhine –

Len's Field Service Postcard of 26 March

Operation Varsity – took place on *24 March. The airborne forces landed north of the small town of Wesel, where the Rhine begins to bend west towards the Nether-lands. It was the biggest such action in history, and it was a complete success, although it came with a heavy cost to the 6th Airborne Division of over 1,000 casualties. Len's first communication to Mona afterwards, dated 26 March, was a preprinted "Field Service Post Card" which stated "Sentences not required may be erased". His choice of words was "I am quite well. Letter follows at first oppor-tunity. Greetings and best wishes." His first proper letter followed ten days later and described something of his experience in the drop.*

RAMC, Att. A COY, 1st Canadian Parachute Battalion, BLA
– 6 April 1945

I have a little time to devote to letters, so perhaps I can get one off to you without interruption. Yours are beginning to come in regularly, and since I am more or less permanently with this battalion now, you may as well write to this address until further notice.

I have been unable to contact my unit since the drop, because I jumped with the Canadians & have since been put into a Coy so have nothing to do with the MDS now my work being confined to the company. So I have been unable to find out about some of my pals. A few I know are dead but of the others I'm uncertain. James Bramwell & John Petts cause me most anxiety, because they were taken prisoner shortly after taking a casualty from Dunster & I. Apparently they couldn't get their batch back, as with Dunster & I, but whereas Dunster & I got back the same day or the next, I hadn't heard of James & John before I lost contact. Capt Chaundy, our anaesthetist & dentist, who was a great chap to get along with, was shot as he dropped in the trees. Geordie Hall, a typical Tynesider, who had seen service in Burma, the Middle East, Normandy, Ardennes & Holland was killed too (rather strangely wearing a leather belt of mine which Betty once wore). Others I'm very vague about – I realize how lucky I've been when I remember Capt Chaundy & the Colonel of this battalion, both killed in the drop. – I landing just off some trees, & the first people I saw were 3 Jerries, pale with terror, I suppose, in a deep trench with a Spandau. They were quite harmless & nobody took any notice of them it seemed as we gradually accumulated & trekked back to our respective rendezvous.

The worst part was the flight, I think – nearly 3 hours of intense strain & I felt hardly conscious as I saw the Rhine below, & the red light went on. By the time the green light went on the flak was terrific or so it seemed. I was behind Dunster and we approached the door with our long heavy bundles, there was a burst of flak which tilted the plane, making us a sort of hill to climb before we could get out. So that when I finally climbed up to the door I had to take a big lunge to get out & I seemed to dive & ride on my bundle like a witch on a broom. There was so much flak & small arms fire below that I hardly remember my chute opening. I can remember my bundle swinging in a wide arc below me as I released it & that I seemed all the way to be landing on a house, but I didn't.

The Canadians attained their objective – we moved in – Dunster & I went out to get casualties but were cut off by a party of Jerries who were a bit of a mystery but infested the woods all around. I'm very vague about the whole position, but the rest of the story is in my parents' letters of today. I was alone from about noon till 7 & the only reason I was left alone by the Germans was because the house (a small peasants' place) was the German dressing station, abandoned with its Red Crosses still draped about. As they were wounded, they kept coming to see me as though I were the German orderly in charge, & I remember one rather old Jerrie's astonishment when after asking if I was "Deutsch" I said "Nein, Englische"[…]

I wish this was Rilke's Germany & not Hitler's. The people are difficult to understand – they appear to welcome us – but I wonder. My chief reaction is that, looking at them impartially as though they were not enemies, I don't like them.

Marie Madelaine's [sic] letter is very sad & after seeing certain things, after speaking to the Belgians in particular, I can feel their satisfaction at this repayment for past wrongs.[7] That is the past & how can they forget it! But what of the future?[…]

Over the 40 days after the Wesel drop, the 6th Airborne Division was in the vanguard of a drive 275 miles across the north German plain to the Baltic. Whenever he had time – which was intermittent – he would write to Mona describing some of his experiences.[8]

1st Canadian Parachute Battalion, BLA – 12.1.45
[sic – postmarked 13 April]

[…] We have liberated many Frenchmen, you will be pleased to hear – the few I have managed to speak to were very happy – none of them came from Lens & district so I couldn't send a message to Marie Madelaine. I expect by now you are getting letters & parcels, perhaps, to her.

I often think, like Jim, that there will be no place for the artist in the future. But of course that is proved impossible by the past, & even if artists have to settle inside themselves, be self-sufficient as it were, for a generation, the time will return when their place will be there for them without the feeling of futility & sterility that is bound to prevail for them at present. For a generation then artists may only write paint compose for themselves & not for a dead public – but so long as they create, the time will arrive when the world will accept. In any case, as with Hitler's régime, the people can't feed indefinitely on untruths, & the old swing of the pendulum will bring the world back to truth ultimately.

Some of Germany I like – the barns in particular – half timbered with the names of the first owner & his wife on the huge beam above the door – sometimes in Gothic, sometimes in Roman, but always well done, with a motto of course. But Hitler is stamped everywhere too & one can see how hateful it has all been. I really think that Germany will split up again into her small principalities would work [sic]. The main thing is to get this episode over. They're too damned obstinate to give in.

Cheerio for now.

1st Canadian Parachute Battalion, BLA – 18 April 1945

[…] Your letters, I do remember, mention the preparation for victory day of some of the fools at home. There is nothing more disgusting to men out here, since they are seeing what the price is, & many, after victory here, will have to start over again in Burma. So where is the cause for celebration? They talk of drinks & frivolity while men are still dying or being wounded. I can understand the relief at Germany's final conquest, but what of Japan? And I agree with you, that because of the price, victory is no sign for empty celebration but rather for relief in the present, hope for the peace to come, and memory for those who gave their lives in the past, and gave their years, though living. One can only feel blind rage & indignation at such people[…]

[Signed "Yours ever, Len".]

On 1 April the 6th Airborne Division crossed the Dortmund-Ems canal near Ladbergen. In a dramatic incident here fate smiled on Len. On 5 April the 1st

Canadian Parachute Battalion reached Minden, which is probably the "very old & famous" town mentioned in the following letter.

1st Canadian Parachute Battalion, BLA – 19 April 1945

Perhaps I can get a fuller letter than usual off to you this time. I hope so. I'm afraid that during these few weeks the slightest extra weight has had to be discarded and I have none of your letters to answer except the first one to this address which I received this morning. You had just received your first letter from me. I can't remember if there was much in it, but I know you must have been pleased to get it, even if it was terribly incoherent. Even now you mustn't expect a very good effort because I still can't think properly and I feel in a queer sort of haze all the time, and have the most aggravating stammer in my speech – Costigan says it's only temporary, fortunately.

Time is strange, too, and doesn't seem to matter much. The days, especially, are undistinguishable, and the hours too except for an hour at dawn & an hour at sunset, i.e. "stand-to".

I suppose for the sake of record I'd best tell you a little of "combat experiences up to a fortnight ago" – that is the allotted time. I think that would be up to the time when we took a big town that you mention.

After the drop, which I partially described I think, we linked up with the ground forces who were pleased to see us. We evacuated our wounded, buried our dead, handed over our prisoners and then as the *Times* puts it we were chosen as the spearhead of the British advance. So we marched out to the (then) front and we never rested. 2 hours sleep when we could get it was all we could manage. Perhaps at 4 in the morning, we'd be roused from a heavy slumber & off we'd go. We didn't have a rest till we took our first town. That seemed a pretty fierce engagement, but I know now it was quite a minor affair.[9] A day's rest and off the battalion went on tanks and we made a huge advance of many miles, the tanks only stopping for road blocks and intermittent opposition. It was black dark when we dismounted, well past our objective I think & moved towards a town which had two rather important little bridges. It was ghastly that night, wounded and dying Germans screaming in the darkness & nobody knowing what the score was. One bridge was attained intact, the other blew up just before our men got there. The Germans obviously hadn't expected us & civilians in the dark at first thought we were a column of Germans. A woman shouted in German something like "You're late tonight Hans", and Shweedic, in our company replied in his perfect German that he hoped the bed was ready. We didn't expect Germans either thinking they'd have fled. The shooting was quickly over, & next morning the streets were strewn with German dead. We got some German wounded in – mostly very young. I remember one, who could hardly bear us touching him. A huge ammo dump explosion shook the place – everybody was obviously shaken by the blast & we didn't know what it was. That German moved with the quickest crawl I've ever seen, he was so terrified. One German gave another with a stomach wound a drink without our knowing it and naturally he died.

Next morning the shelling was terrifying for some reason, quite demoralising. We moved to our bridge. I was called to get 3 badly wounded on the other side. Capt Freeman & Cpl Underwood & I clambered by the damaged parapet – an armoured car had fallen through the shell weakened structure & was stuck half way across blocking the whole road – it was only a narrow bridge. We had to get the stretchers over the top of the car & we'd hardly got them over & on to a jeep when everybody scattered – a Messerschmidt 109 came along. Whether he saw the red cross or what I don't know but he never opened up. We crossed the bridge again when the car was removed & the bridge reinforced by RE [Royal Engineers].

That night was our worst – we marched on a few miles & "dug in", in a wood near a canal. The wood got the worse shelling we've had yet, & the second shell got many men altogether. Next morning was a relief. One stretcher bearer lost his arm (Hunt) and Amaolo was wounded in the leg and hand. SP airbursts still continued to demoralise us, but we clambered over the shattered bridge with an ill-will I suppose, because we felt terribly weak without our tanks & transport. We captured the village on the other side & the guns that had caused us the trouble & held the village till a bridge was up next day. Then off on our tanks, or marching, or riding trucks until we were in front of our town, a very old & famous one. That was a nightmare attack, moving in the blackness, trying to make as little noise as possible over the broken glass – debris of the streets. Dogs barked sometimes & no one dare shoot. We apparently startled a woman emerging from a shelter. She became hysterical, screamed & yelled and I know the fellows must have felt like shooting her. She died down & still no sound of Germans. In fact, we went on & on till about 3 am terrified all the time, & reached our objective, a church, with only a little fire towards the end & no casualties. The Gs had apparently pulled out & crossed the river. Next day we rested. The town was freed from Nazism etc and the civilians were strange. They had been used to such rigid discipline that all they did when we arrived & daylight came was loot a cigar warehouse & a liqueur store. No joy, no sorrow, no thought at all, in fact, just a flock of sheep following the leader who looted first. That was my impression of the crowd – individuals I must tell you about when I see you.

Since then I've been in two very exciting engagements of more importance than the rest – but I don't suppose I can tell you about them. Perhaps later.

As you see, I'm right with the company now & never leave them. Before I was with the RAP [Regimental Aid Post] & had to go out and help company stretcher-bearers when necessary & then vacate casualties. Now I dress the wounded as they fall, hand them over to an RAP man & then carry on. So I am now in every assault from start to finish, & though I'm often scared stiff, I know that I'm the man for the wounded. I can save his life more than doctors further back, who often get badly dressed cases too late. So it is just the job for me as you can imagine, though sometimes it's a strain. But I'm with a great company, the general's special favourite, & we've never failed him yet. Don't you feel the soldierly pride now I'm a regular infantry wallah. When we rest we have our own little sick parade, diagnose & treat & only send the bad or mysterious cases to the MO.

So you have a rough idea of my job & since you asked, I thought it worthwhile to describe. It is a great job really & I love it, feeling a sort of amateur doctor with my own practice. I'm not a cog in the medical unit any longer. Only there are the sickening moments before assaults, but everybody is the same. The experience is amazing and though the threnody has gone, there are separate moments that I remember vividly & shall never forget. Horrors too, which nauseated me & have often had difficulty in thrusting from my mind. Being in a victorious army is sickening too, in a way. At first it was just plain savagery & barbarism, with draws emptied on the floor, everything turned out, locked doors burst or shot open, civilians turned onto the streets & wholesale damage everywhere. Then it was just a tidy looting & search for food & souvenirs etc... I'm out of it where all that is concerned, but the Cannucks now accept my attitude and I get along with them very well. They just can't understand anyone not deliberately destroying & looting[…]

224 PFA, BLA – 25 April 1945

At last your letters have caught me up again. I have time to answer them but don't really feel capable. It is so hard to turn inwards these days from the outward life that all I feel capable of most often is to say I'm well, & suddenly dry up. But I must try.

What you say of Father interests me most, and I can understand him to a certain extent. Obviously (to me), of course he is exaggerating in his own mind and it is only natural. Sometimes I wish I could switch on a sort of television show to you to reveal to you just the sort of life I'm leading. Two hours ago, for instance, you'd have seen James Bramwell & I laughing fit to burst. Neither of us was meant to play football I'm sure.

Even in attacks, which certainly don't come every day, I'd have switched you on, to see me rather scared, but shouting bawdy remarks with the rest, then moving in, rather pale, eyes wide open, keeping my place as accurately as possible and then attaining the objective, lying in the sun in a ditch, waiting, perhaps dressing wounded, my heart returning to normal as the noise subsides, being probably relieved by the next company or battalion – then handing over my casualties, following the sergeant-major to our position (he always looks after the "medics"), digging in & taking over the nearest house – a meal, relaxation, perhaps even a bed (bugger the slit trench – they've moved off for the night) and so on. You'd enjoy it partly, your curiosity would be satisfied – a day then perhaps of basking in the sun, mending the men's feet, attending to small needs, frying eggs & other food, ragging the cookhouse for its poor efforts, taking photographs, recounting yesterday's attack, making much of it & remembering the brigadier's pride in our company especially, oh yes! You'd smile then, you wouldn't worry, except you'd hear an occasional remark, "When is it our turn on the tanks again" "Oh, to hell with the tanks – relax!" – and you'd wonder a bit then, as a serious moment crossed each face – then away it would go. You'd be very interested – then would appear a long column of men, marching on either side of the road, dust rising, the men rather tired, some cursing, and moving past columns coming "back", we shouting "Ruski?" – "Yah" – "Good old Joe" – a dark column "Francais?" – "Oui!" "Bon voyage" – then a tired worn-out mob with hands clasped on head – no jests now – just an occasional jibe "Shoot the bloody lot" or "Keep your hands up! Up!! UP!!! Run, you bastards, run!" and so the column passes on. Forward a village in flames – when did that happen? – we don't know – nobody knows – but here's some Jerries. Always vague.

You see, it's just like that & I really would switch you on most of the time, even to laugh as you watch me drop double quick as a machine gun sputters (rare of course).

There's not much to worry about, and there's every reason to say I'm in the best place really, because if I'd been safely back in England, still cutting timber, I'd have been nattering myself to death, just like my Father, wondering about the fellows in Germany & wishing only to be with them. So I'm quite content in that respect. My chief sore point these days is that it's now almost five years out of normal & the prospect, as far as I can see, of absolute freedom, will not come for perhaps 5 years. Germany is almost finished, but not the war. Petts & I have agreed that going East now will just cap our travels, but it is the time that hurts. We both now want to lead our own lives (like me, he spent 3 yrs on the land, then volunteered) & the years ahead seem hard to face. I'm almost certainly for the East – the East itself is a delightful prospect, but the years and the unnecessary but inevitable worries one leaves behind are hard to bear at 30 – to begin rather diffidently again where one left off at enthusiastic, vigorous 21. That is my little worry (not overwhelming) and my Father's worries about me in Germany are quite a small thing, if only he knew. In the meantime, one gets courser [sic] and wilder, incapable of being at home in a quite intelligent household, getting rustier & forgetting all to the point of ignorance and at 30 I shall be far more rough, gauche

& uncouth than I was at 20. You mustn't take it that I'm depressed – I'm not. But when I do think, I think on selfish lines, & my thoughts are like that – when will I be free to go back to normal life![…]

British and Canadian forces liberated Bergen-Belsen concentration camp on 15 April, the 1st Canadian Parachute Battalion being among the first units to arrive. Len's description is terse but eloquent. Although he was probably only there for two days[10], his experience "left an ineradicable mental scar", he wrote late in life.[11]

224 PFA, BLA – 28 April 1945

I got some mail today, from home, George, a forestry girl, Joan, Flo & you. Yours was the note of 22nd, and like George's couple, it was a bit "fed up". You were beginning yet another cold. It's no use hoping it's better – you're probably as chirpy as ever by now[…]

The most discussed thing here, of course, is the recently liberated concentration camp at _____, the big one. All the newspapers say & portray in photographs is true, I'm afraid, and many of the people were intellectuals from all over Europe – doctors, students, artists, scientists. They were so weak that they had no shame & just defecated where they sat or lay. Medical work has attended to those who weren't past hope, the dead were buried in thousands by bull-dozer (the only way, though it sounds callous) - delousing (because the lice were carrying typhus, of which they [sic] were 1000s of cases). The whole thing is too awful to talk about.

I'll try to write a longer letter later. Not much time now.

The 1st Canadian Parachute Battalion arrived in Wismar on the Baltic coast on 2 May. They were the first Empire troops to link up with the Red Army coming from the east. Len stayed in Wismar for almost three weeks, tending to casualties (mostly German) in a Luftwaffe hospital where 224 PFA set up its Main Dressing Station.

224 PFA, BLA – 7 May 1945

Your mail has rolled in – I hardly know how to answer you. I am terribly busy as you would have me be, I'm sure, and I have lots to tell you.

The devastation at Wismar

This is a single hour I have – it should have been 3, but a sister & I couldn't leave a patient we were dressing, & he took over 2 hours, he was so bad.

I had to write at your vision of Cortes, ending with "I hope you are having a nice quiet time".[12] Some day I must tell you all, for mere interest, & even now I think the censor will allow me to tell you some, since the press keeps you informed of our action anyway.

Can you imagine arriving in a town at midnight, all pitch black, and entering a hospital where all is chaos and neglect. The staff had moved out, in their hysterical fear of the Russians, and all we can see is wards of stinking, dirty patients, their wounds in various states of decay; pus, excreta, urine everywhere. No electricity, no heat, *no water,* no food.

The first night, & the first day, was one big sweep out, and the patients began to roll in, old ones with wounds as bad as or worse than the inmates we already had. The staff, whilst shipping off, had tried to take some patients with them in hospital trains. They all came back, had to be housed somehow – I don't know where they all came from but we have hundreds, mainly German. In our little sector we look after 120 & that is only ½ a floor & it's a big hospital. We had amputations, infected wounds, tubed lungs, diphtheria, typhus, starvation. I cannot give you individual cases – I wish I could, because by now I've got to know my lot very well & can see progress & so on. The tide has turned by now – those that had to die, died – & those who have a chance are looking up. Feeding has become organised, the Germans are getting together again, we have water for several hours each day & light intermittently. We have dressed them all by now, & some were so horrible as to be almost unbearable but by now I have become inured & I think I can cut away gas gangrene for an hour and not turn a hair. Most cases are in old plaster and over half are for the surgeon again but of course surgeons are short, so surgery, though over-worked now, cannot possibly cope with them so they just lie there & we dress & feed them in the hope that their turn will come some time for the table. The attitude of the patients has changed immeasurably. At first they seemed resigned to death in many cases and I know one young boy who could move neither to eat or defecate and sullied his bed. Now he is struggling to the lavatory himself, & he is one less to spoon feed. Penicillin, sulph-aguanidine, all the familiar drugs have begun and really, you'd be surprised at the difference. Each man works on his own particular cases with a sister & cooperation is running quite smoothly & efficiently.

But probably you have read elsewhere what this victory march has meant for medical staff in the various armies. Even the press is incapable of exaggeration in cases like Buchenwald & Belsen. I stopped playing soldiers when my address changed[…]

P.S. I'm so glad to hear of Tom Emerson.[13] I suppose he can hardly believe he's alive, and at home. I met an American last night who gave us a picture of the Nazi hell, and of the advancing Russians. He had just brought his wife into hospital after being raped by them (the Russians). L.

P.P.S. I am now quite an expert at injecting penicillin intra-muscu-larly.

224 PFA, BLA – 13 May 1945

There is some Mozart being played on the gramophone – it is most fitting on this warm sunny evening, with the lovely natural silence all round, the war far away and only birds, and people talking quietly as they stroll, to join Mozart. A cool breeze blows from the Baltic, making things more pleasant still. This afternoon, I went with 9 others to a concert show given by the Russians in town. It was most exciting. I have never seen such spirit & enthusiasm in singing & dancing by "non-pros". The occasion was a great one of course, and bouquets were passed between the respective brass-hats, amidst a terrific ovation from the "lads". Put on the West End, the show would bring the house down, and one is so impressed by the spirit of the Russians that it would form the best propaganda. It was quite unlike any other show I've seen. I've never been so spellbound for so long by male voice singing. The slightest nuances were registered perfectly, and they were perfect in a full-lunged passage or a delicate whisper. And this articulation in tight wordy little passage[s] (which apparently often occur in Russian song, tiny syllables racing on top of the other) was perfect too. But it was their unity & spirit which captured us all. Such singing is a privilege for Western ears surely. They danced, too, doing the impossible in physical exertion it seemed. The applause was the greatest I've ever experienced I think, & it was genuine.

I have been out yachting, boating & swimming too, so you must find this letter a strange contrast to the last. Well things have got organised at last, and only a few of us continue with dressings, I included fortunately. I still work with my Sister and we work in perfect accord, despite language differences over which we often laugh. Except for little Erich, whose brain was steadily coming out from behind his ear, we find an improvement in most of our patients. Erich died last night, after suffering agony I'm afraid. I felt almost tempted to give him a shot of morphine, but of course the consequences would have been terrible. I have access to all the drugs now, since I myself inject now, but I mustn't be tempted, of course. It is wonderful to see penicillin working, but I'm afraid it is often difficult to inject intra-muscularly, since most of the patients having it have hardly any muscle left[…]

[Signed "Yours ever, Len".]

224 PFA returned to an England celebrating victory in Europe. Len and his comrades, however, expected to be sent to the East to confront the Japanese in what it seemed would be a fight to the death. First, though, he could enjoy a decent spell of leave.

224 PFA, Carter Barracks, Bulford nr Salisbury
– Sunday [20 May 1945]

I flew back from Luneberg (near the Elbe) yesterday, in two hops, stopping at Brussels. My first thought was that by all means I must join you & your guests at the reunion on Wedn. night. Unfortunately it is not to be – I shall probably be home on Thursday eve at about 1.30. Hard lines.

But at any rate, I can wish all there a very happy evening, & best wishes for the future. I'd like to hear everybody's story of the last 5 years, particularly Tom's, but we must have another reunion, after the final victory.

I am almost deliriously happy to see English roads & hedges & rain again – I shall have a month's leave to enjoy it to the full. Then we are all going East, so I shall have my friends there with me.

Len went first to Tyneside. His meeting with Mona did not go well. She wrote to her brother Tony on 29 May: "Hookie turned up on Friday morning. He has told us a little about his experiences in Germany but he's in one of his unsettled moods. I think he dislikes all of us here and thinks we are not as brilliant as his artist friends. When he came on Friday he sat and read a book, so I did the same!" Len then moved on to Yorkshire, where he spent time with Fred Lawson and George Graham. He met up again with Mona in London, and once more their encounter was troubled. He felt that something had fundamentally changed and was deepening the gulf between them – perhaps his own psyche in reaction to all he had seen.

224 PFA, Carter Barracks, Bulford – Sunday [24 June 1945]

I have been waiting for this opportunity to write to you. Naturally, you expect rather a "full" letter from me, since so much seemed to be happening the other day, beneath the facade of pleasantries over the luncheon table[…]

It has been difficult returning this time, and I cannot abandon myself to the army so easily this time – then my leave was a strange one – it was unsuccessful in one way, yet in another way, so much happened inside. Sometimes it seemed a sort of finale, I was saying goodbye to some people & things for ever perhaps, and the feeling crept in so persistently that it seems the only 'hangover', the only thing about leave which constantly recurs. So I was brought to earth today when unloading a lorry of our tropical stores and the box I happened to be carrying was crosses – 'Airborne Crosses' ran the legend, small easily portable crosses for the few who won't return. I mustn't become preoccupied with death, & yet the poet, Alun Lewis, who was killed in Burma over a year ago, compels me with his letters. I have nothing to go out there for, & yet I have said goodbye to so much, because my informal 28 days made it that way.

For a long time now, despite our resistance to it, the door has been closing on our friendship. I know I'm mostly to blame, and this last week it has been in my mind more than anything else. I have thought many things, but they have gone, so in any case this letter will be inadequate (Interruptions aren't helping!). My chief memory is of the depth of unhappiness I could see in your eyes when we met in London. I had noticed it throughout the leave, but there most of all. And there I had to inform you of another meeting after lunch, which despite its perfect innocence, was hurting you very deeply. Please don't protest, I knew that – and you were hurt with my manner and general attitude, rightly so, I should think, & yet – I couldn't for the life of me alter one little bit. It seemed quite out of my hands – in fact the door was closing willy-nilly, whatever. Before we met, I had been thinking about you, wondering where I was with you, & what I was doing – I knew I was hurting you, & that you are as conscious as I of the closing door. So much lay in my hands and I have failed, Mona. I know how much you can reproach me, and you of all people can lay a finger on my inner fears & weaknesses. You have done so sometimes, but I don't seem to learn. So perhaps it is time something drastic was done. I can remember the unhappiness & weariness of your face, & we must do something. Do you think, perhaps, that we are wrong in trying to be friends, or rather by trying to keep as much in touch as we do. You are still my most constant correspondent by far, & I write more to you than anyone (though your natural reaction appears never to believe that kind of remark – it is quite true). I wish I could write all I've thought this week – I seem quite empty now. Things had got to an impasse, and my conduct for a long time will make it appear as though I am suggesting this for my own convenience. It isn't however, I can't help thinking again & again of your own sorrow, and I want to help. The opposite always happens as things are. We meet – I am as puzzling as ever to you and to myself, and hurt you more & more. Is it not better therefore to do what you've often suggested – break off our relations completely, so that I shall not constantly reappear to aggravate you. Unconsciously I have resisted this hitherto, I suppose, thinking it was possible for time to mend matters, but when I see you now, I realize it's wrong. Whether complete separation is the solution or not I don't know – what do you think? Even our talk the other evening, though quite frank, seemed to make no difference to me – if anything it was all leading to the door, already closing beyond recall.

You must find me a horribly changed person, I'm sure, and I often wonder what has happened to me. It is the easiest thing for me to lose a friend these days in spite of myself, and I can't blame the other all the time. It must be me. I even think I saw the slightest turn between George [presumably Downs] & I, we, who had seemed to fit in perfectly. But perhaps I was wrong. Anyway, the old person you knew seems to have disappeared – why, or where, I don't know. The main thing is that I mustn't make you unhappy for the rest of your life – for I find you changed too, though I tried to fend off the idea of change in either of us. The old bubbling humour has gone, the twinkle, the Lovell – because of me partly, and partly because you're tired out. So make a complete break (if you think it best). I suggest you leave Felling too – have a rest (a woman can work it) and find a better job[…]

I have brought back some old letters of yours – the bundle I once spoke of. It is sad, oh very sad, to read them – after all that, I am asking you if it isn't better never to write to each other again. I try to make excuses for myself. Forestry did me no good ever, the NCC was good in spirit but the slave-driving was killing me and though I have good work in this unit, nobody can ever grasp what happens inside one on a day like 24 March [the crossing of the Rhine]. All I have talked of it has sounded like mere heroics – that's what it is to most, but to a few of us it is something much more far reaching & deep. Poor excuses – all I want to show is that while I'm hurting you, I'm not enjoying the selfish social existence you perhaps imagine. There isn't much for me now – I'm getting remoter & remoter and India seems a finishing touch.

I feel rather tired now – it is 1 am. I must close. If you feel like reply-ing to this, please do so. If you wish to ignore it, just carry on as usual with your letters and the poems you send me. You must think of yourself, not of me. If I sound in despair, it isn't sympathy I require – it's probably a good tanning I need.

The bugs begin to teem forth on to the floor of this picquet room, the other three men snore & in short, it is the Army – what a contrast.

[Signed "Good night, Len".]

224 etc [Bulford] – Thursday [6 July 1945?]

I've been sick with some sort of fever, so my letters are very much behind. I'm sorry, because I wanted to reply to yours immediately, but I could not think straight. A vaccination, 2 cholera injections, a stren-uous game of hockey & so on, and I was flat out for a couple of days. But I have been thinking about your letter of course, and about you.

Will you believe me when I say that I thought that our meeting in London was a sort of quick meeting between train times, & that after lunch you were to catch your train to Bath. You never mentioned that it could have been all day, & yet when you say you presumed that George had made some plan for the afternoon, I think that you must have suggested something like that to him & not to me. Your letter suggesting a visit to Bath came after I'd arranged to meet my other friend in the afternoon, and of course there was a clash, in my usual style. But it's no use offering excuses, though they are true. Why must you clinch such mismanagements of mine! – that isn't the fault, because it was nothing but clumsiness on my part, of which I'm capable, even when it isn't intended. My letter to you was trying to find out why we had drifted apart, not explaining mistakes. But you are relentless about such matters and will apparently never forget, nor forgive, some evening when I seem to have preferred a crossword to you (how untrue!) At any rate, it constantly reappears in letters & so will my clumsiness in London.

But they aren't the problem. The problem is inside of myself, who have changed and in you, whom the change has hurt. We might both say "Why struggle – to hell with the whole business. I've had enough." Probably we have – but for my part, I protest as ever, that I can't let you disappear from my life like that. And you say "He's always saying that & acting the opposite." And so we proceed.

So there is nothing more than to repeat that at heart I realize what you have meant to me, & still mean, that your friendship & your love have had a great part in moulding my life, that the best of me I owe to you, & the worst to myself. With people like me, I see now it is the self that wins and if I'd been great enough to have absorbed & retained your spirit, I'd have been sounder and happier. And now, you have seen such a lot of the bad in me that you can hardly believe in me at all, and when I write & try to help, it all sounds bosh. No wonder.

Anyway, I know from your letter that to all intents & purposes we are separate now – the tone of your letters in future will be as for other acquaintances and, of course, I have lost something. Selfishly, I wanted to retain it – but my last letter was an honest attempt to be helpful. Perhaps now, to retain anything of our long friendship, it would be necessary to love you as you have loved me – since I doubt if I shall ever love anyone like that, the fading continues & inevitably we will separate. Perhaps – I don't know. At any rate, as I said before, I really want to help you & leave myself out of it. You are the wiser of the two, and though it seems ungraceful to leave the decision to you, I know you will be wiser & decide best. I have nothing to expect & I understand just what you mean when you say I have lost the place I had in your heart & that that happened some time ago. So be ruthless & say & act as you wish[…]

You describe our friendship as in its winter sleep. Perhaps you're right and it is better, neither to break completely nor continue as we are, but for you to "merely answer my letters", & for me "to just write if you want to or if/when you want letters". Of course that is a sad reflection really – in any case I shan't write merely because I want letters, but because I want to write to you, and perhaps some day, as you say, the winter will pass, & you won't "merely answer my letters", but will write because you wish to. I'm in no position to ask[…]

Bulford, Sunday [14 July 1945]

There is nothing on this morning, and I am half-reclining, half sitting in bed, the sultry weather making us all languorous[…]

I went into a little copse near here last night and suddenly saw something with my old eye which I wanted to paint – it compelled me, there was such an appealing pattern of shapes of dead tree boles and live ones and an old fir had taken on a reddish hue in the dimness. I took some paper & paints but only got wet in a thunder shower. But I shall try to paint it. It was good to feel I'd seen something however, because I felt something was leaving me lately. But it is the shifting about abroad, the shortness of leave and my hatred of this drab plain which has long lost any character[…]

I have been transferred to the resuscitation (i.e. blood transfusion etc) & heat stroke section, which will consist of all old men of the unit, no new men, and all nursing orderlies. If there is time, it is possible I shall go to Bristol for a blood course, which lasts about 10 days I think. But there may not be time, because sailing has suddenly been brought forward again after many postponements, and 225 PFA sail on Tuesday[…]

The result of the general election – a Labour landslide – was announced on 26 July. Len commented on it in passing, but he was more preoccupied with the unit's preparations for its move to the East and with work on the account of 224 PFA's activities in Normandy.

Bulford, Friday [27 July 1945]

[…] Although you admit complete indifference to politics, I suppose the election has interested you. It's a general surprise I think, and I hope there will be some reforms at home. As for the war, I can't see it making much difference – we could be at peace now, but it seems we've forgotten peace & must fight to a finish. America is putting all her power into it & we follow, since we have possessions out there.

At present we are trying all sorts of airborne experiments for jungle conditions and results are mostly laughable – a whole trolley leaving a plane & whizzing straight to earth without its parachute showing any signs of opening. When we get there we look at the hole in the ground, shake our heads and are grateful that parachuting men seems more efficient than parachuting kit, jeeps etc.

Between times, I am working on book production (sounds big,

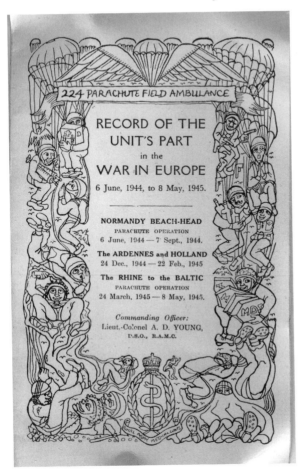

The front cover of the unit's record of action

doesn't it) – actually it's nothing to do with either of us, because it is about the Normandy operation. *Red + Devils* (the Colonel insisted on that silly title): *a Parachute Field Ambulance in Normandy. Written by Members of 224 Parachute Field Ambulance*. It's in folio form, only typescript I'm afraid, & today we've designed the cover between us (only paper) but it looks at least interesting[…] Then we are producing a unit record – a folding card announcing the unit's work, its casualties, awards etc… all in facts & figures. The inside reveals a map showing our progress to the Baltic and it's being hand coloured. It'll take ages to get 3[00]

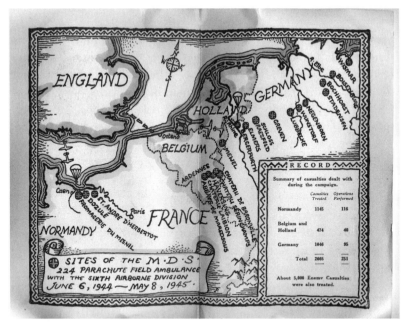

The map from the unit's record of action

or 400 coloured. I'll send you one when I can[…]

Your remarks at the end of the letter provoke me, but I mustn't discuss wildly, because I'm in a miserable mood tonight. How can one "be one with the world & take one's place in the world"? And don't you think, since most people, including the young, let liberty slip away thoughtlessly, that some "young men" are bound to take freedom seriously? One cannot be an ostrich knowing it. And that "frustration" is inevitable? It is not everyone who can be happy in the army, yet conscription is universal – and frustration was the big reward of those who tried to fight against it. Do you think the millions who have now been away from home for 5 years can be blamed if they take "freedom & frustration" too seriously?

My God, it sometimes almost makes me weep! Better to be an ostrich.

Please don't ponder over this, I'm cross tonight. Write, please, when you wish about what you wish.

Bulford, Tuesday [2 August 1945?]

We (Petts & I) are working frantically on the unit souvenir card, against time. The little room we occupy looks like a "Penny-plain, Tuppence coloured" workshop. The card is a rather roughly printed affair, folding with the inside displaying a map of Europe & our places of activity. It is being hand-coloured in five colours, yellow, red, green, brown and blue, with pale watercolours. I hope to send you one, but it is a very limited edition & it's quite possible Petts & I will be left without one in our zeal to provide everybody with one or two. It's a very rough thing, not really our going [sic], but the printing had to be broad to hold the rough hand colouring.

Whatever were you doing to cut your thumb – I thought librarian-ship the safest of jobs. Talking of librarianship, I have been considering more & more lately whether or not I should resign. I become more determined every day to take up art after the war and it's hardly fair to allow the County to continue paying me. Probably I'll have to pay back what they've paid me – I shall do that of course, but it will be some short. The rest I'll just have to save, that's all[…]

At present the East recedes – rumours are rife; we are merely postponed; we are going to America to jump on Japan under US command, as a division representing Britain in the invasion; we are going to Russia for similar but Russian purposes. Take your pick, I can't tell which is most likely, but I think in their order given, they are likely. What it means is a little more time in England, weekends and perhaps a short leave, when I shall be able to get home.

Petts & I are wondering how COs under the various exemptions are being released from their obligations – perhaps the CBCO[14] will be able to tell us something. We presume the forestry & landworkers will be demobbed in stages like the Army, but don't know. Some in the NFS [expansion unknown] have been transferred to the NCC, & their NFS years will count in years for their age-service groups. But John & I, who voluntarily graduated from landwork or timber to NCC, are in a vague position & I was hoping Bill Hamilton had been elected for Parliament so that he could get a ruling on the matter. We aren't allowed to write to our own MPs of course.

[This and the next letter are signed "*Amitiés*, Len".]

In the second week of August, Len went to Bristol for his blood transfusion course, in readiness for action in the East (passing his test with distinction). At the same time, however, the war turned decisively against Japan after the USA dropped atomic bombs on Hiroshima and Nagasaki and the Red Army attacked the Japanese in Manchuria. Japan surrendered on 15 August – V-J (Victory over Japan) Day. Len and his 224 friend Vic Newcomb were swept up in the celebrations for the end of World War II.

With Japan defeated and the war over, servicemen everywhere thought obsessively about when they would be demobilised. The British Government had learned from its mistake after World War I, when all conscripts had been released simultaneously without any preparation. Now demobilisation was to take place gradually, depending on length of service and other factors. Len was to be frustrated; his years in forestry were not counted and he had to resign himself to a lengthy stretch in uniform yet.

Bulford [but envelope postmarked Bristol],
Saturday [11 August 1945]

I have been so miserable that I haven't written to anyone for ages. I wrote to you & Jim Thursday night, but not having envelopes I kept the letters in my pocket until I could get out for envelopes. I got out yesterday, escaping early, hitched to Winchester and, after seeing the magnificent roof in the transepts (of the cathedral), my mood became more calm and patient. Strange! Then the Japanese, having suffered so intensely in the last week, seem eager to end the war now – prospects of freedom are not so distant, and there is the tremendous relief (nobody except the poor victims understand this) of knowing that another operation isn't coming off. Now I can really look into the future, and can look into the past and not regret that I volunteered for this, for I'm to live & what I did in Germany was well worth it, to me at any rate, & the many others I was able to help.

But I have felt miserable for a long time, and I think, once we know for certain that the war is really over, that I shall begin to hope again, and work for the future. So my letters to you and Jim are still in my pocket – low spirited, Oblomov letters, for I have settled into doing nothing, but eat a little, sleep a little, and waste the rest of the time[...]

I still don't know quite what to do about my resignation, but since I'm equivocal myself, I'll let you decide and shall leave things as they are. It seems dishonest though – still, there is a possibility of universi-

ties, colleges & art schools being so suddenly crowded by the demobilisation of 5 years of students at once that I may not get into the first
year's course – in which case I shall be at the library quite a while. So
probably you're right.

                                          Bulford, Sunday [19 August 1945]

I have just written to an old friend of ours, Felling Ministry of Labour,
to ask them for a certificate of my service in Forestry. Was it Oct 1940
I began? I said so, but wasn't sure. If they send it, I'll further it to
Army Records, where it *may* be considered in assessing my Age Service
Group which at 52 just now is quite impossible! If I'd stayed in
Forestry I wonder when I'd have been released. I know if I'd done
ARD [expansion unknown] or Fire Service & then joined the Army
those years would have counted, but because I did forestry where I
worked much harder, it may not count. Apparently the little red
chevrons that Special Constables, Firemen, NAAFI tarts & all service
people wear on their sleeves, are the things that count. But foresters
naturally don't wear them.

So Petts & I have written to our respective MoL officers for certificates & who knows, it may work. We have also written jointly to the
CBCO for information. That would bring my group down to about
30 or 31, which could mean release next Spring, or even earlier.

I just got your Bristol letters OK but regret to say you'd hardly
approve of my week there. In the first place I was so badly off for
money as usual, when I arrived, that an expedition to Bath or my
cousins at Midsomer Norton[15] was out of the question. When one
gets down to 5 or 6 bob, you can only think in terms of one meal & a
short bus ride. Vic Newcomb was the same[…] Normally, I think, I'd
have gone to Bath hitchhiking, penniless as I was, & had the cheapest
canteen bun meals, only to see it, but I was caught in the hysteria and
just went haywire. I had been so miserable, could still have been, yet
the people of Bristol wouldn't allow it somehow, and carried Vic & I
shoulder high, so to speak, till we finished protesting and joined in.
Our 6s never diminished – we were merry, surrounded by Bristol's
clamouring maidens (how they miss their departed Yanks) and
altogether we found it a very strange city. It's no vicious Piccadilly,

mind you, but the positions are quite reversed and all the admiring glances, cheeky whistles, views over the shoulder and general advances are from the poor girls, lonely and deserted. So we went about in danger mostly and had to be careful not to be carried off. Naturally VJ night we were both carried off & didn't see each other till next morning. What a hectic week.

On 1 Sept I am making an effort to get home, it seems so long since I saw you all. Longer than in Belgium or Germany, where I was preoccupied.

The Colonel was back from India on our return – he gave us a lecture and was very scathing about British soldiers there, saying they've "just sat on their arses taking the laurels while Indian troops did the fighting". I can't believe that – he's terribly proud of what we did in Europe. Did I tell you that the ultimate figures of our casualties, treatments & operations constitute a record for a field ambulance in the history of the Army. Generals have come to goggle over them & us and we are quite the boys, according to the Colonel. We got him his DSO you see. Oh the man positively gloats & I'm sure he's disappointed there's not another campaign to show us off again.

I can tell you, since you're a pacifist too, without self-praise, that the cream of this unit all along has been its CO element. COs make the keenest medics you could find, and their impartiality on the battlefield, far from being an embarrassment militarily, was definitely a contribution to the masses of work we managed, because we could always make the German prisoners of war work willingly with us where other soldiers just got their backs up, & that's no use when men are lying dying. It was a pleasure to return to our MDS the evening of our drop on the Rhine & find old Bill Lewis and Johnny Ryder working affably and efficiently with about 10 Germans on hundreds of casualties. We should have lost many more than we did if those Germans hadn't helped us willingly & untiringly as they did. They actually volunteered to work through the night & they did. We shared our meagre 24 hour ration packs with them and I don't know how they carried on. Disorganisation was so complete that they could have gone on the road with their hands up & joined the throng of prisoners already tramping back to safety behind the Rhine. But they wouldn't leave us and I remember some of their faces with pleasure. So, without undue praise for ourselves, I have no doubt about the value of the conshies in this unit, & those that were lost in Normandy & the Rhine must be remembered.

But the Colonel's pride is wrong – his is ambition realised, and we tend rather to laugh at him. Our favourite game is forecasting what he will say in his lecture, when he gives one. We sense his frustration – the war's over, & its possibilities for an ambitious [sic] – a colonel at 30 or so, you know, and all that. But he means to be ahead of everybody else & is already planning pre-demob education schemes and there again the COs will shine – he loves them, they work hard, write his books for him, draw for him, write his signs and generally give him a sense of satisfaction since his men (think of James [Bramwell] & Petts etc) can bring more intelligence to anything than his whole officers' mess. Oh the plans the man has. The parade square will soon swarm like a university campus with students of history, politics, sociology, literature & the arts.

The transition from war to peace is hard to realize – I cannot settle down, but feel my spirits quite slowly subsiding, & I'm hoping to start work shortly. How much we all hope for peace & all it could bring to us, and us to it. But will the world let us? Do you think we are even more wicked and depraved and self-destructive than before the war? Do you think we poor people are more than ever in the hands of vast ambitious powers, helpless to escape, & unable to shape our own little peace because of it? Now more than ever we have to close our eyes to some threat we know over the horizon, and try to live as though it never existed[…]

Bulford, Wednesday [21 August 1945]

I've had a reply from the CBCO secretary, someone called Nancy Browne, the name sounds familiar. From what she says, there's no hope for me, or John, and our land service won't count. It has come as a blow to me, for I was beginning to be so sure[…]

As it is, my spirits leave me and it's so difficult to be cheerful. Once the job has gone & the [word indistinct] in the RAMC this is an unendurable waiting period – mine instead of being Xmas or Spring, will drag on for goodness knows how long.

WITH THE COMPLIMENTS
OF ALL RANKS.

224 PARACHUTE FIELD AMBULANCE
R.A.M.C.

You must tire of me and my wavering. Especially as you so often feel the same and it doesn't help to try to share one's weariness. We need real peace, inside ourselves, of course, and even though the war has ended, it will be a long time before we can settle into peace. I'm certainly not at peace – this not knowing what to do with myself, understanding my friends less than ever.

Next day. […] I feel more philosophical about it today. Perhaps it is because I shall probably have something more to my heart than I'd expected in the last months of waiting. Under the pre-demob education, James & I are to lecture on literary history & drama. How many periods I don't know, but there are 3 periods daily of 1 hour each. I'd probably be covering the former, so I'll have to not only rub up my knowledge, but improve it too, because I was never qualified enough to lecture on the subject[…]

In addition I've been appointed editor of a unit monthly magazine *As You Were*, the first number to appear late September. I don't fancy that job, however, though it sounds good. It will be difficult to please, because the unit tends to split rather sharply into highbrow & lowbrow, each rather resenting the other in spite of themselves.

Then the unit volume on Germany is already taking shape & my account is required. Have you any letters relating to the drop & subsequent action that you would care to lend me during my weekend of 1 September? It would help me to sort out my mind.

So, suddenly, you see, I'm busy, and I'm glad – it takes my mind away from my little troubles[…]

The 6th Airborne Division would not be going to the Far East – but it would be needed in Palestine, where the postwar situation was becoming tense as the Jewish community campaigned for survivors of the concentration camps and other displaced Jews to be allowed into the country. The British Government wished to restrict immigration in order not to provoke conflict with the Arab population. The threat of attacks by the Jewish terrorist groups lurked in the background. Len's next two letters were written on NAAFI airmail letter forms.

[No address – probably sent from Bulford],
Tuesday [17 September 1945?]

Thank you for your long letter, the best I have received from you for years, I think. Don't ask me why. It made me happy for some reason – though lately you seemed to have come to believe I didn't care what happened to you, materially and in the spirit, I *have* always thought about you, & wondered, & hoped. And it seemed no use – what mistakes I had made in the past seemed too dreadful & *life-taking* to ever hope for repair. So your letter seems to me to hold a new life. I am concerned about you, & only in moments of distraction when I was far too worried about myself have I forgotten ever. That must take some believing – I know it's true – I have a tender conscience, but it doesn't prevent me from acts that hurt – I regret them afterwards.

Anyway, all this packing up & sorting out (we sail Thursday or Fri) have made me once more go over some old letters of yours – the fateful year 1941 – some are "hedgers" and contain little, so had to go (space is limited) – but others I shall always keep – they are you, & me, in the strangest situation people ever got into, I'm sure. That sounds cold, unfeeling – how can I express myself! I think I know how very much 1941 meant to you – how much you suffered then (although we cannot ignore the happiness before – that brings tears more than the other). I often think of writing at length & at leisure & at peace to you, but opportunity for all 3 has never really occurred.

Now I am going [airmail letter torn at this point]

Bulford, Wednesday [18 September 1945?]

[…] I was so happy to get your long letter yesterday – rather happier, more at peace than of late, & it was more like your old self. And this morning's letter is you all over, incensed, with nostrils distended in rage at the MoL. I, the poor victim, look on amazed. But please don't tire yourself with them. Trying to be impartial, I think my position is unlucky & unfair, but trying to alter it is hitting one's head against a wall. But I'm grateful – if resigned I'm afraid. George's impatience & groaning don't help me, but otherwise my friends seem to understand the position & don't write things like "Soon you'll be able to get down to your own work" etc. What'll be left of me when I'm finally released I daren't think, it seems I've gone too long to do any good, but I still have dreams. It's nearly 5 years now & apparently my army career is beginning only. I want so much to desert but it would probably cause more permanent damage than patiently waiting.

But never mind, all of us are fortunate to be where we are – the Continent presents a sadder prospect than ever to anyone who cares at all. And I cannot forget the fears a Japanese operation held for most of us. Surely 3 years in the Army weigh well against that.

However, as you will see from part of my letter yesterday, the world & myself are not the whole of my thoughts, and the note, though terribly inadequate, expresses something, so I am sending it anyway. But I am afraid too, & have always been since 1941, of expressing myself quite truthfully, knowing how the human heart will interpret things in its own way, willy nilly. I think we are both wise enough now to speak the truth, however. There is a story of Galsworthy ('First & Last Days' or something) in which a little down-fallen parson, now tramping the roads, has only one regret, that he doesn't suffer, & he is pleased when he is wrongly accused of murder. Well in the light of Almighty God, as he would have put it, we are partly atoned I think – you've suffered, I know, because of me – I've suffered too, whatever you may think. Is that anything – does it mean anything? I'm sure it does. Love has meant little but pain ultimately for both of us, though I don't wish to equalise my blame with your long suffering patience.

All this means to say, again, is that you are not forgotten, and never will be and that whatever is happening to me, part of it happens to you too, for you can be as sure as Lucy Snowe of Dr John in *Villette*, that there is always a place in my heart that belongs to you and is nobody else's.

All this seems cold, comfortless really – whatever I can offer must seem inadequate – indeed you want nothing from me, you will say, but I do want only the good to reign between us & we both have faults, I the worst only, but we must try to bury them. I must not be cruel, you must be free with me, & never try to keep me away from other friends. They all have their place – yet we've misunderstood each other – what has appeared as jealousy to me has just made me rage. Why must we be like that? We know each other so well, yet how careful we shove the dog & ornaments & papers etc behind the screen when we meet. Aren't we queer? I admit to most of the faults – I have been dreadful, but I have been blamed for wrongs I did not mean. Oh why *must* I begin on that. I ride over details, you cannot ever ignore them – so we must meet halfway – I be more careful, you more trustful & broadminded. But who am I to make demands, you'll say. Alright, I'll shut up. I know full well my position. But when I left you to the decision, to be or not to be, or even to decide *what* our friendship could consist of, you left my letter almost unanswered. Since then we *have* been friends – *but* – always but. The letter was never answered – perhaps it need never be, nor this one. But it has been written, &

yesterday's. Both are meant in the best spirit, & are sent with my thoughts &

Love,
Len

Early Months in Palestine

The voyage east along the length of the Mediterranean was an experience both wondrous and trying for Len, as his letter written aboard conveys. He kept a diary, from which he would later quote in an essay 'The Voyage Out From Innocence' published in The Gallipoli Diary *in 1989.*

224 PFA, MEF [Middle East Forces] – 30 September 1945

The voyage is almost over – tomorrow we may see Crete and I think we shall be off Haifa (definitely our destination) by Tuesday night. Just now we are in the hottest quarter of the Med and I'm revelling in it. Heat & sunshine are never oppressive at sea as they can be on land. From noon we can dress as we wish – I go round in trunks & I'm brown with the sun. The voyage has been most interesting for those of us who were looking for things. The most impressive I think was sunrise over the rugged mountains behind Cape Finisterre, the first land we saw after the B of Biscay. It was long silver rays on jagged ranges and I wanted to be there so much. Gibraltar we passed at night – we could see the lights clearly, & Tangier lights twinkled on the opposite coast.

Next morning the high mountains of the Sierra Nevada stood up to the North, the distance & height & shape all making them wonderful – to me anyway. The Atlas Mountains we saw all next day, looking very much like the more rugged of England's mountains in Cumberland, N Wales & Skye, I imagine, only higher, & rising straight out of the sea. The first range, the lowest, was mostly capped with stubbly trees, probably dusty old umbrella pine. A line of puffy clouds hung above the whole range – some freak of condensation – you could trace the coast line by the clouds.

Then Pantelleria, a dream island, stretched before us one morning, with its own little mountains. Bare, cliffs to the south, flat to the north, a few signs on our side of the heavy shelling & bombing it got, but I think the flat N end which is an aerodrome, got the worst.

Sailing between Maltese islands & Sicily vaguely visible as pale shapely mountains on the northern horizon.

All very wonderful, but I can't describe all. In the Atlantic we saw dolphins leaping, whales spouting off Portugal, gannet off C [Cape] St Vincent.

A swallow & a finch seem to be migrating with us – an old soldier's trick to save flying. The swallow is plebeian & flies on the men's deck, the finch confines itself to the boat deck among the officers.

We are very crowded, I find the constant crush & noise unbearable sometimes, and there are few retreats – but I can't say I'm not enjoying the thrill of a Mediterranean cruise. The food is good, we have had 2 oranges, 1 apple & tobacco issue of ½ lb cost only 3/9. Fish, plaice, lettuce even – what a refrigerator this ship must have. It's the *Dunnottar Castle*, a Union Castle liner – i.e. England to S Africa in peace.

I'm looking forward to a letter or two at Haifa.

I'll leave this open till then. Despite the interest of all this for me, the 'experience' as people call it, I still long to be free and I hope I shan't be too long in Palestine[…]

Wed, 3 October

Just arrived Haifa. Awaiting disembarkation.

The unit was at first sent to a camp near Gaza in the south of the country. Len's first letter from Palestine on 10 October described the heat and dust, the "general state of discontent throughout [the] Brigade", and a "general deep longing for England already".

Unsurprisingly Len took an interest in the political situation in Palestine. While he was instinctively sympathetic to the Jews – his experience at Belsen had only strengthened that – his initial conclusions leant more to the Arab case. He was critical of British policy and of the conduct of army officers.

224 PFA, MEF – 17 October 1945

[…] As for the situation out here, I am not very happy about it. The situation is very "delicate", and the longer one is in the country, the more one forgets the Jewish case in the outside world & supports the Arab. One thing is certain – the policy of Britain is divided between great military strength (it is terrific out here – I can't tell you how many divisions in case the letter is opened) and the supposed enlightened imperial policy of "guidance". As far as the Arabs are concerned, they feel out of it but don't wish to make trouble. I have contacted the HQ of the Labour Movements in Gaza which is an Arab stronghold & no Jews at all. The men I met spoke good English, were very frank & outspoken & fair, I thought, & represent a very large section, the majority, perhaps, of Arab feeling. They maintain that in the early days of Jewish immigration, with the Jews in a small minority, they sought cooperation with the Arab with all apparent sincerity. But as their numbers & power increased (the proportion in numbers is 1 Jew to 2 Arabs approx but power is the other way) the Jews became more high-handed and finally wrested all municipal power etc from the Arabs who have now retired to well-separated "quarters" where, unaided by Jew or Briton in local government services & social services etc... they gradually lapse into filth and disease that has now made them almost taboo. In the meantime the Jews develop amain, have created, by subsidies & assistance (natural favour etc) modern European districts, with broad gracious streets, well-swept, and with adequate drainage & waste disposal. Educational facilities are hopelessly disproportionate. I think only 9 Arab students are accepted each year at the University, which becomes inevitably [a] Hebrew University.

These are facts. What are the reasons for them, I haven't sorted out. The Arabs say Jewish domination, monopoly, dictatorship (this is really felt – important) & wealth. The Jews say Arab decadence, corruption and indolence as against their industry & thoroughness. The real division is on what might be called territorial rights – whose land is it. Here British Imperial perfidy is at its worst – after the Arabs pulled off our Middle East flank in the last war (equivalent almost to the advance from El Alamein in this war) we broke all our promises made through [TE] Lawrence, almost broke the latter's heart & discredited him in the minds of his greatest Arab friends who looked to him for everything. Lawrence, like themselves, had believed the promises & suffered. There is no doubt the Land of Judah is one of the richest parts of Arabia – it is on the direct line of communication from the Syrian Arabs to the Jebel Druze, Senussi & Mecca centres – it is definitely Arab, says the Arab. It is definitely Jewish, says the Jew.

The Old Testament, tradition, prophecy, natural economic reasons (they do develop land better than the Arabs) & a more or less world backing support their arguments. The difference is that the Arab wants peace (I do know that) & is prepared for neighbourliness with what Jews there are if they will cooperate – which the Jew, though in the main peaceful & waiting patiently the will of the United Nations, probably supports in sympathy, if not in practice, the extreme Zionist methods of terrorism, which are fearful.

Quite a lot happens here & things are so bad that I feel the military have broken faith by requiring even the COs in this unit to perform picquet duties. It is quite futile – we volunteered for non-combatant duties & only two, Petts & Bramwell, have taken arms, but though we remain non-combatant & still carry no weapons we are placed in the most annoying of anomalous positions. Picquets are so big in numbers that it comes twice a week & even then 2 hours, 2 hours off, so that two nights a week are almost sleepless. There is no time off to make up (except two compulsory periods per week swimming). There are regular "stick-ups" etc but so far nothing has happened on our area. In action, the CO relies on his ability (by artificial means (red cross) or natural, personal) to express his good faith to both sides & I could usually manage that. But this, you can imagine, is awkward, embarrassing, stretching our promises to the furthest point. It isn't that we mind night duty, for the battalions are as badly off, but since they know our ideas of policing a place are so vastly different from theirs, they might spare us the stupidity and embarrassment of such a position. I can't explain it properly, but that, briefly, is how the situation affects us – I am rather unhappy about it, as you can imagine. Mind, there's little danger except for an accident – I feel that having survived an operation, I shall pull through as far as that goes – but I think you will understand how things are partly.

There are many complaints, general & specific, but I won't moan about them. Officers in Palestine are mainly incorrigible & their chief occupation is drinking & the result neglect of the men's welfare. The COs will be hard to hold I can see – our ideas on the Army Education Scheme are almost opposite the Army's out here. Young men make up most units now & even I am quite an old soldier. Only a comparative few of us have seen action & yet those young men, even though

it's peace-time, are being allowed to stagnate in mind & spirit. Many
of them are fine young fellows & would be keen – why should their
minds be sacrificed to mere physical training for the Army's requirements when so much could be done? […]

Tomorrow. After lunch, noon.
It is hot & still outside. I am writing this in the cool of our big spacious
shed which holds the carpenter, cobbler, tailor, sign-writers cum
editors cum printers. A lizard basks on the window sill (they are all
over this place) – some sparrows quarrel above me in the eaves, there
is no ceiling, just the roof laid on the walls. Do you see it! Outside roll
after roll of pale dusty land, with Arab tents, camels, dogs & people
about them, and on the Eastern skyline, a distant pale, hazy mountain
range, which is deep purple at sunrise. Do you see that? It would need
a great painter to bring out the strange quality of the colours & form
– most would merely convey a vast nothing plain with a low skyline.
But there's the heat, the parched earth, the slight break into whiteness
here & there, a bleached stillness[…]
   By the way, Bramwell & I gave a transfusion of glucose-saline for
dehydration (heat-stroke) yesterday. It was most interesting –
performed in same way as blood transfusion, only instead of blood or
plasma being in bottle there is glucose-saline. GS is part of blood, of
course, a clear fluid, lack of which, due to extreme perspiration etc,
causes collapse. The recovery of the patient was visible – his parched
lips and taut skin became more normal. Transfusion is my sole
medical work now[…]
   [Signed "With my thoughts, Len".]

*According to Len, the British troops "detested" the local Jews, and in this letter he
comes close to sharing this view as he complains of the high prices charged by
shopkeepers – before remembering that the Jews have no homeland except Palestine,
"the natural & traditional home for them". Some of the opinions and terms
expressed here would draw a storm of condemnation in the early 21st century; they
were common currency in 1945. For Len, as for most of the troops serving in Palestine, this was the first experience of foreign countries other than those he had passed
through during wartime. These young men were not to know that the local Jewish*

shopkeepers were hardly unique around the world in trying to extract whatever they could from foreign visitors who in any case were not welcome. Len's views evolved as he saw and found out more about the situation in Palestine.

224 PFA, MEF – Tuesday [23 October 1945]

I'm at the Military General Hospital at present, but my address remains the same as before. I'm still getting your mail alright, thank you – a jeep brings it in a few hours from our old camp. 8 of us are on attachment nursing here, where they are short staffed, so I'm pretty busy. This is a sort of pleasant military suburbia, at Sarafand, 10 miles from Tel Aviv & very near Lydda. We came here at very short notice on Saturday morning – it was a very pleasant ride back into cultivated territory & civilisation. From Arab territory, we have come into Jewish territory, so that everything is very Westernised and very expensive. But we don't get out much & therefore can't spend. In any case I'm broke after sending 1 parcel of fruit to Wardley (of which part is for you) and 1 parcel to the Downs family. You've no idea how high the cost of living is here and I must say that there is nothing like a Jewish community for just putting everything slightly beyond one's means. Our own unit canteen dealt wholesale with Jews for some fruit for home – here is the price as it was for us. 1lb raisins, 1 lb sultanas, 1 lb of lemon peel – posted & export duty paid 500 miles 10/-. I rejected that, because it seemed extortionate. But I had to submit. The two parcels I sent contain 1lb more, but do not include peel, which I could not obtain anywhere. Shopping just makes me mad every time I even think about it. Now take this writing-pad (this is a phoney sheet, but I mean the big lined page). About 150 pp I suppose – 2/- – and that's through official Army channels. Toothpaste in England at 1/1 to 1/3 a tube is 1/8 to 1/9 here. I don't wish to complain, but the constant drainage of one's pocketful of mils is just maddening. The trouble is, I think, that people at home expect parcels of fruit, clothes etc from Palestine where everything is coupon-free and to see it all here & yet be unable to buy is extremely annoying. I liked Gaza for its prices much better – had my eye on some native carpets which were much better value than any of this Jewish stuff here.

It is almost impossible to be fully pro-Jewish in this question, for only a blind person could ignore the fact that the Jews create their own difficulties. Here is a community of them – Tel Aviv is their city, 4,000 absolutely Jewish citizens and from there radiate power, wealth & conditions which cut out the Arab altogether, & leave the Tommy, whose presence is a military matter, penniless. The boys detest the Jews, it is reciprocated, & there lies the making of an incident. Yet nothing happens – yet. The Arabs will steal, will corrupt you, pass on disease, but are peaceful, and I can assure you, without prejudice, & from reliable sources, that the Arab is not resorting to violence, either by riot or raiding any more. But the Jews are a potential source of both all the time, and the Stern gang is dreaded throughout the land.

Irene Ward's article was typical of most knowing viewpoints – a knowledge of the issues, an absolute inability to come to any decision. S. Phillips letter comes to a very nice decision, but doesn't know the facts. (1) Promises were made to the Arabs, for military reasons, & broken for political reasons connected with the Balfour Declaration which had to ignore Arabs to a large extent. (2) is stupid. Raschid Ali represents Arabs even less than Laval represented France – he had certain Powers, like Laval, & used them backing the wrong horse – like any adventurer – but a great mass of Arab feeling is Socialism unexpressed & suppressed, but there.[1] (3) The White Paper took a limited policy (75,000 Jews in 6 years) because in the political state of the world (remember 1939) it had to make a commitment but could not ignore Arabs, so limited numbers till further reference. Now is the time for decision. No wonder American demands are insistent, since Jewish power in America controls all the banks & a large part of industry. America, in fact, with her loud mouth, would do well to help herself towards the problem by forming a Jewish National Home on her own territory if she wants one so very badly. (4) Too stupid to answer, since even the silliest ass knows that the one-fifteenth referred to is richer than the vast areas of Saudi Arabia, the Yemen, Transjordan put together.

So you see my prejudice against Jews seems whole now. But it isn't. I cannot forget the outside world in its attitude to Jews, & I pity them in their wanderings. I realize that Palestine, & not America or Australia, is the natural & traditional home for them, and I must admit that it is their very superiority that makes them disliked (they do know how to tackle a problem, how to create, write, compose, paint, understand medicine, commerce & so on, about 5 times quicker & better than other people). I realize that they will cultivate land to richness where Arabs would keep merely a few goats & that is what they have done. They create employment, attract Arabs from other states & there lies another problem; too many come, are disappointed & go begging. So amid all the wealth & prosperity is seen the direst poverty & wretchedness. But – a Jew rarely works after making a beginning, when he is very industrious – an Arab feels, & is, exploited, and I think it's probably true to say a Jew will always be a Jew & all that means, & a Wog (Army for Arab) will always be a Wog. I think even a small enlightened & educated community of Arabs could guide the rest to their own wealth & prosperity by reorganising the former irrigated richness of the Arab lands which once made them the most fruitful corner of the world[…]

224 PFA, MEF – Sunday, 4 November 1945

[…] The HQ of our unit has arrived at the other side of Sarafand, & the Colonel asked me to go to see him about the magazine – it's to be done quickly now. I'm to join Petts & Ryder to get the Press going. We pulled off our first proof yesterday, & it isn't bad, though the gilatine [sic] roller has been damaged in transit. The Verona type-face looks very good. We also have 1 fount of Caslon bld [bold] face for special work (vaguely future)[…]

I'm still nursing, of course, but since I can't do two jobs at once, the Colonel is recalling me to the Unit. I've got quite attached to the Hospital, and of course, it's the first time I've worked under women since I worked under you. Sisters are funny, but now I think I know how to humour them – here the broad essentials are (1) a cup of tea at 10 am, 3 pm & 7 pm (2) tidiness in the ward (3) an appearance of efficiency. Is that right? With a man it is (1) Efficiency (2) a cup of tea (3) tidiness. Correct (?)[…]

224 PFA, MEF – 6 November 1945

[…] Despite the Colonel's talk to me the other day I am still at Hospital, & having a fairly easy time now I've got the routine. But I shall be going back to the unit when they've fixed up billets. The printing press is ready, and I've sent Page 3 and Page 7 paste-ups for them, so the magazine has gone to press[…]

Thank you for the part of Jim's 'Sleeper in the Earth' – the prologue is an exquisite piece of poetry and reminds me of Rilke trying to take the reader by the hand into the mystic regions which the poet has experienced. It is as tender as a flower and the words will bear as little touching as petals, they are so lovely & free & of the essence of poetry. I shan't say anything about the whole poem until I get the other part. It is very good of you to type it out for me. I still carry round with me the wonderful Hart Crane threnody you typed out for me.

I am concerned because you tell me I may be destined for a branch in Durham Co Library. I should feel dreadful if I deserted a position of responsibility and as the time nears I begin to see what a queer position I'm in. I do want to take up art, & am sure of myself – but if Mr Hamilton is planning responsible positions for us all, what am I to do. Should I write & tell him? My plans are so indefinite, that is the trouble. Mr H *will* think I'm a funny man, & an ungrateful one, skipping off after 3 or 4 months as a branch librarian or something at a good salary. I think I'd best fritter my time away at some less responsible job – making tea for HQ staff or something, or driving the exchange lorry. In any case, I'm a very ignorant librarian by now[...]

Enclosed a picture of the very Eastern Via Dolorosa in Jerusalem, the street up which Jesus climbed with the Cross from the Garden of Gethsemane. I have a bible, thank you, & have re-read the journey – it is a very steep & arduous climb to Calvary. All the streets are like this, some hidden from the sky altogether & little shops open out to the sides so that you have to squeeze between customers. Garbage litters a street like Via Dolorosa, which has few shops & is very mediaeval. It makes you sad. With all the world can offer, people can live in filth, poverty, disease & wretchedness. Without doubt the woman in the picture would approach you & beg "Baksheesh".[2]

Len's time at the hospital came to an end; it was his last sustained medical service. Col Young needed him to print the account of 224 PFA's activities during the cross-

ing of the Rhine and to edit the unit magazine As You Were. *This would keep Len occupied for the next few months. His work with the Canopy Press – 224's print operation – would be a good apprenticeship for his later collaboration with John Petts at the Caseg Press in Wales. Len/Jonah published an essay on the Canopy Press late in life.*

224 PFA, MEF – 9 November 1945

[…] I moved from 91 Hospital yesterday, to get down to printing the magazine. We've got Page 3 set & will print tomorrow. Perhaps I can run off another rough proof for you. I was sorry to leave the hospital, I'd been very happy there. I finished up in charge of a convalescent surgical ward, without a sister, & it was pleasant running things for myself. But I suppose the Colonel was right in getting me back – because the difficulties in setting up even one page are quite enormous[…]

Next day

[…] We've had bad news this afternoon – James Bramwell's mother is very ill, & he has been granted a compassionate posting near home. So he left us to fly to England this afternoon. We shall miss him badly. He seemed to be the centre of what the colonel calls "The Inner Circle" – the little band of select conchies who run everything in the unit. I hope I shall see James again – he is one of the finest people I've met – gentle, cultured, introvert, but affectionate & kindly too & he was never sarcastic or moody with anyone[…]

Sarafand, 14 November 1945

[…] This morning has been spent folding 1,000 sheets of paper in two for the Unit Xmas card. There are more to do, but we have begun printing the little greeting inside, and have about 400 done up to press. It's a tedious job pressing the old lever down 400 times and we are taking turns. We are the only Unit in the Division with Xmas cards, and a Colonel was almost on his knees to us yesterday to beg us to do 'Just a simple one' for the 8th Battalion. We had to refuse but he was so polite that it was very difficult, but it would have put off the printing of the magazine for a while and we can't have that any more. As it is we have had a job dealing with the various little problems that keep turning up. The chief problem is that it is impossible to get any help from local printers such as borrowing the letters "as you were" in bold type for the heading – apparently the body of type here is a shade higher than ours and impossible to use in our press or any English standard press. So we had to cut a block in lino and cutting letters for heading a page of type is no joke. Then we had to have a colophon for the Press, which is called The Canopy Press, so I had to carefully draw out a design in ink for the block-makers in Tel Aviv to make a block for us. In the middle of all our activity the officers had to send an invitation card for us to print. We hadn't meant the press for such trivial jobs, but then the officers can't get over the idea of having a Unit press. The magazine is ready for printing but we haven't got any further than page 3 yet but it promises to be a very high standard and quite unique in Army production[…]

There is one thing about all this activity – it keeps the army at arm's length, and even the colonel comes in occasionally with an air of mystification and afraid to touch anything[…]

[Signed "Bye-bye, and cheer up mate. Len".]

Keeping order in Palestine was a difficult job for the British troops, but sometimes their conduct made it harder. The soldiers of the 6th Airborne Division were superb fighting men, but perhaps for that very reason they were not ideal for policing and peace keeping. Len deplored the behaviour of some of them off duty.

Sarafand [no date – envelope postmarked 19 November 45]

The rain has started, although we've been having glorious weather while you've been having the old indifferent English autumn, I think we must have caught up with your rainfall in two days. It began to blow first of all and we had an awful job controlling papers in the "printing house". So we evacuated into the more public "quiet room". But before we had completed the move, there was a brilliant flash of mauve coloured lightning, a peal of thunder, and we could hear the rain beating along the ground towards us like fleeting horses. When it reached us, it was simply a deluge – in a moment, drains were blocked with sand, paths were buried under rain-washed dunes, and water rushed & swirled everywhere to the roar of the cloudburst on the tin roof. It was deafening. And it's rained on & off since.

AS YOU WERE

PRODUCED BY
224 PARACHUTE FIELD AMBULANCE
FOR ITS MEMBERS IN THE FIELD
AND ITS FRIENDS AT HOME.
VOL. I   DECEMBER 1945   No. I

A MESSAGE
FROM THE COMMANDING OFFICER
Lieut.-Colonel A. D. Young, D.S.O.,R.A.M.C.

Some day I hope there will be a reunion of all ranks who served with this Unit since it started its parachuting career. One of the purposes of this magazine is to form a link between past and present members.

"As You Were" has, I think, two implications. For those of you still serving in the Army it conjures up thoughts of 'civvy street'; for those of you who have already been demobbed I hope it will mean equally pleasant memories of the Unit. We have all, soldier and civilian alike, pulled well together in war; let us make sure that we do not forget each other in peace.

In launching this little magazine I wish to take the opportunity of wishing all former members of the Unit all the very best of luck from all of us here in Palestine. Wherever you may be Go To It!

I am beginning to lead a harassed existence like you – the magazine presents some strange difficulties, and in addition to that, the unit library has arrived. Vic Newcomb is to be librarian since I'm too busy already to take it on. But I've worked along with him, classified them all, catalogued them, & arranged a ticket issue. Unit libraries usually just disappear or disintegrate & gradually finish up with a ragged Penguin or two. But this new issue, under the Army education scheme mustn't do that. There are about 300 altogether, including books we'd bought with unit funds[…]

So now there is a system & I've outlined rules for the Colonel's perusal & it's all ready. I hope this lot does[n't] disintegrate.

We've got the front page of the magazine printed[…]

You will have heard something of more disturbances in Tel Aviv. I don't [know] much about them – I do know that if British troops are hated it is because of the arrogance, drunkenness & indiscipline of idle 6th Airborne Troops of our brigade (Tel Aviv is our area, as you'll probably have gathered). So the riots are not only political but social – an expression of resentment against these swaggering Red Berets who think they conquered Germany & who now presume Tel Aviv is theirs to make mischief in. Tel Aviv is the Jewish capital of the world, and you can understand their resentment. I have said I dislike the Jews here for some of their doings – but I have never gone so far as to express that to a Jew, shout it in the street, to presume a Jewish girl is mine for the asking, to generally contaminate the spirit of a fine modern city loved by the Jews. In fact, though I have got a permanent pass to Tel Aviv, I haven't even been there. I am ashamed of my red-bereted comrades – mind you it's a minority, but it's a strong noisy mischievous minority & they have upset the Jews even more than the political situation has done. I'm glad I belong to a unit like 224 – it has a certain spirit which keeps it much apart from the battalion spirit as a few private individuals from a football crowd in revolt. We just go our own simple way – most working in hospitals, a few with the battalion, & the rest of us at this HQ doing our own job as I am at the moment. And we are the best of friends with the Jews we know and I hope some day to visit Hulda, a Jewish Settlement where I've been invited to ride with a boy I nursed recently in hospital. So don't think of me mixed up with any of this business.

I think the behaviour of some of the 8th Para Battalion has been so bad that we may be withdrawn to Germany or England[…]

Sarafand, 22 November 1945

I'm full of cold and feel quite seedy but it is several days since I wrote to anyone. So I must make the effort. I went to Jerusalem yesterday to get a roller for the press and we seemed to spend an awful amount of our time going from one printing house to the other. Eventually we saw a very nice Jew who makes them and he is making one for us in three days. By the time we had finished our business with him it was lunchtime. It was a good meal wasted because I wasn't in the mood for food.

It was beautifully sunny after the rainy spell and everything seemed to be at peace in Jerusalem. In the afternoon we decided to go up

Mount Scopus to Hebrew University. We left the road and cut straight through the Olive Groves in the Valley of Kedron, where men and women were picking the olives, the men up the ladders and the women on the ground picking the fallen olives up into a cloth. It was very quiet and peaceful, and the people were very friendly. It isn't that often they see a British soldier off the beaten track and I suppose our trustfulness pleased them. Everywhere it was "Salaam" and the old Arab greeting touching the head and the heart. We were sweating by the time we had climbed to the university. We made for the amphitheatre which they built into the east sloping hillside – this is a particularly fine position because as you look from Jerusalem east the view is interrupted by the nearness of Mount Scopus and the Mount of Olives. As you climb Mount Scopus there is no hint that it is the last height and that once you have reached the top you will look down in a steeply descending landscape. So you reach the top tired, search through a small wood towards the amphitheatre and it suddenly hits you, you can't possibly [believe] what your eyes see. There, behind and below the colonnade of marble pillars, is a magnificent view – Mountain slopes right down to the Dead Sea which is clearly visible with the mountains of Transjordania rising up steeply on the other side. The nearer mountains are very strange – like rain-washed humps of sand. The Jordan lies along the flat bed of a deep valley, and we could see the salt beds at its mouth. The amphitheatre itself was surrounded by umbrella pine and in the cracks of the stone seats Autumn Crocus were in bloom[…]

[Signed "Salaam, Len".]

In late November Len paid his first visits to Tel Aviv. He was extremely interested in the Palestine situation, and devoted much thought to it. In this letter he shows the first signs of changing his attitudes and swinging his sympathies behind the Jews, while recognising that there was "no solution to the problem really".

Sarafand, 27 November 1945

Tonight we finished the magazine – it is a great feeling and I am rather proud of it. It has been a labour of love which is a lot to say for a single little unit magazine, but when you see a copy, you will see how much care we have taken on the typography – so much care was taken that some of the contributions were below its standard and it was the editor's painful duty to persuade the authors to make certain improvements in style form and content and so on and in one case the contributor was so bad that three times he had to be pacified and eventually I persuaded him that a mere simple leaf from his journal would be a grand thing. And now it's all finished – there have been several things to learn. The chief one is that it is no good cutting the heading out of lino as we have done because it is such a vastly different medium from type face that it needs extra inking and in this case it has shown through. But we apologise by saying that it's only an experimental number which it is of course. I'm afraid that we have had so many spoils that we only have the bare amount to go around, so it is impossible to send you a copy but I shall be sending a copy home for myself and it shall be one of my treasures in the future[…] Jim will probably think it is only a glorious opportunity lost but it must be remembered that it is a magazine for the unit, which for the most part consists of quite ordinary blokes, and the articles reflect them and in this case do them credit I think[…]

I can't find the first part of Jim's poem, which seems awfully ungrateful of me after all your work but I have been so busy that I have hardly been able to sort out any letters. I'm pretty sure that a thorough search will find it because I know I didn't tear it up. So I cannot tell you what I think of it as a whole. At the first reading it struck me as being very beautiful; it is very like the 'Drowned Sailor', but with a more consistent flow. The imagery too is beautifully apt throughout and seems to sustain that strange atmosphere more deliberately and convinceingly [sic] than in the 'Drowned Sailor'. Jim is rather like Byron you know, in that every poem is another aspect of the poet and it seems quite impossible for the poet to escape himself. But just as it is useless to even wish for another Byron – more than useless, rather stupid and unappreciative of the poet's innate gift which is himself – so it is stupid to wish for a Jim that wrote a more detached and less egoistical poetry.

I haven't written much about events in Palestine recently – I myself am far away from them except for two very cautious business visits to Tel Aviv. But they were sufficient to show me just what the Jews think of us and on one occasion I was called an English swine by a passer by. My ideas have changed considerably since I last wrote about that question, chiefly because much of my time has been spent trying to find out how the various parties stood and how just were their claims. As far as I can see there is no solution to the problem really and an arbitrary ruling in favour of the Jews and at the expense of the Arabs is the only way out. It is now such a matter of life and death to the Jews that they are prepared to die for their cause, and when a mob charges British soldiers it is the most fanatic and determined mob you could imagine. So shots have been fired and I'm afraid boys of 14 and 15 have been injured and the effect has been terrific on the Jewish population, who are making capital of British soldiers shooting Jewish children. Well it's a fact – a horrible fact. But I must say in justice to the British soldiers who shot those children that the children are being brought up in political ideas similar to the Nazi methods – they have a society clothed and organised just like the Hitler Jugend which used to distress me in Germany. And these children throw stones get out of hand and [a] situation arises which leaves most parachute troops (trained for quick action) nothing else to do but shoot it seems. I hate the whole business, and as you know I will as soon see the other side's attitude as my own, so I must say that though I cannot agree with the men who shot or the officers who ordered it, I can understand them very easily. But the effect on both sides has been enormous – the Jews hate us as a type of SS soldier, and the trouble the Jews have caused only has the effect on the ordinary irresponsible and non-thinking Tommy of making him even more indifferent and careless in a situation which is extraordinarily delicate. They are quite the wrong troops to bring in – fresh from looting in an enemy country they come here and expect the same. So that a situation is caused by our very presence[…]

[Signed "Sahida. Len".]

With this letter Len enclosed a letter dated 20 November from Nancy Browne, secretary of the Central Board for Conscientious Objectors, to Len and John Petts confirming that "No serving members of the Forces are allowed to count civilian service before enlistment for demobilisation purposes." He also enclosed a typewritten note stating: "Enclosed a letter from the CBCO recently, which isn't very encouraging. It is in answer to a further enquiry by John and I since the introduction of the new bill. Apparently we are still not covered by the bill and my group is once again 52 and I feel there will never be any freedom. If only I could explain to the powers that be that I am doing extra service and losing three years service only because I wanted to help. I am determined not to let it depress me but it is a horrible thought that I can't come home in Summer and must wait over a year." Len would continue to fret about his demobilisation at regular intervals in his letters until he left the army, while Mona loyally continued to lobby on his behalf.

Sarafand, 30 November 1945

I've had several letters from you the last two days, one of 25 Oct, a much belated reply to one from me at Gaza. It was rather interesting, since it was quite out of its phase, and referred to things we were talking about at that time. Apparently at that time I'd just seen my Arab Labour Party friends. Unfortunately, I haven't been able to see them since, but hope to go to Gaza in the near future. Anything I say on Jews or Arabs is bound to be inadequate. So you must reserve judgement on what I say – it is bound to sound inconsistent. I enclose 3 cuttings from the same paper *Mid-East Mail* on the same day. How can one decide? I put (1) first in strength & need – but it isn't a truthful statement (2) Second, because the Jewish claim & need is greater & not because the Arab is wrong (3) The Army attitude just stinks. If I had the strength & were willing to undergo 2 or 3 years in detention (it would harm me for life) I would desert. In fact, if it weren't for my parents I would go & hide in a Jewish Settlement. But it means a complete abrogation of life, the life I hope to live in future, & the renunciation of friends and so much of myself.

I am really concerned about the situation. The rather lovable, ignorant and blustering parachutists I served [with] in Germany were bad enough there – I excused their behaviour because I thought it went with war, and I was too absorbed in my own work to see everything. But now I look on with my eyes open and hide in disgust in my own little "Inner Circle" as the Colonel calls it. Oh Mona, why are men as they are? My own brothers make me sick and Mowat, Petts, Newcomb, Dunster & one or two others with myself turn inwards & towards each other. What else can we do? We don't talk much about it, but the same feeling is in us all, I think. I was in the Wilderness of Judea yesterday & I began to know why ascetics crept away from mankind & its ways to seek solitude & inner fulfilment in the wilderness. None of us is perfect, but at least we strive after something, but the huge empty-headed mass which has no brain, no struggle, nothing to do, is the problem. I at least excuse myself that if ever I am on one of these searches as a medic in attendance on troops, I shall do as I did in Germany, make it almost impossible for a man to loot & destroy in my presence without his feeling absolutely aware of the horror of what he is doing & feeling ashamed. And believe me, I am absolutely detached from whatever horrors the Army perpetrates out here. The Colonel knows my position for one – if I'm not employed on *As You Were* & educational things I work in a hospital fulltime as I was recently. For the rest, I am friend to Jew & Arab alike & hope that if & when we go (as I hope we may some day) they may live in peace together[…]

Three newspaper cuttings were enclosed with this letter. (1) 'Ben Gurion challenges statement'. The political leader of the Jewish community (and future first prime minister of Israel) declared three things for which "we Jews are prepared to die": "freedom of immigration, the right to rebuild from desolation and an independent political future for Palestine". (2) 'Arab reply to Bevin postponed'. Delegates to the Arab League Council meeting postponed their reply to British Foreign Secretary Bevin's statement on Palestine. "Arab rights in Palestine have been explained scores of times before and there is no need for a commission to consider the question. Zionist immigration should be stopped and an independent democratic Arab state set up in Palestine." (3) 'Palestine troops praised'. The British High Commissioner expressed his satisfaction that troops who had fired on Jewish settlers "had acted with restraint and discipline". Len added a handwritten note in the margin: "There is a Jewish statement absolutely denying this, which I think is true. Can you sort it all out? I can't."

In early December Len spent some time in and around Jerusalem. He gave his impressions of the Dead Sea, which prompted a surprising comparison with the Lake District.

Toc H Jerusalem, 4 December 1945

I was quite tired after a 10 mile walk yesterday to & from the Dead

Sea. We left the Jericho Road about 5 miles from the town & cut straight down to the sea. It was very hot, much hotter there than up at Jerusalem. We were very thirsty and had to pay 3s. for a cup of tea and a cake.

It's not out of the ordinary as a lake – there is no vegetation of course, but the Mountains of Moab run down into its depths just like the scree East of Wastwater. We couldn't see the other end of course, since it's nearly 50 mls away. There are great evaporating beds at the head of the sea, and they are full of tons of salt. A plant sorts out the various chemicals & lorries are struggling out all day long on the steep climb to Jerusalem, each one with about 3 tons of fertilizers or other chemicals. There is one small Arab settlement of small European bungalows; one Jewish settlement, strangely in tenement flats about 4 storeys high, as though the builder had been pinched for room in the middle of a city. He had whole acres to play with and built flats right up to the sky.

From the Jericho road to the Sea is a gently descending slope, for it is already the floor of the great depression. First it is scrub country – soft greens, ochres & that strange grape-coloured purple that the dead scrub has. Looking back over this expanse of soft coloured scrub to the hills of the Wilderness is an amazing sight.

We got a lift back when we got back to the Jericho Road. Dinner & then to an orchestral concert being broadcast from the YMCA auditorium[…]

In his next letter from Jerusalem, Len reported that Vic Newcomb had received an encouraging note from an official who had spoken about demobilisation to Ness Edwards MP, parliamentary secretary to the Ministry of Labour. He then described a walk with Vic in the hills towards Bethlehem.

Jerusalem [YMCA notepaper], 5 December 1945 (New Year's Day in the old city)
[…] Vic brought this [the letter from official R Sorensen] to Jerusalem himself today. Now we are away into the hills round Bethlehem for a good quick ramble in the cool sunny air. Two letters from you today, thank you.

I wish you could see all the Arab women in the best clothes today for the New Year or something [Muharram]. What a *feast* of colour – On top of their tribal robes they have plaid jackets against the cold, vermillion with black & gold needlework. There is one beggar whom we call George who is clothed thickly in rags tied together, & squats in the smallest bundle you could imagine inside his thick sacking. He's always there, never speaks or moves, & shows only a mass of falling ringlets of dusty black on the well shaped head. I think he is a mad carrier who has just squatted into a final rage & disgust with the world.

More later.

Later. Well, we got right off the road into the queer hills & valleys S of Jerusalem. I don't suppose English feet have trodden much there, except that where we left the road (at a Greek Monastery on the Bethlehem road) there was a nice cool tone seat, inscribed in English & Greek, to the memory of Holman Hunt. There we [ate] an orange each & offered one to Holman, who sat dejectedly between us but he refused it. He is very depressed about the world's attitude to his *Scape-goat* and the other day at the Dead Sea, we thought we saw him with his sketch book under his arm, but he left the path to get out of our road. Perhaps he didn't want to show us his work, but we thought it was more likely that, like us, he had neglected his sketchbook that day & [had] nothing to show – a perfect disgrace for any good Pre-Raphaelite.

We were among the olive groves again and in the queer field they make in the hills by collecting the soil on the bare land, plough it in & leave it. It's rather amusing, this soil-scratching business & hasn't advanced a bit since Jesus lived. The plough is only a tree bough with a long iron spike[…]

If you read my book (I mean the Unit book) of the Normandy Campaign, you will find a section on the German strength at Brevelle[3] & how the Black Watch ran away, dropped their arms in headlong flight. The 6th Airborne Div then in reserve after a hard fortnight, pulled them out of the fire. In Holland we relieved the 15th Scottish Division on the Maas Front, and owing to their then poor spirit, the Germans on the opposite bank were very pugnacious at first and red berets had to [be] worn before the bridgehead could be freed just before we came back to England. After our drop on Germany, the same Division relieved us, yet after only 3 days we had to go out into the line again to relieve the situation which they had caused by digging in & stopping prematurely. From then on the 6th Airborne Div was the unrelieved spear-head across Germany[...] As a fighting mob, the 6th Airborne Division was the cream I can tell you, and we all say (listen to the man!) we'd have pulled off Arnhem for them. Their morale & cockiness & cheekiness in face of the enemy was amazing, & when I was in with the Canadians, we used to move on & on & never dig in until the very last minute. I know now it shortened the war by never allowing a pitched & ordered battle or counter-attack, but at the time I used to swear with fear. They were superb – but send them into a delicate situation like Palestine & they are the same blokes, eager for a fight, & it's all wrong, of course. Here they are despicable, to say the least[...]

Sarafand, 11 December 1945

[...] My leave has been a very fruitful one. I have got to know Jerusalem well, and its character and types have fascinated me. But most of all I have begun to draw and I am convinced on the slight showing so far that I ought to take up art in the future. I have been trying my hand at figure drawing, mainly from Greek and Roman sculptures, and the main reaction is that I must do some more as often as I can. It's like a drug and I must have some more. I have bought a little piece of wood to try some carving too and want to attack everything with enthusiasm, but there is too much to do. The success of the magazine is quite turning my head and I have to go to Division to see the Education Officer about *Bellerephon* the Division Magazine, which they are ashamed of having seen our little effort. But I don't want to leave 224 and shall tell them that I'll help them from outside. I must get back to normal and just peg away at *As You Were*, and not be tempted to do other jobs. In any case, the Inner Circle, as the Colonel calls the few who run things in the unit, is already disintegrating - James Bramwell in England, Bill Godfrey leaving tomorrow for England on a class B release, John Petts probably leaving to join the Education Corps (that is one reason why he renounced his status I think, particularly as the opportunities now the war is over are great for him, and he is feeling the pinch as far as money is concerned and he has to pay for a divorce and get married some time in the future)[...]

The sojourn in Jerusalem led to Len carving his very first sculpture, a tiny but accomplished piece of work which he described in his next letter.

Sarafand, 15 December 1945

I've begun setting up No 2 of *As You Were* and am having to do all the composing alone, because everybody is either on courses or otherwise occupied, or on leave. But I don't mind, except that composing is tedious. I have cut a little woodblock for a tailpiece.

But the chief thing is that in my moments of resting from the magazine, I have been carving a tiny female torso of some wood like cedar or dark olive. It has turned out much better than I'd ever hoped & I'm quite in love with her. She is almost finished and the wood polished beautifully. She is very small of course (less than 4 inches) which made the various recesses difficult to scoop out & polish, but I am very proud of her & she is something to show the professors if I apply for an art scholarship. I shall send her home when I can bear to part with her. It is the result of my studies at Jerusalem, which as I said was a most fruitful leave[…]

George Downs is quite ill poor soul, & that is why you & Mother have been so neglected lately. He is rather weak, since it is his stomach & he can hardly touch Army food, it makes him so ill. So letters & so on have been neglected as you can imagine. He is being X-rayed for a suspected gastric ulcer and it may mean his discharge from the Army, which in itself is a good thing, but not if it means being very ill. Even when I was with him he used to suffer with his stomach on account of the vile food at Barby. I have a little trouble sometimes, but nothing serious, & it is soon put right with a short fast or some fruit, easy to get out here[…]

Sahida,
Len

P.S. Oh yes – *Sahida* is a pleasant Arab greeting – untranslatable I suppose – less formal than *Salaam* (Peace be unto you) but similar. L.

Sarafand, 16 December 1945

[…] The Colonel came into my work room this morning, and I was quite unshaven (though washed) since it was Sunday morning. He didn't seem to mind & as I was alone he seemed to want to chat as man to man. First he wanted to know how the men were using the library. I was able to give a good report, with records to prove it. I have been encouraging men to read technical books on subjects that interest, and also leading them on from westerns & detectives to better fiction & I could quote the example of the cook corporal who started with them and is now accepting my recommendations, & thinks Francis Brett Young is grand stuff, *I Claudius* is "good meat" & Grahame Green [sic] is "just his going" & so on. The colonel seemed pleased. He was also very pleased about *As You Were* which he keeps sending to this big-wig & that, rather in the spirit of a creation of his own private circus, but nevertheless is good strong enthusiasm. Then he picked up my little nude, which is almost finished, and went off his head, & I couldn't get a word in edgeways (that's how he talks, all in one gabble) – wanted to know where I got it & would I sell it to him. When I told him it was my own work, he was most impressed – but I said I couldn't sell it as I wanted it for scholarship & so on. So you see, he isn't a bad Colonel, is he?

The little nude pleases me very much - it has been a very great boon to me and probably means about 3 months tedious study at an art school in one effort, though my work at Jerusalem inspired it, & must be included[…]

Like me, you cannot easily sort out the conflicting statements of the Press on Palestine. Perhaps Arthur Raistrick, if he were here, would form definite views. I defy anyone in England to decide. Take for instance the pure bilge uttered in the H of Lords the other day. The Archbishop of York was worst, talking of not allowing P to become overcrowded & making it one vast slum! He just wants a good kick in the pants for being in a position to speak such utter nonsense from so high a place! He doesn't even understand the first things.

Though I deplore the extreme Jews attitude & pugnacity & nation-alist spirit, I think more & more that they are right in essentials. Anti-Semitism is rife in the Army, because the Arabs are so peacefully subdued by comparison with the progressive & spirited Jewish movement & if you are killed out here, it will be by Jewish terrorists. But that is an ignorant & empty reason for refuting them, or for holding Anti-Semitic views. But nevertheless Palestine police & soldiers serving here go back to England just hating the Jews, like Kitty Leaske's[4] brother & glibly declare the Arabs are in the right. That view influenced me at first, as you know, especially as the first people I contacted were Arabs. Their views were sound, I liked them but beside the urgency & strength of Jewish demands their story pales. Both are right in many ways, & both are wrong in just as many others, and I'm sure that if England & America & Russia weren't playing power politics so hard, & interests like oil, the Suez Canal, & other imperial claims weren't at stake the Jews could have just what they wanted, & a sort of peaceful penetration would soon arrest their full claim to Palestine & the Arabs, after an initial struggle would gradually fall back into Syria, Egypt, Iraq & similar Arab states, especially if the latter were encouraged along more progressive lines as [King] Farouk in Egypt seems to aim at.

Your letter from Wilson Harris was most encouraging & such a similar tone to Sorenson's to Vic [Newcomb] [both about demobilisation] that I think there is real hope. One reason for urgency is that jumping commences in January & it is all aperture exits – i.e. instead of from a door in the side of the plane as in a Dakota which we are used to, it is from a hole in the floor, which is a precision job & requires skill & extra nerve if you aren't to knock your parachute pack on your chin coming out. [Small ink sketch of a parachutist illustrating this]

It is even more nerve-wracking than door exits & it scares me & I know it will upset me. The planes are old Halifaxes, since Dakotas are in such demand for transport demobs etc.

Anyway, your letter does cheer me. You do work hard & I'm sure half the house must wonder who this persistent woman is[…]

Sarafand, 17 December 1945

I am very depressed tonight for no apparent reason. I try nowadays to put depression down to slight ill-health or some obvious cause. But this refuses to lift. But I think it is some sort of homesickness, because it keeps re-occurring. I suppose it is understandable with Xmas approaching, but that seems a silly reason. Perhaps it is because I have finished my little nude & the job of working on her is spent. Perhaps it is because I went to Tel Aviv this morning & the coldness & even hatred I read in people's faces made me think the whole human race was like that. Or perhaps it is because it seems months since I talked to a member of the other sex.

I don't know, but it is there. The trouble is, of course, that there is no real balm for the troubled soul out here – not even the comfort of a rosy fireside (though I'm not cold) but one is constantly thrown up against the same poor friends day after day, hour after hour, till you think friendship would be quite worn out[…]

When we are depressed we are failing ourselves and it is a confession of weakness of mind & spirit. Well, like all depressed people, I confess! And that is all there is to it. Tomorrow I hope it has passed. But I cannot tell you how much, all the time, I am longing to return to England & begin real life again[…]

I must work – all the time. As soon as I begin to ponder I'm lost. So now my little lady is finished I must begin something else, because setting up the magazine all the time almost sends me mad[…]

Sarafand, 21 December 1945

I think you would find my last letter not very cheerful. It's bad when we get depressed in a foreign country and so far I can't pull up. I don't know what's the matter with me, but I think it is fairly general. We can't wait to return home, where for a while at any rate, we can forget there is still a war on. I wish the Labour Government could know the full facts of Palestine for one country [sic] – I feel they are being duped by the military, who are enjoying themselves making ready for real war in Palestine. Road blocks are flying up faster than during the German threat of invasion of England, and the most strategic positions are being chosen for machine-gun nests. 1 whole train-load of 17 pound guns was seen by John Dunster at Haifa today. Poor John is terribly depressed & is probably worse than me.

Surely the Labour Government will put the local people's interests before British Imperial matters. I can't believe that a Labour Government sanctions all this.

Oh for peace from all these squabbling people, & from the army, even though it leaves me alone.

Today it got hold of us all however and took us about 20 miles to an aerodrome for some synthetic training for aperture exits. We used the Halifaxes themselves and the nervous exhaustion after only one afternoon is terrific. I hate it. And what is it all for? None of the high ideals that made us transfer for a jump on the Continent fire us now. I was so pleased to do what I did on the continent – I was impartial and can honestly say I helped more Germans than British, because circumstances called for it, and I found it easy to break down national enmity & become friends. Here the frigid hostility is impenetrable. It is impossible to declare your trust and good faith as one could in Germany. Here I am an SS man whatever my aims are. The thing is of course, that no individual Jew or Arab needs help, as Germans or Belgians or Dutch did – they need help as a nation, & I am one of the big army of obstruction. The Jews are so wrong-headed too about so many things that they are dangerous & I can understand, without condoning, the Army's precautions. They were arming while the British Army was fighting desperately at Alemain [sic] in 1940 – with stolen British arms. They blow up this & that, slander beyond measure the only nation that has truly sympathised with their plight in Germany under Hitler. They forget so easily. So as usual, it is 6 & two 3s. I never knew such a complicated problem, with so many wrongs & rights on all sides[…]

Sarafand, 27 December 1945

It has been a dismal enough Army Xmas – when one must make the greatest effort to be "merry", and yet feels conscious all the time that only 1 blessed hour at home would have made us happy.

So it is best forgotten as a Xmas. There wasn't even any mail – in fact mail has been bad and nothing is more depressing out here.

On Boxing Day, though it was officially a holiday, I just started work again, set up another page & printed it today, so that is 3 pages finished[…]

Johnny Ryder, Vic and John Dunster have gone on leave to Beirut today, and John Petts has been posted to Haifa – Mt Carmel College (an AEC – [Army] Educational Corps – instructional place). So Hugh

[Mowat] & I are left alone. We work pretty solid all day & go for a 3 or 4 mile run before tea, or so we plan, as we have been doing it mostly for several weeks now. We must keep up a sort of high physical tone, or parachuting is impossible[…]

Sarafand, 28 December 1945

Stacks of mail today – I wondered why all my friends were neglecting me, & thought it was to punish me for recent depression. It cheered me and it was exciting. For Bill Hamilton finally writes to me & we are reunited by letter anyway – he's actually at Mt Carmel College Haifa, where John Petts has gone on the same Army Educ Formation course. I could go too, but I won't renounce my status even to educate the masses. Then, following your advice that I might turn some of my recorded experiences & observations to good account, I sent a little article on the Orange Harvest to the *Manchester Guardian* & this mail there was £2 for me. I've forgotten what it was all about, but I know it wandered from oranges to lady's dresses in very quick time, & it was very short. So it was worth it – I'm not a writer, but this was written after a day in the groves & it took very little time. It was just like writing a letter. It happens too that I'm hard-up[…]

Sarafand, Hogmanay [1945]

[…] I want to write about the Jews but haven't time I'm afraid. The terrorists were murderous the other night & I think even the Jewish population think it has gone too far. Several Basutos were killed & wounded in Jerusalem; an Arab killed in the Jaffa police station, & in another raid, one man was killed while paying a visit to the lavatory in his vest & pants (which seems particularly pathetic in its innocence). Two British Policemen were killed in Jerusalem, one leaving a widow who lost her first husband in a similar affair in 1942. 1 parachutist was killed. The raids were murderous & cowardly, made secretly in the night with several armed men going for one guard. Nobody, not even the Jews, can condone it, and the general feeling is that it is embarrassing the Jewish case. I am just irritated by the stupidity of such tactics which do nothing but cause a few needless deaths and breed violent anti-semitism much more permanently & deeply than any Hitler campaign could in the ordinary un-thinking British soldier – & there are 10s of thousands out here, as you know. The change in Tel Aviv is interesting – I went there this morning to have some blocks made for *As You Were* & other little things. Last time I went with the little colophon (The Canopy Press) block, they were difficult, & said it would take a fortnight. This time they said "Good morning", treated me with professional understanding, as between illustrator & block-maker, as it were, & said it would be ready in two days. The scowl & sulk is almost gone, & though one feels we are still frowned [on], there is an atmosphere of apology & care.

I'm sorry the colophon wasn't ready for this inset when I sent you a copy of *As You Were*. It was printed later & enclosed in overseas members' copies. I designed & drew the colophon.

[Enclosed: Colophon for the first number of As You Were*, the unit magazine, printed by the Canopy Press]*

Palestine:
An Educational Experience

The New Year began symbolically with Len's first visit to the functionally named No 1 Command Education College Wing, otherwise known as Carmel College in Haifa. The place would have a profound effect on his life. On this occasion he met his old friend Bill Hamilton, who since joining up in 1941 had undergone lengthy training and risen through the ranks without ever seeing armed action. (The start of 1946 was also marked by a change in Len's way of opening his letters: his customary "Dear Mona" became "My dear Mona". This does not appear to be particularly significant.)

Sarafand, 5 January 1945 [sic – clearly 1946 meant]

I have been out all day in a jeep to Haifa, and was very lucky, for an officer took me straight to Bill Hamilton. I hadn't heard from him, & knowing the Army, thought it quite possible for him still to be at Cairo waiting for the movement order. He'd just seen Petts yesterday, who gave him my letter (Petts has gone to the same college on a course). We were both almost delirious with excitement when I entered his room. We must have looked like two young school-girls, each chattering above the other & almost in tears with joy. Bill is a great fellow and his commission hasn't made the least difference. He is soon to be made a captain and is a lecturer in modern history & political economics. He is very friendly with the Major who runs the place. There is a job for me there too, but it would entail renouncing my status, so I mustn't yield to temptation. I shall end my army career as a humble private.

What a lovely place, set high on top of Mt Carmel amidst the fir trees, overlooking the great bay round to Acre on one side & the Mediterranean on the other. I could see Mt Hermon in the distance, snow-capped & pink.

Bill is happy for the first time in his Army career and he has a good job, which enables him to study in peace. Naturally we talked & talked, except for an hour's interruption when some Major came in to chatter about nothing in particular.

It was a long ride, 140 miles there & back, but it was worth [it] [...]

Many of the fields on the coastal plain are fresh & green now and it is quite unlike the light brown dusty landscape I saw when we travelled down from Haifa to Gaza. After seeing Haifa again I have decided that it is the best city in Palestine. There are only 2 more, of course, Jerusalem 80,000 people, Tel Aviv 40,000 (Jaffa is very small of course & is on the outskirts of Tel Aviv, though 20 years ago it was the other way round). Haifa has 40,000, and it has a wonderful site on the edge of the bay, on a great point, and on the slopes of Carmel itself. As you climb the slopes up the winding road, it gets better, with the cypresses giving way to firs & heath, and the view is breathtaking. The expensive Jewish houses, set in big gardens, remind me of Hampstead[…]

Sarafand, 11 January 1946

All your recent letters are packed away in my kit somewhere so this is not a reply but only a note. We are moving; in fact, we've moved, and so far it's just terrible until the "flap" gets over. I am worked off my feet trying to keep up with the demand for signs "This way out" "That way out" – "MI Room" – "Dental Centre" – "Vehicle Park" – "commanding Offices" and so on till I'm just browned off. To think that John & I went to such great trouble to paint most of the unit signs at Gaza, & even evolved our own alphabet, Gaza Roman as a medium. They were beautifully done, believe me, but just because the unit has been split up since then & only now unites again, they have to lose them all. This time I'm on alone, Murphy the present signwriter being in hospital, and I'm just hurrying them through in the worst bastard lettering. In the meantime *As You Were* No 2 is held up for want of a page which I can't find time to write (since it's about the unit sports etc) or set up & print.

So you can imagine a very low-spirited fellow this end. It's not because of the above really – I don't care (I really don't take any notice of attempts to hurry me now) if they never get their signs, and I've given up worrying about January's number of the magazine appearing in February sometime. I've tried my level best & I'm just not allowed to keep at it, because it looks like a "racket" I'm working, and privates, sergeants, officers alike would rather not have a magazine than see a man with a good job producing it.

No, I'm just like that most of the time now, and I'm sure you must find my letters poor ones lately. I can't wait, you see, and since the fellows around me are much the same, especially the older ones are much the same, we are all a mopey lot these days I'm afraid & no help to each other. Several things contribute. The Army's attitude to the education scheme is showing itself. Education is not the Army – it would never do to educate soldiers, and even if the authorities above want it, and the privates below want it, it is the people in the middle who run things, and I'm afraid it is just those same people who would suffer if the masses were just a little more intelligent than they are. Just think of what could be done. I don't think the Army would be a university – but think what little classes like Eric Canning's could do – they wouldn't teach much, but they would start most fellows on a trail – think of the millions who, once having got a scent of what there is in life & living really, would never again be satisfied merely to eat & drink, sleep, read the *Daily Mirror* & go to sleep to a background of jazz on the radio. But no. It would never do to have private soldiers even starting to think. So those people in the unit who try to get things going are just obstructed – sometimes wilfully, sometimes just because it interferes with military requirements. So I begin to reflect – am I to go on through life hitting my head against the wall & finding no response & feeling desperate half the time, or am I just to recoil, take no notice, and settle down comfortably in my own little niche as soon as they'll allow me. So far, I have continued to hit my head. I am noted for shouting & screaming and the QMS [quartermaster sergeant] is afraid to ask me to say "Sir" to him though I pointedly omit to say it, for a man who is such a sucker and panders to the army at the expense of the army education scheme is no gentleman.

(Later) The same QMS has just been into my room where I was quite alone and he knew I was fed up. He asked me what was the matter and for about an hour I have been going at it until I was almost passionate. And do you know, my head has made the slightest hole in the wall. He has listened, I have pleaded, and all the time he, who never visits people personally like this, had come to tell me I was to go to Haifa on about 10 Feb on a unit instructors' course at Mount Carmel College. So I shall be with Bill for a whole month and it will be just a holiday for me. It will help me, even if it doesn't help the fellows, which sounds selfish, but I think I do need some help myself, for things are beginning to get me down. I am pining and fretting & fuming all the time and that isn't a nice state to be in[…]

Sarafand, 17 January 1945 [sic – clearly 1946 meant]

[…] You very tactfully discourage me from writing about what I saw in Germany. Well, I know what an utter bore a man can be when he begins to tell how he won the war & narrowly escaped from death. The truth is, if he was in a war at all, he must at some time have narrowly escaped death & there is forever afterwards a bug in his brain. But it is a painful job for people like Jim or George Downs to listen, making them dwell on the little they have done, & feel that they've missed something. It is bound to happen, & no one could have convinced me I had missed nothing if I hadn't been to a front. It is all too recent and 2 or 3 years will even it all out. Our achievement in peace will count not how we won the war, how heroic we were. So treat my malady as a bug – don't take much notice[…] After all, this was my first visit abroad. So you will forgive me, I know[…]

I'll not discuss the Palestine situation except to say that the terrorists are very much in the black books among the Jews themselves who declare in the Press that they do not represent the people & are Fascist in their aims & practice, & embarrass the Jewish diplomatic battle with Britain[…]

[Enclosed copy of As You Were *Vol. 1 January 1946 No. 2]*

In later life Len/Jonah was a respected and popular arts educator amid other strands of work. He began as a teacher in Palestine, where he taught various subjects, most notably English literature. He enjoyed the work and it paved the way for his time engaged in arts colleges, which would form a significant part of his career.

Sarafand, 24 January 1946

[…] I have just finished an hour's teaching, preceded by ¾ hr with a short break between. I'm quite hoarse and I'm sure the poor pupils must be sick of hearing me. I have had to take all the English since Hugh [Mowat] left on his course, as well as Mechanical Drawing, whereas I usually only take literary appreciation and Drawing. Hugh usually does Grammar and composition. The Exam (Forces Preliminary – equivalent to matric & recognised by most universities & Professional Bodies) is in February sometime, but most pupils are the younger men & are sitting in July.

I didn't have much time to tell you about Sunday. It was a real Jewish day of course because Mrs Goodman, who is a hostess at a forces club there, always gets hold of any pacifists she knows and has a gentle *tête-à-tête* in some corner. She has got to know of the COs in 224 and knows us all by now. She is adept at getting to know people (probably it has been her job throughout her life) and she calls me Jonah as much as to say "We haven't known each other long but we are friends enough for that surely!" The Ark, as the club is called, is full of lovely Jewesses making pleasant silky conversation for our benefit and flashing pearly smiles at us. That makes me sick to be frank, but one of them knew I was one of Mrs Goodman's cronies and called her from her inner sanctum. She has the art of making one welcome off very well. I was ushered in & invited to lunch. This was at a little table on a tiny balcony outside her office and almost on top of the promenade overlooking the thundering breakers. It was scorching hot but pleasant in shirt sleeves. Like July at Whitley Bay. I was left a while with a pacifist Jew who acts as a sort of host & arranges tours of Palestine, talks about the country to troops and so on. He is an ardent communist, loves the country and especially the communal life of the settlements. He is all politics – knows the answer to everything and was so vehemently, enthusiastic and apologetic for the misdeeds of my own country that I couldn't stick him.

Mrs Goodman came in & Ben went out. She & I had a splendid lunch on German lines and I was far away from camp talking to a woman. She is very charming, and has much experience of life – she can speak many languages fluently and though she is not insincere, she has all the tricks of attracting men still. She is Russian and when

I say she knows how to attract I don't mean the obvious cheap way that many English women have, but the subtle courtly way that noble-women have in Tolstoy, say; it presumes some intelligence in the male & also presumes his vulnerability, despite his intelligence if you know what I mean. In Mrs Goodman it is well practiced and she is an easy conversationalist, talks about art with taste & sense, and about people & the world at large with a gentle melancholy which says "I used to have great hopes when I was a young Comrade, but now I am old enough to realize human nature cannot be changed. Only in striving is there any reward, and it keeps our head above water, if nothing more." In that respect I come more and more to agree with her. Her sorrow for the plight of her people is very real. Two days ago the independency of the Transjordan was promised & a seat in the UNO[1] guaranteed for them. Egypt, Turkey & such states "sat on the fence all the war" as she put it, can vote at UNO but the Jewish State is not even held to exist nor the Jewish Nation. Frankly, she cannot under-stand a people who proclaim they are fighting for certain things & when they get victory turn their backs on them. The Four Freedoms[2] were believed in by most Jews and they fought at our side for them – yet now they see the nation they pinned their faith in backslide, show gross ingratitude, & forget the horrors of Belsen & Dachau as though they were a mere local riot. That is how she, and all her people, look upon us, and the best of them are dumbfounded. The worst of them blow up railways, raid & kill as a protest.

So I had to discuss politics for a while – I didn't mind though, because Mrs Goodman is sensible about it & not fanatic and has, as I say, that Tolstoyan view of life which comes with wise and long experi-ence. I enjoy talking with anyone like that, & I am lost with people who hold bold & definite views to the exclusion of all others. Mrs Goodman was very young in the Revolution, just a girl, I imagine, but she was an ardent Comrade and though she declared she disowns her old country now for its misdeeds, she still admires Communism as a working principle. She is proud to be a member of the War Resisters' International & has travelled all over Europe on its behalf. She has lived in America too & has their accent.

It was very good to talk to Mrs Goodman – I suppose in her own way, for tolerance, good sense and experience she is as near George

Carr as any of our friends, though she is always a woman first and I should think she has had a great many lovers in her youth. She is the sort of woman who has a great & varied story to tell, but is always inevitably silent on that point[...]

Sarafand, 26 January 1946

I've had one helluva day – just like you on pay-day. I went to Gaza with £10 in my pocket, hard-earned savings or shall I say hard-saved earnings, and I just flung it right & left and enjoyed myself, came back with my arms full and my pockets empty. And I'm content. Tomorrow I'll start packing, and in 2 or 3 months time if we're lucky, you will get a little praying mat. I do hope you get it, because I can't register it I'm afraid. And I do hope you like it. Gaza mats are famous all over Palestine and are a tough, rough, plain & natural rug, hand-woven and just good solid raw wool[...]

I haven't heard about my Haifa course yet, but I'm still hopeful. Only I wish they'd let me know in time so that I could let you know my address in good time. Re-addressed mail from the unit goes back to Cairo and takes over a week to reach its new addresses. I shan't change my rank, because it requires renouncing my status as a CO. Petts did renounce his and is now a Sergeant Instructor, which means he'll get 8/3d a day – quite a wage. He's terribly in love with Kusha and I know he intends to marry her as soon as he is free (you know he awaits divorce proceedings with his first wife Brenda Chamberlain). So the money has largely dictated John's actions, though I know he felt cramped in this unit & wanted to join the Education Corps badly too[...]

Just before he left Sarafand for his month in Haifa, Len found time to write Mona a long description of his friends in the "Inner Circle" and the daily routine in camp. The negative remarks about John Ryder are ironic, since Len and he eventually became the closest of friends after the war.

Sarafand, Sunday 10 February 1946
(write to Mt Carmel College, Haifa MEF please)

[…] This week I have been fully occupied printing No 3 of *As You Were*. I have been trying to print a page a day, working in the evenings, but it is a strain, and in such a close job as printing it harms the eyes. But I don't mind, since I am leaving the number more than half-finished with the rest of the copy pasted up ready for my printer's devil, a lad I have been trying to teach what I know about hand printing[…]

Vic [Newcomb] is very pleased about your comment on "Bessie" – he will never live it down, but he now quotes you as an authority who had the taste & judgement to like his stuff. Actually Vic is a boon to the magazine. I have so many things to do, that I cannot write as much as I'd like. Actually, Vic writes the column about old members "They still remember", and I do think it is entertaining, considering what a dull list of names it could be. You can see, he is cheery and affable, rather like Arthur or Leslie Taylor, and you'd like Vic very much I think. He is a voluble talker and when he is warmed up, it is difficult to get a word in edgeways. When there is a discussion on a subject like the Palestine problem you can rely on it being warm & heated if Vic is there and he's difficult to wear down, even if he is wrong. That part of him sometimes irritates me, but we are old enough now, & love each other in our own way, that it makes no differ-ence. He probably benefits from the mistakes I have made with my older friends[…]

The other prominent member of the inner circle is Hugh Mowat – we have been separated for a long time by class, I think. My working class origin, rather rough & direct outlook on life or whatever you like to call it, have kept Hugh at a distance for a long time – he is the son of a wealthy parson, now dead, and was a student at Cambridge. He is a typical English gentleman in his manners, precise, extremely polite, the essence of patience & was almost unbending. The latter kept us apart probably. He is an ascetic, an intellectual who abhors loose thinking & mis-statements and is silent corrector behind you as you talk somehow. So that intimacy is difficult – Hugh is the walking ghost of your own conscience, I suppose, and you stand constantly corrected before him. Therefore not an easy friend – but all the work you put in to reach his fastidious nature is worth [it] as you can imagine. He now understands me, very well, I think, and we are intimate friends by now, and he is no longer my conscience, nor I his errant spirit. I have made him bend and I think he is grateful, though that sounds like self-aggrandisement. I mean he mixes more now, and seems to find more joy in people than when I first knew him. And I, constantly corrected, audibly & silently have benefited from the strictness and austerity of his mind. One respects Hugh – it is impossible to love him as one loves Vic – but nevertheless, one is constantly grateful to Hugh, for his patience, his zeal for work, and his essential purity. He is rather saintly, and his asceticism has led him to make permanent contacts with similar spirits we have met in our travels. Thus he is in constant correspondence with the brothers at Maredsous Monastery in the Ardennes, and has already made himself acquainted with the Carmelite Brethren at Haifa. If Hugh had not been a CO he would have had a great Army career because of his great capacity for work, contacting people, talking with precision & intelligence, organising, and for his great endurance (he runs 3 miles in under 17 minutes) – his brother is a Lieutenant Colonel (if that means anything). And that is Hugh.

John Petts, as you know, has left us, is now a sergeant, and you probably know him reasonably well from my letters. Johnny Ryder, an authority on book-production, was the mainspring in the establishment of the Canopy Press. He taught me all I know, except what I've read, about printing, tasteful layout and so on. But we never got on. He is a morose, sarcastic & bitter little man, and his attitude to life was too joyless and empty for me. He hated women, did not understand them at all, and if he had his way, all dance music, religion, sport and things that bring warmth & feeling to life for other people except himself would be abolished. One of the most bitter, intolerant, agnostic men I'll ever meet, I think. Everybody found him hard to live with, but I had to be with him more than the others lately, and explosions were often, I'm afraid. Again, however, we got over them – we had to. I write of Johnny in the past because he has been away 3 weeks on a course in Cairo before his demob (Group 27) and he'll be away homeward bound by the time I get back from Haifa.

The other member of the Circle is James Bramwell – he left us not long after we came to Sarafand on a compassionate posting (his mother died shortly after his arrival in England). Browned off with Army life in England he has wangled his re-posting to 224 & has been back 3 days. It is great to have James back among us. I can't describe him, except to say he is an aristocrat in the best sense, a poet, and has a certain spirit which it is easy to worship. He is a great friend, & has some great friends, among whom are a few of the older generation, John Masefield, Eric Kennington[3] (a particular friend of James's I know) and TS Eliot. His face is fascinating. It is like some old bronze in its character (though I don't mean in complexion) and might be some Medici with his silky bleach curls.

I ought to count John Dunster too, but since he was forced into the job of ration corporal we haven't seen so much of him. John is just a big lovable Englishman in spite of himself, for he continually raves against the British Way & Purpose, Britain's attitude to love & sex & all the inhibitions of British life & so on. But he is an intensely loveable lad, with his blonde hair, his strong ruddy face and his great moustache. A great fraterniser in Germany where he made friends (literally) with SS men & avowed Nazis in Wismar Hospital because they interested him.

And there, very poorly I'm afraid, is a picture of the Inner Circle or what remains of it. We has [sic] one young man, who we picked as the most intelligent of the young ones, to replace those of us who may go. But he can never be part of the Inner Circle – the spark is missing, he lacks fire.

We have our friends, mostly those who like music, literature or the arts, for which at least one of the Inner Circle can supply a lead. People call in, talk, have tea with us in the evenings and use our lodge as a sort of club. All people with a social conscience come to us, if only to take part in one of the heated discussions that constantly rise. The other night about 8 of us nattered about the Jewish problem for 2 hours – it was surprising what different views could be held. Economists Vic & George Fox excitedly reeling off facts & figures against the broad humanist claims of John & I, with others chirping in every now and again.

And we have our enemies – the cross, ignorant, stupid who cannot bear to see us printing, teaching, organising lectures and gramophone recitals, making paste-ups of pictures & generally looking after their interests in education – to them we are merely running a racket – to get out of route marches, fatigues & all those things that make the army distasteful.

And our actual life? It varies according to the station – here we are in a part of the NAAFI buildings (NAAFI is closed). We have a big room, with tables, chairs, blackboards, pictures, posters illustrating Levant ruins like Baalbec & Crusader castles etc... Here the men may read, write, peruse the pictures etc... Straight through this room a door opens on another smaller, but still spacious room. Here the first thing is the library, nearly 500 books, good fiction & non-fiction by any standards, with a sure system working efficiently so that the library doesn't disintegrate & disappear (same system as Felling Library, ahem). Behind a slight partition is the Canopy Press, one table with type-cases & galley etc, one with ink plate & press. Discreetly hidden behind all this is Pte Jones's bed (Editor cum Printer cum English Lit Professor). Another table holds various manuscripts in preparation, *Over the Rhine*, forthcoming lessons etc... As discreetly is hidden Pte Newcomb's bed behind this (sub-editor, sub-librarian, Geography Professor). Another corner holds Pte Mowat's bed (librarian, joint author *Over the Rhine*, Asst Lecturer in English).

Rise about 6.30. First up gets the washbasin, makes a helluva row to annoy the other two, and starts the general rush through shave, breakfast & dressing up, towards parade. Always late. Parade 8.15, attended by frequent return of greasy sausage & cookhouse reconstituted egg. Perfunctory inspection. Back to our sanctuary, sweep up Quiet Room, & our own, & begin work, printing or whatever is on. 11 o'clock classes start – about 20 pupils are taught by the very highest rate professor you could wish for, with help from outside in unearthly subjects like Maths. Two ¾ hr classes till 12.30 – Dinner, continue work unless, as on Monday, Wed & Friday, we are required for sport, which we cannot neglect, for reason of policy – health. So Mowat plays Rugger & is Capt of Cross country team, Newcomb plays soccer, Jones Rugger & Cross country (all in respective first team mark you.) So we balance our intellectual activities with the physical – and we can't grumble, because really, we're all very healthy, and you'd envy us our sun-tanned faces. Teatime and unless we are orderly room runner (1 in every 4 nights – a little arrangement whereby we do runners & not guard) the evening is ours. Tuesday night we run a gramophone recital, with tea provided – bring your own mugs. Thursday night we run an Art Club (at least I do). Other nights are spent reading, writing, talking and sometimes a visit to the Garrison Cinema, where sometimes an occasional good film appears. There isn't much else we can do. Tel Aviv usually means a whole day, being 9 or 10 miles away, so it is reserved for Sundays. But that is described in separate letters, I hope.

Seems quite a pleasant life, in a pleasant climate, surrounded by pleasant people. And yet – there's not one of us who would think twice if he was offered release – in other words, this definitely isn't the life. Don't ask me why. It's still the Army. I often feel a great big turn of homesickness. Who can explain it all! I can't. So there's a brief picture of the life, very incomplete – it's so serene for Army life that it is impossible not to feel the dread hand will fall at any moment. It has already threatened. There is always a jump in the offing, and that isn't pleasant – but there it is – a grand life – shall I sign on for 12 years? Not on your life. Just give me my ticket and I'll be in England just as sharp as transport can take me[…]

[Signed "Goodnight, God Bless, Len".]

Len now began his month's course at Carmel College. It was part of the network of "formation colleges" organised after World War II by the Army Educational Corps. This played a significant role in preparing to return a national army to civilian life. These establishments can be seen as something of a precursor of the Open University two decades later. As Len makes clear, the courses offered were truly challenging.

No 1 Command Education College Wing (Modern Studies),
MEF – 16 February 1946

I am beginning my most studious month since you so patiently laboured with Latin & me, and am very busy browsing in English Literature. I have come here on a First Instructor's Course (which is in teaching methods) but through Bill's influence, I have been able to take the Modern Studies course proper, which is reserved for schoolteachers, or people with degree, or were studying for a degree before joining up, as a refresher course before demob. It is an intensive course in English Literature from the beginnings to the Present Day, & we must submit two essays each fortnight. A month is not long enough, but it is going to be an excellent refresher. I have got to know Major Champion (in charge) quite well, & though I'm not too keen about his proposal, he is considering having me transferred to the Education Corps. I don't think it is possible, though he said, since I did not wish to change my status, that I could have acting unpaid stripes if I were willing to have a job here and wasn't worried about the money.

The idea rather confounds me, and I can't think why he is so keen, except that the staff is constantly being thinned out, and an experienced librarian is quite lacking (& it is an excellent library here). So, as far as he is concerned, it could easily be done, & I'd be a sergeant, since that is the lowest rank in the AEC [Army Educational Corps]. But I don't think I'd like it really, especially since I have so much to do with the unit & it would be unfair to leave them suddenly. It would release [me] from jumping of course. So I leave it to be decided. I'm content either way, which is a nice position I suppose.

It is marvellous here, though my first rhapsody over the view & position has been flattened rather by the most wicked rainstorm these last two days that you could imagine. It is so bad that it would make the best place miserable.

But when it was fine, I was completely entranced by the views from this ridge which is the topmost of Mt Carmel. The foreground is the humpy slopes, covered with stunted pine & cypress, down to the narrow plain stretching out to the sea, & narrow white margin of apparently fixed breakers. And the sea's surface, stretching far away – it's incredibly beautiful, with the sunlight playing on the surface – it is almost like silk gently ruffling.

On the other side the mount descends steeply to the town and the perfect curve, a clean mathematical parabola of the Bay stretches round to Acre, faint in the distance. Behind are the humped Hills of Galilee[…]

Mount Carmel, 19 February 1946

[…] I am very very busy, almost as though I were cramming at a university. I am on a Modern Studies Course in English Lit. About 2 lectures a day, the rest private study. 2 essays each fortnight on certain set subjects. My first essay is "That the Ballad cannot exist in a sophisticated society". My second choice is discussion of a quotation from TS Eliot "The poets of the 17th century, the successes of the dramatists of the 16th, possessed a mechanism of sensibility which could devour any kind of experience".

My other two will possibly be "Great writers could not accept the religion of the 19th century. Discuss with reference to Tennyson, Browning, Hardy or Wilde" & "Eliot is a poet because he has no axe to grind: Auden became one when he stopped grinding his. Comment on this opinion."[…]

And there are more purely literary questions of course. It is all very interesting, and a good refresher. The chief instructor, Major Champion, is a Cambridge MA. The other instructor, George Urwin (Capt) is BA London, & shares Bill's room, so we are good friends. Only 8, I think, are taking this course. I am the only private, but Major Champion takes quite a special interest in me and is trailing a great red herring across my life by saying I could polish my studies by taking a Cambridge degree. I know how easy it would be really if I said "Yes". He makes out a report which carries quite a lot of weight in requests for Army grants which amount to fees + £160 a year to live on. He thinks Cambridge is best by far for Literature. But I must resist such a great tempting red herring[…]

[Signed "*Amitiés*, Len".]

Haifa, [no date – envelope postmarked 4 March 1946]

I am neglecting you all, I'm afraid. You know why, of course. Certain demands are made of one on such an intensive course as this and there isn't much time left for anything else. Even now I might be wading through some more work. My next two essays are 1. A rather facetious but serious inquiry into the nature of poetry by examining the question "Is Gray's *Elegy* a great poem?" What do you think, off hand? I'll be interested to hear. (2) A continuance of my "metaphysical" studies

"Examine the poetry of TS Eliot in the light of your knowledge of the Metaphysical poets."

So I have plenty of work. Your letters continue to arrive, of course, although I know how much you have to do. Still your work is like you on a frosty day – "All spread out". Mine is sheer concentration – at least, examining the mechanism of sensibility of the 17th cent. poets was. I must send you the result sometime, though it is hurried and an awful mess[…]

You talk of this "holy" land. I can never think of it as such except on rare occasions. For instance Nazareth is anything but "holy" – pimps & touts selling postcards is anything but "holy" and the streets crowded with scores of lovely Polish girls who flaunt silk stockings and make Nazareth a place of pilgrimage for sex-starved troops, if only to come & look. They are bonny lasses, almost taking your breath away so that sitting down to a cup of coffee in the canteen, I was swept away by a lovely pair of eyes that kept darting into mine – that is Nazareth – I swept out of it as quickly as possible like Ulysses past the sirens. Nazareth is distinctly dangerous. Galilee to me is a lovely country. Green hills, fertile little valleys, a plain above the Lake, and the Lake itself (Oh so very like Semerwater in many respects) in a hollow. Tiberias rather a pleasant lake-side resort set on the slopes. All round the lake, particularly East & South of it, Jewish settlements of the best type.

I visited (I was forced there with a party) the Church of the Annunciation. Below it is a grotto where the holy family lived – but I just wanted to burst out laughing at the old monk repeating his story (probably a fairy story anyway) like a parrot.

So nothing "holy" here. In fact Palestine if anything is forcing me into a quite new position as regards life & religion. I'm not agnostic – that is just giving up the ghost. And atheism is senseless, impossible.

I always was a vague sort of 18th century pantheist or deist but even so I fix my mind on altogether different things now. Why after all, should we be immortal? What does that mean to us? It begins to mean nothing to me. Death "itself is nothing" – dying can be – I was afraid of Death last year because dying could be so awful – I saw it so often. But now – why do we even think of it. Life is our problem, our force, our everything. And I come more & more fully to that every day.

"We who are living are now dead"[4]
How true of the vast vast majority of us.
[Signed "*Amitiés*, Len".]

Mount Carmel, [no date – envelope postmarked 7 March 1946]
Your long letter of 26th Feb came yesterday, among others – with a delightful poem by Jim and a really shocking thing "Would that wars might end for all soldiers like this ...."[5] Whatever made you forget yourself to copy out such a thing[…]

Another thing you might have given to someone else was the little book on Jews – not that I'm ungrateful, but it does contain one or two home truths which someone else has not access to. George Carr provokes me, of course – Jews lazy – not on your life. He should see them working on the land, working on buildings and in the factories. Vic Newcomb & I were once introduced to a secretary of the Histadruth [Jewish trade union federation] in Tel Aviv and he gave us details of their cooperative movements and much more, which I can't outline here, but which reveal a hard-working community in which there is a pioneering, communal spirit in which no drones are tolerated unless they are old and infirm. I have been steadily plodding at French Symbolist Poetry with a French Jewess, who is a philosophy student, and who recently submitted a really brilliant essay on the shift of idealism from Plato to Descartes, and I wish you, and George, could see it, if only as an evidence of industry. I try in vain to think of any English girl of my acquaintance who could even begin to think of such things (even philosophy students wouldn't apply such industry)! And I, in turn, have been helping another two to understand Metaphysical poetry – yet one only began to learn English after escaping from a concentration camp a few years ago. Lazy! Oh no, I can't accept that. At this College, the number of Jews taking Greats outnumbers the British, though the British must outnumber Jews in the Army of Palestine. And they work industriously and intelligently. There are so many common fallacies abroad concerning the Jews that one naturally takes up their position, though Zionism isn't all that is good. Terrorism is disowned by Jews at large by now and all patiently await the findings of the Commission, part of which arrives at

Jerusalem tomorrow. It is difficult to be patient of course, when all the facts are known anyway and so many still wait in Europe, in camps that are not home for them, even after Belsen & Buchenwald. The Commission might first of all have been taken to Belsen last May, along with some Arabs, and all the UNO representatives. Then they wouldn't have quibbled and argued & sent commissions here, there, & everywhere. And anyway, the British won't take any notice of it unless it suits their policy[…]

P.S. I had a perfect day on Sunday. Megiddo, Jenin, Sebastia (old Greco-Roman town – superb) Tulkarm & home. Must tell you about it some time. I want to write about Sebastia.

Mount Carmel, Sunday 10 March 1946

The weather has continued warm & sunny, springlike, till last night, when there was an ominous ring about the moon. This morning the sky is dark, greyish yellow, and hot oppressive wind blows in gusts, but for some reason it doesn't rain. Yesterday, however, was like an English summer's day – like our day on the Severn, when all seems at peace. I walked down a deep wadi with an RAMC corporal who in the early days of the war, I found, was a CO, and who suffered the deepest soul-searching tinged with a certain cynicism which still impoverishes his spirit. He has been studying Modern Greats under Bill. We talked about ourselves and life in general, and it was an afternoon to remember. It was a very deep wadi, with the bare rock showing in great slabs, but with green slopes above prinked with all the lovely spring flowers. Our only companions were two old shepherds, with their flocks, black long-eared goats, with the old ram ringing the sweetest, most resonant of bells which filled the wadi with their music. At the very bottom was a deep well of crystal clear water. The shepherds came down as we sat smoking there, and washed their feet, shared an orange with us and then the two pairs, one English, one Arabic, talked in their respective tongues, at peace with each other and with nature. It was so still and quiet except for the tinkling bells that we could hear the grass rustling across the way and saw a tortoise emerge, scrutinise us, and then proceed on its urgent errand – for it seemed in an awful hurry.

How you must envy me this possibility of peace, even in a hostile land like Palestine. I can read the austerity, anxiety and almost privation of England in your letters and I realize that I am the one who am [sic] well off and you who are in need of comfort. There is so little I can do, except to hope that you especially, since you are so capable of it, can find peace inside[…]

Your last letter to Carmel came yesterday[…] I got your syllabus, too, which seems very good indeed to me. This course at Mt Carmel has quite a different aim, if it is of interest to you. It presumes the reading and knowledge of your course, and its purpose is to extend the background, and above all, to develop a critical facility in the student. I think it succeeds, if you are alive to its real implications and I am very grateful for what I have been able to do here. My last essay on TS Eliot and the Metaphysicals probably indicates that I have benefited considerably from it all, and I am rather proud of it because it impressed Major Champion and in a seminar he asked me to read it as a paper to the course, which I did, rather like the proud child reciting at the Sunday School anniversary. It is really an essay on the problem of communication and it really pinned me down to the essentials and made it impossible to gloss over the least statement. It required some close thinking, which was worth it, of course, and which has helped me considerably. Although the essay does not appear half as good now as when I was struggling to find expression for its thought, I think it has some good points and some day, if I'm not finally disgusted with it, I shall send it to you to see what you think.

The thought of returning to the unit is painful now – I have been so happy up here, on the hill top, with the sea on either side and the wind blowing fresh from the Mediterranean. As Tolstoy said, unhappiness does not spring so much from privations as from superfluity. Having tasted the happy superfluity of Carmel I shall be miserable on the plains and have to readjust myself.

However, let us adopt your old philosophy – *Carpe Diem*.

So Len returned to 224 PFA at Sarafand, to complete the printing and binding of Over the Rhine. *As he had feared, he found himself restless back there. This made him only more homesick and obsessed with his demob date.*

Sarafand, 16 March 1946

I shall have a big job trying to catch up with my correspondence. The worst of a course like Mt Carmel, where one works hard voluntarily, is that one becomes remoter than ever from friends at home. Indeed, you remark in one letter that we seemed to be a little out of touch, and I know that is largely my fault. I have gradually got into the habit out here of keeping on the move all the time – not fussing around all the time, but attacking every job with a single mind and working hard at it, while it lasts. I don't want to feel as I did over Christmas again, because however much one longs to get home, there is simply nothing to be done about it. So in my apparently endless preoccupation, I perhaps neglect you, without intending it. And it will probably continue, because on my return to 224, I was welcomed with ½ ton of paper and a manuscript. It was such a blow to leave Carmel where I had been so happy, that I attacked that paper with a vengeance, printed the little pages (two printings – 1 black, 1 red), the verso behind it, and am now printing the frontispiece plan (in black and red). I don't think much, and I certainly shan't have much time to read. I reckon it will take nearly 3 months of solid work – but it will be worth it. In the meantime, you must forgive me if I tend to drift. I do think something is happening inside me – I'm afraid to look into myself, but I am changing and sometimes it is not good to know. I don't want to begin all those horrible morbid introspections that I used to bore you with long ago, but nevertheless it is happening. I think it is part of a necessity to adjust myself to what at Christmas would have appeared to me a suicidal & hopeless position – to be needlessly & (rather unfairly, I still think) separated from my beloved England and my more beloved friends, without the slightest chance of doing anything about it. Bill Hamilton & John Petts have both had negative replies about demob and both (not that Bill's is quite the same case) have settled down to the fact that they are Groups 37 & 52 respectively, instead of about 31. And I haven't had the final reply yet, but I know it will be the same.

So I have to face up to it – I am to endure till next year, and I must make it more than merely "endure".

Your letters were very mixed up yesterday – there were a few from the very beginning of February. One discusses a recent visit to Tel

Aviv. And you tease me about falling for Mrs Goodman. Well it is about 6 weeks since I saw her – but probably you're right, I did fall for her. She has all the charms, all the allurements of her sex, and all the maturity which will ultimately "catch" a man like me – I like 'em machoor. To be serious, however, I think you would like Rose, because she is sincere at heart, and all those graces are cultivated through being a hostess for so long. She is an ardent pacifist, and speaks out (because Rose could say anything, anyway, & nobody would dream of taking offence) and yet Brigadier Lathbury[6], and our General have called on her, and she teased Colonel McEwen (the man who organised Parachute Medical Services) for wearing a Czarist medal. And Judge Singleton (a Member of the Palestine Enquiry Commission) was told in England to call on her, since she represents one Jewish point of view, and the Judge & two other members did call on her yesterday, I'm told, and no doubt they too "fell" for our dear Rose[...]

I have been working between paragraphs on the book, and have now completed title page, frontispiece & verso of title-page & have set up the little first recto heading "Over the Rhine" ready for tomorrow – I'm too tired tonight to do any more[…]

Sarafand, 23 March 1946

[…] I've just had news that I was accepted as sergeant-instructor at Mount Carmel College. But, of course, the posting has had to be waived because of the book. I'm only praying that they won't reject me when the book is completed and I can take a job there.

The book goes well, 10 pages of text completed, and is ahead of my schedule. Perhaps I shall get it finished in 2 months. Tomorrow is the anniversary of that terrible day – it seems so long ago, much more than a year.

Our new General, General Kassell [Cassels], visited us today to speak to us, and is a horrible individual, preaching the most incipient anti-Semitism. "Don't throw beer bottles about the streets of Tel Aviv – you'll get your turn, and very shortly, I should think, so be patient, and probably you'll find something more pleasant to do in the near future than merely wait for these terrorist acts". I just went red and was on the verge of getting up & shouting a protest to the roof tops.

Surely that is not interpreting the Labour Government's attempts at impartiality. There is so much misunderstanding that when you tell me of George Carr's cock-sure attitude, I just go wild and could make the same dreadful *faux pas* I made when I was about 19 by accusing him of "loose-thinking".

But I think I am a bit upset this week, so will make this a short letter. All the peace, study & discourse on poetry of Carmel are gone, and printing from morn till night makes me temperamental I think.

I went into Tel Aviv on Wednesday night with the other COs to see Mrs Goodman who wanted to see us about new WRI aims and so on (she's so keen). It was a pleasant evening but I got tired of discussing world affairs. Of course, she's as charming as ever and I have completely fallen. James & I think she's a spy, because she has all the tricks and we are anxiously waiting to be robbed of some secret or to have our pay-book stolen or something.

Sarafand, 26 March 1946

This morning I woke up late, because I was working late the previous night. I did not shave, thinking I'd be left alone with the press as usual – but a message came from the CO who wanted to see me so I had to whip off my beard and dash across to see him. He had a "confidential" report from Mt Carmel about me and he wanted to let me see it. Actually the chief clerk had already given me a copy yesterday, though the CO wasn't supposed to know. It was rather flattering and the old man beamed with reflected glory I suppose. "An excellent student. Prepared to think clearly and deeply before giving opinions and to proceed slowly, but very thoroughly. Advantage of beginning course well-read. I recommend Jones's transfer to the AEC and have already made application." Signed A Champion Major CI[…]

Sarafand, Monday 1 April 1946

[…] I have had a final letter from some under-dog in reply to mine to Ness Edwards (I addressed it to MP, House of Commons so I presume he did read it and then fobbed it off on some subordinate). Anyway, I am Group 52 once & for all, unless Harding Pritchard at Cambridge can help me. He will if he is able. What annoys me most is that the people I write to just ignore the whole point of my letters and reply as though I'd surely asked for some civilian service to be tacked on to my army service. I begin to see their difficulties of course, because Army demob counts only "whole-time service in the Armed Forces since 3 Sept '39 which counts for Service Pay"[…]

I promised myself that I would base my future plans on this reply from Edwards and so I presume I'm unalterably 52, and must therefore leave the unit and give up my "long-preserved" privacy. I have left the whole book in definite plan and (?Lees) is quite ready to carry on & can. It is nearly half-finished and I only have to get some more blocks made at Jerusalem, fix up the binding, leave instructions about collation & cutting etc... I saw Bill [Hamilton] yesterday and I can still have a job at Carmel, but it is an urgent matter, so I'm probably too late for that. If only I could get to Carmel, I could at least begin to read and study again and should be as free as it's possible to be in the Army.

But sometimes the desire to be in England comes so forcibly that it turns into absolute detestation (for the moment) of this country and its people. I remember wandering out of a bookshop in Allenby Road in Tel Aviv and onto the very busy side-walk (equivalent to walking out of Bumpus on to Oxford Street) and feeling absolute nausea for all those Jews. "My God" I remember saying to myself "what in hell is an Englishman doing here among all these people?" Which is a bad feeling, for you know I like the Jews here now and come more & more to see their point of view. I think I must have been just sick, but it is a recurring feeling. I have liked the country, its hills, its flowers, its splendid winter, its warmth – but it could never be the rapture of the discovery of the Vale of Evesham or Semerwater, or the Roman Wall.

I think your letters are happier than they have been and I am glad, for you seemed to be having a pretty lean time all ways during the winter. It is good to be your friend when you are bubbling over – you are supremely Lovellesque then, and I can see your eyes twinkling as you suffer Arthur's torments. I'm sure you'd all lift my spirits up if I could only be at that grand reunion of the Old Guard[…]

Sarafand, 6 April 1946

[...] Today I dashed into Jerusalem to get some blocks, bought some books for the Unit Library (light classics to help our students to develop taste in reading by gradual stages – [John] Buchan, HE Bates, [Somerset] Maugham & so on) had lunch, a haircut and dashed back to finish printing page 35 – so you see how we are progressing[…]

I think we move from Sarafand in a week or two to our "jumping" station in the wilds further south. On the bare dusty semi-desert again in tents. How we shall be able to print there no-one knows. Already temperature is playing the most alarming tricks with paper and ink, and even with the wooden plates, so that the book is going to be a sorry mess. The heat makes me past caring somehow. I have come in any case to expect criticism for even one's best efforts, so I might as well be criticised deserving it. We are now over half finished.

My transfer is now going ahead with the CO's approval since the book is well on the way to completion. Major Champion has been very kind to me and is working it so that I shall not need (until my demob query is settled finally) renounce my status. If of course the answer is still "no" (I'm afraid Ness Edwards has already been final in his "no") I can renounce if I wish, for the purpose perhaps of being granted a job with a commission though in practice the Education Corps is non-combatant like the RAMC – more so, as you can imagine. The job which will help me most (in that it means few lectures & plenty of opportunity for study) is Capt Unwin's job. He leaves 16 April and Major Champion was rather cross with me over my unwillingness to renounce my status because he needs a substitute for Unwin & there simply is not anyone in the ME [Middle East] that he can think of. The job was mine, only it entails a commission & he can't wangle that as I am. It's nice to think however that there are still possibilities for me if the M of Labour will not free me this summer. Mount Carmel, if not England, is virtually civilian life & I could do more or less as I liked there.

Your comments from Ralph Connolly[7] are most interesting. I can quite understand his reaction to Rose Goodman – one hardly knows whether to laugh at her (& with her, she's utterly charming!) or to take her seriously. Perhaps her approach to pacifism is a sort of emotional outlet (rather like Gertrude Robson) but of course one hardly thinks of judging dear Rose, she's too perfectly nice. She smiles angelically at me, says "And when are you coming to see me again Jonah – you & I must have a quick talk together some evening." And of course, you know me. I just melt with sheer worship & love, blush deeply & blather some loving nonsense. Do I hell! I'm hard as nails! I listen attentively and play up to it. But heaven forbid a "quick talk together". When Connolly says the Arabs had the "good life", the Jews the "efficient life", I'm a bit lost. Either his remark is too profound for me or he is basing his statement on only half observations. My reaction is that the Jews are leading the efficient life, but like Turgenev's Nihilism it expresses a potentiality for very much more, & only remains confined to the merely efficient level by the nature of their situation at present. Much of their life is still pioneering, colonisation, struggling – like our own early Canada, Australia, it must be practical, efficient before the rest can come. Much of their life is potentially bad, mind you. I can see dangerous elements even now. Tel Aviv is 'The Waste Land' in spirit, without the aged sordidness of Tiresias's Unreal City. But only because it has made a false start. After all, look for one second at what has happened to this nation in Europe in the last 10 years, and the panic conditions their life here. The peace of English life is impossible for one minute, there is no time for reflection, there is even no room for affection, the opportunity to open their gates to their brethren seeking a haven from persecution or its threat.

Now the Arabs leading the good life makes me smile rather. The Arab is a friendly, lovable rogue, though you have the quiet contemplative occasionally, and a few personalities, usually educated, like the Sheik of Gaza, are capable of leading the quiet contemplative life of the Oriental which is a contrast to the busy almost unnatural progressiveness of the Jew.

But to say that the Arab in general leads the good life is hardly possible surely. You should see the majority knocking the hide of a bony donkey, flogging a dog till it has no spirit left, you should see them even flogging each other, the poorest carrying sheep's carcasses for a mere pittance, bent doubled, stinking outcasts. The rich man or the merchant doesn't turn a hair so long as business is good – it is all cut-throat business, looks marvellous to the European, but what a terrible, painful struggle behind it all. The town Arab is not, I'm sure,

leading the good life – even the lower classes, knowing their brothers
are oppressed, merely say "Maalish"[8] and shrug their shoulders.
Except for a few effendis[9] (like those I met in Gaza) who are more
politically aware & have formed unions – even they render this
movement ineffectual by squabbling.

I wish this Palestine [problem] could be solved amicably. For the
Jew, the only hope is a Jewish majority in a Jewish State. Since it has
come to such a pretty pass for world Jewry, I can understand their Life
or Death, All or Nothing Policy. But it cannot possibly suit the Arabs.
In other words, the compromise we would desire is quite impossible.
Especially as Britain is playing ball with the Arabs, since a Moslem
bloc, with Indian Pakistan, is our best answer to the Russian interest
in the Middle East – the Jews can't help us there. The Jewish claim
does not fit British Middle East policy, & I'm a little disillusioned over
the fact that this policy, an inheritance of Tory imperial methods,
overrides a long Socialist support of the Jewish race[…]

Compromise being impossible apparently, one must choose, and it
eventually evolves upon the moral right of either side. I think the
Jewish moral right to unlimited immigration & development in Palestine is greater than the Arab's moral right to refusal. But who am I to
judge? And any decision must be taken at least against the whole
background of the Middle East. There is no doubt at present that the
Arabs are being treated handsomely and the Jews shabbily – that
incenses the Jew, who is much more politically conscious than the
Arab. The two blatant examples are the sudden award of independency to Transjordan by Britain (I see US has questioned Britain's
right to do this). And Transjordan, a cruel, feudal backward country
whose Ruler exploited the rights given by Lawrence's overthrow of
Turkish domination to his own end & left the people in the same
plight, is accepted at UNO.

But these temporary grievances must not weigh ultimate decisions
– I hope the Commission in Switzerland sees the question from its
ultimate – not only its immediate standpoint. I think they will extend
immigration, as an expedient for those still in camps in Europe. They
may suggest a sort of Jewish autonomy in their own areas, they may
even suggest Partition, or extension of the Jordan Valley Scheme
(similar to TVA)[10] – but I don't think they will grant a Jewish State. If

they did, the British would only ignore it anyway. So the problem won't be solved. The tension will remain – it will burst into open revolution of the whole community, Arab & Jew, and bloodshed is so accepted out here that it will come easily. Oh for England, the peace of her countryside – can you imagine what Wensleydale comes to mean – it remains ever a place that cannot exist in any other country. Its beauty can be surpassed perhaps, its people can be, its history, its anything, but what a depth of eternal peace, stretching from time immemorial! And more of England can be like that. No wonder we worship her.

And yet how much of that peace (and plenty?) depends on those very politics which cause trouble in the Middle East, in India, Greece, and so on?

Enough about Palestine. It was peaceful today in Jerusalem. And now it is peaceful here. But who knows – a bomb may go off anytime, anywhere – terrorists may try again to break into the camp to rescue other terrorists in hospital here from wounds sustained on another stupid railway raid the other night.

Thank you for my favourite Rilke elegy.

Sarafand, 16 April 1946

It hardly seems worth writing, because now we are not only cut off from the rest of Palestine, but also from the world, as far as our mail goes. However, I am trusting the Army will improvise some service of its own now the railway isn't functioning. With all its transport you'd think the Army need not depend on railways to bring its mail from Egypt to Palestine. But the reason why road transport is not used is because there is only one road across the Sinai Desert & that is narrow and at present crowded with convoys of evacuating troops. Why not air transport? Our mail comes and goes by air between England & Egypt, yet when the railwaymen strike (& quite right too) the mail is just stuck in Cairo & ours in Sarafand.

Palestine is paralysed – the hunger strike in sympathy with the 1,000 or so people held up at [La] Spezia I thoroughly approve of. I think this passive form of resistance by known leaders bears more dignity and is more far-reaching than the terrorist tactics which I think

Dear Mona: Letters from a Conscientious Objector

bring only discredit to the Jewish cause. Already the Colonial [sic] has got moving and after 100 hours hunger strike, the authorities agreed to grant the people of Spezia immigration tickets.[11]

But besides the strike & its effect on our mail, I have not been able to write letters as I'd have wished. I had to go to Jerusalem to get blocks, fix up with the binders, and visit a Jew who has just come back from England & told me all about his stay at Whitley Bay etc; and the rest of the time has been a ruthless progress with the book, in an effort to get it finished before anything drastic happens to the unit[…]

[Signed "*Amitiés*, Len".]

Len enclosed with this a typed letter from a civil servant at the Ministry of Labour and National Service dated 18 March 1946, which confirmed that "only whole-time service in the Armed Forces since 3 September 1939[…] can be taken into account for the purpose of determining the order of release from the Forces[…] I am afraid, therefore, that the period spent in forestry cannot count towards release from the Forces."

Sarafand, 18 April 1946

[…] It is Good Friday today – while I write this, *The Dream of Gerontius* is being broadcast from records. Otherwise I would hardly know that in this, the Holy Land, this is Good Friday. Perhaps, if I'd gone to Jerusalem, as I might have done, I'd have watched the sacred processions up the Via Dolorosa & perhaps felt more of the spirit of the Crucifixion. But somehow I could not face it. That part of it, the celebration and pilgrimage, hardly seemed to matter, in fact I felt that being jostled in the seething mass (as I'm told people were on Xmas Eve at Bethlehem) would only bring on that human sickness and nausea which level us out however great the occasion might be.

So I just mark time, feeling rather unwell I think for some reason, and nursing my right foot which is not yet right after that accident at Manchester. Apparently I'm not walking properly and it is so bad at present that I'm shuffling around like Byron. For the first time in my Army career, I'm not A1. But I'm not complaining about the Army – if I do so often rail, it is because of my delayed demob – I think joining

224 was one of the best things I ever did and it has been a rich experience in many ways, not only in the men I have been with, but in the work it has permitted me to do[…]

Sarafand, 24 April 1946

We now rise at 5.30 and finish work at 12.30. It is so hot in the afternoon that there is compulsory rest – siesta. But no laws in the unit seem to affect me these days: I cannot sleep, so I sit here quietly perspiring and writing some letters.

Easter came suddenly upon me – we were forbidden weekend passes, so I just ran away on Saturday morning and did not return till Monday night. In that time, I must have travelled about 300 miles, saw two settlements and got plenty of sun & fresh air. At Givat Brenner[12], I was entertained by the brother of Enzo Sereni, a Jewish hero who tried very hard to get refugees through from Northern Italy in 1944. He died at Dachau.[13] What a marvellous family. Italian Zionism is best of all – it is a gentler ideal than that of the other Jews, not based on malice, since anti-Semitism hardly existed in Italy despite Mussolini. They speak lovingly of Italy, home & Florence in particular, and even of the people, and converse among themselves in the graceful rhythmic Italian rather than the harsher Hebrew. And how well they entertain – they know how to cook, how to set a table, and how to laugh and smile with a guest & not take the opportunity to pump him with Zionist ideas. Imagine a full drinking set in dark Venetian glass.

Givat Brenner is a flourishing collective settlement and some day I must tell you all about it. I wish you could have seen "The Fiver" as they call it. Little houses for 5 children of up to 6 years – a little bedroom with five tiny divans, five little chairs, five little baskets, five of everything, with these five children living and playing together (they have their own little garden outside). A girl or woman looks after each five; that is her job, and when they are older they go into bigger houses, boys & girls together, & they look more after themselves, make their own beds, keep their own place clean & so on. So that with school lessons goes a general regime of domestic responsibility which the children accept & enjoy. They have a higher school for older children, but those worthy of a special education & who want it can be sent out at the settlement's expense, to high schools outside, and also to the University. So that children are no trouble to a mother – indeed, since they feed communally & there is a communal laundry, a woman is finished with work like a man when she is finished in the fields or the small orange (juice & preserves) factory, and she can develop her own interests. Not that motherhood is cut out – she can still take an interest in her children, can tenderly watch their progress through the various stages & be with them when she pleases.

But there is so much to tell you about collective life that I cannot even start here. Later, I met the former editor of the Italian Zionist paper, *Israel*, which has a great cultural background. He was a laughing fellow, Italian rather than Jew; his wife was a pretty, jolly woman & they had 4 of the most delightful curly mopped children. His library was superb (how cultured these Italian Jews are – I met several & all had beautiful libraries)[…]

Sarafand, 30 April 1946

I'm so homesick – you describe spring in England, the little birds singing. It is all so wonderful in England when the winter is finally over and the soil begins to dry. By heaven, I know how much I love England now – there can't be any doubt about it – they are joys in England which are untranslatable, but there is some of it to be found translated in Wilson Steer's *Blue & Gold* (the rhapsody of gazing over the Vale of Evesham), in Elgar's *Serenade for Strings*, in Constable, in David Cox, in countless others. That is what I'm missing – the sight of Penn Hill [Wensleydale] in a warm haze, the black mass of trees over by Aysgarth, the falls themselves with the Church over the shoulder of the hill.

Indeed I'm quite sick at heart and am in no state to write letters[…]
[Signed "Bye-bye for now, Len".]

Sarafand, 6 May 1946

I'm in that dreadful state when each day is too short to fit everything in. Jerusalem Thursday, Friday; Haifa Saturday, Sunday; move to Qastina tomorrow. So it is 4 or 5 days since I spent a day at home, &

it will be Wed before I'm settled in Qastina, if at all, for it is all tents.

I wish I could answer your letter properly. But George D is complaining of 3 weeks' silence on my part (quite unintentional) so you will understand my poor replies.

First the book is already sewn & glued, & will be finally trimmed & bound this weekend. So that is that – except that I am trying to evolve a suitable dust jacket – got the design, but can't find a way to print it yet.

Second – I'm sorry Jim's visit has been so awful for you. He can be an utter cad sometimes, and even more cruel than myself in his thoughtlessness. From all accounts he seems so selfish that one had best treat him rough. I was bitten so often that I soon learned the way to treat Jim. He often thinks I'm rough, uncouth and un-gentle, and even thinks I'm cruel to him. But I find he thinks a deal more of me when I am blunt & direct with him. My attitude is that my time is my time and my wants my wants & Jim only shares them in so far as it suits me. He is as unreliable as the worst type of woman, as wayward as a child (as spoilt and as selfish too) and as thoughtless as the worst type of man. That sounds pretty bad, & I'm afraid it is when one suffers, and you have. But you allow yourself to be wounded so easily – I don't mean you are needlessly piqued, but you should assert yourself more, make it clearer to people how valuable your time & wishes are. In fact, you ought to be a lot more selfish than you are in the right sort of way, if you see what I mean[…]

Qastina was the last place where Len was based with the rest of 224 PFA. Situated further south than Sarafand – thus hotter and dustier - it was not a congenial location and he felt out of sorts during his brief spell there. He was affected by a debilitating lassitude for much of the time. He did not know it then – in fact astonishingly would not realise for another four years – but he was showing the first signs of tuberculosis. It was a sad, downbeat end to his association with 224 PFA; in many ways it had been a life-changing and enriching experience for him.

Qastina, 7 (or 8) May 1946

I have been put on an advance party to this new camp, and the rest of the unit arrives in 4 or 5 days time. Last week I forgot to salute the Captain Quarter-Master *en passant* and he pulled me in front of the 2 i/c [2nd in command]. He asked me (again *en passant*) if I'd finished the book & when I said it was at the binders, he said perhaps a little hard work would wake me up and remember my station. I submitted graciously to his judgement and am serving my punishment by doing fatigues at the new camp – i.e. putting up miles and miles of barbed wire from morning till night. I am given 2 Italian POWs and since one speaks French, we find out about each other and we work like Italians rather than like Englishmen who are far too energetic anyway. So my punishment means a pleasant break in the open air, without any worries & responsibilities and just moving along easily without a care in the world. There's absolutely nothing to do here – it's miles from anywhere. The aerodrome is nearby and jumping is in progress, but the latest scheme was such a flop that I think it will be a while before there is another drop. Our neighbours the 8th Battalion sent 108 men on a practice drop last week. You can believe this or not, please yourself, but wind currents went all wrong and of the 108 over 90 were casualties, with 1 fractured skull, 1 fractured spine, 2 broken legs, and the rest minor injuries ranging from minor abrasion to sprains etc... Naturally my ankle got "worse" and I seem to be permanently down-graded to A4[...]

Qastina, [no date – envelope postmarked 22 May 1946]

I'm afraid you will find me the very poorest of correspondents the coming months. I wish I could write you a proper letter, particularly you, since you are the only person who has been the consistent & unfailing recipient of all my moans, groans, joys & sorrows & every experience & impression. And now I seem to write to nobody, not even you.

It's an awful effort, but it's no use trying to explain why. It is impossible to make other people understand why you can't write, why you've completely dried up. No one could understand Oblomov, but as far as he was concerned the chief thing was that he didn't even care if they understood. So it didn't matter. It is so difficult to care – and when you do care, as I do (because I know & value my friends at home) it is so difficult to do anything about it.

You must not even hint it to my parents, please, but I'm almost always in a poor way these days, with a constant depression hanging over me. I know now it is wrong to moan and expect sympathy, so don't get me wrong, and please don't take me up. Probably my return to England will bring renewed hope – I have often been depressed during the war years, often without need, so it is nothing to worry about. It does worry me, however, and I keep giving the Unit a deadline and saying on such and such a date I'll have reached the end of my tether. I thought I had yesterday, but I just flopped on my bed in the heat of the day and stayed there till reveille next morning not speaking to anyone, half sleeping, half moping. And another day started.

The Rhine Book seems neglected in a box – nobody seems interested in it, and I'm on fatigues anyway, the whole 2 or 3 months work seems futile, and I don't even care. I can't believe where our early enthusiasm came from. And yet, looking at it objectively, I know it's quite an achievement. Anyway, 300 copies lie in the stores, so much more Army stationery.

Then again, perhaps I shall pick up if my posting to Carmel comes through. But I despair of that. Probably my status has proved a stumbling block after all, and there's a hitch somewhere.

Vic leaves for England in 9 days. I don't know how I shall manage in 224 without him[…]

[Signed "With my thoughts, Len".]

Palestine: Carmel College

Qastina was Len's lowest ebb during his time in Palestine. Fortunately he was rescued after three weeks by an opening as Command librarian in Jerusalem. His health and spirits soon recovered, and he enjoyed exploring the city, although he continued to worry about the rising tension in Palestine. Increasingly he enclosed with his letters cuttings from the local English-language press about the situation. After less than a month in Jerusalem, Len moved on to Carmel College in Haifa.

Jerusalem [no date – postmark unclear,
but clearly end May-start of June 1946]

What a week! I've trailed round the Levant, trying in vain to ignore an attack of gastro-enteritis. In Cairo I felt really ill and seemed to be floating in a haze, and felt I was going to faint sometimes.

From Cairo, back across that worst of all countries, the Sinai Desert, up to Lydda, wait with oriental patience (or is it sheer indifference to life or time?) for 3 hours, then the train (3 hours to cover 40 or 50 miles) to Jerusalem. Nobody seemed to know anything about me here, and knowing the MEF, by now they shall probably never know, and I shall drift about pleasing myself and looking important.

However, it is nice to stop travelling. I went to Cairo to understudy Michael Rix who is editor of *Pictorial Review* (Rix leaves in July). John Petts is Art Editor. Captain Howell seemed well pleased with me, and John put in a terrific blurb about me, of course. However, a Colonel Hadden had been looking "rather anxiously" for a qualified librarian and intervened before I could get dug in. I felt quite pleased because I thought that he was going to insist that I went to Carmel after all as librarian (I like Carmel) as had already been suggested. But it was more – I was to be Command Librarian. The Command library is quite an imposing array of non-fiction for postal service to students all over No 9 Command, i.e. Palestine, Transjordania, Cyprus & the Lebanon. A job rather like Mr Hamilton's, only much simpler, since

I have only 3 people working for me and as far as I can see it works alright. So I haven't done a stroke of work yet. I need a rest. This morning, however, I dashed off to 224 to say goodbye to my beloved sub-editor, Vic. It was terrible to say "Goodbye" to Vic. I'll never forget his last words to me "And thanks for just being you". I appreciated that, because Vic has had to suffer me as well as like me. He leaves tonight.

Then I borrowed money from poor James (I'm always hard-up and Cairo broke me). And finally got a lift back, just too late to have lunch.

Of course, there is no need for me at Jerusalem, and I'm a bit fed up not having a proper job. But then you'll say I'm always fed up[...]

No 9 Command Education Library, Jerusalem, MEF – 5 June 1946

I am wondering where you will be by the time this gets to Iona Road. I have an idea you will be in France or somewhere. Since I've lost track, I'm continuing to write as though you were still present, to let you know some sort of address, though I may not even stay here. But if I do change my job, this address will find me, since I shall stay in Jerusalem. Ah, the Holy City, it is so cool and windswept after the heat of the plains and Egypt. I think, if I could settle down here, I could recover myself. I need something, because I have felt "down" for a long time now, so that I seem to be a mournful individual like George D so recently. It is so terrible to become detached from life and see it only as a petty, worthless existence. I seem to have run down altogether – is it that which makes it difficult to write?[…]

[Signed "Shalom,[1] Len"]

No 9 Command Education Library, c/o 90th Bn RAPC, Jerusalem, MEF – 14 June 1946

My fate has been undecided for another week, and yet I'm still here. Apparently there were two postings from Cairo for me, one to Jerusalem and the other to Mount Carmel. They are still wrangling over my body and Colonel Champion at Carmel seems determined to have me there while Colonel Harper is just as determined to keep me here, though the Carmel posting bears a date two days previous to the other. I have shown my complete indifference to their choice, for either place will make me happier than I have been for months. Already at Jerusalem I am picking up and feel as though I had been ill. I have been mentally sick of course, so I know my move has been a good one. It is easy to find friends in Jerusalem and it is almost like old times being able to go out and call on some friend and have a quiet talk in the comfort of a home. Despite the fact that I am no socialite, I have deliberately accepted invitations from civilians here and I have found them very kind and the talk and discussion has taken me away from myself. Personally, I hope I stay in Jerusalem, because I am beginning to get used to it, and I think I may be able to work here. I have got to know an artist who is a first rate technician and has a soul – Anni Sternheim – and it has been good to talk to her. I know too that I have been able to help her, even in a material way, because she is just about starving though she tries to appear otherwise. However, it is rather fun to make a bargain that if she will provide the tea, I will provide some NAAFI buns.

I have become a librarian again too, so you will be pleased. I often wonder what you would think of this place – it has such a splendid collection of books. It is so wonderfull [sic] in fact that we seem to be able to satisfy almost any request. There was one today, for instance, that I'm sure would have made Felling library sit up but we had just the book – on yacht construction! Then a Commercial College sent a request for 30 books – I know they were all standard works - but we were able to supply the lot. So you see it is a library that works. Since I have arrived here we have had a blitz on the place and all the books are accessioned and catalogued by now, and we're in the process of rectifying some shocking errors in classification that some former serjeant must have made at some time. Then at my suggestion we have inaugurated a permanent loan scheme to units, of those books which we possess in triplicate or more, discriminating in subject according to the type of unit. And they all seem very pleased with what they receive.

Of course, too, it is rather a thrill living in Jerusalem. Until the trouble starts I am exploring as much as possible and will tell you all about the various places when I see you. When the explosion finally occurs we shall probably be confined to barracks, because it is to be serious this time. I think the British government, good as it is, has [sic] the foggiest idea what it is playing with. To repeat the old game of creating trouble and making it appear to be the local population's fault is too bad. They are trying very hard indeed though, and they are bound to succeed if only they keep it up. It is very awkward of the population not to have rioted yet, because it forces Mr Bevin[2] to hedge and hedge – it is difficult to delay a decision, and after all, this is the second lot of committees to sit on the Palestine problem and even the greenest horn can see through that. Anyhow, the second lot of committees is now being appointed, and one must allow the dear souls at least three months to find out all about the subject – though the last committee did hurry it and got it down to just under three months. But even these committees don't seem to cause any more than mumblings.

So it is necessary to be more personal. To show discrimination at the law courts always incenses one side or the other, so they are going all out. One Arab in charge of firearms – 3 months. One Jew in charge of firearms – 18 months. That should work. But now the real cases are coming up. Those terrorists who have been appearing are making a tremendous impression. I'm afraid I have let the account get lost of a young girl who appeared the other day. She had lost all her family in Europe, and was caught trying to get illegal immigrants ashore near Tel Aviv. She took no notice of the proceedings and merely submitted to her sentence of three years. One can see they all appear in the dock with rather the same kind of sympathy that used to go with us at the tribunals – only here it is a whole people, even though most of the people deplore terrorism. I have no sympathy with terrorism as a means of fighting a cause – but one must admit that there is a cause – and after years of passive resistance they are only following the rest of this wrong-headed world in trying to get things by force. Indeed the cause is so good and deserving of sympathy that it is most embarrassing for even a Labour Government. We have delayed as much as possible and there now seems only one way out of our plight – if there is trouble here then there is no need to make a decision. It will then be our duty to suppress the trouble and of course declare that it is no fit time for immigration and so on. So having already done our little bit towards it, it only needs a spark to set the whole thing ablaze.

The chief thing against there being trouble out here lately is that the Arabs, since their desperate struggle from 1936 to 1939, have never got together again to make more trouble. In any case their great leaders have all been in exile for co-operating with the Germans. So we have released one Jamal el Husseini[3] who is now nicely incensing the Arabs and things are going very nicely except for a few Arab left-wingers who see through the effendis at last, and who somewhat spoil the show. It is necessary to let the Arabs have their great leader back – the Grand Mufti of Jerusalem – but he has been the subject of awkward questions in Parliament and has been conveniently kept in Paris, where he could not be tried as a war criminal by Britain as some MPs wished.[4] But now the Arab world is alive – there is to be a second coming – the Grand Mufti has escaped, and though his whereabouts are so far unknown, his name is on every Arab's lips, and it is even rumoured that he is already in Damascus.[5] Yesterday was an Arab day of rejoicing and flags were hung out and songs sung, and in the Bazaars there was free Turkish coffee.

So things are going quite satisfactorily, and though it is regrettable that some ordinary British lads will lose their lives, at least we won't have to make any decision. And then our Arab bloc against the Russian zone of influence will be assured. It would be a terrible thing if we were forced for conscience sake to help the Jews and so mess up our Middle East policy in general. So any time now you can expect a bloody three-cornered fight which will delight the world. At least it will take one's eyes off the other places that are causing trouble – unless they take example [sic] and start their own little fight – then we can safely say we are on the way for another war, and our foreign policy and Russia's and America's and France's (good job they are weak or they'd be the biggest rat of all) will have succeeded in their nerve campaign against the common people of the world.

I'm afraid that things are so bad out here in ways that are difficult to explain, that it has had quite an effect on me. You see, if you think and observe at all, it hurts, and there is no escape. This is such a small country that you bump into the old problem everywhere. And yet I know the ordinary people of Palestine, the Jewish *Kibbutznik*[6] and the Arab *Feallahin* [sic][7] can live very happily together. Henry Kornreich and I were out riding one day and met an Arab from the neighbouring village, also on horseback. Although Hulda (Henry's settlement) is a typical Jewish collective settlement,[8] they stopped and we chatted in very strange English for quite a time and I could sense the comradeship that existed between the two tillers of the land. There was no question of political quarrelling. But the Grand Mufti, like his brother Jamal, will soon prove how evil it is not only to sell land to a Jew, but even to talk to him. Long live the Mufti.

Just back from a cup of tea in town... I don't know where the Mufti is, but the whole Arab population is bringing out gaudy pictures of him and decking him with sprigs of olive and hibiscus. The pictures have been hidden all through the war. I hope it is all a false alarm. I must close. I hope to hear from you soon. I haven't had a letter from anyone for three long weeks, but it is my own fault and the Army's.

Jerusalem, 17 June 1946

There was a huge pile of old mail from you this morning, which was most entertaining after such a long silence. I think it must be the longest silence ever and it seemed as though I hadn't heard from you for years and years.

Since beginning this letter there has been a phone call from Education HQ to ask me to go down to see Colonel Harper who has just returned from England after some Edn Conferences there. He was very nice and matey, and told me about his trip back with Montgomery, who is touring the Middle East at present. Anyway, Colonel Champion is so worried about his college library that he has won my body and I am going to Carmel on Wednesday.

I am quite pleased, though I have already got so used to Jerusalem that it is hard to leave it now. And I have had a blitz on this library and would have liked to have stayed a little longer to see the results of a new system of permanent loans I have organised whereby the books, instead of staying here on the shelves are sent out to units to be used and a record kept here of their whereabouts so that requests can be traced at any time and either sought by Special Delivery Service or DR. Paddy had no idea how a county library was run so I have been of some use in the short time I was here. Indeed, I think this library is the more important service of the two, but that is probably because

I was a "public" librarian and not a university librarian. One is for the mass – the other for the specialist. Mount Carmel is a fine library, of course, as nearly as possible on the lines of a small college or university Library. It is beautifully laid out, with carpeted floors for silence and tables covered with blue baize for the students. It is nice to have the choice (or rather the Colonel's choice) of the best two places in Palestine – for coolness, pleasant surroundings and nice people.

I think I shall be happy on Carmel as I know I was going to be happy in Jerusalem. They are both good places, and both jobs are good, so I think I am lucky. Another thing pleases me, and that is the way Colonel Champion has taken such a personal interest in me. That sort of thing is very nice, if it is only one's own pride which is gratified, but I know Colonel Champion treats me as a friend and kindred spirit. There are his remarks which are at the end of my essay on TS Eliot. So I shall have a good friend as my boss and I suppose it is almost my return to Civvy Street – for it seems I have turned my back on the army altogether and it is like old times. In fact Champ [sic] has been behind this move since my course in February, and only the book has held me up. I must send you the book sometime, but various people are having a *shufti*[9] at it at present[…]

Palestine fills me with despair. Every day the picture becomes more complete in my mind and I begin to see the real tragedy of the Jews. Even now they know they are not wanted here any more than anywhere else, and the Balfour Declaration has been a vast red herring. Now they are here, and must be taken for granted or else hounded out again as out of Germany and Poland and elsewhere. And in the coming struggle the British and the Arabs will be united against them. In the final anti-Semitic drive, Britain is going to be a big power, and it horrifies me. I give an example of the way in which even now the spirit against is working. I was waiting at a military pick-up for a lift and a Jewish Engineer in British uniform and with medals for the African and Italian campaigns was with me. He was going on leave to his settlement. A truck pulled up – he was so willing to pick me up and seems a kindly sort of bloke. The Jewish lad of course jumped up with me, and the driver snarled at him, and told him to get off. I simply couldn't bear the look in the lad's eyes. To be such a pariah in such an institution as the British army is a terrible thing, and I cannot bear to see people hurt so horribly and openly like that. I told the driver that as a British soldier the Jew had done his bit and that it was a rotten attitude to take. But he remained obstinate calling out "I'm not taking any ----- Jews on this truck". So I had to get off on principle. And even that did not move him. He drove off in a temper. The British driver goes off having fed his anti-Semitic spirit to the full – the Jew has his pride like any other person and will not forget the action – he will leave the army in disgust and determined to do his best against the British intruder, and so more anti-Semitic feeling will result. And so it goes on, with compound interest. And yet when they are your friends they are such fine people and understand so much. I wonder where it will all end[…]

Thank you for the honeysuckle – a little souvenir from the Leigh – from England. Ah! What a country – Switzerland and Sweden are also fit to live in, but they didn't have to suffer the actuality of war. More and more I bless England.

Command Librarian!!!!!!

Please reply to No1 Command Education College (Modern Studies), MEF

Len took up his post at Carmel College just as the tension between the British mandatory authorities and the local Jewish population – the Yishuv – deteriorated. The army imposed curfews and searches in many areas, increasing the resentment of the Jews. Len was in despair, and condemned British conduct trenchantly. But Carmel College, at least, was a convivial refuge from the hostile atmosphere.

No 1 Command Education College Wing (Modern Studies),
MEF – 27 June 1946

[…] Despite the heat and homesickness, I must admit I like Carmel, with its gorse[10] and pines, and its wonderful views of the coastal plain and the great curving bay round to Acre. Since we are now well & truly immured, it is as good as any place to be imprisoned. I still get out though, unarmed, in civilian clothes, by climbing through the barbed wire and posing as a *kibbutzim* [sic], or settlement man. I think I shall continue to go about Palestine as a civilian, even if the trouble lifts. The College is a refuge from the Army. I only work from 8 till 1, 5 hours and the rest of the day is my own. What a glorious opportunity you will say. But the heat neutralizes all in the afternoon, and in any case I seem so empty inside that I neither do anything for myself, and what is worse, don't wish to. Truly distressing, isn't it – I who used to be so keen. Oblomov all over. Yes, Oblomov.

Carmel welcomes me, however, so I can't grumble. I am called Len by the Colonel downwards and my fame as an apologist for the Metaphysicals is remembered – next month, when I lecture on them, there will be a record attendance, Champion having prepared the way. He leaves us this weekend, and it is a great pity, for we were already good friends. I am having lunch with him on Friday, when we shall both sneak out in civilian clothes and crawl into the Arab quarter for some Laban and arak. I do wish he had been staying, for he was a great friend & maker of friends. With him, Arab, Jew & British meet in comfort & friendliness, and I like to think I can do the same, if on a lesser scale than he. He recognised my potentialities anyway, and we got on well from the first. This cold aloofness of the average British, soldier & official alike, was anathema to him. It is a shocking thing. Both Jew & Arab detest us for it. When I think what we might have done with a little friendship & cooperation. British administration under the Mandate has been as rotten, partial, unfair & mischievous as is possible in a "nice" English way. And even Arab revolts could not break a cold stubborn Anti-Semitism from the start.

So I am a little ashamed of England out here – though I respect her more than I did, and even now apologize for her – after all, she is better than the rest of them put together. If I were a Jew however, I think I would become so bitter and impatient that I'd probably be a member of the Irgun Sva [Zvai] Leumi or extremist Nationalist Army. But when I go out and meet Jews, I am a friend and yet do not let them disparage my own country – rather show them that there is another point of view, and that in any case, violence will do more harm than good. I often wonder whether I meet a member of the Irgun – one never knows here who is a member and who is not – & how far my preaching goes. But I think I only meet the common people, helpless & only wanting peace, peace from us, Arab & terrorist alike.

Mt Carmel, 29 June 1946

Three letters at once from you, and some bundles of papers, thank you. The last one was a very beautiful letter from Castle Bolton, and it made me so sick to be there. It was such a contrast to Palestine, which today has merged into a state of war. The Airborne Div has gone into Tel Aviv and occupied it as we used to occupy towns in Germany. The only difference is that we used to look for cooperation and invite it in Germany – here we resent it and snub all Jews. The general feeling is that it is time to finish Hitler's task and exterminate the remnants of this unhappy race. I feel so sorry for sincere well-meaning Jews – they can be such splendid people, and I know they form the majority by far. But a militant minority can cause enough trouble for all of them. Our policy is so puzzling to the intelligent Jew. I know Professor Grossman of Haifa Technion[11] and talking to him the other night, he could only knit his eyebrows and puzzle over it – he just cannot understand any of it – and if anyone is capable of it, he is, for he is like Arthur Raistrick in his thinking – not led by newspapers, but seeing things in their setting.

Today there is a 24 hours curfew throughout Palestine – no news, no communication, nothing and all the people confined to their homes, even the workers. No traffic on the roads. We await the explosion and I am confident that it will come, much to our satisfaction, very shortly, probably in Tel Aviv. I think the people, unable to stand any more, will riot and our troops will be given the opportunity to shoot. I know many of them want to – I can understand it; they are absolutely fed up out here, for it is a miserable enough life for the ordinary infantry lad, doing his guard & twice a week standing-by, being called out, & being generally detested all round. It isn't much of a life, is it? It is cruel that men must be asked to do such things.

The comment from the *New Statesman* you quote is "right on the ball". The Government's advisors have coldly calculated exasperation from the Jews and as the NS puts it "this expectation has been regularly fulfilled".

Your own suggestions that now the Governments of Europe are de-Nazified the Jews need not leave, is rather naive. Even when I was in Germany, I could see what a problem the Displaced Person was going to make. Between Celle & Wismar (the Belsen area) there were literally more of these broken people wandering round than soldiers. Some nationals, like Frenchmen, were already courageously beginning to track back. Others had no such goal. They were just – well "displaced". Nearly all Jews are like that. Their roots have been destroyed, not only as individuals, but as a community. Even if a genuine attempt at rehabilitation were made (which [it] is not of course) could you ever convince such people that they were now secure, after all that has happened! Possibly, however, they have no right to refuse if such rehabilitation were available. The truth is, however, that most Jews are still languishing in camps which amount to nothing better than Belsen cleaned up. It is impossible to keep such people disciplined as soldiers in an Army Camp. And you cannot expect British or other occupation troops to keep them clean. From what I saw of Belsen people, they looked mainly as though they could never live again. Those few who get to Palestine prove me partly, for apparently those of middle-age & over never do, or show no hope of any life again – younger ones only emerge slowly & begin to work & live as a member of the community. Some of these live too intensely too suddenly and I suspect that terrorist gangs can easily recruit them. In Germany, of course, they are still wretched, their minds so warped that they carry on rackets among themselves & even riot (it is all – here & in Germany – a sign of sickness & injury – and my heart goes out to them). It needs the absolute compassion of the "Forgive them, for they know not what they do"[...]

I have just heard the glorious story of thousands of Jews arrested in Hadar Hacarmel (the Jewish centre of Haifa) and herded off in lorries to a barbed wire enclosure. The boys were just waiting for a move to shoot, but I think it did not happen, because Haifa is a Socialist stronghold & and it is more difficult to provoke them than Tel Avivis. I don't know if any of my friends were caught. These mass searches of individuals are typical – 3 British officers are still held as hostages – possibly they are in some Jew's dispatch case or under some typist's shirt – so let's arrest the lot and see what we can find. And we are always disappointed. Pity, isn't it.

God Bless the Human Race,

Len

Carmel, 1 July 1946

I can't tell you how very bad things are here. The British are behaving extremely badly I'm afraid and BBC reports etc at your end on the restraint of our troops etc is distorted to satisfy the British Public. Yesterday was better for LOOT than anything in Germany. Tell me if you want silk stockings looted from Jewish shops while the owners were held by curfew at home. Or a watch or a ring from some home or individual – one cannot protest when facing a Sten gun. Those who do are shot.

Yes, British people looting. It's hard to believe – but worse still – shooting (to kill) on the slightest provocation. I have tried to keep sane & sensible, to see how difficult our position is (for it is) but I find it hard not to burn with hatred of my own race after yesterday's glorious effort to restore peace. How the settlements suffered – corn trampled down, property destroyed, homes turned upside down, people shot & arrested for passive resistance. We WANT war with the Jews. Well we're going to get it. If I were a Jew, I'd fight to my last breath, & start right now.[12]

It is terrible to feel so powerless before all this cruelty, indifference and plundering on the part of British officers & men. I can just fret and fume inside and look on with disgust. I think every Jew must hate our guts by now. We've done our worst, have not given a single concession and we glory in a frenzy of anti-Semitism. We must have some scapegoat, & why not the oldest and best.

I am a quiet (outwardly) prisoner in this pleasant sanctuary and yesterday was my last escape in civvy clothes. I got back just before a big round up, so was lucky. How awful to be arrested as a Jew. I can't risk it any more, and I think it might be my last walk out – for if there is war, we'll be permanently immured in our ivory castle. There is no place better in Palestine of course, but I know I'm in the wrong camp, as far as sides go. However, Carmel College staff are communist & Zionist, and are as neutral as it's possible to be. We have lost a grand fellow in Champion who even in his parting address joked that he had been proud to fly three flags at Carmel – the Union Jack, the Red Flag, and the Star of Judah.[13]

Mt Carmel, Monday [1 July 1946]

Your two further letters from Wensleydale arrived today. They are so full of the peace and beauty of the Dale that they are very dear letters to me. It is hardly believable that such a place really exists in this weary world. Forgive me if I must break the spell with more dreary news.

Here are a few of the pictures of our devastations in Palestine. In nearly every case, safes have been blown open in such a clumsy military fashion that the four walls of the room have fallen in. The contents, far from being examined, have been wantonly destroyed.

A minor incident consists of a private press with a novel set up ready for the press being absolutely destroyed. A book of short stories, also set up was damaged beyond repair by a sharp instrument destroying the type face. I know exactly how the printer must feel.

A major happening is a settlement near Haifa which is being systematically devastated by small safe explosions, floors of houses being ripped up and property damaged almost beyond repair. As a settlement it is slowly but surely being raised [sic], and 25 years of hard work are going west.

In Tel Aviv, one street of shops has windows broken from end to end.

These facts are the truth.

I have just heard Mr Attlee's self-satisfied statement. Obviously relying on distorted reports from officials & the military in Palestine, he is satisfied in this war against the terrorist minority that the Jewish community at large has not suffered. He reveals the amount of arms & explosives found in various places – they are a vast quantity, & I think there are probably more. We are quite right to try to root out such things. But our method has merely precipitated a situation that is beyond recall. There is nothing for the Jews to live for, even in their National Home. They realize that, after Europe's tale, they can only die. I cannot blame them if they die fighting. If it is not war now, then they must be the greatest people in the world. Because no race has had to stand more than they. Dr Weizmann, the Jewish leader who has done more than any other to bring Britain & the Jews together, is ill. I have no doubt it is of a broken heart. There must be many broken hearts today. For to most Jews this land has meant hope, the promise of security and opportunity to build a new life.

Perhaps they have brought the wrath upon themselves. I can only say that they have shown restraint throughout the years, against provocation & obstruction from Government officials & only now, after the war have they tried force. They had the precedent of our yielding to Arab force in 1939 and the White Paper which prevented free entry of Jews into the country at a time when many could have got there from Germany but were refused entry.

Thank you for the news of Mrs Dinsdale. I shall try to write to her, but naturally it is difficult to write personal letters when one's mind is so full of the acts of a looting, raving mob systematically destroying & plundering. I don't exaggerate – I know their methods well. The Natanya settlement was searched by 2nd Parachute Brigade. They love watches & cameras & know how to loot.

Do you feel like writing to an MP. I hate to get you busy again, and I know one should produce documents. But it does distress me to think of even the Cabinet's ignorance of the true facts.

Carmel, 2 July 1946

There was a person at the gate this morning to see me, a girl called Esther who is the fiancée of a Jewish Brigade[14] lad I know – I only know them both as Rafael & Esther. She had a message for one of the Jewish ATS[15] girls who is staying here to study – her father had suffered badly in the British raids.

Rafael's settlement, a small fishing one further down the coast, has not yet been searched so Rafael is alright so far. Esther looked worn-out however. Her office had been ransacked on Saturday while she was kept at home by curfew. Her boss had been arrested but she can't understand it for he is very old and has nothing to do with politics or anything. I tried to comfort her, but there is so little one can do. Can you imagine your library turned upside down for nothing. She had dreadful news of Yagour, the settlement which is being destroyed.[16] It is now almost flat, all the men have been taken away, even boys of 12. The women are just left trying to salvage things from the wreckage, but they have to compete with the Arabs who have now just walked in, put their flocks in the vineyards and groves and are just wandering unmolested in one glorious ransack. Yagour, one of the finest and oldest settlements in the Yishuv, can now be written off. Tel Aviv has now suffered very much, the Jewish Agency (though I have to rely on only Jewish statements for this) is badly smashed up & files & documents by the thousand have been destroyed by safe-blowing etc... In fact, it seems as though it can be written off as an organisation.

Many settlements have suffered, mostly by personal looting, and only a few, which Esther was ready enough to admit, got off with slight damage.

My information about Yagour has come from 3 different sources, and since it is not far from Haifa, and the three pictures seem to fit together, I think you can take it as reliable. Probably there will be further information in the Press, which I will send. Papers are late.

I enclose the British interpretation of the events, with the glorious heading "Restraint".

As soon as the Yishuv recovers it will be war, & on our head be it. If they haven't enough arms, it will be with sticks and stones & then with their hands, for no Jew could live through all this plundering of their National Home without a deep sense of hurt and despair. There is nothing for it but national suicide, and I have no doubt they are prepared for it.

In Britain, people will only hear of the arms discovered. There will be no reasons for the presence of those arms, no description of the means taken to root them out, and a glorified picture of British restraint in the face of provocation.

I think we just stink.

I have written a letter of sympathy to Professor Grossman, his wife and daughter, for they have been very kind to me. I feel ashamed to think my own people are committing this wholesale damage & destruction. But what can one do? I feel so helpless.

Len's next missive from Mt Carmel enclosed the typescript of an article entitled "Anti-Semitism in Palestine: The Jewish Case". It argued that events in Palestine were spiralling into ever-worsening hostility between the Jewish population and the British forces, which in turn were lapsing into anti-Semitism. The Labour Party had previously been highly sympathetic to the Jews' aspirations in Palestine, but Clement Attlee's government had proved a great disappointment to them. The recom-

mendations of the Anglo-American Committee of Inquiry into the Palestine problem must be implemented urgently; "the delay in giving a decision one way or the other has played a large part in the increase of terrorism and hostility to the British Government." Len added a note date-stamped 8 July 1946:

This article, written by Bill [Hamilton] & me, was composed in the heat of the moment for the *Daily Herald*. Things were going badly we felt, & events were causing the balance to tip most unfairly. As the *New Statesman* put it, the Government could rely on the bulk of the Press to support its policy, whatever. This is a rather feeble attempt, in political journalism for the mass, to keep that balance fairly weighed. I don't like the article – it is Bill's approach, my introduction & smoothing out (bad English & all) – we didn't have time. Time is important.

I personally don't think for a moment that the *Herald* will publish it, but if so, it will probably have appeared by now. Bill being a Scottish candidate, it is probable that it will appear in the Scottish edition – Bill is a personal friend of Dolan, the editor, anyway. Fancy me, dabbling in politics.

On the same day Len sent another lengthy polemic.

Carmel, 8 July 1946

I didn't think I ever had such vivid letters as those 4 or 5 from Castle Bolton. Your stay there has been alive for me too, and though you cannot send a piece of England, you have sent a lovable picture of the dale and the places that have come to have a special meaning for us there. All that country has a very special place in my heart, and even if I'm changing all the time & my views of life change & so on, I am still the same – that I can't, & don't want to uproot that part of me. You can possibly imagine how hopelessly homesick I am sometimes, especially under the unfairness of my position. I am always the Daddy of the party now, somehow, & though in itself that isn't an unpleasant sensation, I know I belong to that group who formed the first militia before the war, & if I wasn't due to be demobbed with [them?], at least I should have been by now. So Wensleydale only becomes more heavenly & desirable.

Palestine settles down uneasily again. The purge has left a nasty taste. I was out over the weekend in civilian clothes for the first time since before the operation. I went right into the Jewish quarter with a Jewish schoolteacher friend, Uloo Vilna, where I bought some grey flannels – £4!! The people seemed quite normal of course, especially since Hadar is out of bounds to troops. There was one queer incident though, which had a queerer effect on me. A big car went quickly by, tooting urgently, full of Palestine Policemen, & a very young one, in plain clothes, was clinging heroically to the running board and brandished a pistol in the air with the biggest cowboy flourish possible and you could see how much he loved it, how much he was showing off. And it made [me] so angry, I wanted to pick up a stone & throw it at him. It must have been the effort of the heat upon me, but it shows I'd make a nasty specimen in a mob.

The *Spectator* article you sent, by an Airborne Officer, was very sound indeed I thought, and there is nothing wrong with it – except that one must go further. There is something wrong with the Jews, & whatever it is is making them their [own] worst enemies. Even an Arab leader admitted recently that there was no better fighter for the Arab cause than the Jewish terrorist. Of course, the terrorist thinks differently, naturally. But since there is something wrong with the Jews, one must face up to it, see it in its proper light, and go further back. As a nation they are sick. They have been increasingly persecuted in Europe, & the more persecuted they were, the more they appeared to deserve it – and by God, they know it. It's like a child. A child may be strange, & you beat it – it only becomes more strange then and the trend to normality is defeated – it becomes more strange & deserves more beating. The Jews are rather like that, though one cannot simplify it so easily. At an unfortunate period in their history they were forced into exile, & became a wandering tribe again. In Europe they appeared strange – therefore they were a little (if not more) cast out & had to resort to the jobs outside the community. They never became the farmer, the blacksmith, the cooper, the weaver, & so on – they are all integral members of the community – & kept the Jew out. He, being oriental, found a means of eking an existence in spite of the community – he soon became a money-lender of course, & in fact soon found his place in that walk of life which is outside the actual part of life, outside the intimate working parts of the machine – he became a parasite because he could get no further on. And so he became hated, and it has gone on and on, the more he was hated, the more he deserved it apparently. And he knew it too – he became self-assertive, *different*, & became the natural scape-goat. That's somewhere about the root of the problem, in brief & simple form.

The British seemed to grasp the idea in 1917 & there seemed hope for the Jew – that hope may be defined in a simple phrase – hope for a return to normality. At the very first, things went well – he was a real member of the community again. Indeed, as a communal, social-ist experiment, the average settlement was & is a shining example to the rest of the world. But was he allowed to become normal! Oh no, far from it. It was soon apparent that even if he could overcome Arab hostility by sheer hard work & raising the Arab up with him, the British policy, or at any rate, the administration of the Mandate, would not allow it. Perhaps the neatest account is that in John Gunther's *Inside Asia* if you have it. So I won't go into it. And once they knew they were not wanted, that even here they were not secure, that the "return", in fact, was no more than a makeshift, & that England was as ever, afraid before & regretful after the event, the hope for normality gradually died, and as Matthew[17] would put it, the bottom of the boat dropped out. They are in a mess – one cannot but help laughing at Uloo's funny face as he declares with a shrug of the shoulders "We are quietly doomed" – and if you could meet the ordinary Jew here, especially the *kibbutznik* or settlers, you would be sorry. It seems such a tragedy. And so much might have been done if there'd been a sincere attempt to deal with the world problem of Jewry.

So the officer's article is a very sound (& fair) picture of today. But there is so much more to it. It is typical of their own desire for the same fairness & soundness that the same article was published last week in full in *Davar* (the popular socialist paper) in Hebrew – before you had even sent it, I had had bits of it translated to me. And yet they seem to do the wrong thing every time. Sometimes their own fault, often that subtle way we have (you have no idea how subtle & inevitable it is) of putting them in the wrong[…]

A few days later Len sent a letter printed in The Palestine Post *of 8 July from R Ginzberg, honorary treasurer of the WIZO (Women's International Zionist Organization), accusing the army of "wanton destruction" and "pilfering" during a search of the organisation's offices. He added a cryptic note:*

When the women begin to natter, they are hard to answer. But when the case is so strong in Palestine, one simply does not answer – or merely laughs – or simply denies it.

So I merely send this letter as a little social document. As a good British citizen, you must not take any notice, understand?

If only there were less good British citizens & less good Jews in the world and a few more people.

> No 1 Comd Edn College Wing, [no date
> – air letter postmarked 22 July 1946]

I have been very busy with Bill and other people on a project – the Palestine problem, of course – so have had little time for anything else. I'll tell you what happens to it, but I think it is going to England, as soon as Bill & I can sort out the various contributions – either to Gollancz or the Fabian Society as a pamphlet.

Palestine is quiet again – Britain is a fine artist at procrastination. The hand dips into the lucky bag, is about to withdraw the prize & nothing happens. No wonder the baby screams sometimes.

This library takes some licking into shape, and I often work over into the afternoon. But at least I have a system which gives me a record of where every book is, or should be. Do you know there was no accession register, yet there were accession nos – very mysterious ones, which written on a reader's card when he took a book out. You can imagine the chaos. All I knew was that Capt A had a 1098 out.

> Mt Carmel, 21 July 1946[18]

I'm hopeless with letters, first of all a spate from me, then nothing for 3 or 4 weeks. I have been busy &, let us be truthful (since it happens abroad) disinclined to write. Everyone has suffered, or otherwise, and you must feel that your letters don't make any impression whatsoever.

Well they do. I'm grateful for them many a time[…] Palestine forces your attention once you have anything to do with it, and there is little room for anything else in my head. We (a group of us) have just finished a project on Palestine & I'm heartily sick of it by now – I loathe politics, even writing, speaking or thinking as a humanist[…]

To return to the Palestine problem, have you read the report of the Anglo-American Committee yet? An excellent document, but with a few flaws I think. Who can say? The Memorandum submitted to them by the Jewish [sic] is a revealing document and I would like every anti-Semitic person to read it. It is not propaganda – an official report to such a committee must stick to the facts & be careful. Well, it is a fair enough report, or memorandum, but its facts are horrifying – facts which can be confirmed & which must be laid at the door of the British Government, I'm afraid. The Arab Report, too, can bring facts against us, but its basis is not half so sound nor is it as well written & put together. It need not be of course, because the Arab knows he has his rights without even speaking. The next important document is the British Communist Party statement to the Committee (ask a communist to get it for you). It is the only statement from a political party in Britain, & is therefore very courageous. But what is more, it is extremely sound, sane & understanding & it earned the praise of the Committee. It is so often easy to overlook Communist literature since it is so often lurid, unfair & bad. But this is thoroughly good & fair.

I see Kingsley Martin[19] is quoted in the *Palestine Post*, he himself quoting from a British soldier's letter which sounds suspiciously like me. So our views do get about & keep the party clean, I think.

I'm afraid my outraged sense of fairness has given you a lot of work, writing & so on. I hate to involve you, especially as good people are snubbed by politicians. Questions are asked in Parliament & I know for a fact that the answers are wrong, inadequate or twisted. Anyway, on whom does the Foreign Secretary rely for his answers – the very Administration and military that are causing the trouble. As bad as asking a Jewish Terrorist for his facts on Palestine[…]

PS Cuttings in a separate envelope on explosion at David Hotel.

On 22 July the Irgun carried out a bomb attack on the King David Hotel in Jerusalem, the British administrative headquarters for Palestine, killing 91 people and injuring 46. The victims were British, Arabs, Jews and others. The bombing drew widespread condemnation, including among Palestinian Jews. Len felt that those like him who sympathised with the Jewish cause would be ignored more than ever, and that all Jews would be blamed for the actions of the terrorists (in contrast to the sensitivity shown after the war to Germans over their relationship to the Nazis). He was horrified by the bomb attack, but was also outraged by the British military commander's reaction with its anti-Semitic overtones.

Mt Carmel, 25 July 1946

[…] Palestine has paralysed whatever there was in me that made me dabble [in art]. A pity, for it's a grand thing to put into shape or form or colour your own thought and feeling, even if it is a simple little comment on some familiar rock or stream[…]

The King David explosion has cooked their goose. American support is greatly diminished I feel – sympathetic MPs have felt compelled to withdraw their support (and I cannot blame them), and people like myself who could not look on and remain silent have been discredited and must now remain silent. My views are the same – it is the world which changes its views daily – and even if the whole Jewish nation was behind this outrage (believe me, I am certain only a score or so people knew of this) I could argue a man stiff if he was reasonable at all. But the Jews do not depend on people like me – they are dealing with the world, with politicians – all too ready to find reasons to prove the Jew is always wrong. While we took such care over our arguments of Nazis and the German people (were they, or weren't they!) there is no doubt that every Jew is always wrong and a single act, or a series of acts from a minority, damns the lot. But the subtle print in the publication of evidence against the Jewish Agency – very subtle, because while in fact it means nothing, it amounts to corruption and sabotage in the mind of outsiders. Everybody knows Jewish Agency leaders were in the Haganah. The nearest equivalent to it is the Home Guard. Necessity (as they saw it) forced them underground like the Maquis, and even [to] co-operate in exploits with the extreme Irgun[…]

Carmel, 26 July 1946

This time we seem to be facing real imprisonment. On orders today it all appears rather ominous.

Discipline:- All Jewish places of entertainment, Jewish premises and private dwellings are out of bounds to British Troops.

No British soldiers will have any social interaction with any Jew.

All business with Jews will be conducted as briefly and formally as possible.

Well, there it is. No loophole whatever this time. There were good Germans like Pastor Niemöller, Thomas Mann and so on – but there are no good Jews.

There seems little hope in Palestine now, and I feel very bad about it, because this latest measure, I feel, is not military only, nor political, but racial too, and even considering the staggering events of the last week, I think it is a measure which bodes no good.

There is so much hate on both sides now that I'm sure nothing but war can clear the air. But the Jews cannot wage war, except for comparatively small terrorist groups who do quite the wrong thing. Sabotage activities by the Haganah have been on the right track I suppose, particularly since they took special care not to take lives – but the Irgun seems to have taken over and being less responsible (to people, I mean) than the Haganah, it has gone too far and its fascist methods lately have brought the Jewish race into complete disgrace.

You've no idea what a wreck of human relationships Palestine is. It is a fact that, left alone, young Englishmen and young Jews get on marvellously together and troops stationed here during the war will always speak enthusiastically for the Jews. Individuals still get on well (or they did till today) but the two races are now bitterly opposed. The trouble is, of course, that the mass of the troops now in Palestine has not contacted the Jews, and Jews, in disillusionment, have ceased to make the effort. What riper moment for hate.

I want very much to leave Palestine now because the air is poisoned. Even in war, one could get away from hate in England, and even in war, in Germany, there were contacts where love shone through. But here there is coldness, a disillusionment and an *unreasonable* hostility. I think I have put more *work* into friendships in Palestine than ever before. I have not defended one side from the other, have not apolo-

396 *Dear Mona: Letters from a Conscientious Objector*

gised, but have tried to show Britishers that the Jews have a point of view and vice versa. We are much to blame and so are the Jews. The people I feel extremely sorry for are those (and there are many) who have clung faithfully to the moderate approach of Chaim Weizmann. But Weizmann, who did so much to build up the National Home, can only look on with despair (or rather cynicism, I'm told) at the Jews themselves and the trustees, the British in Palestine, and realize what a wreck he is left with.

Later. A fresh Order has been published, and I copy it word for word for your perusal.

Terrorist activities in Palestine

The attention of all troops to Lt Gen Barker's Statement on "terrorist activities in Palestine" published as Appendix "A" to these orders

Appendix "A"
Terrorist activities in Palestine

1. The Jewish population of Palestine cannot be absolved from responsibility for the long series of outrages culminating on Monday with the blowing up of a large part of the Government offices in the King David Hotel, causing grievous loss of life. Without the support, active or passive, of the general Jewish public, the terrorist gangs who actually carry out these criminal acts would soon be unearthed, and in this measure all Jews in this country are accomplices, and bear a share of the guilt.

2. I am determined that they shall suffer punishment and be made aware of the contempt and loathing with which we regard their conduct. We must not allow ourselves to be deceived by the hypocritical sympathy shown by their leaders and representative bodies, nor by their protests that they are in no way responsible for these acts, as they are unable to control the terrorists. I repeat that, if the Jewish people really wished to stop these crimes they could do so by active co-operation with us.

3. Consequently, I have decided that, with effect from the receipt of this letter, you will put out of bounds to all ranks all Jewish places of entertainment, cafes, restaurants, shops and private dwellings. No British soldier is to have any social intercourse with any Jew and

any intercourse in the way of duty should be as brief as possible, and kept strictly to the business in hand.

4. I appreciate that these orders will inflict a measure of hardship upon the troops, but I am confident that, if my reasons are fully explained to them, they will understand their propriety and they will be punishing the Jews in a way the race dislikes as much as any, namely by striking at their pockets, and showing our contempt for them.

(Signed) E.H. Barker

Lt Gen Comd British Troops in Palestine and Transjordan

I leave it to you, without comment. Naturally it is official and therefore secret, but show it to anyone you can rely on.

My only reaction is that it distresses me and my first reading made me sick at heart, I can tell you. But you must decide for yourself which of it is right and which wrong, which justified and which not.

After the King David's Hotel crime, I wanted to keep quiet, but statements like the above and the New White Paper make me rave again. I wish I could explain certain things to my own people. But already there is the deliberate closing of the ears, a turning away from the truth when the truth is inconvenient, and one is easily dubbed "Zionist" for suggesting a single item against Britain. I sometimes think it must be nice to see yourself as always right and the other fellow always wrong.

Enough.

Len's next letter, on 30 July, apologised for "harping on about Palestine". He concluded: "My letters are pretty empty now, aren't they? A pity, I suppose, but I'm quite dried up. You know, I've been away from England too long. I feel completely cut off."

In a letter postmarked 10 August Len accepted Mona's suggestion that he sit one of his librarianship qualification exams. "I'll take you on – for 1 paper, just for honour[…] What shall it be? I say bibliography." He went on: "Demob news is bad and my morale is very low. [Group] 46 (only part of) by end of year and not 50. And strictly 2 groups a month which makes me beginning of next April […]" Meanwhile he was tied up cataloguing the whole library – "I started at No

1 and have reached 1,060."

Mt Carmel, 14 August 1946

All day I can look down on Haifa Harbour and watch the warships moving, with little helpless looking steamers among them. I know what they mean, and I cannot settle to anything. I am ashamed, not only for England, but for the whole of mankind if it is possible. I look on, as helpless as the Jews themselves, and I want to cry from the roof tops. Is there any sense, or feeling, understanding or sympathy left in us? It does not need absolute love and compassion, just common sense and a plain live & let live attitude. The events of Haifa this last week are a symbol. The dregs, the outcasts, one might say the ultimate victims of the war are drifting into this port as a last resort, in despair, and yet hoping, and at the last step they are denied.[20]

I suppose it all sounds very simple and human in the British press. I despair of the truth ever appearing. I will not say the *Palestine Post* will give it (it is just as biased as, say, the *Daily Herald*) but I shall send you cuttings because today, it is trying very hard, almost in spite of itself, to be objective. And I can get facts at first hand. I shall send cuttings from the British Army paper, too, to balance the Post.

There is a move towards martyrdom, the ever reassuring masochistic tendency, people throwing their lives away uselessly. But can you wonder. Can you for a minute imagine what it feels like to be in your home and know that members of your race are packed in ships and denied that last step to security or comparative security? They want to welcome them and in their enthusiasm and desperate movements are killed.

And before all these moves, the British Government's conscience so patently pricked it that it had to issue a historic statement of past friendship and so on. We wallow in it and are puzzled and hurt when Jews spit at it.

Perhaps I am a sentimental fool. I'm taking up a Zionist "line" perhaps. And I conveniently ignore the Arabs. And I am ignoring the fact that it is a difficult situation for Britain.

Well, there they are, the dregs, in their little boats, called "Haganah", "Yagour" and so on. I see how difficult it is for Britain –

I see how right the Arabs are to protest – I see how wrong it is of Jews to mob and sacrifice their lives in "bags of martyrdom" as soldiers call it. But I know what I'd do with these people. And Russia, Britain and America with all their power haven't the foggiest idea.

In the meantime, Jews are still dying, the Arabs are laughing, and we are ever so neutral and all that.

By the way, in my queer state of mind, I forgot to warn you that my library gets every Hansard and we have everything from about 1941 to the present and it arrives about 7 days after publication. I read everything on Palestine and for a long time I have been considering Mr Bevin's tricks of thought and I wonder if I'll remember to go over it all someday with you and prove categorically how wrong, and often, I'm afraid, how hypocritical he can be. He is not alone. But how foolish of us to expect absolute integrity from Labour leaders[...]

At present, the College is empty and the library closed. I am re-cataloguing and making out the new accession register starting from No 1 and have reached 1,600. My assistant ATS is working independently and starting at 8,000 has reached 8,400. And it is automatically taking stock. But what a mess!

Mt Carmel, 19 August 1946

A sad little note from you, rather depressed. Was anybody so ineffectual as you, you ask, and however did you forget it sometimes. I often wish I could have kept all your letters (I can keep only a few) and present them, with an "honest and unimpassioned" account of our story, to some interested psychiatrist. Perhaps my letters to you would have helped him too. And he'd have a lot to say, I'm sure. However, I can't psychoanalyse you, and don't want to, for the piles of letters we have written to each other must make a pretty complete, yet minutely detailed picture of the other in our respective minds. You have kept on filling in details even to date. You rightly reprehend me for not giving my details. For 5 solid weeks nothing but Palestine and politics in my letters. I'm sorry. I do feel strongly about it, of course, and the propaganda on all sides (Jews included) is as subtle, dangerous, and filthy that I shout in spite of myself[…]

But to try to get into your letter and forget about Palestine. It's difficult you know – as I've said before, I feel quite cut-off and seem to be away ages and ages. It is difficult to project one's mind on to problems like Leslie Taylor's[21] reaction to your kindness in providing a typewriter for him. The times you have had to put up with that sort of thing, that latent bad taste among us uncouth Northerners, ought to have made you a bitter woman. Thank goodness you never are really, but one could understand it if you were. Perhaps you have a surfeit of grace which enables you to continue in spite of rebuffs and selfish reactions. And that grace is the answer to your complaint that you are ineffectual. You know quite well that you aren't, but are leading a life which, however unimportant and ineffectual it appears in its tiny impact upon this big, rough, selfish world, is a precious and glorious example of the good life. And just reflect – is there any place for goodness in this world at present? Not really – it is cried down, it goes unheeded, and is actually unwanted. But even so, think how much more terrifying it would all be if that little leavening lump of goodness did not continue to exist in latent form. It exists in you. You must either be grateful or treat it as a burden, presuming you must consciously consider it. In depression you are bound to regard it as a burden, I know, for it is hard to bear these constant rebuffs, even from those like myself whom you count your best friends. At other times you are grateful. But mostly you are quite natural about it, and that is how it should be[...]

And I'll not say anything about Palestine this time, except that the Haifa trial of terrorists (18 sentenced to death for a raid which cost 11 terrorist lives and no British) has inevitably aroused sympathy in the people who cannot forget that the trial took 3 days while Goering etc still live.[22]

Over the two months since Len had taken up his post at Carmel College, Mona must have been struck by his extreme preoccupation with the Jews' predicament. Suddenly she heard of a personal dimension to this identification – and it must have been an enormous shock that changed her life. The old friendship between them would never be quite the same again.

Mt Carmel, 21 August 1945 [sic – clearly 1946 meant]

My dear Mona,

Since writing the last letter to you things have been in a whirl, and you are going to be shocked by this letter. After months of resignation and unhappiness that I could not marry a girl I loved in Haifa, I hear suddenly that it is possible, without Army approval, to marry her. And so, on 5 Sept (provisionally & DV)[23] we shall be married by the District Commissioner.

The girl is Judith Grossman, daughter of the Mathematics Professor at the University here and a Russian lady. We have known each other all this year, and were on a course together at the beginning of February. Before that, Judith was Education Serjeant (ATS) for the Jerusalem area, but like the rest of Palestinians, is now demobbed. Normally, she is a law student & was on with her finals, but some governmental upset prevented her from taking her exams this July. I am lamely trying to describe her, knowing all the time the effect this letter will be having upon you.

Perhaps the last thing is first to explain why I have been so mysterious, or rather secretive about all this. It has been very difficult all along, owing to the situation in Palestine. In all these months, I have only seen Judith legally 5 times. The rest of the meetings have been illicit for some reason or another – I have travelled the length of Palestine from Sarafand to Haifa & Jerusalem to Haifa without a pass, & now I am in Haifa, I can only see her as a civilian, which is breaking the law. And yet nothing, not all the Armies & Governments in Palestine could prevent these meetings. We were always very happy together, and the impending separation (through my return to England) was always hanging above us & prevented complete happiness, the possibility of planning our future, or even thinking of our future. We both decided it was to be a Palestinian affair, ending in my return to England, something only to be remembered as precious & fragmentary in our lives. It was hard to believe that stupid armies, governments & a political situation could prevent our marrying, but so it seemed, & we were resigned. We decided, moreover, that since it was only to last for my stay in Palestine, I should say nothing about it to my people, because it would only cause worry, & perhaps cause unnecessary ill-feeling. I would have returned home, perhaps have

Judith Grossman

recounted the sad episode, & waited for Judith's possible visit to England (a vague chance).

At our first encounter, we both presumed I was leaving Palestine this July or thereabouts – perhaps I'd have returned, & lost Judith had my demob been corrected, so it's an ill wind that blows nobody any good. Then we presumed the New Year, & though Judith genuinely regretted my delay in demob for my sake, I knew it was another lease for her. And now it's March or April 47, which gives me a month's leave in England. And now you are again making efforts to obtain my early demob. I wonder what you think of all this. (I must say here that all the time, I have tried very hard to obtain my demob, because I knew it was my duty to others & to myself, & because Palestine was gradually making me ill. Judith backed my efforts, though it was not in her interests really.)

And now, after tentative enquiries, I have got round the normal procedures, and the DC will marry us. It is very sudden, & I am in a whirl. The chief trouble is that though it has seemed the natural sequel to our relations as far as Judith & I were concerned, it does not appear so to others, & it has come as a shock. So although it is quite natural to ourselves, the job of announcing it to those who must know is not easy. First I had to ask the Professor's permission & I could see it was a great shock to him, for Judith is the only child & he loves her dearly. He would not give permission until he had a long talk with Judith – but everything is alright – he approves of me. It is sad that marriage will then separate Judith from her Aba and Ima[24] – Ima in particular will feel lonely, and I feel sorry about it for her sake. But she likes me and she entrusts her Judit [sic] to me.

   And now I must tell you, and my parents. It is particularly hard to tell you. I know what we have meant to each other & still mean. It is 10 years now, and 6 of them have been apart, and still we are each other's most constant correspondent, I suppose. And it is a friendship that has been through every phase and survived all. I have often wondered (I think I have mentioned it in letters) what marriage on either part would mean. The point has been ignored or pushed aside, till now, when our friendship must face it, as the biggest obstacle yet. Or is it? Need it be? I realize how hard it will be for you. I leave this question open; I must not laud my friendship & offer it heartily, nor plead rather guiltily for yours. There must be no pride nor guilt about what I am doing, for it is the natural thing to do, the best & most beautiful thing to do considering what Judith means to me now. Perhaps when I return to England, you & I shall be able to have a *tête-a-tête* about each other. In this letter it is difficult to discuss you & I. All I want to say is that you are still in my thoughts & shall never leave them, and that precious part of you which has gradually been revealed to me over the years has had full meaning for me in spite of my wayward spirit at times, and I will always cherish it for its influence upon me, its guidance and example.

   Judith – you will wonder perhaps. What is she like, who is she? Tiny, thin rather, a little worn from malaria and the recent tension. Not beautiful, I should say: in fact plain, except for sparkling eyes (very like you there, I must say). Complexion rather pale, features expressive – she laughs easily, twinkling her eyes. Perhaps her greatest feature is her volatile temperament. In such a tiny creature it is irresistible, and she is intensely lovable (I have many rivals!) Intelligent, a good psychologist, has no complexes (rare in people of Jewish extraction), an indefatigable worker, and highly sympathetic to others' moods and tantrums. She gets on very well with English people – and I hope she gets on well with you. She already knows you, and I know she likes you & respects you for what is best in you – that past in particular which wrote to me from Wensleydale. I had to read those letters out to her and believe me, her appreciation of you is unaffected and sincere.

I must write to my parents now, and send this letter.

With my blessings,

Len

As if in some tale by Thomas Hardy, there was to be one final, bitter twist to the episode.

Mt Carmel, 2 September 1946

My dear Mona,

It came as a shock to read in your two letters that the news of my marriage was broken to you first by Betty. I can think of nothing worse.

After such a thing, it is practically useless to say that I did in fact write to you before I wrote to my parents; that far from wishing to keep you all in the dark, I had nevertheless to debate whether to announce to you all a *fait accompli* this week (since the situation in Palestine is too tense to suppose that arrangements go smoothly); that far from my letters home being diametrically opposite to yours in content, I have "deceived" my parents more than you.

The rest of your letter is so bitter that I feel I must not try to reply. The damage is done & I can do no more about it. I can only say that, in spite of your words, I remain

Your sincere friend,

Len

Epilogue
A Friendship Winds Down

Mona reacted with fury to the news of Len's marriage. The bitterness of her accusations can be gauged from Len's attempt to shoot down her barrage of missiles in a letter (dated 9 September) so long he had to send it in two instalments.

I'm so pleased you did, after all, reply to my letter[…] However, this second letter is better than your first, which was too sweeping & bitter, even considering the facts. In some ways it was an important letter, but oh! how small-minded you can be sometimes – instead of sweeping aside such trivialities, you dwell on them & bring them out as trump cards. But since they are so important to you, & you are trying your best to hurt (cowardice, dishonesty, disloyalty, an admiring petticoterie *– really Mona!) I must lash out too & answer things to which you already know the answer[…]*

Do you realize that since leaving you, Judith is the first woman I have embraced? And Palestine has been a bed of roses! I have told you one long fictitious yarn, have I? My family is conventional, sends conventional letters, the conventional soldier's cake for my birthday, & gets worried conventionally (merely for the sake of getting worried). I have rarely given them a true picture, & if I had spoken to my Mother of my unhappiness in Palestine, she would have been quite ill. To discuss the same unhappiness with you was quite natural. Why? Because we have continually wrote [sic] in that tone of intimacy for years, & though I have overloaded you with my loneliness & unhappiness at times, I know too that when you were 'low' too, I was as likely as anyone to hear of it. But the intimacy ended as soon as a woman's name had to be mentioned. Let's make no bones about it. In that point our friendship has been unnatural, as you say. I would be the last to dispute it. There seems no way of telling you about such things. The happenings of 1941 were not so easily erased, were they? I was guilty there alright, & the guilt has made me unnatural - & you too in your turn. But I do not think that has made the cowardly, deceitful & disloyal friend you try to paint[...]

My friends have not been too loyal over this business if it comes to the point. I could never discuss another woman with you, I admit, but once I told Jim casually, since he likes gossip & to mention a girl discourages him from writing in a rather offensive manner. I was a fool to think he could be trusted – when the time comes, like a woman, he blabbers over the phone something I did not even know myself, that I knew in June I was getting married. Just to hurt you, & impress you. Such a thing is despicable I think, & Jim might know its effect on our relations, always unnatural where love is concerned. I had told one or two other people (not my parents or sisters), but your network of spying and checking upon me is already quite elaborate, though goodness knows why. After all, if you disbelieve a friend to the extent that you disbelieve me, the best thing is to tell him to go to blazes. The fact that you didn't made me think that you still cared for me, & I could never be comfortable then.

But, like you, I should get down to brass tacks. This wife of mine. This is what makes you detest me so much – that my friendship was not real enough to be 'candid & trustworthy' enough to say a word to you. And worse still, I painted a picture of unhappiness & frustration that you say is quite untruthful. How do you know?[...] The situation here is so bitter & hateful (& the weaker nation is always worst) that a gang of political thugs for months now have been tipping nitric & sulphuric acid into the eyes of girls who 'fraternise' with British soldiers. Jerusalem (the saddest of cities now) is worst, Tel Aviv next, & Haifa next. Judith, living high up in Carmel, is safer than most, but she was terrified at one stage, just before we were married, & the precautions I had to take over secrecy were quite elaborate – no banns please, an Arab taxi, a carefully planned route & so on. Not ideal for complete happiness[...]

There is much more to answer – your accusations are endless, & my ingratitude for what you have done for me & my family knows no bounds apparently. I have gone wrong very often, I know, but Heaven only knows I am not the utter cad you paint me[...]

Three days later Len sent a brief cover note: "I had nothing to do with the enclosed – Judith wrote it while I was at work[...] Judith had realized I wasn't too happy about you." His new wife's olive branch was a model of tact and grace:

The photograph sent to Mona by Len and
Judith, after their wedding

I feel I ought to write to you, having looked upon you for all these months as Len's best and most understanding friend. Len told me a lot about you, always with warm and sincere affection when referring to you. So much so that I began thinking of you as a potential friend.

I feel rather guilty, because I do not want to come between you in any way whatever. What existed between you and Len belongs exclusively to the two of you, and I hoped it would continue as it used to despite my marrying Len. I should be most disappointed if your affinity were to be damaged through it[…]

Judith would continue to write short letters to Mona from time to time over the following months, seeking to build a rapport.

Thankfully relations between Mona and Len now took their usual course after each of their bitter quarrels. She regained her composure (outwardly at least) and her essential generosity asserted itself once more with a conciliatory letter to Len (before she had received Judith's). For the next three months the flow of letters continued between Mona and Len almost as before. The newlyweds "subsided into a very steady domestic existence, punctuated by terrorist activities which confine life rather painfully", as he reported on 21 September.

Throughout this period Len was working long hours sorting out the Carmel College library. He knew by now that he wanted to escape from librarianship, although he took his bibliography exam in December as he had promised Mona he would. He expected to go back to work in the County Durham library system for a period, but thought he might then take a BA degree in fine arts at Newcastle to launch him into "the right world". On honeymoon in Cyprus at the beginning of November he found himself "among things to excite me again & make me realize I wasn't dead, but only asleep", and drew or painted energetically.

Len's demobilization seemed to be forever receding into the future. He wrote on 26 November of having to wait until August or September the following year. Mona was still fighting his corner, writing indignant letters to figures of authority about the delay.

Around the turn of the year Len got an urgent message that his mother was seriously ill and in intensive care. He was granted compassionate leave so he could visit home. Fortunately his mother was out of danger by the time he reached England, but he stayed anyway until mid-February 1947. While there Len met Mona a few times. Early in the year she moved to Oxford, having taken up a post as reader at the Oxford University Press. It was a step down in status for her compared with her old post running two public libraries, but life in Felling had exhausted her and she needed to escape back to her native South. Len wrote from his family's home in Wardley on 11 February:

I felt we helped each other by our few talks together & I wish we could have had more. Perhaps you don't. It was a strain for you in amidst other strain[…] There is so much sadness, yours included[…]

Mona clearly felt by now that Len had slipped from the centre of her life for good. Yet he still cared deeply for her, writing the next day:

I realize that any brave resolutions to ignore each other for ever will break down[…] I could never break with you upon a decision & we've been like that for years. This isn't weakness or we'd never write as we have. Even today, the first person I must write to is you. That's not a habit, but a token of something.

The situation in Palestine deteriorated while Len was away and the army decided to move all non-essential personnel out to Egypt. Judith, worried sick for her parents, was among those evacuated as was Carmel College. Len left England in mid-February, arriving in Port Said late in the month. He was reunited with Judith, and busied himself once more with the library at the relocated army college at Gineifa in the Canal Zone. For the first time since he had left the North East for Exmoor in 1940, he did not write to Mona for several weeks. He finally broke his silence to explain on 12 April:

I felt it might be better to let time have a chance, to let myself become "normal" about you by letting time & distance separate us for a while. I like your term normal. The separation has helped me, and I hope you too[…]

I hope J & I can settle on the warm toe of Wales at Llanystumdwy but cannot tell you yet whether our plans will work out. They are certainly going well. Petts and Kusha (now married) have found a place there, there is a place for the Press, and I hope there will soon be a place for us too.

This was the first indication of a plan to move to Wales. Len needed a way out of Tyneside, an exit from librarianship and somewhere to live. If he could work with John Petts at the revived Caseg Press, and find a house, he would be able to gain an *entrée* to life in the arts and crafts.

In February Len's demobilization date had unexpectedly been brought forward. Finally, at last, Len's longed-for freedom arrived. He was demobbed in late May and sailed home with Judith, arriving in Liverpool on 7 June. At first they settled in with the family in Wardley, but shortly travelled to North Wales to stay with John and Kusha Petts while hunting for a home of their own. Len wrote to Mona on 1 July from the peaceful confines of Cwm Pennant, in the hills of Caernarfonshire (now Gwynedd) near Criccieth. It was almost certainly Len's first ever visit to Wales. It was an idyllic place, but it had been marred by a health scare for Judith; in the early stages of pregnancy, she had suffered a serious haemorrhage. She had to spend time in hospital before she could be driven back to Tyneside (staying overnight with Bill Hamilton and his wife in Huddersfield).

Before Judith's illness Len had found a house for them, dating back to 1280, which had not been occupied for 15 years and now required extensive repairs. The rent was only £14 a year, though. High up the western flank of a small mountain by the sea, Bron y Foel looked out towards Criccieth Castle and down the Llŷn Peninsula. Len had also agreed to join John Petts at the Caseg Press once he had completed four months' work at Felling library. Intermittently he returned to the house to make it fit to live in.

Mona and her German husband, Willi

Len's last letter of the year to Mona was written on the train between Criccieth and Newcastle on 26 July. Almost a full year passed before he managed to write again, on 12 June 1948, from Bron y Foel.

Len and Judith had moved there in February with their baby son David, who had been born in December. Mona too announced life-changing news, reporting in a letter in July that she had got engaged to Willi Pehle, a German ex-POW she had met in Oxford. He was a storeman and the son of a railway signalman from Bad Driburg, near Paderborn in North Rhine-Westphalia. They got married on 9 April 1949. Mona was 44, Willi 29.

Len sent his belated congratulations on the engagement on 21 November 1948; "I was rather touched to learn the news, naturally, and I am sorry that my own carelessness has caused such a gap in our correspondence." The truth was that life and work had kept him fully occupied since before the move to Wales. As well as his job at the Caseg Press he had still had much work to do on the house, but now it was a comfortable home where the family lived blissfully.

It appears that Mona's letters to Len were by now as intermittent as his to her. The mutual affection was still there, but with a greater distance now, for both had plenty to fill their lives, and alternative centres of emotional existence.

It was not until 28 August 1950 that Len next wrote – from a sanatorium in Llangefni, Anglesey. He had worked hard at the Caseg Press for almost two years, eventually growing tired of the restrictions in his role as John Petts's assistant. He wanted to become a sculptor and letter cutter, so early in 1950 he went to be trained at Eric Gill's old workshop at Pigotts in Buckinghamshire for six weeks. It was not practical to leave Judith and David alone in Bron y Foel for so long, so they left for Israel to spend six months with Judith's parents. In their absence Len completed his training and returned to Wales to begin his career with a number of commissions. He was doing well, but his health let him down; it was a recurrence of the illness that had debilitated him in Palestine four years earlier. By June he was so sick he could not continue. He was diagnosed with tuberculosis and sent off urgently to the sanatorium. He told Mona:

Bron y Foel has been certified unfit for me in the future – I shan't be able to tackle the 300 feet climb to it. So the house I restored with my own hands has to be written off and we are all sorry[…]

I seem to have lived much nearer to the bone since then. And latterly, I was

Len, with John Petts, a friend and his son David

enjoying it immensely, really tasting life to the full, throwing placidity & serenity to the winds in my enjoyment. I was getting known as a man of letters, literally I mean - in the sense that I was drawing and carving (& printing) good letters[...] And then this enemy within. Strange, "Oh what a falling-off was there". Well even so, life is even more intense and lovely now, I know. I trust that you and Willi treasure it. Never mind placidity and serenity – per se, no good. Be happy and alive.

Len wrote thrice more from the sanatorium at two-month intervals. Before the first of these letters, on 8 October, Mona had gone to Germany with Willi to meet his family, a good visit from the impression Len got. He attributed his tardiness in replying to having undergone artificial pneumothorax, which involved collapsing a lung with a kind of stiletto. He added wryly: "By the way, where do you think I might have got this plague? Yes, Germany[…] All those poor Stalingrad lung cases at Wismar, which I fussed over for a month or so."

The final letter from Llangefni was dated 12 February 1951. By this time it would appear that Mona and Len had not met for four whole years. An opportunity had arisen before he entered the sanatorium, but fate had dashed it, he explained. "I saw Cowley[1] from the train last year, returning via Oxford from H Wycombe where I'd had a month at Mrs Gill's, Eric's wife[…] I might have called to see you, but I was already hopelessly ill and feeling as if I had been run over by a tram."

Another two full years lapsed before Len's next letter, on 9 February 1953. Having recovered sufficiently at Llangefni, he had been sent to complete his rehabilitation at Leysin sanatorium high up in the Swiss Alps. After five months there he came home in the spring of 1952. By now the family were living in a council house (named Carmel by Len and Judith) in the village of Pentrefelin, near Criccieth. In July that year a second son, Peter,[2] was born. Mona, generous as ever, sent a cheque for him. Len had resumed work, had done well, but winter had taken its toll of him.

The final letter in the preserved correspondence, written on 5 December 1955, was far more cheerful, for Len had finally conquered his illness. The family had moved to Plas Afon, a big house in Pentrefelin, in the summer; the space was needed as there were now five Joneses, daughter Naomi having being born in November. Mona, of course, had sent a gift. Once again Len had to apologise for not visiting her.

I nearly called on you this year, in August, but found all my time taken up finding a chest clinic at Churchill Hospital. I've been to Oxford three times on work but never found time to visit you. This year I cut a headstone & footstone in Cheltenham for Bishops Cleeve, and travelled on, via Oxford, to Thame, to make a slight alteration on my memorial to HJ Massingham. But Judith, being very heavy by then, couldn't be left for long and I had to fit the whole lot into a week, and I had to resist temptation to visit.

Len reflected on his life's progress from assistant librarian to established artist-craftsman.

I've moved far since I studied McKerrow etc[3] under you. Though all on the same line – I print a little, & am this week publishing a book (5,000 edition) by a Criccieth mountain guide[…][4] But mainly I carve letters, and apparently well enough to get work all over GB from Sutherland in Scotland to your parts, and even abroad, in Nigeria. When I'm in funds, I carve freely according to inspiration, and my Deposition *is in a New York Collection and* Bathers *is owned by the Arts Council.*

But whether it will ever earn enough to feed my flock I don't know. I'm overloaded with work & I'm strong again; praise be, & finished with doctors.

The transition marked by the 475 letters is complete; Len the librarian has become Jonah Jones, sculptor, letter cutter, polymath… This final letter reads like a typical Jonah missive, full of a love of life and work, devoid of the agonising over Mona's emotional welfare that had surfaced repeatedly over the years of the correspondence.

The two old friends had stopped writing regularly to each other in 1947. Len's marriage meant that their relationship was bound to change, yet it was not directly the reason for its fading into a more distant bond. The tone of loving concern for Mona in Len's letters of February 1947 indicate that she still occupied a special place in his feelings then. Clearly, though, one reason for her sadness that so troubled him was her having to accept that another woman had taken centre stage in his heart. It would seem that Mona decided to draw back a little; she had moved back south, had a new job and finally found a husband. Len, for his part, was swept up by life's exigencies. Caring for a sick wife, travelling back and forth between Tyneside and North Wales, rebuilding a broken down old house, starting a new career, battling a life-threatening illness; he perhaps did not intend to wind down the connection with Mona, but after all that had happened he found he was only writing to her every two years, and the relationship was not what it had been.

Besides, he was no longer dependent on Mona as a soulmate and as a lifeline out of the isolation he had lived in for so much of the earlier years. Judith was not his intellectual equal in the same way, but she was a lively conversationalist, and crucially she gave him room to find himself, to indulge his need to be an artist even if it meant a life of semi-bohemian insecurity. Together they had overcome extraordinary obstacles, and the mutual love and loyalty these engendered would keep them together for the rest of his life in an odd kind of happiness. This was no hermetic marriage; Jonah (for such we must now call him)[5] had a talent for friendship and for sustaining it with streams of beautifully written letters, as he had with Mona. Over the years he would correspond regularly with such close friends as John Ryder (who, after 224 Parachute Field Ambulance, built a distinguished career as a typographer and book designer), the Marquess of Anglesey, the writer Jacqueline Wheldon and the North East painter and art teacher Derwent Wise. He built strong friendships too with local friends like his early patron Sir Clough Williams-Ellis and his wife Amabel, and Mary Burn, a woman of depth and great kindness.

It is not clear that Jonah and Mona met again after 1955. They continued to exchange letters intermittently, with gaps extending to years, giving news of their respective careers and family life. Ironically, as the intervals between their letters to each other stretched out, it seems that over the decades after the war Mona became closer to James Kirkup. They had got to know each other well after 1943, and he stayed with her at Oxford in 1948. They maintained a correspondence (Jim addressing her as "Mo") during his extensive travels.

Kirkup enjoyed a successful career as a writer and lecturer, publishing over 30 books. From 1950 to 1952 he held a poetry fellowship at Leeds University, making him the first resident university poet in the UK. He worked abroad after 1956, finally settling in Japan for nearly 30 years; the country had a profound influence on his writing and he found a long-term partner there.

In the mid-1970s Kirkup held a post in Dublin for a while. He wrote to Mona from there on 23 April 1975 about a surprising encounter:

I thought you might like to know that I met Jonah Jones last night for the first time in 30 years and found him really very little changed. He seems to have made a success in arts administration and examination, and has been all over the British Isles evaluating art schools and so on. At the same time, making quite a good living as a sculptor. He seems to be getting on well during his first year as Director[6] in Dublin[…]

He spoke very kindly and feelingly of you and of all our common friends. Indeed, he invited me to join his staff, but I don't think that is for me. We have a lot of common acquaintances from my Bath Academy of Art days. His Professor of Painting, a Scot, has bought my house here with a minimum of fuss and trouble, and Tamaki-san and I are leaving at the end of the month for Sheffield, where we'll stay a few weeks before he flies back to Japan. I myself am expecting to return to Tokyo either in July or October.

Kirkup achieved some notoriety in 1977, when the last successful prosecution for blasphemy took place after the newspaper *Gay News* published his poem 'The Love That Dares to Speak Its Name', on the fantasies of a Roman centurion about the crucified Jesus. The paper and its editor were found guilty and fined.

After retiring in 1988 Kirkup moved to Andorra, where he remained until his death in 2009. Over the years Jonah and he exchanged occasional letters.[7] They never met again. Jonah kept a journal from 1981, but he never mentioned Jim Kirkup once. As with Mona, a passionate friendship once central to his life had drifted to its outermost periphery.

Mona stayed at OUP until about 1956, when she moved with Willi to his home town Bad Driburg. By this time her German was probably quite proficient, but her time living in a small provincial, very Catholic town must have been testing. The marriage broke down, and they were divorced in late 1959. Mona returned to England, taking up a job as a mobile librarian with Wiltshire County Council. She appears to have retired in 1964, when she turned 60.

It was not in her nature to settle down to a life of gentle leisure. Mona had long had an interest in Africa, probably due to her sister Doris living in South Africa and later Bechuanaland (now Botswana).[8] In the mid-1960s she visited Swaziland, then in 1967-70 she did voluntary work at the National Library of Botswana. During this time she formed a close friendship with the mixed-race South African writer Bessie Head, who had sought refuge in Botswana from the deepening political crisis in her homeland. They began a deep and passionate correspondence about religion and philosophy, Mona on occasion expressing herself as trenchantly as she had in letters to Len.[9]

She took the opportunity to visit neighbouring countries during these years, and worked for about two months in 1977 in the central library in Windhoek, capital of South West Africa (now Namibia). In between these journeys Mona lived quietly in Warminster, her health now declining. She was shortly to leave on another trip to Botswana when she suffered a heart attack on the street. Mona died a few days later on 15 November 1980, aged 76.

Jonah did earn enough to feed his flock. He was one of a tiny number of full-time artists in Wales who managed to eke out a living through the relative austerity of the 1950s. At first he was in demand mainly as a letter-cutter, producing inscriptions for all sorts of clients from the Marquess of Anglesey to the University of Ibadan in Nigeria. Sir Clough Williams-Ellis gave Jonah much work at Portmeirion and elsewhere. Gradually he started to get commissions for public monuments in Wales. In between jobs he would make his own sculptures, small figures carved in stone, later branching out into bronze bust making (he modelled Bertrand Russell, John Cowper Powys and Sir Clough, among others.)

During the 1960s Jonah undertook much work for newly-built Catholic churches around England and Wales. Not only did this include lettering and stone carvings, he also learned the new skill of making glass windows (both leaded glass and the new technique of *dalle de verre* or slab glass).[10] He was perhaps at the peak of his creative powers during this period from the early 1960s to 1974. In the late 1960s he moved to greater abstraction in his work (both personal sculptures and public commissions); he made impressive wall sculptures at Mold Crown Court and Coleg Harlech in Gwynedd.[11] By now Jonah had gained widespread recognition as an artist. A token of this was his inclusion in the National Council for Diplomas in Art and Design, which totally reorganised the UK's art colleges during the 1960s. He also became a regular external assessor and examiner at art faculties and colleges, an activity he continued for three decades.

By the early 1970s the economic climate had worsened, and Jonah found the flow of commissions slowing down seriously. In 1974 he agreed to become Director of the National College of Art and Design in Dublin, an establishment riven by internal dissension and in chronic need of modernising. Jonah showed a genius for conciliation; divisions were healed and teaching transformed. By the time he left the NCAD at the end of 1978 it was a vibrant, modern art college.

While he was in Dublin Jonah began writing a novel based on an incident during the Easter Rising of 1916. He completed the story after his return to North Wales, which was published as *A Tree May Fall* in 1980 (it was received favourably). He would go on to publish a further novel, a guide to the lakes of North Wales, a collection of essays and a biography of Sir Clough Williams-Ellis. Jonah also resumed letter-cutting and sculpture after his time in Ireland; and in

1981 returned to his first artistic medium, water-colour painting. He became quite prolific in this field. After 1994, when he ended almost half a century of working in stone, he concentrated on writing and painting. He was still making fine images in water-colour – particularly his painted texts which were much admired – until shortly before his death aged 85 on 29 November 2004.

Jonah ended his days well respected for his contribution to the arts. As a man he left an impression of amiability, humour and humility allied with a quiet authority. David Sherlock, his deputy at the NCAD, recalled in his eulogy, "He gave everybody he met that wonderful sense of having touched the hem of the garment; of having been joined to something grand and first-rate."

There seems to be no record of how Jonah heard of Mona's death, nor of his reaction to it (he only began the daily journal he kept up for the rest of his life the following year). This seems a particularly cruel irony, given the profound closeness between the two of them up until the late 1940s. So it is sad that we have to turn to James Kirkup for a fitting epitaph for Mona: "She was one of the most understanding, compassionate, intellectual and saintly women I have ever known, and I cherish her memory."[12] It feels right that Jonah should have been on Tyneside, working as artist in residence at Newcastle University, at the time she died. Their lives, of course, had drifted apart. But if he reflected on Mona, he must have recalled how much she had helped to set him on his course towards a life in the arts, a life free of the poverty of circumstance and expectation that he had grown up with – how, in short, she helped Len to become Jonah.

Notes

Introduction
1. Jonah Jones, *The Gallipoli Diary* (Bridgend: Seren, 1989) and *Clough Williams-Ellis: The Architect of Portmeirion* (Bridgend: Seren, 1996).
2. Peter Jones, *Jonah Jones: An Artist's Life* (Bridgend: Seren, 2011).
3. Susan Williams, *Colour Bar: The Triumph of Seretse Khama and his Nation* (London: Penguin, 2007). The British colonial authorities banished Seretse Khama to England from 1950 to 1956 for daring to marry a white woman, to appease the apartheid government of South Africa. In time he became first president of independent Botswana. The story is told in the 2016 film *A United Kingdom*.
4. Sadly most of these expressions of gratitude for Mona's kindness have had to be omitted from this book for lack of space.

Exmoor, Kirkcudbrightshire and Tynedale
1. Presumably colleagues at Felling library.
2. Probably Len got into this through his father's medical activities at Follonsby pit.
3. For an alternative account of this episode, see Willie Hamilton, *Blood on the Walls: Memoirs of an Anti-Royalist* (London: Bloomsbury, 1992), pp 34-35.
4. The Women's Voluntary Service helped civilians during and after air raids, knitted socks and gloves for servicemen and carried out other charitable social activities. Now Royal Voluntary Service.
5. Presumably Library Association exams.
6. Myrddin Emrys-Jones, probably the first Welshman Len ever met and presumably the "undiluted boyo" with whom Len first saw Wales from Exmoor, as described in Jonah Jones, 'Gwynedd Freeman' in *The Gallipoli Diary* (Bridgend: Seren Books, 1989), p 28-29. His brother J. Emrys-Jones was assistant editor of the *Sunday Dispatch* and then a senior journalist on *The Daily Express*.
7. Removal of branches from a felled tree.
8. Peace Pledge Union, a mass pacifist movement which Len had joined in the Thirties.
9. Tyneside acquaintance.
10. A kind of cake made with boiled fruit.
11. John Armstrong had been ill with toothache.
12. C.E.M. Joad (1891-1953), left-wing philosopher and broadcaster.
13. Newspaper of the National Association of Local Government Officers.
14. Trilogy by Australian writer Henry Handel Richardson (Ethel Florence Lindesay Richardson) published between 1917 and 1929.

15. Reference unknown.
16. By Charles Harold Herford (1897).
17. Two-act play by Noel Coward (1935).
18. Colleague of Len at Felling library.
19. Friend and colleague of Len at Felling library.
20. Another library colleague (not Len's father).
21. The last line of John Keats's sonnet *Bright Star* – except it should read "And so live ever – or else swoon to death".
22. The German invasion of the Soviet Union.
23. Friend of Len living at Grasmere in the Lake District.
24. Words from William Shakespeare's *Julius Caesar*.

Jervaulx
1. This is the first mention of Len having tried water-colour painting before.
2. No more is heard of Mordue in the letters, so presumably he did not cause Len further trouble.
3. Reference unknown.
4. In fact Mona and Jim did meet in 1944.
5. E.M. Forster, *Howard's End*.
6. For Willie Hamilton's brief account of his time in Wensleydale, see *Blood on the Walls*, pp 37-38.

First Months in East Witton
1. Len's roommate at 23 East Witton, and a fellow Tynesider.
2. Presumably Tarran, the foresters' manager.
3. Len had been back to Tyneside over the weekend.
4. Scots phrase here meaning restricting output, going slow.
5. A German U-boat attacked tankers in Willemstad harbour, Curacao, on 16 February 1942 as part of an assault on oil refineries and tankers between Lake Maracaibo and the Caribbean islands.
6. Austrian Jewish writer (1881-1942) exiled from Vienna, who committed suicide in Brazil on 22 February 1942.
7. Reference unknown.
8. *He Will Watch the Hawk* by Stephen Spender.
9. *Oblomov* by Ivan Goncharov, published in 1859. Its central character is a case study in slothfulness and indecision. His faithful servant is called Zakhar.
10. Len's sisters.

East Witton: Beginnings of an Artist
1. Jackson lived with his mother and sister in Ripon during the week.
2. Jackson had spent much of the First World War in a German POW camp, where he suffered considerable privation.

3 Teacher and Tyneside acquaintance with an interest in art.

4. There is no further mention of Kramer in the letters, so it is unclear whether Len did meet him.

5. Muriel Metcalfe (1910-1994) was born in Wensleydale. Such was her precocious talent, she won a scholarship to Armstrong School of Art, Newcastle when she was only 14. She married Fred Lawson in 1933. He was 22 years her senior, and despite being of the same mind artistically the marriage was difficult. Muriel suffered from Graves' disease and depression, so she was unable to care for her daughter Sonia, who was born in 1934; the child was raised by her aunt in Leyburn. This is probably the reason why there is no hint of her existence in Len's letters. Sonia Lawson became a respected painter and was elected to the Royal Academy in 1982.

6. Nothing came of this plan of Len's – Muriel did not respond to the book.

7. In fact Kirkup went on the run, stopping in the Penrith area before he found farm work in Essex for a while. Then he took a post as a home tutor in Cornwall. He finished the war once again working on a farm in Northumberland.

8. Reference unknown.

9. One of Mona's friends on Tyneside – probably a Quaker. She built the Little Theatre in Gateshead (letter from Mona to her brother Tony, 28 September 1943).

10. First novel of Christopher Isherwood (1928), concerning the clash of generations.

11. Could this be Kate O'Neill, the Irish girl who Len was seeing at the end of 1941? There is no way of telling. Clearly there was no shortage of attractive land girls in the area.

12. In other words, homosexual.

13. Reference unknown.

14. George Graham (1881-1949) came from Leeds. He trained in architecture, then studied under Frank Brangwyn. During the 1920s he settled in Sussex, but came back to the Dales regularly. He worked in both oil and watercolour. During the 1940s his paintings took on a visionary quality.

15. 'Der Tod und das Madchen' ('Death and the Maiden') a song by Franz Schubert (1817) with words by Matthias Cluadius.

16. *Polish Painting* (1942) by Henryk Gotlib and R.H. Wilenski; *Seven Pillars of Wisdom* (1922) by T.E. Lawrence.

17. Tyneside acquaintances.

18. Len had been reading Thomas Hardy's *Tess of the d'Urbervilles*.

19. Tyneside acquaintance.

20. Doubtless this exercise would also prove invaluable for his training as an army medic less than two years later.

21. Henrietta Lister (1895-1959), watercolour painter of scenes in Wensley-

dale and other parts of Yorkshire.

East Witton: An Unforeseen Crisis

1. Albert Wain, the young art teacher at Middleham with whom Len had become friendly.

2. In *Jonah Jones: An Artist's Life* I attributed this incident to George Jackson. I hereby apologise to him!

3. *Mr Norris Changes Trains* (1935).

4. In fact Ernst Röhm was chief of staff of the *Sturmabteilung* (SA), the Nazi party militia. By June 1934 he had come to be seen as a threat by Hitler, who had the SA crushed in "the Night of the Long Knives"; Röhm was executed.

5. Tyneside acquaintance of Mona and Len.

6 Probably Barden Moor, north-east of Leyburn.

7. George Jackson's watercolour portrait of Kirkup was used for the cover of his memoir *I, of all People: An Autobiography of Youth* (New York: St Martin's Press, 1988). Kirkup writes of his stay (p 90): "Later, when I ran away from East Witton, I spent some weeks in hiding at George Jackson's cottage in Castle Bolton[…] When I was hiding out there from the Ministry of Labour, I wrote a number of poems, and a strange group of sonnets I called 'Ten Pure Sonnets' [referred to by Len in his letter of 27 February], which were finally printed in my collection *Refusal to Conform* by the Oxford University Press in 1963." Kirkup's account of his actions is not necessarily to be taken as gospel: he was notoriously given to embroidering his life story.

8. Angela Petter, pacifist and writer, who lived near the George Lansbury Farm in Essex where Kirkup had been working.

9. Hugh l'Anson Fausset, writer and literary critic (1895-1965).

10. A quote from *The Starlight Night*.

11. The first line of William Wordsworth's sonnet *Surprised by Joy*.

12. Len did indeed paint the falls – the picture (one of his more modest efforts, it has to be said) is still in the possession of his family.

13. Naomi, the little daughter of Mona's younger sister Doris and her husband Alan, who had settled in South Africa, was killed when a gun went off accidentally.

14. Ronald Firbank (1886-1926), novelist, aesthete and gay.

15. Mona had promised a painting by Len to Doris and Alan.

16. Charles Ricketts (1866-1931), artist, illustrator, printer, designer and author. He met Charles Shannon (1863-1937), painter and lithographer, at art school, after which they became lifelong partners in both their artistic and personal life. Jacques-Émile Blanche (1861-1942) was a French portrait painter who worked in both Paris and London.

17. Corydon, a shepherd in Classical mythology and poetry, was in love with a young boy named Alexis.

18. Sir Thomas Wyatt, poet and diplomat (1503-1542).
19. Is this a strange premonition of Jonah's conversion to Catholicism in 1955?
20. Friends' Ambulance Unit.

Last Months in Wensleydale

1. Len had been working near West Burton.
2. On 26 July 1943 Mona wrote to her brother Tony that she had been typing out some short stories for "our poet friend, Jim Kirkup[...] The first two were very peaceful stories about a small boy, but the third one is quite Edgar Allen Poeish."
3. A quotation from W.B. Yeats's *The Lake Isle of Innisfree*: to be precise, the line reads "And I shall have some peace there, for peace comes dropping slow".
4. Both places are a little further up Wensleydale from East Witton and Castle Bolton.
5. Friends from Tyneside.
6. Not previously mentioned in the letters, but clearly another young aspiring artist.
7. Mona wrote to Tony on 12 October 1943 about Len's impulsive decision to go to London.
8. Baron de Charlus, the homosexual aristocrat in Proust's *In Search of Lost Time.*
9. Mona mentioned Len's wrist injury in a letter to Tony on 26 October 1943.
10. Fellowship of the Library Association.
11. Halifax JB926 crashed while on a training flight at Slipstone Crags above Colsterdale at 0115 hours on 23 November 1943.
12. In fact it ultimately led Len/Jonah to author five published books, and various unpublished efforts.
13. The other two are "*une femme*" and "*un cheval*".

From Non-Combatants Corps to 224 PFA

1. John Lockett, one of Len's companions from Buxton.
2. I.e. qualified as a parachutist.
3. There was a camp for Italian POWs next to the NCC camp. Len became quite friendly with one of them.
4. Acronym unclear – possibly Len is referring to the Royal Engineers.
5. Reference unknown.
6. Inseparable young Bedouin friends who stayed by T.E. Lawrence's side, as described in *Seven Pillars of Wisdom.*
7. Assistant Director Medical Services.

8. In other words, preparations for D-Day.
9. John Farleigh (1900-1965), wood engraver, painter and art teacher. In a 1987 letter to David Sherlock, Len recalled "the friendly welcome people like John Farleigh accorded poor benighted souls like me" during visits to the Central during this period.
10. Benno Moiseiwitsch (1890-1963), Ukrainian-born pianist.
11. Len is probably referring to 'Implicity', published in James Kirkup's volume *The Drowned Sailor,* as was 'Moorland'.
12. George Downs's mother.
13. Type of two-engined bomber, superseded during the war and then used for auxiliary purposes such as paratroop training.

War Experience and Aftermath
1. Orroir, in the Mont-de-l'Enclus area not far from the French border and south-east of Kortrijk (Courtrai).
2. See letter of 27 January.
3. Main Dressing Station, the unit's central point for medical and surgical treatment in any engagement.
4. Character in John Cowper Powys's *A Glastonbury Romance.*
5. James Bramwell was another pacifist member of 224 PFA, with whom Len became close friends. He was a poet and writer who had served as a volunteer fireman in Finland during its winter war with the Soviet Union (1939-40).
6. Probably a reference to A.J. Cronin (1896-1981), author of two popular novels about mining life.
7. Marie Madeleine was one of Mona's friends who she had befriended during one of her stays in France.
8. Mark Celinscak, *Distance from the Belsen Heap: Allied Forces and the Liberation of a Nazi Concentration Camp* (Toronto: University of Toronto Press, 2015) provides a summary of the 1st Canadian Parachute Battalion's path from Wesel to Bergen-Belsen, making it possible to corroborate some of Len's movements.
9. This is probably Schermbeck, about 10 miles east of Wesel. Ibid. p 28.
10. Captain Costigan, the Canadian medical officer under whom Len was working (see p 250, 261), was "among the first doctors to provide medical aid to the inmates in the camp. Costigan spent two days treating the ill in the camp before returning to his regular duties." *Ibid*. p 36-37. We can infer that Len arrived and left with him.
11. Peter Jones, *Jonah Jones: an Artist's Life*, p 46.
12. Mona may have been quoting from John Keats's sonnet *On First Looking into Chapman's Homer*, which contains the lines "Or like stout Cortez when with eagle eyes/He star'd at the Pacific". This is a reference to the Spanish

conquistador Hernán Cortés.

13. Tyneside acquaintance who had joined the forces.

14. Central Board for Conscientious Objectors.

15. Len's grandfather John Jones had originally come from Midsomer Norton, Somerset; the family can be traced back in the area to at least the start of the 19th century.

Early Months in Palestine

1. Rashid Ali al-Gaylani was prime minister of Iraq in 1940 and 1941, pursuing a pro-Axis policy. Pierre Laval was head of the Vichy France government under Marshal Pétain.

2. Len had made his first visit to Jerusalem during October.

3. Len means the Battle of Bréville, 8-13 June 1944.

4. Tyneside acquaintance of Mona and Len.

Palestine: An Educational Experience

1. United Nations Organisation.

2. The Four Freedoms were articulated by President Roosevelt in his State of the Union address to Congress on 6 January 1941, in which he responded to the Second World War. He proposed four fundamental freedoms that people everywhere should enjoy: Freedom of speech, Freedom of worship, Freedom from want and Freedom from fear. These came to underpin the moral justification for the Allied war effort, and were explicitly incorporated into the preamble to the Universal Declaration of Human Rights.

3. John Masefield (1878-1967), poet, novelist and playwright – Poet Laureate 1930-1967; Eric Kennington (1888-1960), sculptor and painter.

4. This is probably a paraphrase – or a misquote – of the lines "He who was living is now dead/We who were living are now dying" from T.S. Eliot's *The Waste Land.*

5. In the absence of Mona's letters we can only speculate on what she meant by this remark. Perhaps it was a reference to Len's description of the pleasant life he was leading at Carmel College.

6. Commander of the 3rd Parachute Brigade, July 1945-November 1946.

7. Presumably an acquaintance of Mona's.

8. *Ma'alish* means "Never mind" or "It doesn't matter". Len/Jonah would use this word sometimes in later life, but he would say it with a hint of frustration as in "What the hell"; perhaps this can be the meaning too when uttered by Arabs.

9. Persons of education or standing.

10. Tennessee Valley Authority, set up in 1933 by the US Federal Government as a regional development corporation.

11. The Jewish National Council of Palestine called a general strike on 12

April in protest against the detention of over 1,000 Jewish refugees at La Spezia, Italy. It was hoped to persuade the British Government to allow the refugees entry into Palestine.

12. Givat Brenner is a kibbutz in central Israel, some 15 miles south of Tel Aviv.

13. Enzo Sereni was parachuted by the RAF into the Nazi-occupied area of northern Italy, where he aimed to help some 40,000 Jewish fugitives from the concentration camps hiding there to get to the liberated south of the country. He was captured by the Gestapo and executed in Dachau in November 1944.

Palestine: Carmel College

1. Peace – the standard Hebrew greeting and salutation upon parting.

2. Ernest Bevin, the Foreign Secretary.

3. Jamal al-Husayni (1894-1982) was one of the foremost Palestinian Arab political leaders. He was arrested by the British in 1941, exiled to Southern Rhodesia and only allowed to return to Palestine in February 1946.

4. Hajj Amin al-Husayni (c.1897-1974), the Grand Mufti of Jerusalem, was related to Jamal al-Husayni. The British Mandatory authorities regarded him as an important ally up to 1936, but his activities against Jewish immigration led up to a leading role in the Arab revolt of 1936-39. The authorities tried to arrest him in July 1937 but he went into hiding, then escaped into exile. During World War II he allied himself publicly with the Axis cause, meeting both Hitler and Mussolini and urging Arabs to revolt against the British.

5. In fact the Grand Mufti had recently arrived in Cairo from France, where he had been held under loose house arrest since the end of the war.

6. *Kibbutz* (collective settlement) dweller (Hebrew).

7. *Fellah* (pl. *fellahin*), Arabic for farmer or peasant.

8. Kibbutz Hulda is in central Israel, south of Ramla.

9. From Arabic – taking a look.

10. Len is mistaken here – it is broom that is common on Mt Carmel as elsewhere around the Mediterranean.

11. Institute of Technology.

12. The Haganah (mainstream Jewish self-defence force) on 16 June blew up bridges linking Palestine to the neighbouring Arab countries, hoping to stop the transfer of weapons to the Palestinian Arabs. This operation, as well as other attacks around this time, prompted the British authorities to impose curfews around the country and conduct searches for arms caches and militants in the main cities and dozens of Jewish settlements.

13. Presumably what is meant here is the Star of David.

14. The Jewish Brigade was a military formation within the British Army set

up in late 1944, which saw action in Italy.

15. Auxiliary Territorial Service, the women's branch of the British Army.

16. Yagur is a kibbutz on the eastern slopes of Mount Carmel.

17. Len's old friend and Felling library colleague.

18. Despite the date at the head of this letter, it is clear from the reference to the King David attack that it was not posted until at least 23 July.

19. Editor of the *New Statesman* 1930-1960.

20. In early August the Haganah, transporting 2,678 refugees from Yugoslavia to Palestine, was found at sea with its engines broken down and no electrical power. It was towed by *HMS Venus* to Haifa, where the passengers were arrested and interned. A similar fate befell the 758 passengers on board the *Yagur*.

21. Tyneside acquaintance of Mona and Len.

22. In other words, Len is comparing unfavourably the extreme brevity of the Haifa trial with the thorough process of the Nuremberg trials.

23. *Deo volente* (Latin) – God willing.

24. (Hebrew) Father and Mother.

Epilogue: A Friendship Winds Down

1. The part of Oxford where Mona was living at the time.

2. The editor of this book.

3. I.e. bibliography.

4. For some years Len (or rather Jonah as he was known by then) ran a small publishing operation, the Cidron Press, as a sideline. It made a modest profit.

5. Like all Joneses, Len found himself nicknamed Jonah in the army. He took a shine to the name, and adopted it after his move to Wales. Soon only those who had known him on Tyneside would call him Len.

6. Jonah was Director of Ireland's National College of Art and Design in 1974-78.

7. I recall the odd letter arriving from Japan, embellished with Kirkup's acute remarks about life there.

8. I distinctly remember my father receiving one or two letters sent by Mona from Botswana.

9. Gillian Stead Eilersen, *Bessie Head: Thunder Behind Her Ears* (Cape Town/Johannesburg, London, Portsmouth NH: David Phillip, James Currey, Heinemann, 1995/96).

10. Jonah's church artwork, which by definition is non-transportable, deserves to be better known. Sadly, with churches now being closed, much of this work is under threat.

11. The latter was dismantled in 2012 and is due to be reinstalled at University of Wales Trinity St David's, Lampeter.

12. *I, of all People,* p 174.

Index